C0-AWT-426

OF BEASTS AND BONDS

Death and Destiny Trilogy, Book 2

N.D. Jones

Baltimore, Maryland

kuumbapublishing.com

Copyright © 2016 by **N.D. Jones**

All rights reserved. No part of this publication may be reproduced, distributed or transmitted in any form or by any means, without prior written permission.

Kuumba Publishing
Maryland
www.kuumbapublishing.com

Publisher's Note: This is a work of fiction. Names, characters, places, and incidents are a product of the author's imagination. Locales and public names are sometimes used for atmospheric purposes. Any resemblance to actual people, living or dead, or to businesses, companies, events, institutions, or locales is completely coincidental.

Book Layout © 2014 BookDesignTemplates.com
Cover design by Jesh Designs
All art and logo copyright © 2016 by Kuumba Publishing

Of Beasts and Bonds/ N.D. Jones. -- 1st ed.
ISBN-10: 0-9975293-0-X
ISBN-13: 978-0-9975293-0-2

DEDICATION

This book is dedicated to my talented daughter, Najja. She is a wonderful visual artist whose dream of becoming a great graphic designer is well within her capable reach.

Najja created the logo centerpiece for Kuumba Publishing. Thank you.

PROLOGUE

Baltimore, Maryland
29 Years Ago

Rain thundered, a torrential deluge of harsh, whipping water and winds, punctuated by spine-tingling bursts of lightning. Somewhere, deep in the Pacific Ocean, two goddesses dwelled, imprisoned by the sun god Ra for their crimes against humanity. On this prophesized night, with thunder, lightning, rain, and the smell of fire and godly magic in the warm June air, Samuel Williams gritted his teeth, balled his fists, and swallowed down the urge to cry, to curse, to scream.

Doing any of those things wouldn't change the situation. Nor would they help the woman on the other side of the bedroom door. Right now, despite his anger and fear, Sam had to be strong for his wife. The jaguar within demanded nothing less from the man. For both had experienced crippling loss before—one child and then a second, neither surviving long enough to take their first gasping breaths of life. But this one, this third pregnancy, would prove the exception to the awful rule. Makena would see this child born, and a calm, in control Sam would be by her side. His cat spirit bonded and mated to her fire spirit, all wanting, needing the baby's safe delivery.

Sam pressed his hand and forehead against the cool pane of glass, lightning illuminating the night sky and the curse that would be his unborn daughter's fate. He felt it, with each contraction his wife endured, Sam sensed the tiny baby struggling to be born. Only her life wouldn't be hers alone. It belonged to the gods. A family war thousands of years old that claimed and destroyed countless lives, full-human and preternatural.

Senseless.

Bloody.

Enduring.

The prelude to war was now at Samuel and Makena Williams' doorstep, forbidding and crackling with old power but new possibilities.

"I didn't see my daughter pushed into the world, Sam." A strong hand landed on Sam's shoulder, a reassuring weight. "Little has changed in twenty-six years, even though this is the United States instead of Nigeria." Sam turned to face his father-in-law, meeting light-brown eyes that sparkled with concern but also with a touch of rebellion. "Sometimes witches hold onto the old ways too tightly, even when they make little sense. You should be in there, holding my daughter's hand and soothing her silent fears."

Sam glanced over the broad shoulder of Odafe Toure and to the closed wooden door behind the man who smelled of chaconia, reminding Sam of growing up in Trinidad and long August days. He heard the sound of three distinct female voices, none of them his wife's. With the enhanced senses of a jaguar, very little happened in his bedroom turned birthing room he couldn't smell or hear. Yet there he stood, in the hallway of his home. At twenty-eight and the recent owner of his first apartment building, Sam had all too easily allowed the High Priestess of the Witch Council of Elders to push him out of his bedroom and away from his wife and unborn child. Well, that would end right now.

"They all think my daughter is the fire witch of legend." Sam's eyes settled on Odafe, a fifty-three-year-old Nigerian, who shared the same type of inner cat spirit as Sam. Unsurprising since all the women in his wife's family, as far as Sam knew, mated with men who harbored an inner jaguar spirit. Yet his daughter, if truly the fire witch of legend, wasn't destined to have a jaguar as her familiar. No, the man who would fight, maybe even die by her side, would hold a far more dangerous and powerful cat spirit. An ancient cat of myth and legend he would be, or so the prophecy foretold. "What do you think? Will my daughter be the fire witch of legend, the one our people have waited five centuries to be born?"

Odafe raised a solitary finger and pointed to the window. Thunder and lightning roared, rain tumbled, and Makena moaned her birthing pain. "It also rained the day my Makena was born. The Biu Plateau erupted for the first time in decades. So-called extinct volcanoes mean nothing to the old gods. If we were to turn on the news, Sam, how many volcanoes do you think we would find have erupted since my daughter went into labor, spewing their fire and ferocity?"

Makena's moan turned into an outright scream, splitting the night air and challenging the thunder for prominence. "We'll talk more about this later, son. My daughter and granddaughter need you." Odafe stepped aside. "Go. I'm right behind you. And if that high priestess so much as raises one disapproving eyebrow at you, she'll have to deal with me. Now, let's not keep our women waiting."

Sam went, opening the door to his bedroom. As promised, Odafe followed, taking up the position behind Sam and in front of the glowering high priestess. Sam ignored the seventy-something woman, whose straight white hair, aquamarine eyes, and willowy frame did nothing to capture the magical might of the witch. But her magic, no matter how advanced, paled in comparison to Wasola's, Makena's mother. While Sam knew High Priestess Katherine meant well, this was his home, his wife, and his child. And his daughter, damn the prophecy, did not, would not belong to the Council ... or to the gods.

He hoped.

He prayed.

Then she was born, with red-gold hair and green eyes—undeniable marks of the fire witch of legend.

Thunder purred.

Lightning laughed.

The rain raged, battering the city, the state, the nation, the world in unforgiving explosions of water goddess fury. The fire witch of legend, an unwilling champion of humanity, a tool of the gods, and Samuel and Makena Williams' child had been born.

Healthy and hail and without a single tear or scream, her birth brought forth shock and awe from High Priestess Katherine and her daughter Anna, a water witch with hopes of replacing her mother on the Witch Council of Elders. But for now, the women dropped to their knees, heads in supplication and an ancient prayer on their lips.

Sam neither understood the language they spoke nor knew whether they prayed for his child or to the storm and wind goddess Oya, who was known for her lustrous red-gold hair, flawless brown skin and vibrant green eyes, as much as for her destructive battles with her water and serpent goddess sister, Mami Wata. For whatever they prayed, Sam couldn't begrudge them their relieved happiness. For he too was happy, as were Odafe and his wife, High Priestess Wasola.

More importantly, Makena had finally given them a child they wanted so desperately. Even with the threat of the prophecy attempting to mar this beautiful moment, Sam couldn't help but smile down at his tired but mighty wife. "You've made me the happiest man today, Makena. Thank you for our daughter. I love you."

Leaning down, he kissed Makena's sweaty forehead and then the angelic face of his daughter. Unblinking green eyes stared up at Sam with such trust and faith his knees nearly buckled, threatening to send him crashing to the floor like Katherine and Anna. It was then Sam knew, understood there was nothing he wouldn't do to protect his precious little girl.

Three hours later, with Katherine and Anna gone home, Odafe, Wasola, and Makena asleep, Sam, daughter held against his pounding heart, descended the stairs to the basement. Able to see in the dark, Sam didn't bother flipping on the light switch. Instead, he held his bundle even tighter and walked until he reached the couch.

Grabbing a ruffled throw pillow, he knelt, and then placed his silent newborn on the pillow.

Again, those too-knowing green eyes stared up at Sam—haunting in their immature intensity, beseeching him to not do what he was planning on doing.

"This will be for the best. My jaguar spirit agrees. This is the only choice. It's the way of fathers and daughters."

He would confess all to Makena in the morning. But not beforehand, not when his wife would be forced to choose between her husband of her heart and her daughter of her soul.

"Trust me," Sam whispered to his daughter.

Refusing to back away from his decision, Sam bowed his head and began an old prayer he'd learned at his grandfather's knee.

And when Sàngó, god of fire, lightning and thunder appeared before Sam asking with benevolent omnipotence, "What have you named the fire witch of legend?" that his daughter cried for the first time. An inconsolable bellow breached the night sky, cracked it open and brought forth the return of the wind, thunder, and lightning, but no rain.

Sam cried as well, trembled in fact when he said, "Sanura. Her name is Sanura Wasola Williams. And I pray you will do me the great honor of blessing her."

There would be a cost, he knew. With gods, there was always a cost. But Samuel Williams would pay, would make any sacrifice if it meant Sanura would survive what was to come.

Beasts.

Water.

War.

CHAPTER ONE

Alexandria, Virginia
Present Day

Assefa heard the *tap, tap, tap* of Sanura's fingers striking the keys on her laptop when he pulled his cell phone from his pants pocket and closed the bedroom door. A few weeks ago, he'd found his mate in Sanura Williams. He'd gone to Baltimore, Sanura's city of birth, on FBI business. By the end of the case, Assefa had not only captured and killed the adze, a bat-humanoid serial killer of witches, but had fallen in love with a fire witch.

His destined mate.

True, Assefa and Sanura had yet to complete the tri-part wedding ceremony that would bind their lives as well as their inner spirits. Yet they had engaged in the first part of the handfasting ceremony. Assefa's inner cat, his Mngwa, tempted and beguiled by the allure of Sanura's fire spirit, had stalked her in the astrophysical plane. Accepting her siren's call, his Mngwa had loped toward the woman and a destiny of fire, water, and love. Their fate, if the prophecy of the fire witch and cat of legend was true.

Assefa sank onto his bed, back going against the wooden headboard, bare feet onto the duvet, cell phone in hand. Yes, he'd found his witch and Sanura her familiar. The handfasting proving to them their biological compatibility, which meant two things. One, Assefa and Sanura could safely reproduce, not having to worry about their unique genetic composition working against inception and the birth of a healthy witch or were-cat. Two, Assefa and Sanura could perform powerful magic together. Their auras merged and aligned in such a majestic way that enabled Assefa to hold and manipulate Sanura's magical energy while using his cat chi to strengthen his witch's spells.

Pulling up the keypad of his cell phone, Assefa hit the number two, speed dialing the first woman he ever loved. A woman who, no matter the physical distance between them, held his heart in her hands.

She answered on the third ring.

"Hello, brother."

Assefa smiled, the rest of him relaxing at the sound of his sister's warm, loving voice. She spoke in Wolof. And Assefa slipped into his native tongue with familial ease, unconscious of doing so.

"Good evening, Najja. I was hoping to catch you before you sat down to dinner."

Khartoum, Sudan, Assefa's ancestral home, was seven hours ahead of Alexandria, Virginia's time, his home after moving to the United States and joining the Preternatural Division of the FBI. At eleven in the morning his time, it was six in the evening Najja's time. Their father, Jahi Berber, the ruler of Sudan, ate at seven every night. Najja, being the dutiful daughter that she was, obliged their father in a way Assefa had ceased to do once leaving home.

Which, in a way, made Assefa a bad son and Najja an overindulgent daughter. Either way, they permitted their father to have far too much emotional power over them. A bond between twins, which Najja and Assefa were, so great that even their character flaws matched, even when they acted opposite of each other.

"Yes, well, we have about an hour before dinner. You should've called me earlier. That would've given us more time to catch up. It's been too long since we last spoke."

Actually, it had only been two weeks. But Assefa understood how Najja felt. People who weren't blessed with being a twin rarely comprehended the indescribable bond. Closeness and absolute trust didn't adequately capture all that they meant to each other. The only bonds that could rival that of twins were the bond between mates and the bond of parent and child.

So they talked, Najja bringing Assefa up to speed on the politics of their country. As Secretary of State, Najja Berber, the First Daughter of the Sudan, knew the inner workings of the Sudanese government on a level that was both impressive and disheartening. Her knowledge and enthusiasm crackled through the line, as did her passion for the people and the country of their birth.

The selfish part of Assefa had hoped his sister would one day leave Sudan and move to the States so they could be together. But, over the last two years, ever since their father had appointed her to the post, Najja's commitment to her position and the people who relied on her intelligent, strong, and generous nature, Assefa's dream began to slip further away.

Sighing inwardly, he continued to listen to his sister. Sudan, a nation torn apart by too many civil wars, a violent response to what used to be despotic Berber regimes, needed honest and honorable civic leaders like Madam Secretary Najja Berber. His family had done much to destroy the country and exploit its people, namely his grandfather and great-grandfather. So it was only right that a Berber do the heavy lifting of putting the country back together. Their father, Jahi Berber, the country's General Supreme, had been the first Berber to undertake the monumental task. Now, apparently, it was Najja's turn to do her part.

"What's wrong, Assefa?"

"What makes you think—"

Najja snorted a laugh. "I know it's been a while since we've seen each other, but I'm still me and you're still you. Just because you're an American FBI agent doesn't mean I no longer know the were-cat behind the badge."

Assefa found himself smiling again. "I miss you."

Another snort of laughter. "Of course, you do. So, did the package I sent arrive? I mailed it as soon as the jeweler finished."

A third smile split Assefa's face, recalling how pleased he'd been when he'd opened the little velvet box.

"The designer did a wonderful job. I wasn't sure if she would get it just the way I wanted it, but she did."

"It's beautiful. One of a kind, Assefa. I'm sure your Sanura will love it."

He hoped she would. There was nothing like the magnificent diamonds found in the mines of Sudan, which was why Assefa commissioned the ring from a Sudanese jeweler instead of a local one. His sister, pleased to help, oversaw the transaction for him, guaranteeing the piece would be to his specifications. She'd done, unsurprisingly, a damn good job.

"When will you ask her? I suppose American witches do things differently than we do here. I mean, you're already living together and are bonded. I guess the ring is a formality for the full-humans she's used to being around."

Assefa's eyes went to the nightstand on his side of the bed. He'd buried the jewelry box in there under a stack of papers. It wasn't the best hiding place, but Sanura had her own nightstand and no reason to go into his. Still, maybe he should consider hiding it someplace more secure. Now that he thought about it, the lock box where he kept his FBI-issued firearm would be a much better location. He made a mental note to make the swap before Sanura returned to their bedroom.

"The engagement ring is a formality, but I also like the idea of seeing my mate wear a symbol of our love, our bond."

"That's what the mate mark is for, brother."

Assefa didn't respond to his sister's comment about the mate mark. But he did make sure to maintain his side of the conversation without a lengthy pause Najja would catch and question. They may have been twins, but Assefa didn't want Najja knowing the truth. And while his bond with his sister was as solid as steel, his mate bond with Sanura was anything but.

During the first handfasting ritual, Sanura allowed her fire spirit to bond his cat spirit to her. That should not have happened. First the alignment of auras, then the merging of auras, and finally the cat's bite

– tri-part wedding. But Sanura had leaped ahead, aligning and merging their auras during the first ritual. Yet, that night, when they'd made love for the first time, a frightened and unsure Sanura had frozen when Assefa's fangs had slipped from his gums. His inner cat ready to bite and claim his witch, completing the bond and making them mates. Without both, merged auras and cat's bite, only a partial mate bond existed between them.

No one knew he and Sanura weren't fully bonded. Not Makena and Cynthia, Sanura's mother and best friend. And certainly not Mike, Sanura's irascible dwarf of a godfather. Hell, Assefa hadn't even confided in Zareb, his FBI partner and best friend. No one knew his secret shame except the woman who'd shunned his bite.

But things were different between them now. Sanura had moved in with him, accepting his love and giving him her own. And while they had yet to set a date to complete the third part of the handfasting ritual, at which time Assefa would finally claim his mate, he was sure they soon would. If nothing else, what he had planned for Sanura's twenty-ninth birthday would push them to set two dates. The partial mate bond would be no more, and the corrosive doubt he harbored would die a silent death.

No need to confess to Najja or anyone else. He trusted and loved Sanura. They would complete the final part of the mate bond. Sanura would accept his bite and then they would act the role of full-humans and get engaged.

Brother and sister talked a bit more about Assefa's plan to propose to Sanura, the conversation pleasant until she mentioned their older brother and their father's sixtieth birthday at the beginning of September.

"You know you have to come home, don't you? If you don't, Father will be disappointed, and Razi will use your absence to try and turn Father against you. The way he's done since we were children. Honestly, I've never understood his problem with us, especially with you."

"I don't either. But I've given up trying to figure him out. It's enough to know that my only brother hates me."

The truth of that hurt, no matter how dispassionately he'd made the statement. Something else the twins bonded over—a distrust and lack of understanding of their older brother.

"He wants to be General Supreme."

Assefa wasn't surprised. Razi always had illusions of grandeur, as well as an unnatural need to bully and control all those unfortunate enough to be within his reach and sphere of influence. "Father won't allow that to happen."

"I know, but Razi worries me. He's quieter and sneakier than he used to be. I've caught him staring at Father when he thinks no one is looking, and I don't like what I've seen."

That had Assefa darting up, his legs swinging over the side of the bed.

"What do you mean? How does Razi look at Father?"

She didn't respond right away, which sent Assefa to his feet, cell phone clasped tightly in his right hand.

Najja's sigh was wind witch loud. "I don't know, Assefa. He says all the right things and shows the proper respect to the General Supreme. It's just, well, there's something unsettling about our brother. It boils to the surface at the oddest times, then disappears as if it had never been. Just when I think I have it, it's gone."

Assefa relaxed the death grip he had on the phone. "It sounds like the same old Razi to me, Najja, except he must've gotten better at hiding his selfish and nasty disposition. It probably helps that I'm not around to set him off."

"Don't let Razi keep you from coming home for Father's birthday. It's been more than a year since your last visit. That's too long to be away from home."

It was. Assefa dropped his six-foot load onto the side of the bed, accepting his sister's gently given scold.

"I know. I'll think about it. That's the best I can do, right now. Besides, it's June. I have time to decide."

"It's *not* the best you can do. It's all you're willing to commit to, which means you're considering not coming home."

A much harsher scold from his twin. He deserved her anger, her disappointment. But home held few good memories for Assefa, although there were countless people there he loved and missed. Najja and his father being the most important. But he'd never quite managed to be his true self at home, not in the way that he could here. And while Najja seemed to have flourished under their country's flag and sun, Assefa had slowly but surely begun to melt, to wilt.

So he'd abandoned his family and homeland, seeking his freedom and manhood away from his father's and country's expectations he had no intention of living up to.

"I'll think about it." Assefa glanced at the clock, which read half past twelve. "You're late for dinner. I'm surprised Father hasn't sent one of the compound guards after you."

"He did, but I ignored the knock on my office door. But I should be going. If I wait much longer, he'll come looking for me himself. Call me in a couple of days?"

"Of course."

"Good." Assefa could hear his sister moving about in her office. "Think about what I said. Father would love to see you. He's already asked Uncle Ulan to come home, seeing how it's also his birthday. Maybe the two of you could travel together. That would be nice. Our little family all together for once."

Not all together. Their mother, Nyanath Berber, had passed on long ago. But Najja, like Assefa, rarely spoke of their deceased mother. No more than Razi, or their father, spoke of her. That didn't mean her death hadn't left a substantial hole in their hearts and their lives. A hole, Assefa admitted to himself with reluctance, that had yet to heal.

"As I said, I'll think about it."

"That stubborn streak of yours makes a witch want to shake you. I hope you're more accommodating to Sanura than you are to me."

Actually, he was. Because Sanura, bless her sexy, fire witch soul, knew exactly what to do to get her way. Apparently, Special Agent Assefa Berber wasn't above a little sexual manipulation.

In fact, he loved it.

"I'll take that long pause as a *yes*. Anyway, brother, I have to be going. Talk to you later. Love you."

"Not as much as I love you."

Assefa wanted to add, "See you soon," but didn't want to commit. But he did want to see his sister. If his father called, making the same request of him, Assefa didn't think he would be able to turn the old jaguar down.

****

Sanura reclined in her ergonomic desk chair and sighed. The back of the seat changed shape to support her body, specifically her spine. Seat, arms, and height adjusted, creating a perfect body-mimicking fit. Sanura sighed again, appreciating Assefa's exquisite, if not expensive, taste in chairs.

Casting her eyes around the luxurious sitting room, Sanura couldn't help but shake her head. Assefa's exquisite and expensive taste went far beyond the thousand-dollar desk chair he'd bought for her, saying, "Since you'll be spending more time on the computer this semester, you need a chair that will work with your body, not against it."

Yes, Sanura's fall semester would consist of a full schedule of asynchronous classes. The University of Maryland was implementing more eLearning courses, a means of diversifying instruction and meeting the needs of twenty-first-century learners. Sanura, the youngest professor in the Department of Psychology, was tapped by the department chair to create and field test the department's first foray into asynchronous learning. Sanura and several other professors had taught hybrid courses—a combination of online and face-to-face classes—but the Introduction to Psychology and Statistical Methods in Psychology courses would be the first fully online classes the department would offer to its incoming undergraduate students.

Hence, Assefa's excuse to buy Sanura an insanely expensive chair, to match the overpriced changes he was in the process of making to the sitting room. A sitting room that, once finished, would be Sanura's home office. He'd already traded in his signature dark-blue walls for soft, feminine shades of eggshell white and terracotta rose. The combination, lovely and bright, appealed to the woman and her fire spirit.

Gone were the wildlife landscapes of the Serengeti Assefa was so fond of, replaced by three Monica Stewart originals. While Sanura may have liked the ergonomic chair and the rich, colorful walls, she adored the paintings. They were perfection on canvas. And Sanura couldn't help but wonder about Assefa's selections.

Sanura pushed away from her glass-top desk. Chic and fashionable, the sleek lines, champagne finish and rich ornamentation had Sanura's jaw dropping when Assefa and Zareb had carried the grand piece of furniture into the room with a "Where do you want this thing, Sanura, it weighs a ton," from a smiling and winking Zareb. Sanura would have to have a word with Assefa. While she appreciated his earnest attempt to make Sanura feel like his house was as much her home now, he didn't have to go about it by showering her with expensive renovations.

She stood, then took four steps back to get a better look at the painting nearest her. On the wall behind her luxury desk was *Fantasy in Red*. The man in the painting, dressed in a black suit, held a woman in a red spaghetti strap dress from behind. A large right hand held the woman under her full breasts. His eyes were downcast, face turned to his partner, and lips shy of her slender neck. The woman, eyes closed, small right hand over that of the man's holding her with tenderness, grasped the back of her partner's head with her left hand. Hair as dark as a moonless night sky, she wore a white gardenia in her hair, reminiscent of Billie Holiday. Her flowing red dress accentuated a slender and sensual form, one sexy brown leg revealed and pressed against the black pant leg of the man.

The sensual dance caught.

What came before or after this moment, Sanura would never know. But the man and woman radiated restrained desire expressed in the hushed lines of the dance, in the way they held each other, and in the eyes that were closed, keeping their secrets to themselves. The psychologists in Sanura couldn't help but wonder what Assefa saw when he looked upon this painting, what went through his mind when he chose this piece over others.

Did he view Sanura as his "Fantasy in Red"? A fire witch, with the natural scent of a gardenia, beyond his reach, no matter that they lived together, and she loved him? Was this Assefa's subconscious speaking to her, revealing his true feelings and fears about their relationship?

Running a shaky hand through her thick waves of hair, Sanura upbraided herself for being ridiculous, for seeing more into a simple painting selection than there actually was. No, Assefa knew Sanura loved African American art, Monica Stewart being one of her favorite artists. And how many times had her special agent told her how much he liked seeing her wear skirts and dresses because they showed off the long legs he took so much pleasure in staring at and touching?

Sanura was not Assefa's "Fantasy in Red."

She spun away from the painting, which should've put her mind at ease but did not. On the wall opposite the dancing couple was *Promise*. Dressed in all-white with accents of brown and black, a couple faced each other. Hands clasped, they stared into the eyes of the other, their profile momentous for the implication of the promise they were making.

She'd seen this painting many times on the Internet. Her appreciation for the subtle simplicity of its design but the blatant message of love, marriage, and devotion had always appealed to Sanura in a one-day-that-will-be-me kind of way. But now, seeing the painting close up, in a home she shared with the man she'd given her heart to, but who she'd yet to allow to claim her as mate, the painting and its message held even more meaning. The immediacy and relevance of the title were not lost on Sanura.

Her one day no longer a faraway dream she had but never truly thought possible. Because to dream, to want, to desire meant so much more when a woman was the cursed fire witch of legend. A prophecy told to witch and were-cat children as a bedtime story—scary and unbelievable.

Yet the real-life signs of the prophecy were hard to ignore. Everyone Sanura knew, witches and were-cats alike, thought her the mortal incarnation of Oya. Oya, goddess of wind, thunderbolts and fire, thousands of years ago, waged a brutal war against her older sister, Mami Wata, the goddess of water and all its creatures. In the end, the goddesses were imprisoned by the sun god Ra. Unfortunately, the war between the goddesses did not end with their confinement. In time, the combatants changed to include fire witches and water witches. Totems for Oya and Mami Wata, as the prophecy went. The water witch of legend was destined to bring watery chaos and destruction to the world unless the fire witch of legend and her familiar, the cat of legend, stopped her.

With Sanura's green eyes and red-gold hair, the same as Oya's, as well as her sudden ability to cast storm spells, the evidence that she was indeed the prophesized fire witch of legend mounted. Then there was Assefa Berber, a Sudanese with an ancient big cat as his inner spirit. A big cat that should not exist outside of an Aesop fable. Yet he did, Assefa's Mngwa as real as the lightning spells Sanura shouldn't, as a fire witch, be able to cast.

But could.

It was all one humongous headache that had Sanura dropping onto the Italian chaise lounge with a carved camelback seat and scrolled arms, striped seat and gold shell upholstery, and an antique mahogany finish that made a confused Sanura feel like a pampered fire witch.

Closing her eyes, Sanura began a slow temple massage. She'd come into this room to work and to record the strange events that had plagued her life over the last two months. Her meeting and falling in love with Assefa Berber the only event Sanura did not add to the list of strange occurrences. But that had been the only one everything else counted as strange and unwanted events of the preternatural kind.

The adze topped the list, not because the bat creature killed so many witches, which was bad enough, but because the introduction of the adze into her life marked the beginning of the changes that would forever alter Sanura and those she called family and friends. If the oddity of having a bat-humanoid in Baltimore City had ended there, Sanura wouldn't now be nursing a headache.

Of course, it didn't. More of the god's first creations had slithered from their hiding holes, finding Sanura and Assefa. The Raven Mocker, a soul-stealing bastard had been the second creature to taste the combined might of their magic. Then came the three siren sisters, wanting to torture and slay Assefa because he'd killed their murderous sister while on a mission in Alaska, hunting the four killers of men. Yet it had been Sanura who'd killed, eliminating the operatic divas with furious bolts of lightning, with no other thought than protecting herself and Assefa.

Dropping her hands, Sanura wondered how long the calm of the last month would last. If she, Assefa, and the world were very lucky, the Day of Serpents would prove to be a myth. A wonderful prospect but one Sanura couldn't bring herself to believe. She'd simply seen and knew too much to lie to herself.

The Day of Serpents would come, bringing flood waters and Mami Wata's beasts, testing Sanura's and Assefa's magical bond, strength, and perseverance.

Opening her eyes, Sanura searched for and found the third Monica Stewart painting. Beside the corner window, the sun illuminated *Inner Peace*. A naked woman slept in the crook of a sofa, face pressed against the back of her hand, a proprietary arm covering her breasts from the viewer. An orange, yellow, and red blend throw shielded her lower half, yet the woman's thigh, shoulder, and face were exposed in somatic harmony. The woman's true face unmasked in slumber.

She stood and walked to the painting. Not for the first time today, Sanura wondered about Assefa's selection and the underlying meaning. Was this the woman he saw when he watched her sleep? Or was this the woman he hoped Sanura would one day become?

What did her sleep face reveal? Inner peace or inner dissonance? A part of her wanted to ask, but a larger part feared Assefa's answer.

A flicker of movement caught her attention. She let her eyes fall away from the painting and to the window and the scene on the lawn below. Assefa's Mngwa stood surrounded by four were-cats. While the Mngwa, as tall as a donkey and as wide as an elephant, radiated ferocity and strength, the other cats were no less dangerous for their smaller size.

And small was certainly relative because there was nothing insubstantial about the leopard, Bengal tiger, lion, and cheetah snarling at the Mngwa.

Before Sanura could scream a warning, the four predators attacked.

CHAPTER TWO

Baltimore, Maryland

At nearly 2,500 students, PreK-12, Sankofa Preparatory School, established in 1945, served as the only witch-owned institution of learning for witches and were-cats in the northeast region of the United States. Of those nearly 2,500 students, eighty percent were Maryland, DC, and Southern Virginia residents. While fifteen percent hailed from other parts of the United States, comprising the bulk of the school's onsite residents. The remaining five percent represented a growing international population, with foreign-born students from Canada, Cuba, Mexico, and the islands of the Caribbean.

"In the last month alone, we've received five hundred applications. The month before that, three hundred twenty." High Priestess Anna Spencer, the leader of the Witch Council of Elders, leaned forward and handed Makena Williams a micro USB. "Everything we know about the applicants' families is on that drive."

Makena palmed and considered the contents of the small device before slipping it into the wine tooled leather handbag on the sofa cushion that separated the women. The selling feature of the handbag, for Michael McKutchen, Makena's longtime friend and Baltimore City detective, was the gun-concealment portion of the purse. After her husband's death, Mike, feeling the need to protect his best friend's widow, purchased Makena the handbag, with the expectation she would begin carrying the handgun she kept in a lockbox under her bed. Three years later, the mini holster remained empty and unused. But Makena did like the hand-rubbed color, embossed rose leaf pattern and rugged cowhide, as well as convenient compartments that held her cell phone, wallet, and sunglasses.

Anna Spencer, a level five water witch and a decade Makena's senior, the sixty-five-year-old woman, eyes the color of a blue hydrangea, stared at Makena with questioning displeasure. She'd seen this look many times, over the years, from her good friend. With shiny blonde hair having given way to random and persistent streaks of gray, Anna, tall and slight of frame, combined with her intelligent and perceptive nature, gave her a certain amount of appeal that served her well as Council leader. Yet her quiet strength and regal bearing never instilled the kind of confidence from the members of their extensive witch and were-cat network as Anna had hoped, had deserved.

Anna called Makena three days ago, requesting a face-to-face meeting in her office. She'd agreed, of course. Since the Witch Council's headquarters, and Anna's office, was located on the fifth floor of the Administration Building of the preparatory school, Makena figured she could also drop by the K-8 school and visit with Cynthia. As Headmistress of the Lower School, Cynthia often worked a few hours on the weekend, taking advantage of the quiet of the campus to get a bit of uninterrupted work in before the school week began.

Makena had given Cynthia a rough estimate of when her meeting with Anna would conclude so she would know when to expect her. With Sanura now living in Alexandria and Cynthia married and busy with a demanding job and fourteen-year-old sister-in-law she and her husband adopted, Makena relished the moments she shared with her girls. Which meant Anna Spencer needed to get to the heart of this meeting instead of taking the frustratingly long route around to her point.

"We've never seen such an influx of applications, Makena. It's unprecedented."

"I know. But we expected this, planned for the increase."

Makena looked across the room and out the window. Large, loud machines worked just beyond the Administration Building, were-cat construction workers putting in long days on the weekends to offset their limited work hours during the school week. The Witch Council of Elders unwilling to interfere with the focused learning of their students with distracting earthmoving equipment—excavators, loaders, and graders. But their work schedule would change in a week when school ended and summer break began.

"True, but we're months from having the new residential hall finished. And we haven't even broken ground on the new academic building." Anna pursed her lips and crossed her slender legs. Her apricot dress fell to her knees, the spring color bringing out the annoyed pink in her cheeks. "We aren't ready for this, any of this, Makena."

A double meaning. Anna often spoke in double meanings, which had never worked in her favor when confronted with a person of stronger, more direct character. Like Makena. Like Katherine Spencer, Anna's mother, former Council leader and unapologetic traditionalist and bully.

Makena reached over and placed her cool, calm hand over her friend's warm, soft one. The irony of a fire witch pumping cool, calming magic into a water witch not lost on the blue orbs that slid from Makena and to their joined hands.

"We've had twenty-nine years to prepare. You were there that night."

"It rained and rained. I thought, at any moment, Mami Wata would send her water beasts for us, for you and Sam. I swore I heard the rain speak that night, whispering in my ear to kill the fire witch of legend." Anna's frightened but determined eyes lifted, meeting Makena's unflinching gaze. "I believe she whispered the same to Mom, but I could never get her to speak about it. When I drove her home that night, she said nothing for the entire ride. But when I walked Mom to her door, she turned, grabbed me in a fierce hug and said, 'I'm old and won't be here to see the child fulfill her destiny, Anna, so you must protect the baby witch. For our family's honor. For the honor of all water witches, you must protect the fire witch of legend.'"

The news should've shocked Makena. It didn't. But it did quicken the pace of her heart and stirred the protective hiss of her fire spirit. Even then, her child had been in danger from a water witch and Mami Wata. The revelation also explained Katherine's harsh and discriminatory stance against water witches. Two months after Sanura's birth, High Priestess Katherine attempted to bulldoze an edict through the Council prohibiting the teaching of advanced-level spells to all water witches born the year before, of, and after Sanura's birth. She'd even gone as far as to encourage high priestesses from other Witch Councils to support the discriminatory ban. Most ignored her, but a few of the more conservative Councils were swayed by Katherine's appeal, even though her own Council overruled the high priestess. Years of endless internal arguing had been an awful time for their Council, Katherine pushing her agenda, chastising any witch, especially water witches, who dared to question her conservative stance.

Makena patted Anna's hand before releasing her. Upon Katherine's death twelve years ago, a younger and more liberal Council, with Anna as high priestess and Makena as priestess, the second-highest ranking witch on the Council, ended the civil rights debate and growing wariness between water and fire witches.

Since no one knew who the water witch of legend was, only that she would be around the same age as the fire witch of legend, rational and irrational fear produced the kind of kneejerk reaction exhibited by Katherine Spencer and others. Still, Makena found it difficult to totally fault someone for an act of self-preservation, particularly when it came in the form of shielding Sanura from harm by denying her enemy magical skills that could one day be used against her.

Magic that could kill my daughter and unleash Mami Wata's water beasts onto the world. An epic flood, like that found in the Judeo-Christian Bible. Evidence, for many witches, of the truth of the prophecy and the deadly might of a water witch of legend when she wins against the fire witch of legend.

Makena had no idea whether Noah ever existed or if the flood in the Bible had actually taken place, but she believed in the prophecy as much as Katherine and Anna Spencer.

"Now that Sanura is nearly twenty-nine, the prophesized year of her ascension, this city, and this school is a lightning rod for witches and were-cats. You would think people wouldn't want to be anywhere near what could be the epicenter of a great and unholy battle, no less send their children here to learn and live. But no, our numbers have swelled."

Makena understood. Preternaturals, like full-humans, possessed a strange trait of being unable to look away from a horrific but beautiful disaster. Storm chasers came to mind, risking life and limb to record the violent majesty of the "perfect storm." Perfect and beautiful until it wasn't, until it roared and raged and destroyed all in its indomitable path. Proving its omnipotence and the storm chasers' utter naiveté for getting so close, for thinking themselves mere spectators in an event of life and death.

"We have no control over people's morbid obsession with the prophecy and my daughter. We'll accept those students we can and send the standard rejection letter to the parents of those we cannot accommodate this year. It's what's always done, Anna, no need to call me here for a routine matter."

Anna uncrossed her legs, cleared her throat, and then crossed her legs again, all the while growing paler and more uncomfortable.

"There have been rumors, Makena."

"What kind of rumors?"

"Rumors about Sanura and an FBI agent."

Makena smiled. "That's no rumor. Assefa Berber is a Special Agent. He's the agent who protected us from the adze. I told you about him. Assefa is the one who suggested we use wards to prevent a home invasion by the serial killer."

Anna nodded, straight blonde-gray hair caressing the top of her shoulders. "I know, but I didn't know he and Sanura were a couple. If I had, if the Council had, we would've done this sooner."

Makena wondered how long it would take for news of Sanura's relationship with the first were-cat she'd ever dated to reach the ears of the Council. The witch-were-cat rumor mill wasn't nearly as proficient as the full-human one. In the full-human world, the day Sanura moved in with Assefa would've been the same day the news appeared on some social media outlet. Available for all to judge and comment upon, sharing their likes and dislikes about something that didn't concern them.

Whether Makena liked it or not, Sanura's relationship with Assefa concerned the world, particularly the witch-were-cat world.

"So you and the other Council members have made a decision about my daughter without including me?" The question came out as a softly-spoken accusation. The way Makena intended it to, for the thought of the Council turning their magical gazes on Sanura, the way the former Council had when led by Katherine, left a bitter taste in Makena's mouth.

Anna may serve in the role of high priestess, by Council law, however, Makena's higher magical level meant she should've ascended to the leadership position after Katherine's death. But Makena had never desired the coveted role, not the way Anna Spencer had. So when the aging members of the Council began selecting their successors and Anna and Makena were looked to to fill the honored post as high priestess, Makena declined.

A mother, wife, and lawyer on the cusp of earning a judgeship, Makena had no time to devote to leading the Council. More, she and Anna were friends. As friends, Makena knew how much Anna's self-worth and stubborn pride hinged on her succeeding her mother as high priestess. Of ruling the Council with equity, compassion, and excellence, three leadership traits Katherine Spencer had forgotten in her tyrannical quest to protect them all, especially Sanura, from Mami Wata and the water witch of legend.

But old fears and concerns died hard. And while Makena loved each of her Council sisters, she'd never trusted the way they fawned over Sanura. Treating her, even when she'd been but a child with too much power and too little control, as a godling. Such reverence tended to breed envy and trepidation, as well as a desire to possess, manipulate, and control the source of godly power. These were the reasons Makena and Sam became members of the Council. The protection of their only child, their Sanura, the couple's shared goal.

Anna's words had Makena's fire spirit awake and interested in the conversation, a simmering heat in her belly.

The high priestess shook her head. "Of course, we haven't made a decision without you. But the others have heard what I have. It's only a matter of time before they come to me, to us, and request a meeting with Sanura and her FBI agent. They'll want to know, like everyone else, if he's the cat of legend. If he is ... I may not be my mother, but I respect the old ways. People look to the Council to guide and to protect. We've been without an alpha on the Council for three years."

Three years, yes, since Samuel Williams' death.

Their community boasted six alpha were-cats—strong, prideful males willing to step into the void made by Sam's passing. But the Witch Council of Elders had rejected each and every one of them. Deciding, unanimously, to hold the position for Sanura's mate, the cat of legend. Only such a cat would be able to bring the other alphas under his control and dominance. Assefa could accomplish the task. The question was whether he would want to undertake such a monumental responsibility.

"The were-cats are anxious. They will follow his lead if Agent Berber is the cat of legend." Anna uncrossed her legs again, a nervous smile lifting her lips. "But they won't like it, even if he is the cat of legend. Sanura turned her back on them a long time ago, denying so many the chance to become mate to the fire witch of legend."

Sanura had done exactly that, dating full-human males instead of her were-cat brothers. However, it had been Sam who'd protected her right to date whomever she chose without feeling pressured to go out with the sons from powerful were-cat families.

His rationale, beyond the fact that it was Sanura's goddess-given right to select her mate—were-cat or full-human—was a simple one. "Does your son have a Mngwa as his inner cat spirit?" he would ask each father who came before the Council. The answer was always the same. "No, Alpha, he does not." Sam would nod, a little sad, and then dismiss the man.

Those sad little nods had grown with each passing year, with Sam worried about Sanura's safety and future once he was gone. Makena's worry had matched her husband's. It still did, not because Sanura didn't have an alpha cat to rely on, but because she needed an alpha cat to rely upon.

"We need to be proactive. I'm sure you would agree."

Makena did agree, and she'd intended to speak with Sanura about the situation after her birthday party. She didn't know how much of their customs and rules Sanura had shared with Assefa. As it was, Sanura had yet to present Assefa to the Council. While the Oshun ceremony was a mere formality, all newly mated witch-were-cat couples were expected to come before the Council for their blessing. The short ceremony always ended with the baring of the mate marks, a symbol of the couple's physical and spiritual union.

"I'll have a word with my daughter soon."

Anna smiled, but not with relief. "Is he the cat of legend, Makena? I confess, as much as I love Sanura and want her happiness, I can't help but wish Agent Berber had never come to our city." Anna stood, her blue eyes staring down at Makena with age, wisdom, and unhidden terror. "I know it makes no sense, as if the young man's arrival has anything to do with the Day of Serpents. But if Special Agent Berber harbors the cat spirit of a Mngwa, he makes it real, even for us believers. As long as Sanura dated full-humans and shunned were-cats, we could convince ourselves that maybe, just maybe, the prophecy wouldn't come true. That Sanura Williams, despite her unique hair and eye coloring, was just a rare witch and nothing more."

Makena also got to her feet, hoisting her bag onto her shoulder. She reached out and laid a hand on Anna's trembling shoulder, understanding lacing her words of, "Assefa is this mother's greatest blessing for her daughter. He's kind, brave, generous, and quite brilliant." She squeezed Anna's shoulder, offering what comfort she could before continuing, "And he holds the Mngwa as his cat spirit— loyal, fierce, and deadly."

Blue eyes slipped closed, followed by a shallow, resigned nod. "It's as we feared. The prophecy will happen, no matter what we do or think." She opened her eyes, resignation turning to resolution. "But we can prepare Sanura and her mate as best we can. We will lend them our full strength and support, but the ceremony must come first. Speak with your daughter, Makena. Press upon Sanura the importance of having the blessing of her Council, and of her mate filling the chair left by her father."

"I will speak with Sanura. But not before her birthday party. You'll be there, right?"

A deep smile this time, reaching Anna's blue hydrangea eyes. "I'm looking forward to it. Maybe I'll even get a chance to meet that Special Agent of hers." A shake of her head. "What am I talking about, of course I'll meet him. From what I've been told, the party is at his home. When I received the invitation, I didn't understand why the get-together was being held in Alexandria instead of Baltimore. Then I had a conversation with Cynthia, and she cleared everything up for me." A youthful grin split Anna's lovely face. "Cynthia also told me that Special Agent Berber is quite the charmer."

"She said that, huh? Is that all?"

Anna grinned, looped her arm through Makena's, and began to walk her toward the closed office door. "Well, she said quite a bit more than that about Special Agent Berber, but I'm too much of a lady to repeat such things."

They looked at each other, then burst into laughter. Makena didn't have to think too hard to figure out what Cynthia Garvey had told Anna about Assefa. What did she overhear Cynthia say to Sanura about Assefa a couple of weeks ago? Oh yes, Cynthia told Sanura to "smile because with Assefa around it's the second best thing you can do with your lips."

Upon hearing that bit of naughty young woman talk, Makena had decided she didn't need the second cup of coffee she'd been looking forward to, and made a hasty retreat away from her kitchen and back up the stairs. She hoped Cynthia demonstrated more tact when describing Assefa's attributes to Anna. Which, based on how red Anna's cheeks now flamed, Cynthia had not. Perhaps Makena should have a word with Cynthia about appropriate and inappropriate conversations with the high priestess.

The women hugged. "I'll see you at Sanura's birthday party. When you meet Assefa, try not to drool. Or I'll have a devil of a time convincing him the Council isn't made up of a bunch of cougars waiting to pounce. And I don't mean were-cats."

Her cheeks blazed fire engine red. Maybe Anna was the true fire witch instead of Makena.

Makena opened the door, waved her goodbye and left. She still had plenty of time to meet Cynthia for lunch. She could, at least, get one conversation out of the way. The one she needed to have with Sanura would have to wait. Because Makena had no intention of ruining her daughter's birthday with talk of the prophecy.

Although, without a doubt, it would be on everyone's mind.

****

With focused golden eyes, alert gray ears, and keen black snout, the Mngwa took in his surroundings.

The prickly grass under his large, wide paws.

The heat of the midday sun beating down on his thick black-and-gray fur.

The scent of mullah bamyah—garlic, tomato juice, minced beef, okra, salt, and pepper.

The four snarling big cats stalking him.

Scanning each strong, lithe, and ferocious cat, the Mngwa cataloged their stance, their position, and the distance between each other and from the Mngwa. They flanked him, a large cat to his front, rear, and sides. If the Mngwa could smile, he would have. Foolishly, they thought their numbers a strategic advantage that would fell the undefeated Mngwa of myth and legend. Instead of a smile, he snarled, a baring of elongated teeth.

A challenge.

The four cats attacked, their bestial response to his bait.

Four sets of paws struck the ground, claws digging into grass and dirt, brawny legs propelling them forward. Razor-sharp teeth bared, husky growls cut through the muggy June air, and feline eyes glowed with a premature win.

The leopard reached the Mngwa first, snapping and going for the bigger cat's neck. Not wasting time with the youngest of the four attackers, the Mngwa sidestepped the snarling, snapping leopard. To only pivot, turn, and ram the side of the too-slow feline with the Mngwa's massive head. Away from the Mngwa the leopard flew, sailing through the air and crashing to the ground several feet away.

The three other cats spared no pitying glance to the downed leopard, who lay on his side, breathing labored and ragged. A sure sign of broken ribs.

More growls and snapping, each cat trying for a different part of the Mngwa's massive body. The Mngwa was having none of it, so he went on the offensive. Leaping over the biggest threat, the Bengal tiger, the Mngwa landed nimbly, then ran straight at the cheetah. Taking the speckled feline by surprise, the Mngwa powered over the cat, knocking him down before hauling him up by his scrawny neck and shaking. The cheetah's fragile neck was held firm between the Mngwa's curved saber-shaped teeth.

When the Mngwa no longer felt resistance, he opened his deadly jaws and allowed the cheetah to fall from his brutal clutch and slip, nearly unconscious, to the waiting grass.

Smack. Bite.

The lion and tiger claimed simultaneous strikes on the Mngwa. A swipe across his hindquarters and a bite to his side. The lion latched onto the Mngwa, his lethal teeth working to find purchase in the cat of legend's winter dense fur and even thicker hide.

Like the predator he was, the Bengal tiger charged while the Mngwa grappled with the formidable lion. A mix of yellow-and-orange with wide dark-brown stripes, the 510-pound tiger landed on top of the Mngwa. His weight hefty, his claws long, sharp, and dangerous. The maw that threatened his nape even deadlier.

The lion kept up his offensive, kept clawing, kept sinking his teeth in deeper and deeper.

The Mngwa roared, reared back on his hind legs, forcing the tiger off him and to the hard ground. With a side dive, the Mngwa dropped the entirety of his 695 pounds onto the 380-pound lion. His long, dark mane shot up and out with the force of the attack.

The downed lion snapped and snarled but didn't get up. No, with the Mngwa looming over him, golden eyes marble hard, paw raised, claws out and within striking range of the lion's throat, the feline had only two choices.

One would see him dead, while the other …

The lion lowered his eyes and then his head.

Submission.

Pleased, the Mngwa shifted his gaze to the tiger, his other senses having tracked the big cat the entire time.

He knew it would come down to this—the Mngwa versus the Bengal tiger. It always did.

The big cats circled, taking each other's measure. They searched for an opening, an opportunity to attack with the least probability of an effective and bruising counterattack. The combatants knew each other well—style of combat, defensive and offensive tactics.

Speed, size, and agility were on the Mngwa's side. Yet, the toxin from an animal no longer than an inch, the golden poison frog could kill a dozen men. Its tiny size and bright colors deceiving. Not, at a length of 120 inches and forty-three inches of shoulder height, with a tail just as long, there was anything small about the Bengal tiger baring his gleaming white teeth at the Mngwa.

The Mngwa underestimated no one—no matter the outward appearance of the enemy. Even the cat of legend, if incautious, could taste the bitter tang of defeat. So he watched and waited and plotted the tiger's downfall.

The tiger charged, all muscle and menace. His long, powerful legs ate up the distance between them, determined copper eyes all for the Mngwa.

The cat of legend braced himself, choosing to face the big cat head-on. He wanted this fight, the primal challenge that only a great beast like the Bengal tiger could give him. A glorious battle of fangs, fur, and claws that would push, force, and compel the Mngwa to prove his worth, his manhood, his undisputed dominance as the predator of predators.

Crash.

The ground shook. The Mngwa and tiger were locked in a feral clench.

Biting.

Clawing.

Pulling.

Strong. The tiger was so strong. *But not strong enough.*

The Mngwa opened his mouth wide and clamped down on fur and flesh. The neck of his opponent was thick with rigid muscles and delicate veins. The pulse of the tiger's life a strong, fast throbbing beat in the Mngwa's deadly mouth.

The tiger whimpered his pain. Neither loud nor long. But enough, enough for the Mngwa's ears to detect the effect of his attack. Yet the tiger fought on, as the Mngwa knew he would. As the Mngwa wanted him to, the tiger too stubborn, courageous, and fierce to submit so easily.

No, there was much fight left in the Bengal tiger.

He swiped at the Mngwa, vicious claws finding vulnerable underbelly and drawing blood. It hurt, but not enough for the bigger cat to release his vice grip. The Mngwa sank his teeth deeper into the side of the tiger's neck, tasting blood and prideful were-cat magic.

Her gardenia scent slammed into his senses seconds before the Mngwa and the tiger were surrounded by a ring of raging fire. Breaking his hold on the smaller cat, the Mngwa turned to see an angry fire witch barreling toward them—green eyes cold, red-gold hair and long striped sundress blowing in a wind that came out of nowhere. Her deadly focus was all for the Bengal tiger who, unlike when he fought the Mngwa, trembled with fear.

Lightning hissed.

Thunder growled.

And fire witch magic crackled in the blistering summer air.

Dammit, he had to do something and fast. Retreating as far as he could go within the cage of fire, the Mngwa propelled himself forward, accelerating when he approached the heated barrier and jumped. With ease, he cleared the four-foot high ring of fire and landed, with an *oompf* on top of a glaring Sanura.

"I can't believe you just—"

He licked her. From the front ring bodice of her green-and-orange striped dress, up her toned shoulders and around the tie neck, and into thick hair covering an ear, the Mngwa tasted his witch.

"Get off me, you big furball. I can't breathe."

Satisfied and comfortable, the Mngwa nuzzled his witch's face, neck, and her heaving breasts, unfazed by Sanura's angry protestations. The only part of him that pinned the witch down was his massive head and part of his chest. But, the Mngwa supposed, even that much weight could be heavy on a woman who, while five-feet-ten-inches tall, weighed no more than 140 pounds. With a teasing snort that had a lock of her wavy hair flying upward and out of her eye, the Mngwa decided it best to give the fire breathing witch some relief.

With a single thought from Assefa—*I'll take care of our witch, my friend, go to sleep*—the cat gave way to the man. A transformative effect where fur and hide succumbed to hair and skin, paws and claws shrank to hands and legs, and golden eyes, muzzle, and fangs retreated, waning under Assefa's command.

"Is that better?" Assefa smiled down at his hot-tempered girlfriend, right before settling the whole of him on top of the whole of her.

Very nice. Sanura made for the best mattress—plush, lush, and with the right amount of firmness.

"You're naked." A huffed complaint that did nothing to encourage Assefa to move off her.

"Of course. My Mngwa doesn't like clothing." He shifted on top of her, letting Sanura feel just how naked he was. "He thinks pants are too binding. What do you think?"

She closed her eyes and shook her head. "I think you need to worry more about that big damn tiger you were fighting rather than your Mngwa in boxers."

Seeing she had yet to grasp what was going on there, Assefa rolled off her, and then helped Sanura to her feet. He pointed to the three cats staring at her—wariness and awe in their eyes. Dammit, he thought his psychology professor was closeted in her office too busy creating her Blackboard community to pay attention to what was going on below her window. In retrospect, he should've taken the men farther away from the house for their sparring session. Because Assefa doubted Sanura knew how far Sudanese were-cats went when they trained, all they put their minds and bodies through to protect their mates, offspring, and household.

"The cheetah," Assefa began, "is Manute. You remember him, he and" —the hand not holding Sanura's gestured to the leopard— "Rashad take care of the grounds. And over there, that beautiful reddish lion is Omar. He's the finest of Sudanese chefs, which you can attest since you've been eating his delicious cuisine for the last month."

Slowly, understanding entered Sanura's eyes as they roamed from one cat to the next, before eventually settling on the tiger imprisoned in her fire circle. "Oh, and that must be ..." With a twinge of guilt Assefa detected through their partial mate bond, Sanura stretched out her arm, palm raised and faced the tiger and the fire. "Fire of earth, fire of magic, withdraw and retreat."

A gust of wind blew in from the Potomac River that buttressed Assefa's mansion home, extinguishing the flames, freeing the Bengal tiger, and heeding Sanura's command.

Tugging her hand from Assefa's, Sanura approached the Bengal tiger, whose head came nearly to Sanura's chest. When his witch reached out and laid her hand on top of the tiger's head, patting, his Mngwa roared to life.

Alert.

Possessive.

Jealous.

Yet Sanura didn't stroke or caress the tiger's soft fur the way she did the Mngwa's. When she spoke, it was with the same calm kindness she used with her family and friends. "I'm sorry, Zareb. I had no idea it was you underneath all of these stripes. You're a magnificent tiger."

Assefa's Mngwa snarled, and the man stepped forward, not liking the way Zareb's cat lifted his head and licked Sanura's hand.

Tasting.

Teasing.

Flirting.

Rashad, Omar, and Manute, still in cat form, slinked away, smart enough to sense the brewing fight in the air. This time, it wouldn't be another sparring match, no matter that Zareb was Assefa's best friend, FBI partner, and sworn protector.

"I think," Sanura said, backing away from the tiger, her voice still calm and kind, "that my fire saved you from Assefa's Mngwa. The next time you fight him, I suggest not charging the Mngwa outright. You'll never win that way, Zareb." She turned to Assefa, her eyes scanning his body and taking in the few bite and claw marks that were, right before her disapproving eyes, healing and beginning to fade.

Their eyes met.

"I don't like it."

"I didn't think you would. But it's our way, Sanura, what makes us strong and formidable were-cats."

She closed those wondrous emerald eyes of hers, lowered her head and whispered, "I know. Always protecting, willing to kill, to die." Something in the soft, haunted way she spoke those words, Assefa didn't think they were for him.

His Sanura could be the most complex of women sometimes. And Assefa wasn't fool or arrogant enough to believe he would decipher all of her inner workings any time soon.

If ever.

Assefa grabbed Sanura around the waist, lifted her into his arms, and before she squealed her surprise, kissed her.

Hard.

Long.

And with all the love of a were-cat for his mysterious witch.

CHAPTER THREE

In silence, Sanura trailed Assefa as he made his way through the kitchen, down the long hall, and up the stairs. Naked and gloriously made, Assefa strode through his home with the cool confidence of a man who knew his power and worth. Luscious toffee skin coated with beads of perspiration clung to rippling muscles and taut abs, thighs, and ass. The moisture, like Sanura's appreciative eyes, was hesitant to let go of the extraordinary specimen on two brawny legs.

"I feel your eyes on me." Assefa's stride never wavered, long legs taking him up the stairs and to their two-room suite.

"You're in front of me and naked. Where else am I supposed to look?" Despite the spectacular view of his impressive nude form and Assefa's delectable kiss on the lawn, a part of Sanura was angry with him.

When they reached the suite, Assefa stepped aside and allowed her to precede him inside. She walked through the sitting room, a spacious area with a modern design. The room was furnished with pearl wool carpet, two black leather chaise lounges, an oak coffee table professionally scuffed for a worn feel, and a white sofa Sanura adored because it was the perfect spot for snuggling with Assefa when they watched movies.

By the time she entered the bedroom and turned around, hands on hips, Assefa stood just inside the bedroom. With a shoulder propped against the doorframe and arms crossed over bulging chest, the special agent looked too sexy and patient for his own good.

Sanura licked her lips, and her eyes slid, ever so admiringly, over every scrumptious inch of him. By the gods, Assefa Berber, at six feet tall, was all male, muscle, and might. Built like an Olympic weightlifter, his body mass topped two hundred pounds. There was not an ounce of fat on him, just a form honed to athletic perfection. Years of swimming, jogging, and weightlifting gave Assefa a naturally-achieved sculpted look that had women gawking.

She was no different, taking immense pleasure in her lover's physique. The feel of his hard body under her hands, her mouth, and inside her hot, eager body. The carnal thought had her fire spirit whispering tempting ideas to Sanura, veering the woman off course with thoughts of how good Assefa's naked, sweaty body had felt when he'd lain atop her less than ten minutes ago.

"You're upset."

Sanura was more than that, but Assefa, always the gentleman, didn't seek to exploit the lustful craving of her fire spirit. Instead, his frank statement allowed Sanura to refocus and hush the sensual hiss coming from her inner spirit.

"I thought you were in danger. I thought another one of your cases had bled over into your personal life."

Assefa's face, so unreadable in public, transformed into an array of unconcealed emotions when they were alone together. Like now, when dark-brown eyes softened, first with comprehension and then with an apology.

On the same lawn where she'd seen Assefa engaged in a four against one were-cat battle, she'd killed three siren sisters. Killers of men by bloody trade, they'd come to Assefa's home seeking revenge against the man who'd killed their murderous sister. He'd taken the youngest siren's life in the line of duty, of course, but sirens, while cruel and violent toward men, loved each other with a passion rivaled only by their barbaric bloodlust.

So they'd come, drugging Assefa and his household of were-cats with their deathly beautiful operatic ballads. A month later, Sanura had yet to shake the guilt over the glorious wave of pleasure that had radiated through every cell in her body when she'd defended, to the death, Assefa and herself from those three murderous sirens.

She'd killed, and a part of her, the fire spirit part, felt not a slither of remorse for what she'd done. But the woman, the psychologist and professor, abhorred the act with physical revulsion.

Control. Sanura needed it. But that night, that shameful night, she'd lost control, claiming three lives as a result. Tainted, murderous lives true, but lives all the same. She had no right. Although, at the time, entitlement was a succulent fruit she'd greedily consumed. Now, as she reflected on the churning rage that had seized her when she'd thought Assefa in danger again, she wondered if she would have let loose her fire spirit to save him. Would she have permitted the heated beast within to torch and kill Zareb, Rashad, Omar, and Manute? Had fire and death been her intention when she'd run from her office and stormed outside?

The realization that she did not know had Sanura shuddering in self-reproach.

Beefy arms wrapped around her, pressing Sanura's trembling body into a wall of warmth and support. Cradling her, Assefa, who'd approached on silent feet, held Sanura with a gentle strength she'd only ever known while in the presence of her father.

Samuel Williams, gods how she missed him. His death, his sacrifice, bubbling acid of guilt and sadness in the pit of her stomach, ravaged Sanura from the inside out. When the tears came, as they often did when she thought of how she'd stolen a husband from a wife, Sanura didn't fight the liquid rush of pain and remorse.

"Shh, it's all right, sweetheart. You didn't hurt Zareb. You didn't know who he and the others were. That was my fault. I should've told you. I shouldn't have let you find out the way you did. Don't cry, Sanura." Assefa pressed a loving kiss to her damp cheek and whispered, his voice deep and husky, "I've got you. You're in control. Always in control."

Sanura breathed in the sweaty scent of her familiar and burrowed deeper into his reassuring embrace. Assefa thought he understood, but he didn't. Well, he did, just not fully. He knew she fought to keep a tight leash on her fire spirit, lest the beast raged out of control, burning anyone who angered or threatened Sanura and those she most loved. But Assefa knew nothing of the sacrifice Sam had made for his daughter the day Makena pushed Sanura into this world, giving birth to the fire witch of legend.

And Makena, well, Sanura had no intention of letting her mother know she knew the truth. It would only hurt Makena to know how deeply Sam's sacrifice had gutted Sanura, layers of sooty guilt and pounds of ashen sorrow the truth of her heart.

But her secret, the millstone around her neck, did not have to become Makena's and Assefa's burden to bear. Her mother, a widow thanks to Sanura, didn't need more pain heaped upon her. And Assefa, gods, Sanura wished she were the woman he deserved instead of the witch who'd selfishly bonded his cat to her fire spirit. An incomplete mate bond, her displeased fire spirit jeered at Sanura every day she allowed to slip by without accepting Assefa's binding bite.

As for the man holding her, soothing Sanura's silent pains, sometimes absolute control enabled more than bolstered, buried more than strengthened, and denied more than freed.

Back came into contact with a firm mattress, and Sanura gazed up into Assefa's gorgeous eyes. "You didn't have to carry me to the bed."

He settled beside her, as naked as the day he came roaring into this world. At least, that was Sanura's image of Assefa's birth. A healthy baby with lungs aplenty, eyes bright and tiny body fierce with the heart of a poet and the soul of a warrior cat.

Yanking the indigo duvet, a regal jacquard made of one hundred percent Egyptian cotton with a stunningly woven rosette pattern, over them, Assefa tucked Sanura against his side. Once done, he closed his eyes.

For a minute, they rest there in silence, Assefa naked and Sanura in a maxi dress. Her feet were bare, as they'd been when she'd flown from her office and out of the house.

"What are you doing?" she asked into the stillness of the room. The adobe blue-brown multi-stripe flat draperies were doing an excellent job keeping the rays from the afternoon sun at bay.

Eyes closed and arms wrapped around her, Assefa sighed. "I'm trying to take a nap with my witch."

"But it's the middle of the day and you never nap." She wiggled in his embrace, an attempt to free herself so she could get up, go back to her office and get some work done. Now that she'd calmed, she felt embarrassed at her teary outburst. When in the hell did she become such a crybaby of a witch?

As composed as ever, Assefa tightened his hold and ignored her. After a minute of fuming quietly and contemplating all the ways she would repay Assefa for using his strength against her, she realized, with annoyance, that she was actually tired. Tired enough, apparently, her yawn a colossal betrayal, to take a midday nap.

She relaxed in Assefa's hold, no longer viewing it as a trap but the emotional tether he intended it to be. Would he always do this for her? Know what she needed before she did? Be her lighthouse in the storm when all around her, inside of her, exploded, thundered, and seared everything in her heated path?

Sanura planted a kiss to Assefa's chest, over his powerfully beating heart. She wanted to tell him how cherished he made her feel, how secure, how protected and how loved. But she stilled her tongue, fearing he would sense all she would leave unsaid. Instead, she watched Assefa, his handsome face set in repose, thick brows, broad nose, and long lashes adding to the masculine appeal that was her special agent. When he spoke, with the cultured accent befitting a son of the House of Berber, the erotic timbre put Sanura in the mindset of cozy winter nights and sultry summer days.

By the time Sanura raised her lips to his, Assefa was fast asleep. Knowing, in the deepest recess of her heart, her soul, she would follow Assefa anywhere, Sanura allowed herself to follow him into slumber.

****

"They are beautiful. *She* is beautiful."

Sàngó glanced over his shoulder at his wife and smiled. No mere mortal could rival the godly exquisiteness of his wife. In human form or her natural electrical state, Oya stole his heart as much as she crushed it each time she returned to her watery prison. Her battle with her sister was an endless cycle of death and destruction that flooded the world with fear and faith.

And tears. An ocean of crimson tears and bloated bodies of loss, of grief, of disillusionment.

Despite it all, desolate days and unsatisfied centuries, each time Oya returned to him, Sàngó's barren heart bloomed anew. Reveling in, once more, the rejuvenating rays of the sun. Yet the glorious sensation and the rush of euphoria were but temporary states of mind. Joy and serenity, twin beasts of cruelty, mocked him each time Sàngó had to stand by as his wife was ripped from his impotent grasp.

He had sworn, on his honor and the souls of the children he and Oya never created, but had found life in the fire witches who shared Oya's burden, to end the vicious cycle. To reclaim his wife, heart, and life.

To achieve such an end required an unflinching heart that matched his own.

Desperate.

Willing.

Devoted.

He had discovered such a mirroring heart in the body of a were-cat. Were-cat fathers, he'd discovered, made for the best of allies.

Sàngó watched as Oya floated around him and closer to the sleeping couple. Hair the color of a cherry opal bathed in gold dust fell in luscious coils to her waist, green dragon flower eyes stared in adoration and bow lips lifted in a pleased smile. Reaching out, she brushed a lock of red-gold hair from the sleeping witch's face, the color lovely but not as vibrant as the hair of the goddess drinking her in.

"Careful not to wake the child, my love."

A slender hand adorned with nothing more than an oval-shaped black opal ring, surrounded by amethysts and garnets, traversed the mortal's visage, love, hope, and worry in Oya's motherly touch.

"They are under a sleeping spell, Sàngó, worry not. We will be gone from this human realm long before either awake. But you have gazed upon our daughter before? Is that not right, husband?"

Remaining at the foot of the bed, Sàngó looked from Oya and to the slumbering witch. This child was but one of many he had laid eyes upon over the centuries. In their own way, they all resembled the human form Oya most liked to take. Although this mortal seemed to favor the goddess most of all, in facial structure, coloring, and build.

"Yes, when she was but a new babe born."

"And you have watched over her?" She placed a hand on top of the mortal man's head, playing with his dark, short curls the way she would any creature she deemed worthy of her attention and affection. "And this one, Sàngó, have you watched over him as well?"

In his own fashion, he had kept an eye on the fire witch and cat of legend. A god's fatherly machinations, invisible and strategic.

Not that gods comprehended the power and complexity of parenthood in the same way mortals did. In the way Samuel Williams had. But that foreign concept meant little to the god of fire, thunder, and lightning. Yet he was not unmoved by his daughter of fire, which was more than he had ever felt for any other mortal.

"Yes, Oya. These two, more than the others, are the best prepared and capable of setting you free, ending this farce of a prophecy."

Sàngó, with the aid of Samuel Williams, had granted the sleeping witch and were-cat a boon. After so long being without his wife, Sàngó would commit most any act to have her returned to him permanently. But his wife, as self-important as any deity, refused to extend her hand in forgiveness, in sisterhood, in compromise to Mami Wata without her older sister humbling herself first.

Prideful gods would one day be the death of the human realm and all the wondrous creatures therein. The gods' unwillingness to impose limitations on self and to acknowledge their imperfections a fatal mistake of incalculable measure. Yet it was possible, though slight, the young ones sleeping with pitying innocence would liberate them all.

That was the purpose of the prophecy after all. Still, godly hubris was a slow-acting poison for which a cure did not yet exist.

Eyes cast to the witch, Oya asked, "Purple, red, orange, or black?"

"I do not understand, my love."

Oya caught Sàngó's buttery gaze as she lowered herself to the carpeted floor. Her own gaze held ageless power, as well as a timeless capacity for sentimentality and mercy but also for selfishness and wrath. "Which color do you most prefer on your consort?"

Sàngó's eyes began to glow lightning white as he admired his wife's human form. Tall, sumptuous and sinfully edible, the royal purple pleated wrap gown with sheer blouson sleeves and accordion maxi skirt she wore brought out the warmness of her dark sienna skin tone, made even more delectable with the thigh-high front slip that revealed one silky-smooth leg.

He cleared a throat gone dry. "Purple." Although Sàngó also had a fondness for Oya in red silk. He glanced down at the were-cat. The way the mortal held his witch with passionate possessiveness, Sàngó could not help but respect the man. These women, the ones Sàngó and the mortal had given their heart to, challenged and infuriated them on a level no one else could or dared. But the love and loyalty they received in return rivaled the beauty of the moon and the heat of the sun.

Oya fingered the sleeve of her dress. "I thought you would say red, but purple is an excellent choice as well."

Sàngó began to fade, their time in this realm nearly at an end. His corporeal body was unneeded for the trip home. But Oya lingered at her witch's side, hesitant to leave the child to her fate.

"She is my favorite of all our daughters."

The daughters who had failed and died, fire witches too weak of mind and body to end the prophecy and ascend.

"I know."

"I do not wish to see her torn apart by Mami Wata's beasts. Her body cast to the four corners of this land."

"He will permit no harm to come to her. I know his mind, have peered into his heart. But you must come now, Oya. The one-month grace period ends at midnight."

"Yes, but the bargain was for naught. The bond is yet complete. My champion's grief was greater than I had imagined."

If Oya witnessed, as Sàngó had, the tears shed by the newborn fire witch when her father bartered his life away to protect his daughter, she would neither be surprised nor disappointed. As it was, Mami Wata's concession of the one-month grace period had resulted in no gains for Oya. Now, for the next sixty days, Mami Wata could "play" with the fire witch and cat of legend without interference from Oya. If Oya's champion had permitted her were-cat to claim her as mate, forming a magical bond capable of defeating the water witch of legend and Mami Wata's water beasts, in return, Oya agreed to grant Mami Wata's water witch the power of wind magic.

Poor strategy for Oya. He hoped the vulnerable position the children now found themselves would not see the young ones emotionally broken or brutally murdered before the summer came to its sweltering finale.

Leaning over the child, Oya kissed the girl's forehead, stirring the witch's hair with her godly magic. "Be well, Sanura, and have a most blessed twenty-ninth birthday. Enjoy my offering." Floating to the other side of the bed, Oya placed two fingers on the were-cat's chin, opened his mouth and blew. Sparks of gold glitter descended. Like a golden leaf from a quaking aspen tree, the glitter fell from Oya and into the mortal's mouth. Reflexively, he swallowed. Closing his mouth, Oya sealed her gift with a kiss. "Trust her heart, Assefa, and believe in yourself. No matter the challenge, no matter the foe, be brave, be wise, be the undefeated Mngwa of lore."

Sparing the children one last look, Oya took Sàngó's offered hand and faded until nothing remained of the gods but a gift-wrapped box in Sanura's closet and a speck of gold glitter on Assefa's lip.

CHAPTER FOUR

Kansas City, Missouri

Jeremy closed grainy, green eyes and curled his five-feet-five and ninety-pound frame in a tight ball. His home for the foreseeable future, a dirt hole, one of a series of tunnels dug into the earth by the forgotten and neglected residents of Kansas City. People with good-paying jobs, three square meals a day, and a warm, safe place to call home would neither understand a place like this nor the utter desperation and soul-rending need that came with forging a shelter from shattered dreams, stolen shovels, and lost hope.

Two years ago, he'd been one of those naïve people. The kind ignorant to the harsh and heartless underbelly of the city. The kind of person who thought the love of mother and father to be unconditional and forever. At sixteen, Jeremy's world had changed in a violent and pitiful way.

As he scooted as close to the wall of hard dirt as he could wedge himself, away from Ethan and Marcus, twenty-something drug addicts with a mean streak when they didn't get their fix, Jeremy swallowed rancid fear and burning tears. He prayed the men would find another tunnel to bed down in for the night or simply ignore him.

As much as Jeremy disliked Ethan and Marcus, bullies like the ones he'd known all through school, he figured they had a story as ugly and depressing as his own. None of the more than four dozen homeless people who called this shantytown home would be there if their lives, before falling into this pride-stealing abyss of horrors, was an existence they could or wanted to return to. While all of them had a story, some awful tale of woe, Jeremy, as much as possible, kept his mouth shut, eyes averted, and questions to himself.

That's how people survived on the streets. Because the daily, bitter grind damn sure couldn't be called living.

Survival—the best word to describe his zombie-like existence, shuffling from one day and into the next.

Dead but not quite.

He'd done what he could to make it on the streets alone. He hadn't buried his pain in alcohol and drugs like Ethan, Marcus, and so many others. Nor had he made it a habit of selling his body for cash or a place to crash. Although, if the after-hours, off-the-books stocking gig at the warehouse didn't pan out soon, Jeremy would have no choice but to slink back to "Mae West." A piece of shit pimp who catered to women with a fetish for female sex partners who were young, tomboyish, and subservient.

The role of submissive, making him the bottom partner, had resulted in Jeremy being bound, flogged, and fucked with strap-on dicks by soccer moms and professional women who thought a college degree and 401k gave them the right to treat a street kid however they wanted. For him, there had been no safewords, a limit to the older women's edgeplay that would free him from their sexual "game." Unfortunately, powerless people, like Jeremy, endured much worse every single day.

He'd survived so far. But sometimes, like tonight, when his too-thin body cramped and ached from lack of food, he filled his belly on succulent thoughts of ending it.

Once and for all.

Who would miss him? A boy trapped in a girl's body, Jennifer Sara Whitehead, named after both of his grandmothers, was a biological girl with bound breasts, baggy shirts and pants, black combat boots, and a buzz cut that would make an Army Ranger proud. And he'd gotten his ass kicked so many damn times, spending more time in the nurse's office than in class.

"If you wanna act like a boy, then you can take this ass whippin' like one, she-male."

He'd been called every slur imaginable, from classmates, neighbors, teachers, even his older sister. Two weeks before he ran away from home, Jeremy's mother had wept at his hospital bed, the teen's wrists wrapped in white gauze from where he'd slit them, hoping to put a stop to the endless pain, self-loathing and rejection.

"Why can't you be normal like your sisters, Jen?"

With exhaustion and disbelief, he'd stared at his mother. How many times had he explained his feelings to her, asked her to call him by his chosen name?

"I was never meant to be a girl, Mom." Voice trembled and rasped with the repeated confession. "I've always known." Jeremy placed a hand over his still-beating heart, the organ keeping him alive while the rest of him ceased living when his father, unable to handle having a transgender daughter, had worked himself into an early grave. "In here. I'm a boy in here, Mom. I pretended. For so long I pretended to be what you, Dad, and everyone expected me to be. But I can't do it anymore. I'm sorry I'm not the daughter you want. But I can be the son you and Dad never had."

Bluish-green eyes overflowed with tears, red hair spilled onto heaving shoulders, and a face that had aged ten years since the passing of his father had dropped into April Whitehead's hands.

Reaching out, Jeremy had stroked his mother's hair, his wrists throbbing with anguished failure. As if his touch scalded, burning cold flesh to the brittle bone, his mother had jumped away from him, knocking over the chair she'd been sitting in.

"You've always been a selfish girl, Jen. If not for you, our family would be whole and happy. The way it was when Daddy was alive. But you ruined everything. It isn't natural. You were born a girl. That's the way God made you, and God doesn't make mistakes."

Another well-traveled argument. But the hateful, arctic way Jeremy's mother had glared at him, well, that look had been new.

Revulsion, confusion, even anger, he'd seen in April Whitehead's eyes countless times. But never hate.

Yet, if he were honest, he'd felt the emotion long before he'd lain in his bed and taken a switchblade to his veins. The first time he'd sensed his mother's hatred had been the day of his father's funeral, a heart attack having claimed the life of the forty-eight-year-old accountant. In the days and weeks after his father's passing, his mother had spoken little to him, furious with Jeremy for wearing a suit and tie to his father's service instead of a black mourning dress as his sisters had.

Jeremy's life had only gotten worse after that, his sisters shunning him at home, and bullies making school the last place he wanted to be. So yeah, he'd known the cutting lash of hate, of disgust. Still, to have his mother drop her mask and openly reveal the ultimate truth of her bigoted heart, Jeremy knew he had four options.

Stay or leave.

Die or live.

He'd chosen to leave and live. The friendless child inside of Jeremy still cried for his mother's abandoned love, even after two soul-scarring years of emotional and physical destitution.

"Did you hear that?" Marcus' too-loud voice invaded the gloomy space.

Jeremy ignored the guy. He didn't think the question was meant for him, anyway. Besides, with thoughts of the past swirling in his head, he hadn't heard a thing.

"Only thing I hear is your big ass mouth, man. Shut the fuck up and pass the forty."

Jeremy did hear a bit of shuffling from Marcus and Ethan's side of the hole, a mother, one dirt tunnel over, singing to her crying toddler, as well as sporadic footsteps from the wooded area above them, but nothing more than the normal nighttime sounds.

"I'm telling you, I heard something. Sounded like … shit, I don't know. A bear, maybe."

"You're as dumb as a bag of rocks. There ain't no goddamn bears in Kansas fuckin' City. Not even in these sorry ass woods. It's the brew, man. If you can't handle your shit, then I'll down the rest."

"I'm not wasted, asshole. And I'm no dummy."

Marcus, voice angrier than loud, spoke with a hurt offense that bespoke of past pains at having his intelligence questioned, reminding Jeremy of Arthur, a student with special needs in his ninth-grade United States History class. The kid was forever getting into fights with jerks who liked to make fun of him, calling Arthur cruel names like "retard" "dummy" and "weirdo." By tenth-grade, Arthur still read on a third-grade level, but he'd had a growth spurt over the summer and put on fifteen pounds of solid muscle. After that, well, those jerks who took so much pleasure in teasing Arthur gave the linebacker a wide berth.

"And I know what the fuck I heard." Heavy shifting from behind Jeremy, and then a, "I'm gonna go check it out. You can stay here or get your lazy ass up and go with me."

"No thanks. I have your share of this liquid gold to take care of. You can go find Yogi the Bear your damn self."

"You're a real ass sometimes, Ethan."

"Yeah, well, cheers and happy bear hunting."

Thick layers of darkness prevented Jeremy, who had turned on his back and opened his eyes, to see either of the arguing men. Yet he heard, what had to be Marcus, amble out of the twenty-foot deep hole. He waited and listened until he could no longer hear the shuffle of Marcus' tennis shoes.

"You asleep over there, little Jeremy?"

He considered not answering but thought better of it. No way would Ethan believe Jeremy had slept through his argument with Marcus.

"Yeah, man, I'm up."

"Thought so. You're a quiet little bastard. So, did you hear anything?"

"Just the usual."

"Yeah, me too. Marcus is full of shit."

Maybe. Maybe not. The guy, for once, had sounded lucid and sure of himself. Jeremy didn't doubt Marcus had heard something. But a bear? Jeremy didn't know about that, even though black bears did call Missouri home.

Jeremy closed his eyes. The toddler had stopped crying a couple of minutes ago, which meant he could probably get two hours of uninterrupted sleep before the girl started with the waterworks again. Ashley cried a lot, much more than his little sister, Kristie, ever had. But Ashley went to bed hungry every night. What two-year-old wouldn't have a fitful night's sleep, with an empty belly as her nighttime story?

He began to drift off, body relaxing and mind shutting down for the night. The shantytown couldn't be called home, but it was enclosed, cool, and as safe as one could get sleeping several feet away from an unrepentant drug abuser.

Cackle.

Cackle.

Cackle.

Jeremy's eyes flew open.

Cackle.

Cackle.

"What the fuck was that?"

Jeremy bolted upright. "The hell if I know." He listened, hearing nothing but Ethan's heavy, drunk breathing and the rapid *thud, thud, thud* of his pounding heart.

"Do you think it's a bear like Marcus said?"

Jeremy pushed to his knees and peered into the inky blackness and toward the mouth of the tunnel, seeing nothing but morbid darkness. He didn't want to think about what the sound had been or the thread of fear he'd detected in Ethan's beer-roughened voice.

"What should we do?" Jeremy asked.

A large, strong hand wrapped around his arm and yanked Jeremy to his feet. Then he was pressed between a dirt wall and a six-foot-two body that smelled of cigarettes, beer, and sweaty pits.

"What in the hell are you doing? Get the hell off me. I can't breathe, man."

"Shut the fuck up, J. I may not know what in the hell that sound was, but it damn sure didn't sound like no goddamn bear. Not that I know what the fuck a bear sounds like."

Jeremy lifted his hands and shoved against Ethan's wide back. The wall of burly man did not budge. Despite the dude eating little more than handouts from local food pantries, Ethan still had bulk. Enough bulk to keep the scrawny eighteen-year-old Jeremy pinned to the wall.

"Stop squirming. By the way, your tits feel real nice against my back. They would feel better if you didn't keep them wrapped all the hell up like some fuckin' mummy."

Hands dropped to his sides and mouth opened on a shocked gasp. How in the world had I-don't-give-a-shit-about-anything-or-anyone-but-getting-high Ethan figured out his secret?

Cackle.

Cackle.

"Just stay put, J. If something comes through that hole, I'll protect you."

Protect him? Ethan, protect him? No one had ever stepped between Jeremy and harm, not even his family. But this guy, a down-on-his-luck homeless man who seemed to live only for the next high, had placed himself between Jeremy and whatever in the hell was making the god-awful squeaky giggle sounds.

Heart swelled with warm gratitude before tears fell in silent droplets.

Then a screaming Marcus burst through the opening, bringing the giggling, cackling sound with him.

****

Baltimore, Maryland
Sankofa Preparatory School

Serving on the Witch Council of Elders had proven to be a perpetual exercise in patience and restraint. Admittedly, when she shared the duty with Sam all the headaches that came with leading and managing thousands of witches and were-cats in a society parallel to that of the full-human one, the stress of it all didn't bear down so heavily on her. Whenever Makena felt her fire spirit rise to the fore, in frustration or fury, she would only have to gaze across the solid wood conference table and find her mate's reassuring eyes.

With a single, knowing look and a sympathetic smile from Sam, Makena always found the strength to calm the fire beast within. Now, as she stared across the table, the vacant oxblood upholstered chair mocked instead of soothed. And the chatter floating around her only held an appeal because the topic reached deep into her heart, reminding Makena of all her mate had sacrificed. If not for the prophecy, the fifth conference chair, like the chair at the head of her dining room table at home, would be occupied by Samuel Williams. As a Trinidadian, Sam loved three things: his family, his island home, and his gods.

Makena neither shared his love for their gods nor the trust he'd placed in them. As far as she was concerned, the gods had taken too much from her and threatened to take even more. What was there to love?

Why a fire witch? Why not a wind witch? She'd asked herself those two questions since before Sanura was born, and even more after her birth. In that respect, the prophecy had never made sense to Makena. Not that any of it made sense, but gods were capricious beings.

Every five-hundred-plus years, Mami Wata, a water goddess, chose a water witch as her champion. Oya, goddess of wind, fire, and thunderbolts, to Makena's knowledge, had never chosen a wind witch to wage the prophesized battle between water and wind. Instead, only fire witches received Oya's "blessing."

The lack of logic once weighed on Makena, but no more. While she detested it was her daughter who was saddled with the overwhelming and unfair responsibility of saving thousands, maybe millions, of lives from Mami Wata's serpents and her water witch, if not Sanura, then it would be some other witch. Makena had never been a self-centered woman, and she wouldn't, despite her fear for her daughter, wish Sanura's fate on another innocent witch. Wind, water, fire, or earth, no witch deserved to have her life upended and manipulated by anyone, not even by the almighty gods.

"Have you heard a word we've said, Makena?"

Her eyes shifted from the empty chair and to the freckle-faced woman who filled the chair next to Sam's. Barbara Vaughn, born in 1945, the same year as the founding of Sankofa Preparatory School. A level four wind witch, Barbara joined the Council when Salt-N-Pepa was pushin' it and Crockett and Tubbs made sockless loafers and shiny fabric jackets must-have menswear. Stylish with her wavy, short hairstyle dyed a warm and bright mix of golden and auburn, Barbara's sandy-brown eyes and light-brown skin revealed decades of wisdom and a widow's pain that mirrored Makena's.

"You're speaking about my daughter and her future, what part of this conversation do you think I would take lightly, Barbara? Or do you expect me to nod at the end of each of your long-winded sentences just to assure you of my attentiveness?"

"Temperamental fire witch." Barbara leaned forward, her rather large breasts settling on the cherry finish of the conference table. "I know this is a sensitive subject for you. Trust me, we all understand. The sooner we have the ceremony, the better everyone will feel."

Makena doubted the ceremony would bring the type of relief Barbara thought it would. But she understood her friend's point well enough. For the Sankofa community, knowing the fire witch and cat of legend's mate bond was blessed by the Council would put many a were-cat and witch mind at ease.

That wasn't what had Makena on edge. The Oshun ceremony, once Makena reminded Sanura of her witch duty, would be a simple matter of proceeding through ritualistic steps they'd performed dozens of times. Each member of the Council knew their role, even Anna, who'd never engaged in the Oshun as half of a mated pair.

Peggy Bradford, the youngest member of the Council at forty-nine and a level four earth witch, sat next to Makena. By age thirty, Peggy's hair had turned silver, which, surprisingly, made her look even younger. Hair coiled in what Cynthia would call "baby locks," Peggy pointed to the closed conference room door, a frown of disapproval on her oval face. "This Council will not be bullied."

Anna, to whom the statement had been directed, also looked toward the wooden door. Back and shoulders straight, the high priestess kept her chin held high under Peggy's scrutinizing stare. "No, we will not. But he has a right, as every member of our network does, to speak to the Council upon request. We can't ignore our own rules when they don't suit us."

"I'm not suggesting we ignore our rules," Peggy countered. "But let's be real. Paul Chambers has always been an opportunistic bastard."

Knowing where this conversation was headed, Makena stood and moved to the sideboard. On the table sat a carafe of coffee, a plate with pastries and a bowl filled with tasty summer fruit—mango, cantaloupe, watermelon, strawberries, and papaya.

"He tried to slide into the Alpha chair when your father retired and again when Sam died."

Makena selected a few pieces of fruit, using a silver serving spoon to put them on her plate. Deciding between a cherry tart and a chocolate éclair, Makena kept her back to the women, knowing Peggy wouldn't let up until Anna stiffened her spine and pushed back.

"And he's doing it again. Because the only time the alpha of the lion pride requests an audience with the Council, it has to do with filling the vacant seat. He wasn't suited thirty-five years ago when he was sniffing under your skirt, and he isn't suited now. Your parents knew it, and so do I."

Barbara tsked. "And how old were you thirty-five years ago, Peg? Don't speak of ancient history as if you were a front-row spectator."

After making her selection, the chocolate éclair of course, Makena filled her water glass and returned to the conference table.

"That doesn't mean I'm not right. On this Council, we don't lie to ourselves or each other. I'm not saying these things to hurt you, Anna, but they must be said."

"No, you aren't trying to hurt Anna," Makena said, grateful the Council conference room was soundproof, which meant no one, not even a were-cat with enhanced hearing, could hear them, "but you could speak to her with a bit of sensitivity. We all know Anna's history with Paul. And no, he will never be this Council's alpha. And yes, if we could legitimately deny his request, I would take immense pleasure in sending the scheming were-cat home. But we can't. But what we can do is show a united front."

Makena bit into her éclair, the coffee-flavored custard melting on her tongue. By the gods, the dessert was sinfully delicious. No wonder Barbara had eaten two since the meeting began.

Barbara glanced from Peggy to Makena, then finally to Anna. "No matter what Paul may say, we know he only speaks for his pride of lions. But that doesn't mean the other alphas don't agree with him. That's what we must determine. We don't want to install a new Council Alpha who will have to fight his were-cats. That's not the purpose of the role."

No, it wasn't, but Makena had a bad feeling it would end up that way.

"But we haven't even broached the subject with the young man in question," Barbara continued.

All eyes shifted to Makena, the last bite of éclair on the tip of her fork. She bit down. Chewed. Savored.

"After Sanura's birthday party." She'd told Anna this before, and she hadn't changed her mind in the two weeks since they'd last spoken.

Anna considered Makena. "Four days is a long time, Makena, especially since there are so many rumors going around about Sanura's mate. I know you want to wait, to not ruin your daughter's special day, but I'm not sure if it's wise to put it off any longer. I think we should bring the kids in as soon as possible. We can talk about the Oshun ceremony and the alpha position. Can you take care of arranging the meeting?"

She could, and she would, if that was the decision of the Council. While she hated to admit it, Anna, Peggy, and Barbara were right. Paul's presence there today was but a physical reminder of three years of Council neglect. Without an alpha on the Council, the were-cats had no voice or representation. They were owed both. And the Council needed to rectify the situation with all deliberate speed.

"Sanura is on summer break," Makena informed the Council, "so her schedule is flexible. But Assefa is a busy agent, I'm not—"

"It doesn't matter." Peggy leaned back in her chair, fingers tapping an annoying beat on the table. "I leave on a medical conference tonight. I put the trip on our shared calendar."

Makena was certain the event hadn't been placed on their shared calendar until five minutes before today's meeting. It was a wonder Dr. Bradford made it to her surgeries on time.

"I won't return until late Saturday, which means I'll miss the party. That makes Sunday the best option for my work schedule. We can drive out to Alexandria. No point making the children drive to us when we're the ones who want something from them." Peggy sipped from what had to be lukewarm coffee, considering how long she'd been nursing the drink. "Unless the three of you want to have the meeting without me."

"If the meeting was only with Sanura," Anna said, "then I would have no problem pushing forward without you. But Assefa Berber is not from our community. We need to meet and introduce ourselves to him as a complete Council. He'll have questions of us, and it'll be unfair to ask him to consider a request that will change his life without giving him the courtesy of the presence of our entire Council. Dammit, I didn't want to wait, but it seems we have no choice."

They sat in silence for a couple of minutes, a frisson of displeasure wafting from the other side of the door where Paul Chambers waited to be seen by the Council.

"It's decided then. We'll speak with Sanura and Assefa in four days. Makena will see to the arrangement, and we'll get our first glimpse of the cat of legend at Sanura's birthday party." Anna picked up the conference room phone to her right, placing the receiver to her face and hitting a button. "Helen, please let Mr. Chambers know the Council will see him now."

CHAPTER FIVE

"Now, isn't this much better?" Sanura sat on the white-and-pink blanket, shoes off, shades on, and back pressed against the towering white oak, its bright green leaves providing shade aplenty.

Above her, looking far more serious than the occasion warranted, Rachel Foster scanned the surrounding area. Eyes the color of the Sahara Desert at dusk, took in the vacant academic buildings to the east and west of them, the five-story Administration Building to their south, and the Orunmila Library, the Orisha of wisdom, knowledge and divination, to the north. The quadrangle lay in the middle, green grass everywhere except the four stone paths. Each path led to a cardinal point on campus.

East, water.

West, earth.

South, fire.

North, wind.

At Sankofa Preparatory School, witches in fourth through eighth-grade learned basic earth magic together. By ninth-grade, however, their education became more focused, based on the type of earth witch they were. Yet all paths converged at the sacred Tree of Ma'at, by senior year. The ancient sentry tree Sanura now lounged against represented the educational and magical journey of each student. Truth, justice, law, morality, balance, and order, enduring values upon which the school was founded. The principles of Ma'at, instilled in every scholar, was more powerful than the mightiest of were-cats or the strongest of witches. An unflinching belief in Ma'at held their community of witches and were-cats together.

As Sanura watched Rachel give the quad one last cautious look before removing a fashionable pair of flat platform wedge thong sandals and joining her on the blanket, Sanura was reminded, with a hot blast of anger, that neither Ma'at nor the Witch Council of Elders could prevent everything.

"It's just us, Rachel. Even the construction workers have gone home for the evening."

Rachel nodded but appeared no less relaxed. At only five-two and a hundred pounds, Rachel Foster, with her long Bob hairstyle, creamy mocha skin, and dimpled smile, possessed the slim, fit frame of a ballerina and the alert, watchfulness of a survivor of rape.

Rachel sat cross-legged. Her skinny denim capris and white, drop-shoulder tee gave her a sweet summer look. At twenty-seven, Rachel looked like one of Sanura's fresh-faced freshman, not the five-year world and classical languages instructor she was. Sanura nearly laughed. When Rachel and Sanura were in school, instructors like Rachel were simply called foreign-language teachers.

Legs stretched in front of her and crossed at the ankle, Sanura's carnation pink, strapless Jersey dress revealed a good deal of her long legs. She removed her shades to get a better look at her friend.

Despite having to virtually drag Rachel out of her classroom, where she'd been holed up preparing for the first day of summer school, and to the quad, the dedicated teacher looked good. An introvert by nature, Rachel only ever required a few close friends to make her happy. She'd never enjoyed large crowds and preferred to spend time alone reading a romantic suspense novel or watching a gory horror movie that always had her jumping and covering her eyes. But she could also be funny and outgoing with those she knew well and trusted—like Sanura and Cynthia.

Unfortunately, being raped by her familiar, a man who should've protected instead of harmed, had turned Rachel into a wary, overly cautious recluse. As a psychologist, Sanura had helped Rachel as best she could, listening when she needed a non-judgmental ear, crying

when she craved a sympathetic hug and raging when a friend's matching anger made Rachel feel validated and strong.

But the psychological process of moving from victim to survivor
was a long, painful voyage. And while Rachel may still think of herself as a mere victim, when Sanura gazed at her friend she saw
perseverance, intelligence, and strength.

"Stop scrutinizing me. You see too damn much when you look at
me with your second sight."

"I'm not using my second sight. Besides, I wouldn't do that without your permission."

Eyes gone hard softened, and Rachel's unfair accusation bled away
into a russet pool of apology. "Right, right, of course you wouldn't.
Sorry." Rachel shook her head, her relaxed hair skimming thin shoulders. "Every now and again, I catch one of the Council members
staring at me, reading my aura with their second sight. I know they
still worry about me. But they don't realize how much they invade my
privacy when they read my aura without my consent."

For a survivor of sexual assault, consent and control were like
food, shelter, and air, essential for life.

Rachel unzipped her leather backpack and shoved her hand inside.
She had a thing about always making sure her bag and shoes were
color coordinated. Today, that meant a navy blue backpack that
matched her denim pants and Yacht sandals. She handed Sanura a CD
inside a red storage sleeve. Eyeing the sleeve, Sanura couldn't help
but wonder if Rachel would've stored the disc in a green sleeve if she
were an earth witch, or a blue sleeve if she were a water witch like
Cynthia. Probably, since the last two CDs she'd given her were in
bright orange sleeves and the first red like today's sleeve. For Oya's
sake, the woman's obsession with color coordination even extended to
trivial matters like CD sleeves.

Sanura granted Rachel a grateful smile and took the CD from her
hand. "This is the fourth one you've made for me. Thanks."

"You're the best student I've ever had, Sanura." Rachel laughed, a rare sound that had Sanura's heart squeezing for all the hurt her friend endured these last two years. "My students, especially the eighth-grade honors students, think because I'm a level one witch they can use a language acquisition spell during class or for a test, and I won't notice."

Another laugh, a self-deprecating sound that too often had the unintentional effect of causing Sanura to experience a twinge of guilt over how easily she'd mastered spellcasting. While level one witches, no matter how much they read or practiced, their magical capability would never change. For low-level witches, the strength of their magic and aura peaked between sixteen and twenty-one years of age.

Level one witches, like Rachel, lacked the genetic material necessary to perform anything other than basic spells. However, most low-level witches possessed a single extraordinary magical ability. A magical gift from the gods, the creators of full-humans, as well as preternaturals. For Rachel, she had the uncanny ability to proficiently speak, read, and write in any language after studying it for a day or less, which made her, not only an excellent foreign-language instructor but a highly sought-after linguist in full-human society. Even high-level witches, like members of the Witch Council of Elders, went to Rachel for help deciphering old scrolls and grimoires. Or, in Sanura's case, to learn Wolof.

"Casting a language acquisition spell would be much easier than putting in the hours required to learn a new language. Even for someone as naturally gifted with languages as you are, Sanura, this is still a heavy undertaking."

"The best gifts are those that come from the heart and cannot be bought."

Her father used to tell her that when she was a kid and cried whenever she didn't have money to purchase her parents birthday gifts. When she was seven, Sam found Sanura sitting on her bed, face flushed and wet from tears. He'd sat down beside her and gathered Sanura in his arms.

"What's wrong, princess?"

She'd sniffed into his shirt and huddled deep into his strong embrace. "Little kids don't have jobs, Daddy."

Sam had chuckled. "I'm pretty sure you told me the same thing last year. I hope you aren't planning on shoveling snow again to earn money to buy me a birthday present."

Even though she'd been upset, Sanura recalled smiling up at her father, feeling better just because he held her.

"No snow this year, Daddy. Not even one lousy flake. If it were summer, I could sell lemonade or mow Mrs. Jenkins' lawn." Although she doubted she could get the lawnmower out the shed, no less convince her mother she wasn't too small or young to mow the neighbor's grass. But a better idea had come to Sanura, perking her up and widening her snaggletooth smile. "Maybe I could cast a snow spell. That way, I'll make lots and lots of money. I'll buy you the biggest birthday present in the whole wide world." She'd stretched out her arms to show how large she thought the world to be.

Her father had smiled down at Sanura and kissed her forehead. "You're the best gift anyone has ever given me, Sanura. How many times must I tell you? I don't need anything else. Besides, the absolute best gifts are those that come from the heart. Free, but priceless. Just like my love for you and your mother."

Priceless. That's how Sanura thought of Assefa. But love wasn't free. Her father understood that truth better than most.

"Meaning the value of the gift is not only the thought but the effort?"

Sanura placed the CD on her lap and nodded. "Assefa has more designer clothes and shoes than me, you, and Cyn combined. He owns a multi-million-dollar pharmaceutical company, museum-quality artwork, a mansion on the Potomac River, and a sweet limo. I could keep going, but you get my point."

"Yeah. Not much you can buy a guy who has so much. Including enough money to buy what he doesn't already own."

"Exactly. Not that he would ask me for anything. That's not his style. But he gives like he's Santa Claus. Because that is his style."

Sanura plucked at the hem of her dress, knowing there to be one gift Assefa had asked of her, wanted from her. Instead of accepting his binding bite, Sanura had decided to learn Wolof, Assefa's native language. A poor substitution, she knew. It was a gift Sanura had tossed around since the first week of sharing his home. Out of politeness sake, Assefa's household made sure to speak English-only when Sanura was around. But the mansion had been the men's home first. Why should they have to adjust any more than necessary?

More, there was a youthful vulnerability about Assefa Sanura loved to witness the few times she'd overheard him speaking on the phone to his sister in Wolof. It was a part of him she hadn't known existed. Perhaps that side of Assefa was reserved for Najja alone. Maybe the bond of lovers wasn't so great that he'd be willing to converse with Sanura in Wolof, dropping his remaining walls. The possibility that Assefa held a part of himself from her stung. Not even the grudging acknowledgment of her double-standard minimized the soreness in her heart from the thought.

Realizing she'd gone quiet and introspective, Sanura lifted her eyes from where they'd drifted to her lap and found Rachel staring at her. "What? Why are you looking at me like that?" She tucked a wayward lock of hair behind her ear and tried to ignore the quiver of dread that had just sidled up to the perimeter of her witch intuition.

"We've known each other since elementary school. I've seen your happy face, frustrated face, sorrowful face, playful face and whatever types of face that exist between all of those. But I've never seen you like this before?"

Sanura furrowed her brow. "Like what?"

A look crossed Rachel's face, dimming her natural beauty to something akin to envy and regret. "I'm glad you found your mate, Sanura. In Assefa, you have the best of both worlds."

Sanura knew what Rachel meant. For witches and were-cats, only the perfect biological pairing could result in children. But genetic compatibility did not, by default, make the witch and were-cat mates. That had been the complicated and unfortunate situation Rachel found herself in two years ago. Stephen Garvey, Cynthia's brother-in-law, was Rachel's familiar. Being the smart woman she was, Rachel knew not to take a belligerent drunk like Stephen as her mate. Proving her right and himself the selfish, cruel bastard Rachel knew him to be, Stephen claimed her the only way he could—by overpowering and raping her.

For Sanura, however, she'd not only found her familiar, a man biologically capable of giving her children, but also a man she loved and adored. A male, who, by all rights, should be her mate, because Sanura couldn't see herself mated to anyone other than Assefa Berber.

"Well, if you want to meet Assefa, you'll have to drag yourself out of Baltimore and to Alexandria."

"Yeah, I got the invitation to your birthday party. On the finest stationery I've ever seen, by the way. Then there was the lined envelope and an exquisite gardenia-and-flames patterned motif."

That was news to Sanura. Assefa had taken it upon himself to throw her a birthday party, inviting her family and friends and arranging everything from the music to the menu to the decorations. And, apparently, he'd created a motif with the symbols of her witch scent and inner fire spirit. When she returned home, Sanura would make sure to get the details about the motif and its design from Assefa.

Sanura leaned forward and playfully swatted Rachel's leg. "And you haven't RSVP'd."

A noncommittal shrug. "I'm still deciding."

"On whether to attend your best friend's birthday party?" In dramatic fashion, Sanura placed a hand over her heart and delivered her best spoiled three-year-old pout. "You wound me, Rachel Foster."

Rachel rolled her eyes. "Get over yourself, Sanura Williams."

"Okay, fine. Tell you what, since you've never been out to my new place and Cyn has, you can ride with her and Eric."

"And be a third wheel, no thanks. By the way, I may not drive to many places, but I do know how to use my car's GPS."

The point about the GPS was a given, so Sanura ignored that part.

"No one thinks of you as a third wheel. Besides, there will be single were-cats at the party. Off the top of my head, I can name four who would turn your legs to jelly if you met them. Now that I'm thinking about it, Manute is just your speed. He's a cheetah and a real sweetheart. He has this full beard and curly hair with spikes thing going on. The spikes make his hair appear neat and shaped, instead of an absolute riot, which is what I think he's going for. He's a real cutie pie and a couple of years younger than you."

Nonplussed, Rachel rolled her eyes. "I can't believe you're trying to hook me up with a younger man."

"Two years barely counts as younger. Anyway, Manute's a good guy, and you need a good guy in your life. If only as a friend."

They'd spoken of Rachel taking up dating again. She hadn't as of yet, but she also wasn't as opposed to the possibility nowadays as she'd been six months ago. For a woman wading back into the pool of men, Manute Aldama would be the perfect lifeguard. While Sanura didn't know the man's backstory, what she did know of him she liked. Strong and considerate were two primary traits that came to mind. More, Assefa, being the protective alpha male that he was, would never have were-cats around Sanura whom he didn't respect and trust. Over the last month, Sanura had grown to like and trust all the men who'd traveled with Assefa from the Sudan and to the United States. Manute would treat Rachel the way a witch of her smart and sensitive nature deserved to be treated.

Of that, she had no doubt.

"I thought you came here for a language lesson."

That was Rachel's way of saying she was done with being the topic of their conversation. But the woman was far tougher than she appeared or gave herself credit for being. And sometimes Rachel Foster needed a caring friend to push her beyond her comfort zone.

"I'll have Mike pick you up at six."

Psychology Manipulation 101. Detective Michael McKutchen had been the police officer who'd captured Rachel's rapist, nearly beating Stephen to death when he found the creep. Since then, Mike and Rachel had developed a relationship nearly as close as the one Sanura shared with the detective.

Sanura pretended not to notice Rachel's glower and kept talking. "I'm sure he wouldn't mind. But I'll make sure to ask him to clean out and fumigate his car first. I doubt if you want to sit in a pile of takeout containers and sweaty, old man socks." Sanura wrinkled her nose. "By the gods, it should be a sin for a man's car to smell like a dumpster in the alley behind a seafood restaurant."

"You're a spoiled pain in the ass, Sanura." Rachel plucked a stress ball shaped like, of course, a red apple, from her backpack and threw it at Sanura, hitting her square in the chest. "Spoiled rotten. All the way to your fire witch core."

Sanura threw the ball back at Rachel, who ducked when it would've scored her forehead.

Rachel reached into her bag again, and Sanura wondered how many damn stress balls the woman had in there. And whether she should prepare to defend herself against a barrage of squeezable toys she'd recommended to the teacher, never thinking her advice would one day come back to bite her in the ass.

Out came a plastic bag of assorted squeeze toys: squishy farm critters, puffer balls, mesh squishy balls, and foam sports balls.

"My students love these things, especially the ones who find it hard to sit still and stay focused on a lesson for longer than twenty minutes." She threw a yellow smiley face stress ball at Sanura, hitting her in the shoulder.

"Hey, this is no way to treat the birthday girl."

A pink critter whizzed past her face, Sanura moving in the nick of time to avoid being struck by the piglet.

"It's Thursday, you brat. Your birthday isn't until Saturday. If you want, consider these your early birthday licks."

"Well, nice to know you remembered the day. Or did you get one of those Facebook birthday reminders? You may have a way with languages, but I'm pretty sure it was you who called me last week because you couldn't remember when summer classes began. By the way," Sanura said with a taunting smirk, "since I'm not the one who works here, I had to call Cyn to find out."

"You called the Headmistress? My supervisor. Well, aren't you the little traitor." Rachel stood, looked from her bag of toys turned projectiles and down to Sanura. She shook the bag at Sanura, a predatory gleam in her dazzling dark-brown eyes. "I don't have enough balls in here. But, if I use them more than once, I'm sure I can nail your behind twenty-nine times."

She gave Sanura a wicked grin. The one that reminded Sanura how well Sankofa had educated all their students in defensive and offensive tactics. And that Rachel, while magically weak compared to Sanura, possessed the accuracy of a sniper. Stephen, serving a meager four-year sentence for Rachel's rape, would've been dead if she'd managed to get to her gun.

Rachel removed a foam basketball from the bag and began tossing it into the air, catching the toy with ease each time it descended. "No magic, fire witch. Just you. Just me." She caught the basketball and grinned her wicked smile again. "I'll even give you to the count of five."

Sanura jumped to her feet, adrenaline pumping. "Why only five? Why not ten?"

Rachel pointed to Sanura's lower half. "Long legs. A five-second head start is good enough. I'll have to run twice as fast to catch you."

"You have a mean streak, Rach—"

Pow.

The little sneak dinged Sanura right between the eyes, Rachel's throw fast and true.

By the time the sharpshooting earth witch reached into her bag for another assault weapon, Sanura had turned and dashed away. Before she took ten steps, however, a ball hit her in the back of her head.

Sanura laughed and ran faster.

If this were what it took to get her friend to her birthday party, Sanura would run the length of the campus.

Twice. And, damn, she loved hearing Rachel's rich laughter.

But Sanura only made it to Sekhmet Hall, a residential building for were-cats before she, quite literally, ran into a half-naked man.

Rachel, unable to stop her pursuit on a dime, ran smack into Sanura's back, causing the three to stumble and then tumble to the ground. Sanura landed, to her dismay, on top of Gregory Chambers, High Priestess Anna's son. Rachel lay beside Greg, sprawled on her back, lips turned up in a shallow smile and taking soft gasps to catch her breath.

Palms pressed to Greg, Sanura made to push herself off the owner of the lean chest with wet, curly hair that coiled around her fingers. The last thing she wanted, needed, was to have this male's scent all over her when she returned home. Although, considering how Greg wrapped his arms around her waist, keeping her pinned to him, unless Sanura showered before going home, no way would Assefa not detect the scent of another man on her. Especially since, it seemed, Greg hadn't showered after shifting. Were-cats' preternatural scent became stronger after they transformed from cat to human male, a chemical defense to warn off potential threats.

Thank Oya the man had the good sense to cover his vital parts with a towel before making his way from the were-cat outdoor training facility and to the gym where he would shower. Most were-cats, when witches weren't around, had no problem walking around butt naked. Which probably explained why, until recently, Sanura hadn't seen any of his friends in cat form. No doubt, once she moved in, Assefa gave them strict orders as to when and where they could shift.

Instead of helping her out of this sticky, sweaty situation, Rachel glanced over at Sanura's uncomfortable predicament, winked, and then began surveying the grounds around them in search of the bag of balls that had gone flying when she'd fallen.

Sanura turned back to Greg, their bodies pressed indecently close together. "Let me go."

He didn't. Instead, blue eyes twinkled up at Sanura with adoration and sexual interest. How many times had he looked at her like this over the years? And how many times had she returned his gaze with friendship and a stern rejection?

She didn't want to hurt his feelings, as she'd done each time she refused to go out with him. But sprawled here, where anyone could see them in this compromising position, Sanura cared little for his feelings. Greg was doing this deliberately, touching her when he had no right.

"Let me go," she repeated, her voice a lowly-spoken command. Fists balled, she lifted as far off him as his strong arms would allow.

"I haven't seen you in a while, Sanura. I was just saying hello." He released her waist, then reached up to touch her cheek.

Before he could lay hands on her again, Sanura scooted quickly off him. She tried very hard not to think about the part of Greg that had come to life while she'd been splayed on top of him.

Dammit, no way could she leave Baltimore without washing the smell of Greg off her. Already, she felt like a cheating girlfriend, plotting ways to erase the evidence of her infidelity. Not that she'd cheated on Assefa, but after being on top of an aroused Greg, Sanura felt dirty and guilty.

She glared at Greg, watching as the nearly six-foot man got to his feet. Sweaty blond hair matted to head, and his sloped tipped nose, which always reminded Sanura of Tom Cruise, lifted into the air and sniffed.

"You always smelled so damn good, Sanura. A rich godly scent that makes a were-cat want to bow down before you in willing supplication. No other witch can compare."

She hated when he spoke like that, as if she were a goddess to be treated differently and better than her sisters in magic. From the corner of her eye, Sanura saw Rachel gather the last of the squeeze toys and drop her petite frame on the bench in front of Sekhmet Hall. Sanura and Rachel had heard such over-the-top flattery before, from Gregory Chambers and most of their were-cat peers. Greg, and his unnatural obsession with Sanura being the fire witch of legend, was the reason why Sanura, before Assefa, had never dated a were-cat. They only saw prophecy and power when they looked at her, instead of the woman behind the myth.

Experience should have taught Greg that such blatant fawning did not endear him to Sanura. If anything, his insistence on treating her as a powerful but one-dimensional goddess instead of a real woman with scars and imperfections only served to make Sanura want to put as much distance between herself and were-cats like Greg as possible.

"So, um," Greg began, eyes casting around suddenly, as if he expected someone to jump from behind the bushes and knock him upside his fool head, "I heard you're dating an FBI agent. What's that all about?"

Sanura refused to have this conversation. She wasn't, however, surprised to learn of the rumors. From the nervous way Greg's eyes kept darting behind him, she suspected he'd heard a great deal more about Assefa than his profession. Which only went to show how injudicious he'd been earlier, holding Sanura to his half-naked body instead of releasing her immediately when they'd fallen to the ground.

She didn't want to even think about Assefa's reaction if he had witnessed the scene. The man had a lock on his self-control made from the strongest of steel, but he also harbored a powerful possessiveness. In that, Assefa and Sanura were of the same mind.

She was his.

He was hers.

And anyone who dared to come between them would find themselves in the unenviable position of facing their wrath.

"You can stop eyeing every bush, tree, and shadow. If Assefa were here, he would've caught me before I fell into you."

A quirk of his lips and arch of an eyebrow gave Greg a rakish look Sanura found more irksome than charming. "That fast, huh? Then it's true. The FBI agent is the Mngwa of prophecy. How swift is his cat? How large? How ferocious?"

Greg spoke of Assefa with the same veneration she'd heard in his voice when he'd asked her out when she was seventeen and he a first-year college student. She hadn't liked it then, and she liked it even less now.

"It doesn't matter, Greg." She spoke to Rachel over her shoulder. "Are you ready to continue our lesson?"

For a moment, when Rachel said nothing, just stared, with amusement at Sanura, she feared her friend would make her deal with Greg on her own. But, being the longtime and lifesaving friend that she was, Rachel hoisted her plastic bag of toys over her shoulder and got to her feet.

"Sure. Let's go."

Without saying a word to Greg, a man Rachel's known for most of her life, she walked away, heading back to the Tree of Ma'at and their cozy shade and blanket.

"It's been nice seeing you, Greg, but I have to go. I don't want to keep Rachel out too late." Or herself. Thanks to the collision, she had to swing past her mother's house and shower before heading home, which would get her to Alexandria an hour or so later than she intended.

Disappointment darkened his eyes, but he smiled, warm and with genuine affection. "Listen, Sanura. I'm glad we ran into each other today."

"Why is that?" Sanura glanced over her shoulder. Rachel was making her way steadily across the acres of grass. If Greg didn't hurry, Sanura would have to jog to catch up with fast-walking Rachel. She turned back to Greg, who was now regarding her with a friend's concern.

"There's a lot I would like to say to you, Sanura. But now doesn't seem like the best time." Greg readjusted the towel around his waist, securing it tighter when it began to slip. "Just be careful, okay."

"What do you mean?" Now it was Sanura who scanned her surroundings. As before, no one else was around. But the dread she'd felt earlier returned.

"That came out wrong. I meant you needed to tell the FBI agent to watch his back."

Sanura's fire spirit blazed to life. Had Gregory Chambers just threatened Assefa? Why would he? They didn't even know each other.

Fire witch magic began to churn in the pit of her stomach, sizzling at the mere thought of a threat to Assefa.

"Explain." It was all she could say without spewing fire all over High Priestess Anna's only offspring.

"I can't."

"Why in the hell not?" Heat pulsed in her veins, Greg's response unacceptable to the woman and her fire spirit.

He looked around again, enhanced were-cat eyes and ears taking in all that Sanura had likely missed when she'd surveyed the same area. This time, she didn't think Greg was searching for Assefa. Perhaps he hadn't been the first time either.

Leaning in, he pressed a kiss close to her ear and whispered, "Felidae law."

Felidae law?

Dammit, she needed to reach Assefa right away.

CHAPTER SIX

"I'm fine."

"Are you sure?"

"Of course, sweetheart. You sound out of breath. What are you doing?"

"Jogging to my car. I'll probably hit evening traffic, but I'll be home as soon as I can. Are you sure nothing has happened, that everything is fine there?"

"Look, why don't you have dinner with Makena since you're in Baltimore. I'm sure your mother would love your company for the evening."

He heard a car door slam, and then the purr of Sanura's car when she turned it on.

"She would but—"

"I already told you, Sanura, I'm fine. Whatever has gotten you so worked up we can talk about it later tonight. Besides, I'm in the middle of a project with Zareb and Rashad, and I want to have it finished before you get home."

"Are you sure?"

She sounded hesitant, her concern for him evident the moment he answered his cell. But Assefa didn't want Sanura to worry, no more than he wished for her to drive recklessly in her rush to get from Baltimore to Alexandria. While he appreciated her concern, he wanted her mind and fire spirit at ease before she jumped on the beltway and headed home.

And, as he'd told Sanura, he, Zareb, and Rashad were in the middle of an important project.

"Yes, I'm positive. Have a nice, relaxing evening with your mother. I'm sure she misses you since you moved out of her guest house."

"She does."

"Then it's settled. Be sure to give Makena my love."

While Sanura paused, thinking over his suggestion, Assefa mouthed to Rashad, "Let me have your cell phone." Second cell phone in hand, he held his phone between his ear and shoulder while typing an address in Rashad's phone.

"Okay, fine, I'll have dinner with Mom. But I'm coming straight home afterward."

Assefa returned Rashad's phone to him. His friend looked at the screen and nodded. Then he turned and took off, heading in the direction of the garage. Satisfied but not happy, Assefa clutched the phone and forced lightness into his voice.

"As I said, we'll talk later. You can tell me about your day, and I'll tell you about mine. But I'm fine, no need to worry or rush back here."

Another long beat of silence followed by an appeased sigh. "I'll see you tonight, Assefa. Bye."

"Drive safely."

Assefa hit the End button, then slipped the phone into his pants pocket.

"W-what a-are you going to do to us?"

Assefa removed his black suit jacket and handed it to Zareb, whose own suit jacket was somewhere between the front of the house and the corpse of trees where they now stood. A minute within pulling into the driveway of the house, Assefa's cell had buzzed.

"Zareb and I have just parked, Rashad. Can't it wait until we're in the house?"

"Someone is on the estate grounds. The person tripped the silent alarm. I'm on my way to intercept the intruder."

That had Assefa out the car, with Zareb following in his wake, yanking off his jacket and tie and switching from FBI agent to body-guard.

"I can handle this, Assefa." Zareb had grabbed his arm, halting Assefa's single-minded pursuit to reach whoever in the hell thought it a bright idea to trespass on his property.

"Yes, you can. But I've never hidden behind you, and I won't begin today. Now release my arm so we can deal with the intruder."

With reluctance, Zareb had relinquished his hold on Assefa's arm.

"And don't change until we know exactly what we're dealing with."

That order had set less well with Zareb than the first. But he com-prehended the importance of being careful. This wasn't the Sudan where only preternaturals dwelled, and no one called animal control or pulled out a gun if they saw a huge Bengal tiger loping toward them.

By the time they'd reached Rashad, he had two intruders pinned to the ground, a lethal snarl warning them to move at their peril. Then, with a timing too perfect to be coincidental, Sanura had called, anxiety lacing every rushed word.

The two of them would talk later, as he'd promised. But he didn't want her coming home until he knew what he was dealing with. As he'd learned, Makena could protect Sanura nearly as well as himself. And since this was Thursday, the one day of the week Mike faithfully had dinner with Makena, Assefa felt even better about having Sanura go there while he handled this situation.

In a couple of hours, when Sanura would be ready to begin her drive southward, Rashad would be there to make sure she arrived home safely. As stealthy as a leopard, Rashad would follow the fire witch at a discreet distance, as to not alert or alarm her.

Assefa glared down at the kneeling males. From the look of them, brown eyes big and wide, broad shoulders they hadn't yet grown into fully, and the spicy scent of fear in the humid air, they smelled like prey to his Mngwa. The one who'd asked the question, a light-brown

African American in a pair of red-and-black basketball shorts, red-and-black basketball shoes, and a black screen print LeBron James graphic T-shirt, trembled like the proverbial leaf in the wind but had enough courage to look Assefa in the eye when he spoke.

His accomplice, another African American, couldn't seem to keep his inquisitive eyes off Assefa or his jaw off the ground. As soon as Zareb and Assefa walked through the clearing, as deep into the wooded area of his home as one could go and still be on Berber property, eyes that reminded Assefa of a well-cut piece of smoky quartz had lifted to his own and clouded over with wonder and a healthy dose of trepidation.

He'd seen the look before, but not since leaving his home, and never when he wasn't in cat form. Assefa stepped closer to the kneeling males while Zareb took up position behind them.

"When you trespass onto a man's property, you must be willing to accept the consequences of your actions."

Sweat beaded on their brows and fell into wide, blinking eyes. They were afraid. Good. They needed to understand the severity of their stupidity, and how the situation could end for them if they weren't cubs.

"Smile for the camera, gentlemen." Assefa nodded to Zareb.

Cell phone already in hand, Zareb walked around the interlopers and took several pictures of the teens, neither of whom appeared older than seventeen.

"You know who I am?"

The boy with the dropped jaw finally closed his mouth when he nodded his head, eyes transfixed on Assefa.

But it was the basketball and LeBron James fan who spoke. "You're Assefa Berber, the Mngwa of prophecy."

"How do you know that?"

Zareb barked the question out, scaring the boys into dropping their eyes to the ground. He closed the distance between himself and the kid in the faded blue jeans and a burgundy Malcolm X T-shirt that read: The Future Belongs to Those Who Prepare for It Today!

With a large hand, Zareb grabbed the boy's chin and forced it upward. "If you were man enough to come onto private property and risk being torn limb from limb, then be man enough to hold my gaze and answer my damn question."

And this was Zareb being nice and patient. But the fact remained, the teens had put themselves in a situation that could've resulted in their deaths. If they'd pulled this stunt at night when Sanura was at home and Assefa asleep, Zareb would've done what he was trained to do.

Protect Assefa by any means necessary. With Malcolm X emblazoned across his chest, a rifle in his hand, eyes cast out his home window, a warrior protecting his children, wife, and home, the teen should understand the gory sentiment.

"W-we overheard ... overheard our fathers talking about Mr. Berber."

"What did they say?" Zareb released the boy's chin but stayed within intimidation range.

"We didn't catch everything that was said. Just his name, city, and that he was an FBI agent and the cat of legend. When my father caught us eavesdropping, he told us to get lost until the meeting was over."

If these kids were half as good with the computer as Manute, the bits of stolen information would've been enough for them to track down his home address.

"We didn't mean any disrespect, Mr. Berber," the basketball lover said, fear but also sincerity in his voice. "We just thought it would be cool to meet you."

The kid meant he thought it would be cool to see the undefeated cat of myth, the reputed barbaric killer of men and beasts. Up close and dangerously personal. Viewing Assefa's home as a zoo and Assefa as the main attraction. The thought disgusted but not surprised. He knew it was a matter of time before this part of Sanura's world collided with his own.

"Let me guess," Assefa said with an agitation that bordered on anger, "you're students at Sankofa Preparatory School."

The boys' eyes widened again, and they nodded in unison.

Zareb said nothing, which meant he'd reached the same conclusion.

"What do you want to do with them?" Zareb looked as if he had a few ideas of his own. All of which would leave the boys with a week's worth of aches and pains and a lesson they wouldn't soon forget.

However, Assefa had a different and less violent idea.

"Escort them off my property and to wherever they've hidden their car. Then explain to them, in vivid detail, what will happen if they come here again, uninvited."

Unlike Sanura, Zareb knew not to question Assefa's decision. During times like these, their roles were written in the history of both their families. If not their very DNA.

Zareb, taking each boy by the arm, yanked them to their feet. Compared to the six-foot-five inches, 225-pound bald bodyguard, the boys looked like twigs next to him. Pushing one then the other, Zareb made the boys walk ahead of him.

In silence, the three walked until they blended into the trees and disappeared.

Pulling out his cell phone, Assefa sent Zareb a text.

Get their name, address, phone number, and take a picture of the car, especially the license plate. I'll take care of the rest.

****

Before Sanura could unlock the door to the house, no less insert the key into the lock, the hand-carved entry doors opened. Light from the foyer escaped, adding a soft glow to the front of the luxury home. The dusk-to-dawn security floodlight was not yet on for the evening, which meant Sanura made excellent time getting home.

Dressed in black leather loafers, a pair of perfectly pressed black dress pants, and a starched gray-and-black button-up shirt, Omar Wek held the door open wide and then stepped aside so Sanura could enter.

She did, smiling at the tall man who, at six-seven, possessed a stereotypical basketball physique—long arms, legs, hands and feet, broad shoulders and toned waist. If the chef liked basketball, however, Sanura was unaware of it. What he did like, beyond cooking, was philosophy, specifically ethnophilosophy.

"Thank you, Omar." He closed and locked the door, a well-worn book in his left hand. "I see you're reading Okere again." Before meeting Omar, she'd heard of but had never read any works by Theophilus Okere, no less had someone articulate, so beautifully, African philosophy and the hermeneutics of culture to her.

"You're welcome, Dr. Williams."

"Sanura. Call me Sanura."

Omar smiled and nodded, and Sanura knew he would call her Dr. Williams again. The man was formal in the extreme. Polite, kind, brilliant, but reserved and stiff.

"Is Assefa here?" Sanura dropped her keys into her purse.

"Yes. In the master suite."

She turned, ready to hurry down the hallway and up the stairs. But Sanura stopped, and turned back to Omar. "Did anything out of the ordinary happen while I was out?"

"Out of the ordinary? What do you mean?"

As handsome as he was tall, the man's voice was as bland and unappetizing as hospital broth. But Omar Wek was no Special Agent Berber. When he prevaricated, the way he was doing now, his eyes shifted down and away.

"Did he teach you that? To answer a question with a question?"

Omar lifted his eyes and opened his mouth to reply, but Sanura raised a silencing hand. "Never mind." She would do better to get her answers directly from the source. It wouldn't be fair to put Omar in the middle. "Have a good night, Omar. I'll see you in the morning."

He neither smiled nor nodded, but he couldn't hide his relief. It shimmered about him, a weedy pulse of were-cat magic.

"Good evening, Dr. Williams." Omar all but bowed to Sanura. Not for the first time since meeting him, she wondered about his life in the Sudan. While Mrs. Livingston served as the housekeeper, it was Omar who played the role of the humble servant. Although no one, especially Assefa, regarded him as anything other than a trusted friend and equal.

She'd inquired into their background before, asking Assefa one question after another about the men.

"They're my friends, my responsibility. I've known most of them my entire life. Once you get to know them better, Sanura, they'll open up to you. Until then, be patient. But know this, if you ever need anything, including protection, do not hesitate to trust them. They will never let you down."

She believed Assefa then, just as she'd believed him when they'd spoken on the phone earlier. But her special agent was a wily were-cat.

Sanura opened the door to the master suite and went inside. In the sitting room sat Assefa, on the sofa, open laptop next to him and cell phone up to his ear. Unsurprised Hershey chocolate eyes stared back at her.

"Yes, I know, Rashad. Thank you." Assefa ended his call, tossing the phone on the cushion next to him when he was done. "You're home earlier than expected."

She shut the door, moved farther into the room and removed her shoes. Holding the sandals in her hand, she considered whether to throw them at her lover.

His eyes slipped to her mouth, lingered for the beat of a hot breath, then rose. A wisp of Mngwa pheromones joined the space between them, a sweet, heady spice.

The hands gripping the sandals relaxed, and the shoes fell to the floor, the carpet absorbing the sound. Or maybe she didn't hear them fall over the sudden pounding of her heart when Assefa smiled his sexy special agent smile.

Damn him. Halfway through her shower, she'd figured out what had been bothering her about her phone conversation with Assefa. He'd assured Sanura, several times, that he was fine. But he hadn't directly answered her question about unusual goings-on at the estate. And he'd made some vague statement about Rashad, Zareb, and a project. Which, when taken together, meant only one thing. Assefa was keeping something from her. After retrieving an outfit from the clothes Sanura had left at her Mom's guest house, Sanura apologized for not staying for dinner and left.

Her heart raced the entire drive, as her mind conjured all kinds of scenarios that could've happened that Assefa didn't want to tell her about. But the one thought that kept her from going a hundred all the way home was Assefa's assurance that he was fine. He may have committed a lie of omission, but Assefa wouldn't lie directly to Sanura. Still, she'd worked up a good mad on the drive south, intending to confront her overprotective boyfriend when she saw him.

Sanura closed her eyes. Unlike Omar, who'd been dressed as if he were about to head out for the evening, Assefa wore nothing but a pair of red pajama pants made of Lycra Elastane®, a body-defining material that emphasized every curve, muscle, and bulge. And the color, by the gods, Assefa needed to wear red more often, his dark skin all but glowed next to the bright color.

She licked her lips, opened her eyes, and tried very, very hard to focus on finding out what he was keeping from her. But damn, Assefa's pheromones fused with the air, thick and inebriating. The pheromones were a sensual fog that lured her fire spirit to the surface, coaxing the beast with promises of pleasure, of magic, of carnal bliss.

A speck of gold glitter materialized on Assefa's lower lip, a lighthouse in the fog, drawing her to shore.

Step.

She had to taste it.

Step.

Taste him.

Step.

Make both hers.

Closer.

Closer.

Face-to-face.

Sanura leaned in, nose touching, heart racing, need flowing. Tongue peeked out, ran across Assefa's bottom lip, tasting, savoring and then claiming the speck of gold glitter.

Delicious.

The glitter. The man.

Their mouths met, melded, and explored.

Soft, full lips slipped to her neck. Gods, Assefa's mouth felt glorious. His probing tongue had never been this electrifying before, her body an inferno of fire witch need.

Burning her up.

Soaking her sex.

So hot. So damn wet and hot.

For him. His hands. His lips. His tongue.

His. Claiming bite.

Yes. Yes. That's what she needed. She needed Assefa to claim her, his bite a release valve for her boiling body, her panting, hungry fire spirit.

She wanted him, all of him, not just his lips and tongue on her neck but his fangs in her flesh. Tasting her blood. Drinking her magic. And making them one.

Two bodies.

Two inner spirits.

One bond.

Mate bond.

Thud. Her back against a wall.

Shred. Rip. Her dress and panties in tatters on the floor.

Open-mouthed kisses to her shoulders, breasts, stomach.

Assefa on his knees, between her legs. Kissing. Tonguing. Sucking.

Mmmm.

Oh yes, he could bite her down there. Her stomach. Her inner thigh. She didn't care, just as long as he gave her what she desired. Saving her from grief, from guilt, from the unknown, with his mouth, his tongue, his Mngwa's piercing fangs.

More of Assefa's intoxicating spicy scent crashed into Sanura, gouging her senses and whispering magical enchantments of lust and love.

Pushing into his wet, greedy mouth, Sanura moaned at the demanding decadent contact. Assefa held one leg over his shoulder, his other hand on Sanura's ass, gripping tightly and steadying her for his carnivorous mouth.

Her fire spirit shuddered and crackled, raging wild and hot with pending release.

Hiss.

Hiss.

Crackle.

Sanura screamed, bucking into Assefa's insistent tongue. A tongue gone long, wide and ribbed for maximum pleasure. And if that wasn't enough to send Sanura hurling over the edge of sensual delight, the magical tongue vibrated against her engorged clit. It pulsed, Sanura's personal vibrator equipped with were-cat speed and endurance.

Pulse.

Pulse.

Pulse.

Pulse.

She couldn't stop screaming, couldn't stop shuddering, and couldn't stop her nails from using Assefa's burly shoulders to keep her upright. And Sanura couldn't prevent her fire spirit from banging against the cage she kept her locked in, hissing at her to merge completely with her other half.

Sanura wanted the merging as well, more than she ever had before. But there was a reason she hadn't completed the mate bond before now. A very good reason. Not that she could recall what it may have been.

It didn't matter. Nothing mattered.

Except Assefa. Except the tongue working its way up Sanura's hot, needy body.

When he reached her face, Assefa kissed her, another gold speck of glitter on his lower lip. She sucked it off, wanting to do the same to him, his erection straining like a mast against his night pants and her stomach.

She removed his pants and dropped to her knees. His fingers went to her hair, plunging in and pulling her forward. Sanura opened her mouth wide and took him inside.

Assefa purred, widened his stance, and let her love him with mouth, tongue, and hands.

Through the haze that was their lovemaking, Sanura heard him moan her name, felt him push into her mouth with careful thrusts, and sensed everything about her lover that marked Assefa as her mate.

Sanura took him deep. Hand wrapped around his length, she pumped Assefa with mouth and hand, then swirled her tongue around the bulbous head when she glided to the tip before taking him deep again.

Strong legs trembled, hips thrust, and hands settled on shoulders.

Then lifted.

Turned.

And pressed her to a wall.

Long, lean legs were hoisted around strong, fit waist.

More thrusting, inside her, hot and desperate.

Sanura held shoulders gone moist. Her face was buried in the crook of his neck, her legs tight around his waist, and her sex a volcano poised to erupt, spewing ardent lava over both of them.

"Bite me."

With fierce, focused passion, Assefa made love to Sanura. Each slick, hard slide into her body sent a blazing path of magical currents straight to her enchanted mind and overheated core.

Toes curled.

Sex clenched.

Gooseflesh of fire rose and spread.

"Bite me."

Assefa grabbed her hair, yanked her head back and devoured her mouth. The rhythm of his luscious loving never halted. His thrusting hips blinded her to everything except for him, for her, and the soul-deep need to be claimed by this singular male.

Scorching lips roamed her face, worshipping eyelids, cheeks, chin, and jaw.

And neck.

Yes, those wondrous lips settled against the rampaging pulse of her neckline. Her heart the epicenter of her need, but her neck, her throbbing jugular, was the untraversed road of claiming, of mating, of were-cat bonding.

He tasted her. His teeth grazing pliable, willing woman.

"I want you, want this, Assefa."

"So do I, sweetheart. You taste like passion, feel like fire, and sound like breathy sex." He swiveled his hips, picked up his pace and shoved her harder against the wall. "My teeth ache, my gums hurt, and my cat is tearing me apart, wanting you in every way imaginable. Your body. Your magic. Your fire spirit. Your blood."

"Then bite me. Take me. Claim me as yours."

Sanura tossed her head back, exposing the vulnerable underside of her neck to the tips of Assefa's fangs that had slipped from his gums.

When he grazed her neck again, sharp teeth seeking the love and commitment she'd offered, the coveted life force that dwelled within Sanura hummed with familial power.

Assefa opened his mouth wider, and Sanura felt a probing prick from his fangs.

She closed her eyes, relishing the pleasure to come, but not the emotional pain and the spiritual loss that would follow.

Deeper his fangs sank, breaking skin and Sanura's heart.

Tears fell. Shoulders shook.

Assefa stopped, stared, waited.

More crying, uncontrollable and soft.

Heart and soul in his sorrowful eyes, he raised trembling hands to her cheeks and wiped away her tears.

She didn't know what to say, couldn't explain what had come over her. Just now, or earlier, when she'd walked toward him, a speck of gold glitter on Assefa's lower lip, body and cat spirit calling to Sanura on a primal level.

He'd been caught up as well, trapped in a sensual mating fog. Or had he? Sanura couldn't tell, not with the way he held her face between his large, soothing hands. Or the way his golden Mngwa eyes drank her in, his lower half still hard, still pushing into her the way his fangs no longer did.

"Assefa I—"

He kissed her, a silencing embrace that couldn't smother the sting of disappointment, of rejection she tasted on his tongue.

When they peaked, pleasure and heartache propelling them toward an inevitable completion, Sanura sensed a shift in their relationship, a shift in Assefa.

CHAPTER SEVEN

He couldn't bear to look at her, to see fear and sadness in Sanura's watery gaze. In the end, neither of them had known what to say to the other, so Assefa thought it best to give them space to breathe and to think. He'd caused this, driven them to the dangerous intersection of bestial carnality and shattered restraint. And Sanura had paid the price, her tears and rejection no more than a monster like him deserved. Who would want to become the mate to a man with a Mngwa as his cat spirit? A man capable of drugging a witch into a mate bond with the strategic use of his pheromones, without the civility of a proper handfasting?

Sanura deserved to have her fire spirit courted by his cat spirit and to not be magically manipulated into forgoing free will and decorum in exchange for a quick fuck and claiming against a wall.

What in the hell was wrong with him? Why did he attempt to use Mngwa magic to force his mate claim?

Warm wind whipped through his black-and-gray coat of fur as he ran as fast as he could over the acres of property he called home. If he ran fast enough, long enough, hard enough, maybe, just maybe, he could outrun his guilt and shame.

Run.

Run.

Run.

He hadn't felt like this in years, not since becoming a man and leaving home.

Run.

Run.

Run.

Run.

He and the Mngwa had become one, relying on and trusting each other. Assefa had grown to accept the unique beast spirit within, as well as the unnatural power such a creature possessed. He'd even come to accept, though grudgingly, that most witches and were-cats would view him as a freak of nature.

Run.

Run.

While the strength of Sanura's fire witch set her apart, somewhat, from other fire witches, Sanura was one of thousands of fire witches. Whenever she wanted, Sanura could connect with another fire witch, their shared cultural identity a bridge of familiarity and a potential basis for so much more, like friendship and trust. For Assefa, however, no such community of Mngwa's existed. No one else knew what it meant to have a Mngwa as an inner cat spirit. Not Manute, Omar, Rashad, or even Zareb, his best friend with whom he'd confided so much.

The Mngwa rounded the estate for the fiftieth time, heading for the dock and the river. Without slowing, heavy paws landed on the wooden planks of the dock. He rocketed forward and leaped into the dark water, shattering the calm of the still night with his mighty splash.

The cat of legend sank, his big, heavy body and thick, wooly fur weighing him down. Closing his eyes, the Mngwa permitted the Potomac River to do what it would to him. The cool, refreshing river water felt good. Nonjudgmental and silent, the river accepted everyone into its wet embrace, even were-cats with a damned heart and a questionable future.

When his lungs began to burn from holding his breath for so long, the Mngwa paddled his legs, swimming upward, his snout the first part of his body to breach the water's surface. He swam to shore, body heavy and dripping river water. Onto the grass he loped, leaving a liquid trail of beastly weariness behind him. He trotted away from the

Potomac River and up the small hill, collapsing onto his side in front of an occupied gazebo.

An elongated hexagonal gazebo with cedar shingles and a belle cupola, the structure was built by Rashad and Manute. The men could craft most anything for a home if given enough time and proper materials.

The Mngwa didn't bother to raise his head when the person in the gazebo rose from the wicker chair, walked to the edge of the structure and stared down at him.

"Although we can speak telepathically while you're in cat form, I would rather have a face-to-face conversation with Assefa."

The Mngwa didn't move, but he did lift his eyes to Sanura's. Cast in the glow from the lighted cupola, green eyes sparkled and red-gold hair circled her worried face in wild waves. Since returning home and Assefa's abysmal attempt at claiming, she'd showered, dressed, and removed her moonstone. If not for the magically-treated piece of jewelry she wore daily, Sanura's true hair and eye color would be revealed to everyone. But the birthstone masked her witch scent and gave the illusion of brown hair and eyes, both normal for an African American professional woman, which full-humans thought Sanura to be.

It's late, Sanura. You should be inside.

"I hate it when you do this."

He didn't disrespect her intelligence by pretending not to know what she meant. Sanura hated when he shut down on her, retreating to an inner cave that had served him well for so many years. It worked. It kept him sane, and others safe.

I'm fine. Please, just go inside. I'll be in later.

"You said you were fine when we spoke on the phone. I believed you then. I don't now." She reached behind her, grabbed something from the chair and then tossed the items to him. "I'm not leaving, so you might as well get dressed."

I'm not quite myself right now, Sanura. Are you sure you want to do this tonight? It may not end well."

She didn't respond right away, and he sensed her doubt. It was the same uncertainty and fear he'd detected the moment his fangs began to slide into her neck. Gods, the Mngwa could still smell the faint embers of blood that had come into contact with his fangs, feel the tempting crimson wetness and the near-uncontrollable desire to go deeper.

Marking, claiming and making Sanura his.

But she'd wept. Not tears of joy, but tears of distress, of grief. So he'd withdrawn his fangs and gave her the only part of him that pleased her body but didn't frighten her heart.

"It's fine. I'm not quite myself either. You've been out here for two hours. Thinking, I suppose. And I've been in our bedroom doing the same. No matter what happens, we need to talk, to clear the air."

Sitting up, the Mngwa watched Sanura watch him. From the firm set of her shoulders and jaw, the fire witch was prepared to stand her ground. He wasn't in the mood to fight. Well, he was, just not Sanura.

He shifted.

Naked, Assefa pulled on the black shorts and T-shirt Sanura brought out with her. She was dressed similarly, black spandex pants and a black-and-red sports shirt.

"Thank you." Sanura moved away from the edge of the gazebo, and retook her seat in the chair, curling long legs onto the burgundy-and-white cushion. Two sets of flip flops were placed next to her chair, a fun gift Sanura purchased when they were at the mall a couple of weeks ago. The smaller pair read: I'm His. While the larger pair read: I'm Hers.

Seeing the sandals reminded Assefa of the black T-shirts he'd spotted in the same store and had gone back to purchase a few days later when Sanura wasn't with him. One had the word *soul* written in big white letters, while the other, in the same bold print, had the word *mate* written on the front. He'd purchased hers three sizes too big since he enjoyed seeing her sleep in his oversized T-shirts. Until meeting and falling in love with Sanura, Assefa would've never considered wearing silly sandals and graphic tees that advertised his feelings to the whole damn world. Now, well, the couple's T-shirts he'd overcome embarrassment and Berber manliness to purchase, would be relegated to the bottom of his drawer, never to be worn.

Ignoring the sandals that mocked, Assefa joined her, claiming the chair across from Sanura instead of the one directly next to her.

He slouched in the seat, something he never did, and stared at her.

She stared back for several minutes before she finally spoke. When she did, her unexpected words had him sitting up straight.

"I'm sorry."

Surely he couldn't have heard the woman correctly. What in Sekhmet's name would Sanura have to be sorry about?

"What are you talking about? You don't owe me an apology. I'm the one who manipulated your senses with my cat pheromones."

She squinted at him, as if he'd said something ridiculous.

"I rejected your mate claim. I didn't mean to ... I mean I didn't want to ..." She sighed, slammed her hands down on the armrests. "What I'm trying to say is that something came over me. I don't know what it was. It was like an out-of-body experience, I suppose." Sanura swore, low and with frustration. "No, that's not right. It was as if my body had a will of its own."

"It was the pheromones."

"No, aren't you listening, Assefa? It wasn't the damn pheromones. It was something else."

"You're the one who isn't listening." Assefa got to his feet but didn't move closer to Sanura. "At the right magic level, my cat pheromones can induce a heightened pleasure response."

"I don't understand. What does that mean?"

Assefa dropped back into his chair, a wave of emotional exhaustion weighing him down. "Remember I told you there were were-cat sex games we could play?"

"Sure, like the time you duplicated yourself, turning a twosome into a threesome."

That had become a private joke between them, with Assefa claiming Sanura liked threesomes and the witch denying it with flaming
cheeks of embarrassment. But tonight, unfortunately, was no joking
matter.

"Right, that's one of many sex spells a mated pair can cast together. Since we're only partially mated, I couldn't maintain my second
form longer than a few minutes."

"Okay, yeah, I remember that too. But what does any of that have
to do with your pheromones?"

"Were-cat pheromones are used to attract his mate. But it can also
be used to heighten the sexual pleasure between a mated pair. Meaning, the higher the pheromone level, the greater the sexual high when
we make love. But since we're partially mated, the effect can feel
more like a drug."

"Wait, are you saying you drugged me?"

She didn't sound convinced that he could or would do something
so awful to her.

"In a sense, yes. I didn't mean to, though. I can't even explain how
it happened. I didn't feel out of control. The only thing I could think
about was how much I loved you and wanted to make you my true
mate."

"I had the same thoughts. I wanted your claiming bite, your mate
mark. I felt desperate for it. As if I would burn from the inside-out if
you didn't bite me." Sanura ran a hand over her neck, the area where
his fangs had been. "A part of me still feels that way. A shallow hum
of need that won't go away."

"I feel the same, but the sensation isn't shallow. Even now, after all
I've done to you, I want to strip you naked, haul you onto my lap and
let you ride me hard while I claim you with my fangs."

Assefa shut his eyes, hoping when he opened them the lust he saw
in Sanura's eyes would be gone. She didn't mean it. She was probably

still feeling the after effects of his pheromones on her assaulted senses.

"I understand what you've just said, but I don't think that explains what happened between us."

He opened his eyes. When he looked at Sanura, he saw much in her gaze, but lust wasn't among the emotions staring back at him.

"I want us to have a proper handfasting ceremony. During the first of the three parts, you merged our auras, allowing your fire spirit to claim my cat spirit as mate."

Guilt, one of the emotions in Sanura's eyes, flickered.

"When you moved in with me, you said you wanted to continue with the handfasting. In the last month, you haven't mentioned it. Do you still want to proceed, or have you changed your mind?"

Fear, another emotion that showed in her eyes, surged forward.

The way she stared at him, he'd never seen Sanura look so torn and grief-stricken. Eyes watered, face crumpled, and for the second time that night, Sanura wept.

In a flash, Assefa was by his witch's side, lifting then settling her on his lap. He stroked her hair while she cried on his shoulder, her arms wrapped fiercely around his neck.

"You have no idea how much I want you," she spoke through a stream of tears. "At first, I was afraid. Afraid of falling so in love that I would leave my heart vulnerable. But loving you also means trusting that you would never intentionally hurt me."

Hearing that she loved and trusted him eased some of the tightness in Assefa's chest. But nothing she'd said explained Sanura's emotional breakdown now, or abrupt halt to his claiming back at the house.

"I apologized earlier because I gave you every indication that I wanted to complete our mate bond." She lifted her head from his shoulder, face a teary mess, and she was still the most gorgeous woman he'd ever seen. Sanura pressed quivering lips to his. "By all that is magical, I want you so much, Assefa." More tears poured from Sanura, wetting their joined lips. "But I don't know how to have both of you."

Assefa pulled back. "What do you mean by 'have both of you'?"

****

Baltimore, Maryland
29 Years Ago

The god of fire, thunder, and lightning lowered his feet to the basement floor, chiseled dark-brown body bare except for a blood-red sarong around his waist. Head and face clean-shaven, he held a battle axe in his left hand. A leather wrapping ran the length of the weapon's wooden handle, and Sam could see his tense, frightened eyes in the shiny double blades.

Prayer and a father's faith had brought the deity to Sam's home, on this sacred and prophesized night of his daughter's birth. He'd asked the god to bless his daughter, but Sàngó had only stared at him with unemotional eyes of lightning.

When he'd arrived, materializing before Sam's stunned eyes, he'd levitated in the air—regal, powerful, and intimidating. Now he towered over a kneeling Sam, his unreadable godly eyes on the crying baby on the pillow between Sam's bent knees.

His Sanura, who hadn't cried when she'd come into this world, hadn't stopped crying since the god entered the realm of mortals. Taking care to support her head, Sam lifted his distraught daughter into his arms and held her to his pounding heart.

Canting his head to the left, Sàngó watched, as if fascinated, Sam rock his daughter.

This was an odd scene, and not at all what Sam envisioned when he'd prayed to the deity. Uncomfortable with the way Sàngó stared, unblinking, at him, Sam blurted the first thing that popped into his head. "My mother assured me babies like motion and to be held close to their parents' heart." He smiled, a forced response to the god's lack of emotion and response. "I guess you can tell I've never done this before. I must be doing something wrong because I can't seem to get her to stop crying."

Eyes transfixed on an inconsolable Sanura, Sàngó tossed his battle axe onto the sofa. The longer he watched Sanura, the more the sparks of lightning at the corner of the god's eyes retreated until the inhumanness of his fathomless white orbs gave way to something less divine, less forbidding.

"She is a fragile creature."

"All babies are. But I have faith she will grow strong under her family's sun."

Sam wanted to repeat his request from earlier, but the god didn't seem inclined to renew that discussion just yet. So Sam continued to rock Sanura and hoped her loud cries wouldn't wake the household, especially Makena.

To his astonishment, Sàngó knelt in front of Sam, his hands outstretched. "Give me the babe, Samuel Williams."

Sam clutched Sanura to him. A little too hard from her yelp of pain. "Sorry, princess. Daddy didn't mean to hurt you." He kissed her forehead, felt the warmth of her skin. Too warm. Fever warm.

"Give me the child," Sàngó repeated, his voice a sonic boom that vibrated in the small space that separated god from mortal.

"No."

The specks of lightning came roaring back, crackling from the corners of the god's eyes like a Fourth of July sparkler.

Sam didn't budge. The god could strike him dead where he knelt, but he would be damned if he handed his Sanura over to a being who didn't understand the basic concept of soothing a crying baby.

"You would die to protect this wailing child of fire?"

"Of course, she's my daughter. There's nothing I wouldn't do to protect her. Even die."

"If you died, Samuel Williams, who then would protect the child of fire?"

Good damn question. Luckily, Sam had an answer. "The cat of legend. Has that child been born yet?"

Hands still outstretched, as if waiting for Sam to change his mind and place Sanura in them, Sàngó said, "It is not yet his time. But soon the Mngwa will come forth, completing the trinity."

Completing the trinity. That means the water witch of legend has already been birthed.

"You requested my blessing, Samuel Williams, yet you refuse me your child."

"I understand your point, but I can't give her to you. Not yet. I know it doesn't make sense, but she won't be mine forever. I'm right, aren't I?"

Sam tried his best to ignore the lash of pain cutting through flesh, bone, and muscle the thought evoked. Sanura's endless sea of tears delivered devastating blow after devastating blow, his heart a mangled organ anchored to his body by were-cat stubbornness and a father's unconditional love.

"You said you would die to protect the child of fire, the fire witch of legend. Do you understand what you ask of me?"

Sam nodded, no longer able to speak, not over the wails of his daughter. Nothing he did calmed her. And she was burning up, almost too hot to the touch. Green eyes darkened, rolled back in her head and disappeared into an eerie pool of scarlet. Sanura's tiny body began to shake. She coughed with each violent convulsion, spitting up frothy bubbles of blood fire.

Before Sam could process that his child was dying right before his eyes, drowning in beseeching tears and untamed fire magic, Sàngó snatched Sanura from him. Then the battle axe was back in the god's hand and pressed to Sam's throat.

Sam stared, swallowed, and considered his options. It took him all of a second to conclude there were no good options, other than begging for the life of his child.

"Tell me, Samuel Williams, what are you willing to sacrifice for her life?"

"Anything."

Sam reached for his dying daughter. The blade cut into his neck, drawing blood, but not as much as that being purged from Sanura's ashen body. Her newborn frame was coughing, crying, and heaving her way to Anubis' waiting arms.

"Give her to me, damn you."

"A life for a life, Samuel Williams."

"Fine, you have it. Take mine, spare hers."

He reached for Sanura again, but invisible hands restrained him." He fought against them, using every ounce of his were-cat strength to free himself. But the hands that held him weren't of this world. They kept him where he was, on his knees and away from his suddenly quiet, too still daughter.

"What in the hell did you do to her?" His wife's face slammed into his mind, the sadness and grief that had overtaken her when she'd miscarried. Then the look of utter relief and joy when she'd delivered a healthy baby girl. If she awoke in the morning to find Sanura's crib empty and her daughter dead, Makena's heart and soul would follow. "Let me have my daughter. Please, I beg you. Don't let her die."

As if the battle axe had never been, it faded by slow, magical degrees before disappearing. Sàngó used his free hand to run a long finger over Sanura's blood-stained lips.

"One day, the cat of legend will find her, and he will claim her as his mate. Do you understand, Samuel Williams?"

He didn't. He'd only wanted the god to bless his daughter. Sam wasn't arrogant enough to think a god would permit a lowly mortal to suggest the type of blessing he would bestow. No more than he was naïve enough to believe that a god, any god, would grant a boon for free.

"I cannot bless this child. If I do, she will reek of my magic and interference. That I cannot have, Samuel Williams."

Sam slumped against the invisible hands restraining him, eyes full of tears. Sanura no longer cried her disapproval or flailed about in protest and agitation. Within the god's omnipotent hands, his daughter lay lifeless, Sanura's white onesie now bittersweet red.

"Then you can't help me. Just return my daughter to me and go." *This was a mistake. A huge, irrevocable mistake. Makena will never forgive me. And I'll never forgive myself.*

A hand touched the top of a head that had fallen in failure, in anguish. "Samuel Williams, this is my blessing for you. As Sanura Wasola Williams' father and protector, you will raise her, guide her, and love her. You will prepare the child for the war to come. And when you have taught her all you know of witches, were-cats, and the prophecy, you will die for her."

Sàngó placed a silent, limp Sanura back onto the pillow. Sam's tears cascaded onto Sanura, a summer shower that did nothing to revive his wilted red rose.

The hand on his head slid to his chin and lifted. Through a waterfall of tears, Sam thought he saw an ember of hope and humanity in the thunder god's lightning white eyes.

"When you die, Samuel Williams, the balance of the long life you would have lived will transfer to your daughter. Inside of her, an echo of your jaguar spirit will slumber until the time it is claimed by her mate, the cat of legend. Then it will be he who will step into the void left by the father. He who will protect the child of fire. He who will fight by her side. A Mngwa with the added might and magic of a powerful jaguar. This, Samuel Williams, is my blessing to you. So I have spoken. So it will be done."

****

Realm of the Gods

"Oh, but they are most delicious, sister." Mami Wata stroked the warm tropic scales of her Titanoboa, its tan-and-gray head between her large breasts, the remainder of the snake's twenty-foot body coiled about her naked form. The snake's head rose, nuzzled her neck, and then burrowed its face in the sea of her crinkled black hair. "Particularly the were-cat. I think I will enjoy devouring him most of all. What do you think, sister?"

Mami Wata lowered the polished metal disc she held in her hand, an ancient looking glass crafted of gold, pearls, diamonds, and water goddess magic. Through her scrying glass, she observed all—the mortal battlefield of play upon which her well-laid plans would unfold.

Layer by layer by beastly layer.

She turned to her sister. On the other side of the room, a structure designed by Ra and placed in the center of the realm, Oya reclined on a Mngwa print bench. Plush and elegant, Oya all but sank into the luxurious piece of furniture, purple silk draped over her nude form, and emerald eyes staring up at Mami Wata with arrogant, willful familiarity.

Mami Wata smiled. "I will feast on that kitty of yours, sister."

As Mami Wata had done to her Titanoboa, Oya laid a hand upon the Mngwa print bench and stroked. "I think not. He will be the one to feast upon your pets."

Mami Wata's warm smile never wavered, although freezing ocean water ran through her veins, cooling her temper and slowing her immortal pulse.

"He should not even exist."

"Yet he does, and he is mine."

"No, sister, what you should have said is that he is mine. For the next few weeks, I own him. And your pathetic fire witch."

Mami Wata peered into the scrying glass. The fire witch no longer cried, nor were the mortals huddled together outside. They had retreated to their bedroom. From a chaise lounge in the corner of the darkened room, the little witch, legs pulled to chest and arms around knees, watched the were-cat through the glass balcony doors. Though, in human form, he prowled the wrought-iron enclosure, back straight, chin held high, but eyes a savage gold. The first fissure in his chain-mail of self-control.

"They are stronger than you think."

"You speak with such confidence, sister. But that will soon change, for I intend to break the were-cat."

A hand blown glass statue of a Mngwa appeared in Mami Wata's hand. She let it slip onto the stone floor, shattering upon impact. "Break him." A second figurine materialized in her hand, made of stone resin. That too tumbled out of her hand and onto the floor, cracking into a dozen pieces. "Break him." She opened her left hand, in the center slept a newborn Mngwa. She tossed the cub into the air.

"Snack."

Her Titanoboa opened its mouth and caught the cub, devouring it in one smooth gulp.

Mami Wata grinned at Oya. "Break him."

The Titanoboa slithered its massive frame down and off Mami Wata. It hissed at Oya, coiling its lower half and rearing up in a show of aggression and solidarity with its mistress.

Reaching out a hand, she stroked the head of her pet. Such a beautiful and loyal creature. All her pets were, even her mortal pets. They would do her bidding whether they wished to obey or not. No one refused a goddess and lived.

"You and your consort have done much to aid my war cause. The sentimental fools that you are. Thank you, sister, for making my efforts that much easier."

The purple silk cascaded from Oya's body when she stood, her eyes glowing murderous red.

The Titanoboa opened its mouth wide, razor-sharp fangs white and dangerous. It attacked, lunging at Oya with an unnatural speed and grace.

Up in flames her magnificent and stupid pet went. A hissing, writhing snake driven to extinction in the mortal realm, but alive here due to Mami Wata's grace. Now scales of ash and charred flesh befouled the cruel air between the goddesses.

A space where love and sisterhood should have been but where bloody competition had only ever existed.

She could make another Titanoboa. But there was only one cat of legend. Once he was gone ...

Mami Wata laughed. "I will destroy his loving heart. It is the werecat's greatest weakness. And without her lover's heart, the fire witch will succumb easily to my water witch. The wheels of his defeat are already set in motion. Now return to your spectator's bench, dear sister, and watch the destruction of Sekhmet's Mngwa of myth."

CHAPTER EIGHT

Sanura wanted to go to Assefa again, the way she did earlier. From the same balcony where Assefa now paced, she'd observed his Mngwa. After seeing a blur of fur run past the balcony twenty times, she stopped counting and had slumped in one of the balcony chairs. She'd literally sent the man running out of his own damn home. Since learning the truth and returning to their bedroom, Assefa had yet to speak a single word to her.

Now she sat in a chair in a darkened room, unsure how to bridge the divide between herself and Assefa other than putting everything on the table and hoping for the best.

When the house phone rang, Sanura considered not answering it, but she pushed to her feet and made her way to the other side of the room. The phone rang two more times before she reached the nightstand and the phone's cradle. In the middle of the sixth ring, she picked up the receiver. The caller ID screen revealed Makena Williams as the midnight caller.

"Hey, Mom."

"Sanura. I'm glad it's you. I thought that butler would answer."

"I've told you before, Omar isn't a butler. You have a near photographic memory, so I know you just said that to get under my skin. Besides, if you didn't want to risk having Omar answer the phone, you should've just called me on my cell."

"Well, maybe if you hadn't rushed out of here so fast you wouldn't have forgotten your cell phone and I would've called it instead of the land line. And if you want me to stop referring to Omar as a butler, then perhaps you should ask Assefa to remove that very large stick from up his ... Anyway, Sanura, I didn't call about your cell phone, which I will bring to you on Saturday, or even to harass you about Alfred Pennyworth, although that's always fun."

Makena laughed at her joke, which meant she and Mike had an enjoyable dinner together, in spite of Sanura's abrupt departure. It also meant Sanura wouldn't be taking her mother to see another Batman movie any time soon.

Sanura sat on the edge of the bed, wanting to confide in her mother but knowing she couldn't. Makena would be as torn about the situation as Sanura. More, Sanura possessed a piece of Sam she wished she could turn over to her mother. But she hadn't found one transference spell that would accomplish what she wanted to do. Three weeks of research and nothing to show for her efforts.

"I can live without my phone for a day. It's no big deal, especially since Assefa keeps a couple of emergency cell phones in the house. So, did you call because of the way I left the house? I'm sorry about that, by the way. If I worried you, I didn't mean to."

"Are you safe and unharmed?"

"Yes."

"What about Assefa?"

"He's fi ... I mean, he's safe and unharmed." A lie of omission, because neither Assefa nor Sanura were fine.

"You sound tired, sweetie. I should've waited to call you in the morning."

"No, it's okay. Why did you call?"

"Well, there's something I've meant to speak with you about. It's late, so now isn't the best time. I thought we could talk this Sunday. Maybe have brunch afterward."

"Mom, we can talk whenever you like. You don't have to schedule an appointment with me. What's with you? You sound strange all of a sudden."

Sanura turned her head to the left when she heard the balcony doors close. Mutely, Assefa stalked to the master bathroom, entered, and shut the door behind him, all without sparing Sanura a glance.

No, Assefa was most definitely not fine.

Sanura slid onto the floor, back against the side of the bed, pinpricks of tears behind her eyes. But she wouldn't cry. She'd cried enough for one day. Tears solved nothing, and they damn sure couldn't erase the past or fix the present.

"The meeting on Sunday is with the Council."

That bit of unexpected news garnered Sanura's full attention. "Why do they want to meet with me? Because of the prophecy?" She should've expected something like this. The twenty-ninth year of the fire witch's birthday was the prophesized year of the Day of Serpents. The Witch Council of Elders would have a plan for addressing what was to come, not that anyone knew for sure what would happen or exactly when.

"Actually, Sanura, they requested a meeting with you and Assefa. Since he's the cat of legend, they would like to speak to him, to get to know him better. He's a part of our network now, it only makes sense for you to introduce your mate to the Council."

That was true. But more was going on here than her mother was saying. She knew Makena too well to be fooled by her cavalier attitude about the Council wanting to get to know Assefa, which they could begin to do at Sanura's birthday party, no special meeting required.

"What else?"

"What do you mean?"

"I mean you're keeping something from me, and I want to know what it is."

Makena, rarely at a loss for words, paused.

In the intervening silence, Sanura listened to the water from the shower and envisioned a stoic Assefa under its heated spray. His FBI armor on and polished to an impenetrable shine.

Damn, ever since running into Greg, Sanura's day had gone straight to hell.

"You know, when it comes to Council business," Makena said, drawing Sanura back to their conversation and away from thoughts of an emotionally walled-off Assefa, "I'm not free to share the details."

"Even if I'm the topic. Yeah, I know, Mom. But I don't like it, especially since it also involves Assefa."

"I know. But the Council wants the six of us to meet and discuss everything at once."

"Everything? As in more than one issue?"

"Just two, Sanura."

"Then how come the 'just two' sounds like something I should be worried about?"

"Because you're like your father and worry about every little thing. One issue is nothing more than a formality."

"And the other issue?" Sanura asked when her mother paused again.

"Well, that one is a bit trickier, but nothing to worry about."

"'A bit trickier'?"

"Are you going to repeat everything I say?"

"Yes, if you keep saying things that make me nervous and not want to see you or your Council sisters. Maybe I should disinvite the lot of you to my birthday party."

Makena chuckled. "I can't believe I raised a daughter who says stuff like 'the lot of you.'"

"Yes, well, blame Omar."

"Right, the butler."

"The chef."

"Whatever. So, brunch on Sunday? Your house at eleven?"

"I guess. I'll have to make sure Assefa is free, then think about what to feed everyone."

"Gods, Sanura, I can't believe you can't cook. And I tried so hard to teach you. I mean, you are truly a horrible cook. Do you remember that time—"

"Goodnight, Mom."

Makena laughed again then said with a mother's mystical knowing, "Whatever is going on between you and Assefa isn't as bad as you believe, sweetie. It's a trite saying, Sanura, but love conquers all. You only have to believe that it can. But most of all, you have to fight for it."

Assefa opened the bathroom door, a towel wrapped around his waist and looking so much better than Greg ever could. He walked to his dresser, opened the top drawer and pulled out a pair of black cotton boxers.

She dropped her eyes, wanting too much to watch him remove his towel before stepping into his underwear.

"If you ever want to talk, Sanura."

"I know, Mom, I know. I'll speak with Assefa about Sunday."

"Good, then I'll see you on your birthday. Have a good night."

They said their goodbyes, and Sanura returned the phone to the cradle. By the time she did, Assefa's boxers were on and the towel in the hamper. And from the foot of the bed, Assefa stared at her, broad, muscular chest slightly damp from the shower.

Sanura climbed onto the bed and moved to the center, hoping Assefa would join her.

He did, but he perched himself at the foot of the bed, his body as far away from her as he could be while still sharing the same space.

She sighed, recalling their first argument. Back then, a mere five weeks ago, it had been Sanura who'd put physical distance between them. On the drive from Alexandria to Baltimore, after learning Assefa was the son of the reputed civil rights abuser and dictator, General Supreme Jahi Berber, the ruler of the Republic of the Sudan, she'd sat on one end of the limousine and Assefa on the other. She hadn't been upset with him because of who his father had turned out to be, but rather the lack of trust and faith in her that had stilled his tongue.

How ironic, their positions reversed. This secret, however, unlike Assefa's, cut long and deep.

"Two Sankofa teenagers came to our home today," he said without preamble. "That's what I was dealing with when you called. At the time, I didn't know what they wanted, if they arrived by themselves, or the level of threat to this household. That's why I pushed you to stay in Baltimore and have dinner with Makena. I'm sorry for misleading you on the phone, but I had every intention of telling you everything when you returned home."

He'd said all of that as if he were giving an assignment report to his division chief. So, he didn't want to talk about what she'd told him. That was fine. What he'd said to her was also important, and added to what she wanted to share with him. But they would get back to the other matter, the one that had stolen the warmth from Assefa's chocolate eyes.

"You don't seem surprised."

"I am, and I'm not. I assume the students were were-cats and not witches?"

"Two lion cubs. Well, not exactly cubs, but still pretty young."

Sanura nodded, thinking back to her brief but strange conversation with Greg. Felidae law he'd said.

"Do you want to tell me what's going on here, Sanura?"

"I don't know myself." She considered scooting closer to Assefa but decided against it. Now wasn't the time to test those particular waters. "I ran into an old friend today. Like the teenagers, he's also a lion shifter."

"Does your friend have a name?"

Once she spoke of Greg, Sanura would have to tell Assefa everything. She had no problem telling him what happened today at the school. She'd planned on doing that anyway. But the half-naked Greg part of the story would only add to the tension between them.

"His name is Gregory Chambers. He's the son of the High Priestess of the Witch Council of Elders, Anna Spencer."

From there, Sanura told Assefa about her meeting with Rachel, omitting the part about her Wolof lesson, and everything that happened with Greg after they bumped into each other.

"Felidae law. That's why you called me?"

During her explanation, Assefa had retrieved his laptop from the sitting room and began typing, adding notes to an already open Word document.

"Yes, do you know what it is? Does felidae law exist in the Sudan?"

Assefa typed as they spoke, his eyes on the laptop screen, his mind focused on gathering and recording all pertinent information.

"All cat families have laws or rules that regulate and guide internal and external behavior. The Sudan is no different in that respect. But no pride, clan, or felidae law is greater than the laws approved by the General Supreme."

"Within the Sankofa community, felidae law, no matter the cat family, does not supersede the dictates of the Council."

More typing. "Is your network of were-cats comprised of both Pantherinae and Feliane families?"

"Yes. The Pantherinae families are the largest of the were-cat families."

Assefa typed in the information before glancing up from his computer. "I'm not surprised. Let me guess. Panthera tigris, leo, onca, and pardus?"

"Smart man. Tigers, lions, jaguars, and leopards. There is also a small family of clouded and snow leopards, as well as cougars."

Assefa tapped on his keyboard, probably adding Panthera unica, Neofelis nebulosi, and Puma concolor to his growing list of details.

"What I don't get is what felidae law has to do with you. Why would the lion pride concern themselves with a man they don't know? And why would Greg warn me that you should watch your back? He all but said you were the target of his family. Felidae law stipulates what can and cannot be shared with those outside of the family, so

Greg was very close to breaking a major rule of his pride when he warned me."

Assefa closed his laptop, all but slamming it shut. "I don't like this. Any of this. The trespassers. The warning." His face turned thoughtful. "I overheard part of your conversation with Makena. Why does the Council want to meet with us this Sunday?"

"I have no idea. Like were-cat families, the Council is very private. But you think all of this is connected, right?"

"Yes, don't you?"

Yeah, she did. Sanura had never been a faithful subscriber to the concept of coincidence. "Yes. It's odd and sudden. But I suppose it could all have to do with the prophecy. You're the famed cat of legend. I guess we shouldn't be surprised you would be the topic of conversation within the local were-cat community once our relationship became public knowledge."

That statement had taken them full circle to the conversation they weren't having. Everyone would assume, and rightfully so, that the fire witch of legend, who once only ever dated full-humans, had finally found her mate in the Mngwa of prophecy. Of course they would be curious about Assefa Berber, including the women who governed the Council.

Assefa gathered up his computer, secured it under an arm and stared at Sanura as if he'd just arrived at a realization that didn't sit well with him.

"I'm not a brute, you know."

Okay, were they back to him thinking he'd used his pheromones to drug her into having sex with him and begging to be taken by his Mngwa? She did move closer to him then, needing to see more of his face in the lightless room. They were capable of seeing just fine in the dark, although were-cats had far better night vision than witches.

"I know you're not. Why would you say that?"

He pushed off the bed and to his feet. "You showered before coming home. You smelled of the same organic soap Makena uses and the

dress you wore out of the house wasn't the same one you returned in."
He turned away from Sanura and began walking toward the sitting
room. "Did you think I wouldn't notice? Or maybe you think I'm so
insecure about the partial mate bond that I would act the role of bar-
barian because you ran into an old boyfriend who got too damn close
and left his lion scent all over you."

The last words were spoken so low and with such guttural ferocity
Sanura wondered if Assefa realized how menacing he sounded.

Menacing but not unapproachable. Well, not unapproachable for
Sanura, who never questioned her safety around Assefa or his Mngwa.

She got to her feet and walked toward Assefa, stopping when she
was toe-to-toe with the man she loved.

"Let me be clear about three things, my grumpy special agent.
One, Gregory Chambers was never my boyfriend or lover."

"Not for lack of trying, I'm sure."

True, but that wasn't the point, and Sanura wouldn't allow Assefa
to distract her with jealous nonsense.

"Two, I don't think of you as a brute, and I never will. That insults
us both, by the way. Three, I would never disrespect you by coming
home with the scent of an unmated were-cat on me, especially one
you don't know. And I don't care what you say, you would've been
upset if I had. Like you are now, and like you were when I told you
about falling on Greg and him not letting me go right away."

He glared at her, not at all appeased by what she'd said. But he also didn't argue her points. What he did do, however, was back away,
turn, and go into the sitting room.

Gods but she wanted to hug and kiss his pain away, as much as she
wanted to shake Assefa and force him to tear down his damn wall. But
when five minutes turned into twenty and then into sixty, Sanura knew
he had no intention of returning to their bedroom for the night.

"Don't do this, Assefa," she said from the doorway that separated
the bedroom from the sitting room. The sofa, while comfy, wasn't
meant to accommodate a man of Assefa's large size. Yet he sprawled

over every inch of the furniture, head propped on an armrest, feet dangling off the other end. "Come to bed. Please."

Eyes that hadn't been closed when she'd spoken, staring at the ceiling, lowered and focused on her.

"It's not a good idea. I don't want to risk getting too close to you until I know for sure I won't unintentionally drug you again."

"You won't. I trust you."

"Thanks, but I don't trust myself to be that close to you right now."

Sanura stepped into the room and closer to Assefa. "What would you say if I told you I think someone bespelled us?"

Assefa sat up, interested. "I would say keep talking."

"It's the only logical explanation for what happened between us. No one has absolute control over their emotions and urges, Assefa, not even you. But you would never hurt me. Rape me," she added, taking a chance and giving voice to what she believed was at the heart of Assefa's pain, anger, and distance."

Apologetic, haunted eyes turned away, and she knew she'd guessed correctly.

"That's not what happened between us. Yes, you emitted your pheromones. But our lovemaking was consensual." She stood in front of him, then knelt so they'd be face-to-face. "When it was clear I didn't want you to bite me, you stopped. You comforted me and made me feel like a woman, even though I was acting like a grieving child. But none of that was rape." Sanura pressed her lips to Assefa's forehead and arms went around his shoulders and pulled him to her. "You're not like Stephen. You may carry a powerful beast as your inner spirit, but that doesn't make you a cruel, heartless animal."

Predictably, Assefa said nothing. So Sanura kept talking, hating whoever had done this to him, to them.

Assefa was magically bound to Sanura and her fire spirit, which meant no witch should have been able to cast a spell over her familiar. Unless, of course, the witch possessed a higher magic level than the fire witch of legend. Considering Sanura's off the chart magic level, she couldn't imagine any witch capable of bespelling her Mngwa, other than, perhaps, the water witch of legend. If the water witch of legend had discovered Sanura's and Assefa's identity, why cast some kind of aphrodisiac spell instead of something violent and brutal, ending the prophesized war before the first battle had been fought?

No, it couldn't be the water witch of legend. But someone was to blame for today's emotional hellstorm, and it hadn't been the man moving out of her arms.

"I hope you're right." Assefa's back went to the plush cushions of the sofa. "If you are, that just means we have a powerful enemy."

Or a powerful ally, Sanura thought but kept the random idea to herself. After the party and the meeting with the Council, Sanura would think more on today, including a gold speck of glitter she just now recalled seeing on Assefa's lower lip. Glitter that, if her memory was correct, hadn't been there when she'd first entered the suite.

She moved to the cushion next to Assefa and took hold of one of his hands. They were big, like the rest of him. But no part of Assefa was as large as his sensitive and caring heart. She squeezed his hand, raised it to her chest, over her heart. "I didn't know about my father's sacrifice until I moved in here. Well, to be accurate, I began having dreams about my father the night we first made love."

She let his hand go when he twisted to better see her face.

"I remember waking and finding you gone from the bed. Then I noticed you on the floor with your candles. Are you now telling me a dream woke you and drove you out of bed?"

"Something like that. I used to have horrible nightmares when I was a kid. Eventually, they stopped. That night was the first time in years I'd had one. I couldn't really make out what was going on in the dream, but I remembered hearing a crying baby and my father's voice. When I awoke, I had the strangest feeling."

"What kind of feeling?"

"I really don't know. I just felt different, as if something in me had awakened."

Now she knew what it had been, back then she did not. The first night they'd made love, Assefa's fangs had, instinctively, slipped from his gums and Sanura became frightened. Not of Assefa per se, but of the emotional and psychological permanence of the mate bond. After her father's death, Sanura witnessed the devastating toll his passing had taken on her mother. Sam's death had nearly broken Makena, their mate bond link forever severed.

Then there had been the mate mark. A week after Sam's funeral, Sanura returned to the house to find her mother sitting in the bathtub, scalding water pouring down on her. Her shivering body was cold to the touch. And all Makena could manage to say, between a tsunami of tears was, "It's gone. The mark of our bond is gone."

Sanura's eyes had traveled to her mother's outer right thigh. Sure enough, the mark was no longer there. Sanura had seen the mark her entire life, a jaguar's paw print inside a ring of fire. To full-humans who saw a witch's mate mark, it appeared as nothing more than a well-inked tattoo. But to those of the preternatural world, all knew the true meaning of the symbols.

Yet with a mate's death, the bond was no more. And the mark that once symbolized their love and fidelity vanished as if it had never been.

"Your father's jaguar spirit you mean? Is that what awoke inside of you?"

"Eventually, yes. But I didn't know it at the time. When my father became sick, my parents told me he had a rare were-cat disease."

"And you believed them because you had no reason to think your parents would lie to you."

She gave a jerky nod. "I was devastated." Sanura stared down at her hands. "My entire life I was told I was the fire witch of legend, the most powerful witch of this generation." Hands balled into fists, then relaxed. "But I couldn't even save my father. No spell, Assefa. There was no spell I could find that would save his life. And I looked. For six months, I searched and searched. No cure. No goddamn cure."

A single tear escaped, and she wiped it away, angry at her own weakness.

"We don't need to talk about this tonight." This time, Assefa was the one who took hold of her hand and squeezed. "You should turn in. There's always tomorrow. Putting this conversation off for another night won't change anything. Things are as they are."

"What do you mean by that?"

"What I'm saying is that your father was an extraordinary man. I already thought highly of him, considering the kind of woman he married and the daughter he helped raise. After hearing how far he went to protect you, I have so much more respect for him." Assefa kissed the back of her hand. "I would do the same for my son or daughter. But I've seen enough as a special agent to know that not everyone would make that kind of sacrifice, not even for their own flesh and blood."

From the moment she met Assefa, Sanura could see how much he and her father were alike. Sure, they were dissimilar in significant ways, as most men were. But when it came to family and matters of the heart, Samuel Williams and Assefa Berber were formed from the same mold.

They loved.

They protected.

They sacrificed.

But Assefa shouldn't have to also sacrifice the truth. He deserved to know, and Sanura would finish what she started.

"After that first night, I had more dreams. Not every night and they weren't like the nightmares I had when I was a kid."

"Then what were they like?"

"Memories. But not my memories," she clarified. "The story I told you tonight in the gazebo was the puzzle of my dreams. When I slept, my subconscious mixed with the residual energy of my father's jaguar spirit I inherited when he passed on. His jaguar spirit slept for three years inside of me and I was unaware of him being there." She touched her chest again.

"But it's awake now?"

"Yes, fully. But it took about two weeks for that to happen and for me to understand what was going on with me. Once I did, I thought I could find a way to remove the spirit from me and transfer it to my mother."

"But you couldn't because, like your father's death, it was manufactured by a god. Which means the spell, or whatever it's called, cannot be tampered with by a mortal."

"I had the same thought. But I'm not certain that's the case. Or maybe it is and I'm just not willing to accept it."

For several minutes, they sat in silence, Assefa still holding Sanura's hand. But when the quiet was finally broken, Assefa's words plunged deep into her heart.

"I would give almost anything to carry a piece of my mother inside of me, to have anything of worth to remind me of the woman who brought me into this world. But I have nothing, barely any memories of her at all. What your father did for you was a gift. I know his jaguar spirit was meant for the man who would become your mate. To make him strong and powerful enough to protect you by defeating Mami Wata's water beasts and the water witch of legend."

Yes, that was Sàngó's so-called blessing. The blessing also explained her father's words during the last days of his life. "Stop wasting your time with full-humans and start looking for your mate. When he comes, you must be ready for him. Let him love and protect you, the way I've tried my best to do. Accept him into your heart, princess, and let the cat of legend claim you as his mate."

Sanura had accepted Assefa into her heart, and she also wanted to let him claim her as his mate. But ...

"If I had bit you that first night, marking and claiming you as mine, you would've never known about the jaguar spirit inside of you."

Yes, she'd had the same thought.

"And maybe that would've been for the best. But we'll never know. But what I do know is that, in a way, your father has been returned to you. That must be the most wonderful feeling."

Assefa smiled at her, genuine happiness shining from him and into her. Yet in the span of two breaths, the light vanished, replaced by bleak reality.

"I can't take the jaguar spirit away from you. It would be like your father dying a second time. I now understand that's the reason why you haven't mentioned continuing with the handfasting. It's also the reason why you cried when I made to claim you today. You thought about what you would lose if you became my mate."

"I want to become your mate, Assefa. I need you to believe that."

"I believe a part of you may want that, but a bigger part of you is the young woman whose father died too soon. The father she tried to save but couldn't. That young woman misses him and probably feels guilty about his death. The bottom line, Sanura, is that you feel you have to choose between your father and your lover. No woman should have to make that kind of no-win decision. And I don't want you to choose." He smiled, grim-faced. "Actually, you've already made your decision. You chose a daughter's love, which is only right. But I won't pressure you any longer."

Sanura's heart raced at the implication of his words. But she had to make sure, had to be one hundred percent clear about what Assefa was saying.

"What do you mean?"

He let go of her hand. "I'm saying I release you from your handfasting vow. I no longer have an expectation of you becoming my mate. I won't bring it up again. The handfasting or the mate claim. You're free and clear to do whatever you want, without feeling torn or guilty. I get it now. I know where I stand and where I don't."

Stunned didn't begin to capture the hemorrhaging taking place in Sanura's heart. Her soul and future with Assefa bleeding out from every pore of her frozen body. He'd released her from her handfasting vow. What in the hell?

"That's not what I want. For Oya's sake, Assefa, that's the last thing I want."

Why was he being like this? Why didn't he understand that she just needed more time to figure all of this out? Why couldn't he see the jagged wounds in her heart, new ones from this madness and scarred-over ones from when her father had died? No, this wasn't what Sanura wanted. Not at all.

"It's not what you said you wanted, but it's the only way. You don't want to relinquish your father's cat spirit, which I understand. On my honor as a Berber, I do understand your decision, no matter how much it hurts. And because of that, I don't want to put myself in a situation where I'll be tempted to pressure, guilt, or seduce you into changing your mind. Which will happen if I let myself continue to view us as one ritual and one bite away from being fully mated." His jaw set in a stubborn line that didn't bode well for them. "I won't do that to myself, Sanura."

"It's not that I don't want to give up the jaguar spirit," she told him, fear and desperation making her tongue feel thick and heavy, unable to express all she needed Assefa to understand. "It's just that I'm not ready to let my father go again."

Assefa raised a hand and took hold of a lock of hair, toying with it between his fingers before letting it drop back to her shoulder. "That's just it, Sanura, you may never be able to let your father go, not after having experienced his loss once. As I've said, I understand. But I don't want to live my life waiting and hoping for that day to arrive, only to find that years have slipped by and I've grown angry and bitter."

"So you're saying you want to break up?"

Gods, she couldn't breathe, couldn't believe this was happening to her, to them. And she didn't know how to fix it because Assefa was right. Sanura had no idea when or if she would be ready to let her father go again. Having his cat spirit inside of her made her feel happy and whole in a way she hadn't since Sam closed his eyes for the final time. It was selfish, she knew, but her father had been the center of her universe. How could she let him go? And how could she grant herself the very thing she'd denied her mother and father? —a lifetime of happiness with their mate.

But she also didn't want to lose Assefa. She couldn't lose Assefa.

"If I loved you less or thought for a minute you didn't love me with all your fire witch heart, I could back away from you, from this, and convince myself my decision was for the best. But I love you, and nothing you've told me tonight has changed that undeniable truth. So what I'm saying, Sanura, is that I have to learn to live with the situation as it is. I have to accept that what we have right now is all I'll ever have with you. A partial mate bond and no more."

Heartache and icy resignation coated each of Assefa's words. His disappointment and utter distaste at the future he'd outlined showed like a Grimm fairy tale across his face.

Despite it all, Assefa reached out and pulled Sanura into a tight embrace, gut-wrenching because another man she loved was willing to sacrifice part of himself for her.

Neither sacrifice she deserved or wanted. But were-cats like Assefa and Samuel never asked. They just did what they thought needed doing, heedless of their own self-preservation.

"I love you, Sanura, and you love me. That's enough. That's enough for me."

But it wouldn't be enough. For a man like Assefa, a proud were-cat who craved commitment and stability, such an arrangement could never be enough for him. One day, perhaps sooner than Sanura feared, Assefa would realize what she already knew.

Love did not conquer all.

CHAPTER NINE

Assefa gazed around the dining room table. Five men filled the wooden chairs, faces taut, shoulders tense, and were-cat magic buzzing like a deadly chainsaw in the air. They'd come when Assefa had called, gathering in Zareb's guesthouse at seven in the morning. Assefa had left Sanura asleep in their bedroom, careful not to wake her when he'd showered and dressed. She'd had a long, emotional night and needed her sleep. Assefa had as well, but sleep could wait. This conversation could not. Sanura's birthday was tomorrow, and Assefa wanted to guarantee no one and nothing ruined her day.

And these men, Zareb Osei, Omar Wek, Manute Aldama, Rashad Minnawai, and Dahad Siddig, friends and brothers of his soul, were more than capable of making sure Saturday's festivities went according to plan. They'd come with him to the United States, motivated by different and personal reasons, but all loyal to Assefa in a way he still couldn't fathom or repay enough. So he'd purchased the sprawling Alexandria estate, wanting to give the men a stable home and a private, secure place where their beasts could run and roam and be at peace.

Assefa didn't require or ask his friends to support the estate, financially or physically. He had more than enough money to take care of his household. Yet they'd assigned themselves various roles, based on their knowledge, skills, and interests, contributing in their unique way to the maintenance and running of the property. But Assefa didn't like it, didn't like the thought of his friends working for him. Didn't like, despite the thousands of miles they were from the Sudan, how they held onto old beliefs and customs, viewing Assefa as their alpha. Dahad, a man old enough to be Assefa's father, had to still be reminded, on occasion, to not lower his eyes while in Assefa's presence.

Even among friends and allies, Assefa stood alone. His Mngwa, forever seen as the king of beasts.

"Sorry, Assefa. I should've reached the Williams' house before your mate left."

At twenty, Rashad was like a younger brother to Assefa. Shoulder-length hair in cornrows, a yellow-gold black diamond skull stud earring in his left ear and an affinity for hip-hop and rap music, Rashad had immersed himself in African American culture when he arrived five years ago. But he soon learned there was much more to African American people and their culture and history than what he'd seen in movies and read in books. Culture rich but power poor, African Americans weren't so different from many were-cat and witch groups in the Sudan under the old Berber regime. Groups marginalized by a privileged few, where societal structures supported and reinforced a debilitating system of oppression.

A system where young men like Rashad felt it necessary to apologize for something that wasn't his fault. No, Assefa would never consider himself these men's alpha, not if it meant this level of deference. At breakfast one morning, Rashad had pulled out a *Vibe* magazine and began to read aloud an interview by Rapsody, an African American female rapper from Wilson, North Carolina.

"'To me, it's about culture more so than money or anything. I make music for the people of the culture we're in. That comes first. If you touch the people first, the rest just falls into place. That's what it means to me, just preserving and respecting the culture.'"

Assefa could appreciate the woman's sentiments, for he shared them. Not about music, of course, but the importance of touching people, and of respecting and preserving one's culture. For the rapper, her music was her route to people's hearts, as well as an expression and an affirmation of her culture and identity. For Assefa, his work with the

FBI, his humanitarianism, and his family and friends were more important to him than money, than being the cat of legend.

He loved and he protected. But he didn't aspire to be a leader of men or beasts.

"You apologized when you called to let me know Sanura wasn't at her mother's house and likely on her way home." Assefa ran a weary hand across his forehead. "No more apologies, Rashad, okay?"

"Yeah, right. Sorry about that." Everyone stared at Rashad. "Oh, right. I did it again. Shit, Assefa, I'm really sorry." He slapped a hand over his mouth and the assembled group couldn't help but laugh.

Assefa loved them all.

Men of magic.

Men of faith.

Men of worth.

But today it hurt to hear Rashad refer to Sanura as his mate, no matter that the young man called Sanura that from the day she moved in. To Rashad, to them all, Sanura was Assefa's claimed mate. Despite what happened between them last night, Assefa had no intention of disabusing his friends of their erroneous notion. No matter the state of their mate bond, Sanura Williams was the lady of the house, and the men would treat her accordingly.

As would Assefa, mate claim or not.

"I assume you asked us here to talk about what happened yesterday?"

Good, Zareb's question had the men refocusing on why they'd gathered in the bodyguard's home.

"Right. I had an interesting conversation with Sanura last night."

More interesting than the men would ever know. But nothing Sanura confided in Assefa had to do with the gathered men, except one bit of news.

He told them about Gregory Chambers, his warning, and felidae law. Thanks to Zareb and Rashad, Manute, Dahad, and Omar already knew about the teenage trespassers.

"I don't get it," Rashad said. "If they knew you're the cat of legend, why in the hell would they be so stupid?"

"Because teenagers are stupid and reckless." Manute, sitting next to Rashad, punched him in the arm. Nothing hard, just forceful enough to remind the youngest of them that he was only two years out of his teens. "Just like you used to be. Hell, you still are a little stupid and reckless sometimes, especially when we spar."

"I'll show you stupid and reckless." Rashad jumped to his feet, tugged up his Jay-Z T-shirt and bared a good deal of his lean chest.

Manute laughed and yanked Rashad back into his chair before he had a chance to get more than one arm out of his shirt. "I'm joking. Don't get all naked and furry on me. Just calm down, fix your shirt, and let Assefa finish before Zareb has the two of us for a morning snack."

Rashad and Manute glanced across the table at Zareb. Who, sure enough, looked as if he wanted to smash their heads together and then toss them into the Potomac River.

Manute raised two placating hands at the thirty-year-old Zareb. "We're good, Z. And I'll be shutting up now."

Wise man. Zareb played and joked as much as Manute and Rashad, most days. But when it came to his duties as Assefa's medjai, the man's sense of humor died an ugly, painful death.

"Do you think the boys' fathers used the cubs?" Dahad asked.

"I thought about it," Assefa replied.

"The fathers would have to be two uncaring and manipulative asses to do something like that." Rashad adjusted his shirt. "For what it's worth, they seemed like pretty decent kids to me. I scared them a little before Assefa and Zareb arrived. Talked a bit of shit to them, tested their mettle. They could've fought back, gave as much as they got. But they didn't do a damn thing, even though it would've been a two on one fight. I would've kicked their scrawny asses, but a battle with those young lions would've been nothing compared to fighting you no holds barred bastards."

"And all of that means what?" Dahad asked, the older man sipping from a bottle of orange juice he'd grabbed from Zareb's fridge when he'd arrived, happy and sated from his overnight date with Joanna Blackwell, his wind witch girlfriend who lived in Baltimore.

"I got the same feeling when I hiked them off our property. They were scared their fathers would find out. They begged me to not call their parents and promised to never return or to tell their friends where the cat of legend lives."

Dahad replaced the plastic cap on the bottle, brown eyes questioning. "So good kids? Good parents?"

"I wouldn't necessarily go that far," Zareb said. "But I sensed they were telling the truth. I think they just wanted to meet Assefa and didn't think through their plan beyond getting on the property. So yeah, pretty stupid kid stuff. But innocent enough that I let them go with only a kick in the ass and a smack to the back of the head."

For Sekhmet sake, he should've known Zareb couldn't just send the boys on their way without making his point physically clear. And since Assefa hadn't given him an order to not touch the teens, Zareb felt free to handle the situation as he best saw fit. An oversight on Assefa's part.

"Yet none of that matters." Omar spoke from the end of the table, arms crossed in front of him. "Regardless of the cubs' innocence or whether they were used by their father as pawns, they now have information about this property, our security, and the three of you." Omar's eyes roamed from Assefa to Zareb to Rashad.

"I had the same thought," Assefa said. "The bottom line is that our home has been compromised. We already know I've been the topic of conversation within the lion pride. What we don't know is why and how far this goes."

"Meaning other were-cat families?" Manute asked.

"That's exactly what I mean. Sanura gave me a lot of useful intelligence on the Sankofa were-cat network. I'll email everyone the information when I get back to the main house. There will be were-cats at Sanura's birthday party, most mated to her girlfriends. In light of what I now know, and how much I still don't know, I'm not sure if I can trust anyone outside of Sanura's inner circle."

"Her inner circle?" Omar asked.

Zareb answered before Assefa could. "Makena Williams and Michael McKutchen."

"Cynthia and Eric Garvey, and Rachel Foster," Assefa added. "They're Sanura's best friends. They wouldn't betray her."

"What about members of the Council?" Rashad asked. "Are you saying we can't even trust them?"

"What I'm saying is that we have a household to protect. Until we know otherwise, everyone is suspect, including members of the Council. I want to know what the Council wants from Sanura and me and why their men are so interested in me, all of a sudden."

His friends nodded, the desire to know the same in their eyes.

"Tomorrow is Sanura's birthday. We'll have a lot of strangers on this property, preternaturals and full-humans. I'm asking everyone to be vigilant. I want nothing to spoil her day, especially a bunch of lion shifters who want to try my patience and self-control on the fire witch of legend's day of ascension."

"She's ascending to what?" Manute asked, fear lurking behind genuine curiosity. "I mean, isn't she powerful enough?"

Sanura was more powerful than she wanted to be and so was Assefa. As to the ascension, he had no idea and didn't want to speculate about something so personal to Sanura.

"She's turning twenty-nine, let's leave it at that. Anyway, I want her birthday to be memorable for all the right reasons. And I'm asking my closest friends to help me make that happen."

For the first time since sitting, Omar uncrossed his arms and relaxed his posture. "Dr. Williams protected us when the sirens came hunting for male blood and flesh. They drugged us with their songs, leaving you and this household vulnerable. If she hadn't acted, after killing you they would've done the same to us. We owe the fire witch a blood debt. A happy birthday party for Dr. Williams is nothing to ask of us, Assefa. We would give more."

He knew they would. But Assefa would never ask for more. Except, of course, if Sanura was in danger and he had no choice. But these men, his friends, were not his to rule over or to dictate to. Except for Zareb, whose family's fealty to the Berbers went back generations. Still, even with Zareb, their friendship wasn't governed or based on outdated familial dynamics.

"Thank you. But I only want to assure Sanura a truly happy birthday. What happens on Sunday and the days that follow, we'll deal with as they come."

"And what if the lion pride wants to test the might of the cat of legend?" Zareb's eyes narrowed to hard slits, and his lips twisted in a predatory smile. "I think that's what the felidae law conversation was about. They either don't believe you're the cat of legend or they don't think your Mngwa is as powerful as the tales paint him out to be. Either way, these lions may be no different from those fools who thought to challenge you when we were as stupid and reckless as those lion cubs from yesterday."

Assefa recalled those horrible days. Bullies and braggarts who thought to make a name for themselves by defeating the mythical cat of legend. In the end, the Mngwa reigned supreme. But Assefa hated what he'd done, what he'd allowed himself to become to defeat so many boys and to finally put an end to the endless taunts.

His father had permitted each bloody battle when all Assefa wanted was for him to step in and act the role of father instead of General Supreme. But he hadn't, telling a seventeen-year-old Assefa, after he'd broken three ribs, a collarbone, and the fibula of a tiger shifter, "This is what it means to be alpha, son. Were-cats won't listen to or follow a man they don't respect or fear. Fear is good. Respect is better. To have both is ideal. So let the challengers come now. Because when you're General Supreme, they'll already know the might of your Mngwa."

The twenty-year-old tiger shifter had been the best friend of Razi, Assefa's older brother. Razi, as was his personality, hadn't accepted his friend's defeat well at the hands of his younger brother. What happened after that, Assefa wished he could forget. But those harsh, brutal battles had taught him many life lessons. One, to always be in control. Two, the Mngwa would rather die than submit. Three, it was better to be liked and trusted than respected and feared. Four, he never wanted to become General Supreme, even if that meant leaving home and everyone he loved.

"I don't want a fight, Zareb. I have no interest in battling Sanura's family."

"They aren't her family if they start a fight with her mate," Rashad said, cracking his knuckles and looking as deadly as Assefa had ever seen the leopard.

Assefa stood. "No fighting."

"You mean you or us?" Zareb questioned.

Assefa didn't have an answer the men would want to hear or one he felt comfortable voicing, so he thanked his friends and left. He had much to do today, because come tomorrow he planned to spoil his little fire witch rotten.

As he walked the cobblestone path from Zareb's guesthouse to the main house, he corralled his concerns and pain from the last twelve hours and shoved them inside a steel box marked: Do Not Open Until After Sanura's Birthday.

****

Bronx, New York

Detective Pilar Salazar parked across the street from a row of contemporary brick buildings, revitalization having reached this part of the northern borough about a decade ago. Home to a million and a half people, the Bronx was a cultural stew of diverse people. People from the islands of the Caribbean, Germans, Irish, Italians, African Americans, foreign-born Africans, and countless other racial and ethnic groups called the Bronx home.

A New York City Puerto Rican girl like Pilar could get lost there, immersed in the sights and sounds of the place. Latin and hip hop music moved her soul like no other mix of rhythms ever could. The kaleidoscope of rich sounds had served as her melodic companion during her two-hundred-mile drive from Baltimore to the bright, energetic neighborhood that was wide awake and on the move.

She turned off the radio, silencing the CD but not the demon in her head. After returning home from a twelve-hour shift, Pilar's only thought was getting out of her wrinkled clothes, sliding into a too-hot bath, and nose-diving into bed, foregoing a microwaveable meal and an overdue call to her mother. Necha Salazar, Pilar's mother, would only want to know when her eldest daughter would "settle down and marry." That fruitless and repetitive conversation could wait until morning. Besides, the last man Pilar had taken an interest in had been Special Agent Berber. Unfortunately, the sexy FBI agent, like so many good men, was already taken.

If Pilar were less her mother's child and more like too many women on the force, she would've gone after Agent Berber with every bit of seductive wiles she possessed. She knew her worth as a woman, as well as she knew her skills as a detective. Tall, athletic frame, thick onyx hair, high cheek bones, and breasts that, while not bodacious, were real and enough to please a man with that particular taste, Pilar Salazar was a beauty. Yet Agent Berber, while assigned to Baltimore and the strange serial killer case that had gone nationwide, hadn't taken an interest in any of the dozen or more women at the precinct, Pilar included, who'd put themselves in the man's path. Hoping, in vain, to be noticed by the good-looking agent.

And, damn, the man knew how to wear a suit. Impeccable taste. Agent Berber had exquisite taste in clothing, shoes, and jewelry. All of which had to cost the agent a mint. None of those material things, however, were what most drew Pilar to the special agent. Agent Berber was one of those rare men who, when he looked at a woman, actually saw and listened to her. Not because he was trying to figure out how to get into her bed, but because he had a genuine interest in who she was and what she had to say. He had an unerring way of making a woman feel special, respected, cherished even. The very type of man Pilar's mother would welcome with a hug and a kiss into the Salazar family.

Pilar had tossed and turned for an hour. Her body dead tired, but her mind consumed with thoughts of how good Berber's hands would feel stroking her needy body, lips full and hungry on hers, and his strong, relentless hips driving into her. God help her, celibacy was a resentful bitch with delusions of righteous superiority. Pilar didn't need a man, but she wouldn't mind having one man in particular. Yet the man in question, the costar of many of her sex dreams, had a girlfriend. Detective McKutchen's goddaughter, she believed.

Lucky, lucky woman.

Perhaps. Perhaps not.

That had been the first time Pilar heard the demon's voice in her head.

You could be lucky in love yourself. You need only secure the male's attention. Would you like that, Pilar Salazar? To have the undivided attention of Assefa Berber?

She would like that, she'd thought. But her mind was playing tricks on her. Still, the thought tempted. And temptation, on this night, was fraught with magic and danger.

Do my bidding, human. You will serve me.

Pilar had huddled deeper under her covers, hands going to her aching head. The demon's voice was a saccharine static of sound that pounded and pushed and demanded.

So much.

Too much.

"No," she'd screamed, tossing back the covers and getting out of bed.

"No, no," she'd pleaded, dragging on day-old clothes and well-worn leather loafers.

You cannot fight me, human. Your attempts are laughable, and so very tiresome. Do as I say, and this will soon be over. After tomorrow, you will have Assefa Berber's attention. In fact, he will never forget what you will do. New York awaits, Pilar Salazar.

Pilar wondered when the demon had done more than slip inside her mind, feeding off lustful thoughts and a single woman's loneliness. Somewhere between her front door and her car, an evil presence had taken up residence in her body. Not a soothing, kind presence, but a willful, spiteful one.

Violent and loathsome.

Pilar had put her car in drive and sped away from her sleeping neighborhood, too afraid to fight and too powerless to win.

By two o'clock in the afternoon, the building she'd watched all day was full of people. So many that people spilled onto the sidewalk, talking and smiling. Over the hours, cars had lined the street, making for a congested and busy afternoon. But this was what the demon wanted, Pilar knew.

"Please, don't make me."

No answer from the demon but her body twitched and jerked, forcing arms and legs out of the car. Pilar opened her mouth, wanting to warn the people, wanting to scream at them to run, to hide, and to call the police. But she couldn't speak. Lips sealed and pain seized her chest, threatening to drop the thirty-year-old woman to her knees from a heart attack.

Pilar may no longer be the faithful churchgoer she'd been as a child, missing Mass more often than her Catholic parents would condone, but Detective Salazar knew when the Devil was at play, his vicious works and pathetic pawns. She saw evidence of it every day—rape, murder, arson, drug addiction, child abuse. No neighborhood or family was immune from the Devil's sick allure. The Devil, the first equal opportunity employer. And the Devil had come calling last evening, using Pilar to spread his wickedness.

Staggering to the back of her car, Pilar used her key fob to unlock the trunk. Digging inside, fingers skimmed her bulletproof vest, but kept moving, over and up. Pilar began to weep, slow, silent tears no one in the bustling crowd noticed. So the Devil meant to see her dead this day. Not just ruined and imprisoned but dead. Her parents and siblings would mourn her death and pray for her condemned soul, unable to understand what had led her to this point of madness and criminality.

Her friends and colleagues would speak on her behalf, sharing stories of her life and work on the Baltimore City Police Force. But like her family, they would have no explanation for the bizarre turn the last few hours of her life had taken. An autopsy would be performed, the medical examiner searching for signs of drug use, dementia, or any helpful clue to demystify why a good cop had gone bad.

A hand touched the pink-and-black one-pound case the Devil forced Pilar to pull out of her bedroom closet and store in the trunk of her midsize car. Although, with what it kept concealed inside, the case no longer weighed a mere pound.

Trembling, Pilar slid the zipper back and down, unsheathing the hunting rifle within. Hunting deer at State Parks, her ex-boyfriend enjoyed the seasonal sport. So Pilar, an excellent markswoman, purchased the .300 hunting caliber rifle, thinking she could share in Juan's love of hunting. She'd gone hunting with him one time, which was one time too many. Pilar, despite all she'd seen being an officer in Baltimore City, found the act of hunting and killing innocent and defenseless deer an acquired taste she'd rather not sample again. Soon afterward, she and Juan had gone their separate ways. Not because of their difference in opinion about hunting, but the demands of Pilar's work schedule, which made dating a guy with an eight hour, Monday through Friday desk job, hard to manage without a bit of compromise.

Neither wanted to compromise.

She hefted the rifle, closing the trunk softly once the weapon was low and at her side. Her other hand skimmed the ammo pouch wallet clipped to her belt. The durable canvas pouch held more rounds than she wanted to think about because each round had the ungodly potential to destroy a life, a family, and Pilar's soul.

Please. Please. Please. Pilar sobbed, rifle in hand, unwilling heart and legs taking her across the street. Dodging cars and people too rushed and focused on other things to notice a woman carrying a rifle, eyes red-rimmed and screaming on the inside.

But no one could hear her muted screams or her unanswered prayers. In a crowd of dozens, Pilar Salazar stood invisible.

A lone gunwoman, they would call her. Rare.

A hate crime this would be labeled. Not so rare.

Eyes full of tears, but not enough to blur her vision, Pilar raised her rifle, aimed, and shot.

A woman holding the hand of a child fell.

A man followed, his body crumpling to the ground. A slow trickle of blood oozed from the hole in his head. Then more blood, and even more, until red streaks morphed the landscape of the man's lifeless face. Eyes opened, brown, and sightless.

Another woman tumbled to the ground, body jolted forward from the impact of a bullet between her shoulder blades.

More shots rang out, lethal pops of sound in the grisly June heat.

Fa-thud.

Fa-thud.

Fa-thud.

Bowling pins of bodies crashed to the pavement. Rivers of blood drained from them as they wept and shuddered their way into the hereafter.

The screams were no longer limited to Pilar's aching head. They were all around her, a fatal concert of ear-splitting shrieks, terrorized cries, and blood-gurgled gasps.

Pop. Fa-thud.

Pop. Fa-thud.

Pop. Fa-thud.

Yes, Detective Pilar Salazar was a superior shot indeed, top in her class at the Police Academy.

Pop. Fa-thud.

Pop. Fa-thud.

She couldn't stop crying, no more than she could stop reloading, stop pulling the goddamn trigger, and stop the brutal, senseless attack on people who'd wanted only civil rights in their adopted country, but found violence and death instead.

Pop. Fa-thud.

Straight through the neck, a panicked and protective father's escape slowed by the toddler he clutched to his chest and his pregnant wife who struggled to keep up with the hand dragging her along. His rapid pace too fast for her, the bullet quicker than them both.

Self-satisfied laughter echoed in Pilar's head, mocking the detective's revulsion and powerlessness. Her body a human marionette with invisible but indestructible strings.

Ah, I have chosen well. But, of course, I always do. Assefa Berber will remember you and what you did this day. Your death will not be in vain. Sleep now Pilar Salazar, you have served Mami Wata well.

Mami Wata? No, the Devil, a dem—

Pop. Pop. Pop. Pop.

Fa-thud.

CHAPTER TEN

Sanura stared at herself in the bathroom mirror. Hair still wet from her shower, body naked, and eyes clear and focused, Sanura searched for signs of change. She'd performed the same task in the shower, hands sliding over every inch of her frame she could reach. Now, using the full-length bathroom mirror, she could better inspect her body.

Turning this way and that, Sanura looked for any clue she'd changed somehow now that she'd reached her twenty-ninth year. But the form in the frameless oval beveled wall mirror looked as it had the night before and the nights before that. Perhaps then the change would be more emotional or magical, if not physical in nature.

She turned away from the mirror, annoyed at the thought of having no control over whatever changes would occur in her mind or body. An ascension, she'd been told her entire life, when she reached the age of twenty-nine. Well, nine hours ago Sanura had turned twenty-nine. A minute after midnight, she'd rushed to this same mirror, expecting, expecting, hell, she didn't know. But something, for Oya's sake.

Not that she wanted to ascend, whatever in the hell that meant. But waiting for some unknown transformation to come about, or to be taken over by a goddess, had Sanura on edge. Maybe the prophecy only meant Sanura would acquire some of the goddesses' power. Since meeting Assefa, taking him as her familiar and merging their auras, Sanura had developed a fair degree of lightning and wind power. Which, of course, a fire witch should not be able to wield. Perhaps those new powers would magnify now that she'd reached the benchmark year, heralding the Day of Serpents and the battle between the fire witch and water witch of legend.

Well, so far, Sanura felt and appeared the same. She could spend her birthday brooding over something she had no power over, or she could bury the fear the unknown evoked and concentrate on having a happy birthday.

Burying strong feelings solved nothing, but it did allow one to get through a day, functioning at a level they wouldn't otherwise if they permitted doom and gloom emotions to consume them and all those around them. After the last two days, with Assefa spending Thursday and Friday night on the sitting room sofa instead of in their bed, Sanura needed a good day, a happy day, a stress-free day.

She had no interest in arguing with Assefa, not that the man argued in the traditional sense. But he did have a frustrating tendency to clam up and shut down. His way of coping, she knew, but that didn't make dealing with him any easier. Friday, she'd seen him only a few times, although she'd stayed at home and he'd taken the weekend off. Considerate as always, Assefa made himself available to have breakfast, lunch, and dinner with Sanura. Polite conversation filled the awkward silences and when each meal concluded, he'd kissed Sanura on the cheek and said something about "having things to take care of."

She was being handled, in that FBI way of his that kept Assefa in charge and at an emotional distance. Sanura removed her white, silk robe from the wall hook and slipped it on, tying the sash at her waist. What did she expect from Assefa? For the man to walk around with an all-is-well grin on his face and reciting love poems after learning Sanura wouldn't accept his mate claim because she had yet to come to terms with the death of her father?

Under the circumstances, Assefa's response was the best Sanura could ask for or expect. He said he loved her, wanted to be with her, and wouldn't press his mate claim. Sanura didn't deserve so many concessions, but knew, if their positions were reversed, she would extend the same to him. Still, how could they move forward when Sanura clung too fiercely to the past and to her guilt?

Sanura opened the bathroom door and exited, disheartened by how much she'd disappointed Assefa as well as herself.

"If you don't lift those gorgeous green eyes of yours, you'll run into the wall. Then I'll have to give you mouth-to-mouth resuscitation."

Sanura's head swung upward, indeed cast down, along with her slumped shoulders. She stopped and, because Assefa sounded like his old flirtatious self, smiled from ear to ear.

"Mouth-to-mouth resuscitation? For running into a wall?"

Dressed in black shorts, a blue-and-black classic fit camp shirt and a pair of black leather slide sandals with contrast stitching, Assefa sat on the side of their bed, hands on knees and eyes alight with Berber mischief.

"It's your birthday, Sanura, of course I'll give you mouth-to-mouth. I'm a highly trained FBI agent, after all, certified in adult and pediatric first aid/CPR/AED."

She stepped closer, surprised yet pleased to see the return of this Assefa Berber. "Automated external defibrillator, I doubt you'll have to use that particular skill set if I run into a wall." She glanced at the closest wall, which the bed and nightstands were in front of. "If I run into anything, it would be you, not the wall."

"Then I'll definitely need to use the defibrillator on you because coming into contact with me will have your heart skipping an erratic, breath-stealing beat."

Still smiling, Sanura narrowed the distance between them. When their knees touched, Sanura halted and stared down at the playful Assefa.

"Is that right? Can you hear my erratically pulsing heart, now that I'm so close to the charming Assefa Berber?"

"I don't know, come nearer." Reaching up, Assefa tugged Sanura between his parted thighs. Hands on her waist, he turned his head to the side and pressed it between her breasts. His ear to her chest.

"What are you—"

"Shush, I'm listening to what your heart is saying."

Unable to help herself, Sanura laid a hand on top of Assefa's head and began to caress his scalp and toy with the short curls she loved so much. If he allowed, she would do this all day, petting the man or the Mngwa. It didn't matter to Sanura as long as she was close to Assefa.

Touching him.

Loving him.

His grip on her waist tightened. Face turned into her chest. And he purred, a barely-there sound that sent waves of desire through Sanura.

"What is my heart saying?" she asked in a breathy whisper.

Assefa raised his head, dark-brown eyes intense. An ocean of intelligence and self-possession lurked within their brilliant depths, but also the unhappiness he couldn't quite hide. Even though he was exerting a lot of effort to conceal his pain from Sanura. A birthday gift, and yet another unasked-for but appreciated concession.

With her other hand, Sanura touched Assefa's cheek, holding his face, as well as his tender, knowing gaze. When he looked at her like this, Sanura sensed he peered into her soul, viewing her on a level that only his Mngwa's perceptive eyes could understand.

"Your heart speaks to me in many languages. Some I understand, while others I don't."

"Why so many languages?"

He tugged her again, and Sanura went, straddling Assefa's waist and sitting on his thick, muscular thighs.

When he didn't answer, just continued to gaze at her, Sanura placed her hands on his shoulders and asked again. "Why do you say my heart speaks to you in many languages?"

Instead of responding, lips sought and found hers, drawing Sanura in for a delicious morning kiss.

Giving in, arms twined around broad shoulders, head tilted, and tongue found its mate in Assefa's mouth. Gods, they hadn't kissed like this since the fiasco that had been their Thursday night. And while going without the touch and taste of her man for a couple of days may seem trivial to others, it wasn't for Sanura. Not in light of the current instability of their relationship.

"You taste so good," she murmured against his lips, teeth pulling his lower lip into her mouth and sucking. "So, so good."

Sanura wanted to taste more of Assefa. All of him. But she also wanted to know what he'd meant about languages and her heart.

Breathless, she pulled back. "Tell me."

"Not now. Not yet. Not on your birthday." A strong, thick thumb rose and rubbed her nipple through the thin fabric of her robe. "To-morrow will come, Sanura, and our issues will still be with us. But let me give you this day. You only turn twenty-nine once. And it's the first birthday we'll spend together as a couple. Let's not mar it with talk of something I shouldn't have said."

Just as she'd thought. He'd pushed his pain and pride down for the sake of her birthday. She didn't like it, Assefa ignoring his feelings. But hadn't she decided to do the same, no more than ten minutes ago?

"All right. Thank you."

The wonderful finger toying with her nipple and bringing it to an aching peak fell away, leaving a disappointed fire witch in its wake.

"But I want to—"

Assefa grinned, mischief back in his eyes. "We will, but not right now. I have an entire day of relaxation and fun planned for us."

"Relaxation and fun?"

"Don't say it as if I don't know the meaning of those words."

"I'm sure you do. But I don't think we define them in the same way."

He swatted her bottom, a sharp sting that sent her mind to places it didn't need to go. Like those times he'd taken her from behind, face pressed to the mattress, ass in the air and Assefa pounding into her. Left hand fondled her breasts while his right smacked and then smoothed her ass, over and over until Sanura screamed her orgasm. The pleasure-pain of their loving had sent her to and over the edge.

Assefa closed his eyes and growled, "Whatever you're thinking about, stop it. Your scent is … distracting. I'm trying to be good, and you're not helping."

Embarrassed, Sanura slid from Assefa's lap and stood. "Sorry."

"It's okay. I'm the one who started it when I kissed you." Assefa eyed the tent in his pants. "Oh well, by the time you get dressed and we go downstairs, it'll be back to normal."

He stood.

Back to normal? Did the man have any idea how beyond normal his magnificent anatomy was, or how hard and frustrating it would be for Sanura to wait to have him? Why couldn't they fool around for a while? What would it hurt? It was her birthday, and she could think of so many creative ways to have Assefa as her personal, sex toy gift.

"You're doing it again." Assefa spun away from Sanura and stalked toward the sitting room of their suite. "Gods, Sanura, if you keep this up we'll spend the entire day in bed."

She wondered what was so bad about spending a day making love. Sanura opened her mouth to say she didn't mind doing exactly that but remembered Friday. Perhaps the reason why Assefa had all but run from the dining room table after each meal was because he was planning something fun and relaxing for her birthday, as he'd said.

If so, not only did Sanura not want to ruin all his efforts, but she was excited to experience Assefa's style of birthday fun. So she shut her mouth and went to her closet. The quicker she dressed, the sooner her birthday fun with Assefa would begin.

****

Twenty-five minutes later, Sanura and Assefa stood in their kitchen. If the woman had had one more naughty thought, while he waited for her to dress, he would've had no choice but to rip that see-through white robe off her, pin her to the bed, and do all the wicked things he'd seen percolating behind those green eyes of hers. As it was, he'd barely leashed his Mngwa, roused from his slumber by the appetizing scent of Sanura's unmistakable arousal.

But Assefa had other plans for the day, which began with feeding his sexy fire witch. Yet Sanura hadn't made it easy for Assefa to stay focused on his goal of fun and relaxation. Today she wore a sleeveless multi-colored beach dress with double flounce detail at the neckline, which hinted at her ample décolletage. Light and airy, the dress fell to mid-calf, hiding what Assefa knew to be delectable runner's legs. Barefoot, she stood just behind him, eyes wide and untamed natural hair framing her beautiful face in a nimbus cloud of brown waves.

Moonstone in her belly button where she wore it, the jewel made her look less like the fire witch of legend and the goddess Oya. Which, on this day of all days, he comprehended why Sanura felt the need to don the scent disguise charm, claiming what she could of herself on the twenty-ninth year of her birth.

Assefa couldn't be positive that nothing had changed about Sanura, but his Mngwa and magic detected no alteration in the fire witch of legend. No hikes in her magic or any other signs she had ascended or been taken over by the wind and lightning goddess.

"What's all this?" Sanura jutted her chin at the items laid out on the granite countertop. She glanced over her shoulder and at the rest of the kitchen. "Where's Omar?"

"Doing other things."

"So why is all of this food out instead of in the frig? Who's going to …" Sanura began shaking her head, an adamant, vigorous side-to-side reaction Assefa found absolutely adorable. "You know I can't cook to save my life."

"Of course I do, which is why I'll be doing the cooking and you'll be doing the eating."

Actually, if Sanura looked closer, she'd see several dishes he'd already prepared for her to sample and enjoy.

"You can cook?"

Assefa wrapped a lock of her stunning hair around a finger. "Careful, sweetheart, if you arch that eyebrow of yours any higher, it'll stay like that. And yes, I can cook. Not nearly as well as Omar or Makena, but I can manage well enough. I'm not as spoiled as you may think, my doubting fire witch."

Her other eyebrow arched, and Sanura glanced from the counter full of what would be their breakfast and back to Assefa. "I'm fairly certain you, Mr. Assefa Berber, second son of the House of Berber, are as spoiled as I think."

Coming from anyone else, except Zareb and Najja, Assefa would take great offense. But Sanura hadn't meant it as an insult or an accusation of laziness or shallowness.

He gathered more of her hair between his exploring fingers. "I did all the shopping myself, for your information. And today's breakfast menu came from me as well. No help from Omar, the Internet, or anyone else. What do you have to say to that?"

A cute smirk was her response and then a, "Quite impressive, Special Agent Berber. You are truly a man of many, many talents. I had no idea."

Somewhere in those three sentences, Sanura's voice had taken on that low, sexy bedroom tone he liked to hear because it foreshadowed sweaty, magic-curling sex.

Assefa released Sanura's hair and stepped away from her and toward the display of food, his back going to the edge of the countertop.

"Damn, I did it again, didn't I?"

"Just a little."

Assefa inhaled through his nose and exhaled out his mouth.

"I didn't mean to. Maybe I've ascended into a horny sex deity. Wouldn't that be a wild twist on the prophecy? If that's the case, we'll be back to your mate sex magic."

Assefa laughed. "Yes, the threesome. But I wouldn't have to duplicate myself this time. It would be you, me, and the water witch of legend. A cozy sandwich with you witches as the bread and me as the scrumptious deli meat in between." He laughed harder when Sanura shot him a displeased and jealous glower. "Don't blame me, Sanura, you're the one who started down the sex deity road. I only followed the path you made."

"Yes, with far too much enthusiasm."

A shrug. "I am a male."

She crossed arms over her chest, annoyed. "So you want to have sex with another woman? A threesome?"

Assefa returned to Sanura's side and kissed her pouting lips. "Only if the second woman is another Sanura Wasola Williams. And really, sweetheart, as nice as it would be to have two of you in our bed and at my disposal, in the end, I have one penis to go around."

And a mouth, of course. Assefa could do wonderful things to a woman with his mouth, but he wouldn't remind Sanura of that.

Her eyes dropped to his pants, right before she reached out and—

Assefa caught her hand. "Don't, or I'll have you on the countertop next to the whipping cream and bowl of mangos, dress to your waist and legs over my shoulders."

She shuddered.

Assefa swallowed a purr of cold, hard desire.

"Maybe we should just have sex," she suggested, hand inches from the growing bulge in his pants. "To take the edge off so we can make it through breakfast and whatever else you have planned for me. Is anyone else in the house?"

He shook his head, so close to giving in to her seductive reasoning.

Sanura peppered his face with sweet kisses, lingering at the lobe of his ear and sucking just the way he liked.

He did purr then, enthralled by Sanura's nearness and intoxicating scent of arousal. Why not, Assefa thought, releasing her hand and pulling her forward? Why not give them what they both wanted? Besides, Assefa had an idea that would fulfill his witch's desire and still meet his goal of feeding her.

Breakfast with a sexy twist. Not a particularly inventive idea, since he'd seen it done in some American or French film, but the thought appealed and fit into his birthday theme of relaxation and fun.

Assefa yanked the straps of Sanura's dress down before pulling his witch to the kitchen floor.

****

Okay, well, if this was Assefa's idea of a birthday breakfast, Sanura would request it each and every year.

Eyes closed and body naked from the waist up, Sanura sat beside Assefa on the stunningly beautiful and durable bamboo floor. Bamboo. Gods, the man did have the most amazing and expensive taste.

"Open up."

She did, accepting the fork and the cool food he placed in her mouth. Sanura chewed, smiled. "Strawberry with a hint of chocolate and whipped cream."

"Very good. Do you want more?"

She nodded.

Assefa fed her more fresh strawberries, increasing the amount of chocolate with each forkful until he filled her mouth with more rich chocolate than sweet berry.

Sanura licked the chocolate that had fallen onto her bottom lip, tongue meeting Assefa's as he did the same. He tasted her with a sensual, predatory exploration that had Sanura opening her mouth and inviting him inside. Instead of taking her up on her offer, Assefa pulled away.

"I'm not done feeding you yet."

"There's more?"

"Of course."

She heard him stand and move away before returning to her side.

"Try this. I made them right before I came to get you."

She opened her mouth and accepted his gift.

Gods, what was this? It tasted like French toast and chocolate chips. And it was to die for, melting in her mouth and setting her taste buds ablaze with pleasure.

"Gods, Assefa, that's delicious."

"I'm glad you think so. It's cannoli stuffed French toast. I sprinkled a bit of white powder on the top. More?"

"Do you really have to ask?"

He fed her more, each bite better than the last.

"You really are good at this. How did you learn to cook so well?" Sanura opened her eyes, wanting to see Assefa's face as they talked.

Like Sanura, he wore nothing but his underwear. A pair of black, flexible fit boxer briefs that highlighted Assefa's sexy goodness. Her dress and his shirt and pants were somewhere in the kitchen, neither concerned where the clothing landed when they'd stripped each other. Yet they hadn't made love, which was fine because Assefa's version of a birthday breakfast in bed was indeed relaxing and fun.

Assefa had put considerable thought and time into this gift, a romantic gesture that touched her heart.

"Until I moved to the States, servants did everything for me. Cooked, cleaned, and drove me to and from school. I was ten before I'd seen the inside of a kitchen. You should've seen the Executive Chef's face when I stumbled in there, searching for a snack before dinner. His face fell, paled. Who knew a man that dark could pale, but he really did, Sanura. Then he ushered me out of there so fast I barely saw his son sitting at a prep station, book in hand, eyes wide with shock. 'You don't belong down here, Master Berber,' he told me. 'Now go before others see you and your father finds out.'"

For a minute, Sanura was stuck on the title "Master Berber." What ten-year-old deserved to be called Master anything? Had that been Assefa's childhood, reared to think of himself as better than others? That was no way to raise a boy, not if you wanted him to grow into a man who valued different kinds of people, not just those in his economic class.

"Would your father have fired him, if he found out?"

"No, but he wouldn't have been pleased." Assefa shook his head. "The kitchen was the place for servants, not the son of the General Supreme."

"Let me guess, Omar was the child with the book? The Executive Chef's son?"

"Omar has taught me a lot, how to cook being just one lesson of many. Like you said, I'm spoiled."

"I wasn't trying to imply that you were spoiled in the sense of thinking yourself better than others."

He smiled. "I know you weren't. But I am spoiled, just as my sister and brother are. Our father gave us everything we wanted."

"But not needed?" she probed, sensing a wealth of unsettled emotions behind Assefa's words.

"No, Dr. Williams, not what we always needed. A single father, even a wealthy and powerful one, finds it difficult to raise three children alone, especially with a nation of people looking on and judging his every move. And this conversation is far from relaxing and fun."

He was right. The lighthearted, sexy energy in the room had changed. Sanura didn't want that, but she couldn't deny how such conversations made her feel closer to Assefa because he trusted Sanura enough to open his heart and soul to her. Yet there was pain there, in the sharing of his childhood memories, just as there was whenever he spoke of his deceased mother.

Sanura scooted forward and kissed his lips. "What else is on my breakfast menu, Special Agent Berber?"

Ah, there went his smile again, peeking out from behind the growing storm clouds talking of his childhood had conjured.

"Plenty, actually. Too much. I think I went overboard. But I'll feed you some more then we can dress." His eyes slipped to her bare breasts. "Do you mind getting a bit sticky, Sanura?" Hungry eyes lifted, ravenous, in fact. "We can get in the hot tub afterward. That'll clean us up."

Okay, yeah, she damn sure wanted to do this again when she turned thirty. And Sanura refused to give fertile ground to the nagging thought that she and Assefa may not survive the Day of Serpents to celebrate her next birthday. Hell, maybe not even Assefa's birthday, which was in September.

"That sounds good."

Assefa lowered his head and claimed a nipple, pulling it into his warm, wet mouth and sucking.

Oh, gods, he did that so well.

She held his head to her, propping herself on her other hand and leaning back to give him a better angle to feast upon her. And feast he did, drawing more and more of her into his mouth, pulling in the most erotic way. The suction strong, erogenous, and panty wetting.

With a *pop*, he released Sanura, and she nearly moaned her disappointment.

"Stay right there, I have something I want you to try."

Stay? Sanura was going nowhere.

For ten minutes, Sanura listened as Assefa bustled above her head, moving from one part of the expansive kitchen to the other. She leaned against the red-toned island, enjoying the aromatic scents floating around her, the blender a low buzz that had her trying to see around Assefa and to what he was doing.

He hummed. Actually hummed while he cooked. What an unexpected discovery about her sexy, conservative were-cat. Who, as Sanura was learning, wasn't quite as conservative as she'd thought. Well, he was. But in matters of the heart and of the body, Assefa was quite romantic and unpredictable.

Assefa pulled something from the toaster oven, slid it onto a white plate and knelt before Sanura. He handed her the plate, then reached above her head and pulled a fork from a drawer of the island.

"This smells incredible and looks even better. A casserole?"

"Yes, I cooked it last night. Eggs Benedict casserole. Canadian bacon, English muffin, fully cooked eggs, and homemade Hollandaise sauce. I will admit, Omar made the sauce, but I did everything else. So, what are you waiting for? Eat up."

Assefa hovered in front of her, staring anxiously. He reminded her of her father when Sanura was a child, impatiently waiting for her to rip into her birthday presents, hoping she would like the gifts he'd bought her.

Fork in hand, Sanura cut a piece of the casserole and ate it. No longer surprised by how well Assefa cooked, she relished the savory flavor of the casserole.

She moaned.

He beamed. "You know, Sanura, that's similar to the sound you made when I had your nipple in my mouth. Should I be jealous of the casserole?"

"The stuff you say, sometimes."

An arrogant arch of his eyebrow. "You like it."

Yeah, she did, but Sanura wouldn't stroke his ego by admitting to it.

Sanura finished the casserole while Assefa watched on. A self-satisfied smile on his face. Once done, Assefa exchanged the plate and fork for a strawberry smoothie.

"Milk, strawberries, and strawberry jam. Here, drink it with a straw."

Assefa slid a red-and-white striped straw into the glass.

She tasted the smoothie. Thick, chilled, and absolutely yummy.

"I know you love mangos, so I'll make the smoothie with that fruit the next time. Speaking of fruit." Assefa rose and went to the counter-top. He found a bowl of fresh fruit and returned to the floor, sitting in front of her while Sanura drank her smoothie.

In his hand, Assefa held a swirl square white fruit bowl. "This is warm citrus fruit with brown sugar."

She examined the contents of the bowl. "Red grapefruit slices, pineapple chunks, and slices of orange?"

"Yes. It's not as warm as it should be, but I think it'll be fine. Would you like to try?"

"Do you even have to ask?"

An anxious smile was her answer. Dipping a spoon into the visually pleasing, red-and-orange fruit salad, Assefa scooped up a spoonful and fed the fruit to Sanura.

Then it was she who smiled. "I've never had warm fruit salad, and you put more in here than brown sugar."

"Rum."

"Trying to get me drunk, Mr. Berber?"

"If you get drunk from two tablespoons of rum, we're both in big trouble because I intend to serve more than that at tonight's dinner."

He fed her more of the fruit salad.

"So tell me about tonight."

"Nice try, but no."

"A hint. Just a small one."

"I don't think so."

Sanura skewered Assefa with a mock look of fire witch ire.

He kissed her forehead then filled her mouth with a spoonful of warm fruit.

Fine, she got it, no hints.

"Are you planning on eating any of this excellent food you prepared, or just feed and watch me eat?"

"Believe me, Sanura, I intend on having my fill."

Oh, but she did like the sensual way Assefa said that.

After another ten minutes, Sanura had cleaned the fruit bowl and drank most of her smoothie. She knew Assefa had more items on the countertop, some of which still needed to be cooked. But she didn't think she could eat another bite.

"I'm stuffed." Sanura patted her stomach, deliciously sated. "Gods, Assefa, I haven't indulged like that in a long time. During the school year, I normally skip breakfast. And the times I do manage something, it's nothing more than a breakfast bar or trail mix and juice or water."

"Not a good way to begin your day. How in the world do you maintain that luscious figure of yours eating dried fruits and nuts for breakfast?" Assefa lowered Sanura to the kitchen floor until she was prone and staring up at him. "It's a good thing you moved in here."

"So you and Omar can fatten me up?"

A large, possessive hand slid over a hip and down her thigh. "It's nothing wrong with a woman having a little something extra a man can hold onto when their making love. But you're rounded in all the right places." Up her hip and across her belly. "And fit and toned in all the right areas."

"Is that so?" she asked, paying more attention to the hand traversing her body with languid satisfaction than the words coming from Assefa.

"Most definitely." Assefa leaned down to Sanura and whispered in her ear. "I'm a little hungry now, do you mind if I have my breakfast?"

Said the spider to the fly.

"I, umm, no, I don't mind." She swallowed. Hard.

"Close your eyes again for me."

Sanura did.

He stood and moved about the kitchen. But in no time at all, Assefa was back on the floor and next to Sanura.

"If you don't like something I do, let me know."

She couldn't imagine not liking anything Assefa had in mind. But Sanura appreciated his consideration.

What felt like a cool ball touched her nipple. Around the areola it went, Assefa circling her in a slow clockwise direction. Juice from what Sanura guessed was a fruit saturated her nipple, clinging to her skin.

Assefa did the same to the other breast, soaking it in fruit juice and rubbing the nipple until it hardened and tingled with need.

Sanura tried not to squirm each time he circumnavigated her nipple, the flesh fine-tuned to his touch.

His mouth claimed an aching bud, licking off the juice. Around and around Assefa's tongue went, lapping every bit of the flavoring off her. He moved to her second nipple, holding the breast up to his mouth and making it and her his meal.

She sighed, loving the way he devoured her, with confidence and skill.

Holding and playing with her breasts, Assefa kissed and licked, burying his face between breasts and rubbing them over lips and tongue, chin and cheeks.

One hand left her but returned quickly. Something warm and thick was spread over neck, breasts, stomach, and inner thighs.

Beginning with her neck, Assefa tasted her. His wide, long tongue explored everywhere the spread had been placed. Every dip and curve. Every mountain and valley.

Peanut butter and chocolate. The spread smelled like peanut butter and chocolate.

Sanura trembled. Her body sizzled with pleasure and desire.

Pulling Sanura onto her knees, her back to Assefa's front, he placed a finger into her mouth.

Whipping cream.

Hands spread the cream over shoulders and nape.

Cradled between Assefa's parted thighs, erection digging gloriously into her backside, Assefa continued his breakfast feast. Large hands reached around and caressed her breasts while he slurped at her nape and shoulders.

Sanura's head fell forward. So many simultaneous sensations.

Hands.

Mouth.

Hoisting Sanura onto his lap as he stole her senses with covetous hands on her breasts and wicked lips on her neck, Assefa rubbed his raging erection against her. The rhythmic movements titillating and breath-stealing.

Assefa was right, he just may have to use a defibrillator on her after all.

One of his hands fell away, and Sanura felt Assefa reaching for something to their right. Mere seconds later, he said against her ear, arousal thickening his accented voice, "A cucumber. Will you let me get you off with this big, juicy cucumber?"

What? Surely he hadn't just said ... "A cucumber?"

"Not in you. But like this."

He slipped a fat end of the cylindrical fruit over Sanura's wet panties and between her slick folds.

She whimpered at the contact on her heated and sensitive sex. Sanura felt desperate and so close to coming, Assefa's mouth and hands having taken her right to the edge of release. And he still nipped at her shoulders, played with one of her breasts and rocked his long, thick erection into her, keeping Sanura on the knife's tip of bliss.

"May I?" he asked, and rubbed the cucumber against her engorged clit, as if it were his penis instead of food that belonged in a salad and not giving her surprising pleasure. Before she could think of how to respond, Assefa did it again.

Rubbing.

Rubbing.

Rubbing.

Sanura threw her head back on his shoulder, body heavy from lust and want. Her mouth unable to form the words to let him know how much she craved to come from this sex game he'd turned her birthday breakfast into.

Where her voice failed Sanura, her body did not. She dug her nails into his thighs, opened her legs wider for the cucumber, and ground herself against his luscious erection.

Then they were rocking in tandem. The fruit, cold and hard against her sex, Assefa's penis warm and hard under her ass. One hand on the fruit between her legs, the other around her waist, Assefa rubbed and thrust, rubbed and thrust, rubbed and thrust.

Sanura came, bucking, screaming, and not giving a damn she'd let Assefa use a cucumber to make her come.

But after today, Sanura knew she would never be able to look at a cucumber in the same way again.

CHAPTER ELEVEN

Assefa lounged against the hot tub, arm reclined on an edge, legs stretched out and hot, bubbling water all around him, kneading muscles and nerves. He sighed, wondering why he rarely took advantage of the solarium and this amazing hot tub Manute and Rashad installed. Then again, until a few weeks ago, he hadn't had a beautiful fire witch to share it with.

From the contented, dreamy smile on Sanura's face, she found the luxury hot tub as sinfully decadent as Assefa did.

"Enjoying yourself?"

Assefa placed his arm behind her, and then reached up and burrowed his hand in her glorious locks of hair. With purposeful fingers, he began a scalp massage, the kind she always gave him.

Slumping, Sanura settled her head against his shoulder, body close, left hand on his burly, hairless chest.

"I am. This is wonderful. When I moved in while you were on your mission in Alaska, Mr. Siddig ran off a bunch of details about the house." A kiss to his neck. "But I was only half listening to the man. He sounded like a realtor."

"So you tuned him out and missed the part about the house having a solarium and hot tub?"

Another kiss to his neck, longer than the last. "Pretty much. That will teach me not to zone out when someone is speaking to me. Just think, I could've been enjoying this room for over a month."

Sanura stretched, her warm, lush breasts coming into mouthwatering contact with his chest and side. She lifted her swan-like neck when he gripped her hair and pulled, a gentle motion that got her attention.

Sultry eyes met his.

They kissed, leisurely, sweetly, adoringly. She tasted of fruit, sugar, and heat. Assefa wanted to make love to her. The extravagant hot tub designed to accommodate four or five adults was a perfect romantic setting for lovemaking. While Assefa loved that Sanura was on the Pill and they could have spontaneous sex, he didn't have time to drain and clean the tub today. Which he would have to do if they made love without a condom. The chemicals that kept the water clean and sanitized notwithstanding. He supposed he could just tell the men to not use the hot tub for a day or two, but they would take one look at him and know the reason why. And Assefa had no intention of revealing any part of his and Sanura's sex life.

"I have a couple of more things I want us to do before our guests arrive."

She settled against him again. "Does it involve getting out of this hot tub and getting dressed?"

"It does, but we can stay in the solarium. If you haven't noticed, there's a very nice seagrass furniture set not far from the hot tub. We could cuddle in our bathrobes on the loveseat or we could stretch out on the sofa, whichever you like."

"I like the idea of staying right here. But we've been in here an hour and I'm pretty sure I've shriveled like a prune." Sanura nipped his jaw. "What do you have in mind?"

"A game."

She sat upright, eyes glowing with interest. "A game? What kind of game? I didn't know you played games."

"For your information, I play many games."

She laughed. "No, seriously, Assefa, I mean real games. Jogging, weightlifting, and using your friends as chew toys during were-cat sparring matches don't count as games."

Oh, but the woman thought herself a comedian. *Fine, let's see how well she handles the game I have in mind.*

He stood and helped Sanura to her feet and out of the hot tub. Within minutes, they were dry, on the sofa, and wearing thick cotton robes. Sanura sat, back to the armrest on one end of the beige-and-brown wicker, wood, and seagrass sofa, her feet propped on Assefa's thighs, looking like a pampered Nubian princess.

Sanura clapped her hands, a wide smile on her beautiful face. "Okay, I'm ready." She glanced around the room. Triple-paned awning windows were everywhere, letting in glorious rays of the morning sun. "Umm, what kind of game are we going to play in here?"

"You'll see." Assefa reached for and snatched his cell off the glass top coffee table. Hitting the app icon, Assefa scrolled until he found what he was looking for.

The curious fire witch strained to see what he was doing on his phone. "I didn't know you played games on your cell."

"I don't. They're a waste of time and brain cells."

"I play them between classes, sometimes."

Assefa glanced up from his phone to see if Sanura was serious. Apparently, she was, if her I-dare-you-to-judge-me glare was anything to go by. He shrugged. No matter, a lot of intelligent people killed time on their cell, playing games and texting.

"Rashad told me about this game the other day. He's played it with his girlfriend."

"I didn't know Rashad had a girlfriend, although I'm not surprised that he does. What about Manute?"

"What about him?"

"Does he have a girlfriend?"

He'd ignored the bit about Sanura not being surprised Rashad had a girlfriend, choosing not to ask the obvious question of: Why aren't you surprised? No matter Sanura's response, he wouldn't have liked it. But the question about Manute had him narrowing his gaze and twisting toward her.

"Don't look at me like that. I'm not interested in Manute or any of your friends, just to be clear. But you're the one who asked me to move in with you knowing you have four incredibly good-looking friends already living here."

"'Incredibly good-looking?'" he repeated, an angry snarl in his throat.

"Anyway, I only asked because I thought he would be good for my friend Rachel. You haven't met her yet, but I've told you tons about her, and her about you."

Rachel Foster, yes, Assefa knew of her teacher friend. The little he'd heard about the woman, he liked.

"Manute is silly and playful on the outside but serious and driven on the inside."

Sanura beamed. "Perfect, because Rachel is more or less the reverse. Manute is also very kind and sweet."

"He is. But matchmaking can be a messy and touchy business, Sanura."

"I know. I'm only planning on introducing them, nothing more than that. Do you think Manute would mind?"

"You're planning on introducing a single were-cat to a pretty, and equally single, witch. What part of that do you imagine Manute minding?"

Sanura gave his leg a playful shove with the heel of her foot. "Pretty? I showed you a few pictures of Rachel and me and you found her attractive?" Another shove. "I guess you also think Cyn pretty?"

"They both are, but you're the only woman I find absolutely gorgeous."

"Oh, you do have a way with words."

Assefa winked. "You liked that?"

"Of course. Good thing for you I'm not the jealous type."

"I may be from another country, sweetheart, but I have seen the movie *Pinocchio*.

With her index finger, Sanura touched the end of her nose, then smiled sheepishly. "Well, my fire spirit may be the jealous type."

"Your fire spirit?"

"Just a bit."

"If you say so."

"I just did. Now tell me about your cell phone game."

Assefa smiled, pleased Sanura had a jealous streak the same as he did. Not that he liked that trait about himself or wanted to see Sanura in a jealous fit, but shared characteristics, even inconvenient ones, helped a couple to better understand each other.

"It's *Truth or Dare for Lovers*."

For several seconds, Sanura only stared. Not exactly the reaction he was going for, but he understood her surprise, even shock. Assefa Berber didn't play pointless games, no less silly ones. At least that's how most people thought of him, and how he'd been reared. Serious, responsible, and studious, that was Assefa Berber. And he was, but just not only those things.

"Gods, Assefa, you've been one surprise after another today. I haven't played *Truth or Dare* since junior year of college."

"So you like the game?"

"Well enough. But I like the idea of just the two of us playing the game. More intimate and fun that way."

That's what Assefa thought as well, although he'd never actually played. He had, after Rashad showed him the app and explained the game to him, downloaded it and read about four dozen questions and dares before he decided it would make for great birthday fun.

"It seems simple enough. I've already typed in our names. This version keeps score, based on whether we answer the questions and complete the dares. And takes away a point if we pass on a question or dare. But this isn't about winning or losing."

"Agreed. Besides, if we ever did compete against each other, I would win."

Assefa grabbed her feet and began tickling her. Sanura squealed, tried to escape, but only managed to twist herself off the sofa and onto the floor.

Het let her fall.

She glared up at him, then burst into laughter. "I'm going to earn more points than you."

"Because today's your birthday and you're feeling lucky? Or do you think this American game will evoke fear in my heart and cause me to pass on a silly or embarrassing question or dare?"

He helped her up, swatting Sanura's lush bottom before she sat down next to him.

"I don't care what you say, I'm still going to win."

He laughed, never having realized how competitive his Sanura could be, especially over something as trivial as a game. The truth was, Assefa could be just as competitive but rarely over insignificant things like sports and games. Another common trait, which, like jealousy, if taken too far could prove harmful.

"Since it's your birthday, you may go first. Truth or dare?" Assefa hit Sanura's name and then the blue square with the word Start written on it. Under her name appeared the words Truth and Dare, separated by a space.

"Truth."

"Okay." Assefa hit the word Truth and a question appeared on the screen. He handed the phone to Sanura so she could read the question.

"What is the worst thing about being your gender?"

"That's an easy question, even I know the answer."

She smirked at him. "It is, and I don't mind telling you."

"So what's your answer, Miss Competitive?"

She poked a very lovely tongue out at him. "Having breasts."

"What?" He couldn't have heard her correctly. "Having breasts? That's the worst thing about being a female?"

Sanura glanced down at her erection-producing breasts and frowned, covered as they were by the robe. "They get in the way, especially when I'm doing something athletic like jogging or jump-rope cardio. And don't get me started on the nipples. By the end of the day, they are so sensitive I just want to rip my bra off and burn it. No wonder some women did that back in the day. So, having breasts. That's my answer."

Thankfully, Assefa wasn't the type of guy whose mouth would hang open in disbelief. But how could Sanura dislike something so wonderful, so pleasurable ... *so suckable*?

"What about your monthly cycle? That has to be worse than having breasts."

"You really are a man. Of course, I hate that part of being a woman, too. But it only lasts four or five days a month then it's gone. I've had these breasts since I was seventeen, and earlier when I first started to develop at twelve. They get far too much attention, almost as much as being the fire witch of legend."

Assefa still wasn't so sure, but he let it go. "Fine. You have a point and it's my turn."

"This is fun. Are you going to take a truth or a dare?"

"Truth."

Sanura hit the screen and extended the phone to him.

"You can just read it to me."

"Okay, this one is kind of weird, though."

Assefa didn't like the sound of that but had no intention of not answering whatever in the hell was on the screen causing Sanura's face to contort into a look of disgust.

"'Your lover has been kidnapped. The only way to get him or her back is to have sex with an animal. Which animal would you have sex with to save your lover from certain death?'"

Assefa snatched the phone out of Sanura's hand. The woman had to be teasing him. The damn question didn't make the slightest bit of sense. What kind of kidnappers would ask for something so outrageous instead of money?

He read what was on the screen. And swore.

Sanura laughed. "You want to skip that one, Special Agent Berber?"

How had she gotten such an easy question and he got one on bestiality? He was tempted to crush the phone. Instead, he loosened his grip and thought about the question. Even though it was just for fun, he didn't like entertaining such a distasteful thought, no matter that he could turn into an animal himself. Why anyone would think this question sexy and fun was beyond him. Still, he had to answer. No way would he forfeit and subject himself to Sanura's gloating and mocking laughter.

Assefa thought long and hard, tossing around one animal choice after another, none "appealing" to him. After two minutes of Sanura counting him down with the song from the final round of *Jeopardy*, he gave up and picked the first animal that came to mind.

"A dog, I guess," he finally said, feeling like a sex deviant for having voiced his decision.

"A dog?"

"Sure. It's an animal and it's my answer. A dog. You know, man's best friend and all."

His answer bothered Sanura, if her knitted brow was a clue.

"What?" he said, more defensively than he intended. "What should I have chosen?"

"You would have sex with a dog?"

"I don't *want* to have sex with a dog. But if I had to in order to get you back safely, I suppose I would." Although Assefa was sure he would have to get plenty drunk to go through with the horrid act. Even then, he doubted if he'd be able to … well, rise to the occasion.

"That brings disturbing images to mind. You know that, right?"

"I'm trying really hard not to think too much on it."

"What kind of dog?"

"What?"

What in the hell did that have to do with anything? Why was Sanura taking seriously a response to a question that should never be asked of anyone, not even in a game?

"I don't know what breed of dog. That wasn't part of the question."

"I think you would kill the poor animal if you choose a small dog, like a Yorkie or Chihuahua."

"I'm *not* going to actually have sex with a dog, Sanura, so the size doesn't matter."

"Size always matters, Assefa." Sanura gave him a you-know-what-I-mean wink, then blew him a kiss.

Assefa was certain if he were a cartoon character steam would be coming from his ears.

"Since this estate is huge and I've never had a pet, I was thinking of getting a Shih Tzu. Now I'm not sure if that's a good idea. Maybe a gerbil or rabbit would be a better choice. Surely you wouldn't have sex with Bugs Bunny. I would be devastated if the cat of legend killed my pet with his mighty Mngwa's penis of pleasure."

Sanura's teasing laughter had rippled through and out of her before she'd reached her unfunny punchline. Laugh tears streamed down her face as she wrapped arms around her heaving middle, enjoying herself at Assefa's expense.

If Assefa were lucky, he'd get a dare that would challenge him to spank his girlfriend, because Sanura Williams, tease of the first order, was begging to be put over Assefa's knee and shown who was in charge.

"Let's just move on. And, Sanura, I'm going to get you back."

The threat broke through her laughter. The haughty arch of her eyebrows a silent challenge for him to try.

He would. There was no doubt about that. The fire witch would reap what she'd sowed.

Wiping laugh tears from her face, Sanura attempted and failed, twice, to get her laughter under control. On the third attempt, she managed to say, "I'll take another question."

Assefa found the next question and read. "'If you were a porn star, what would be your stage name?'"

Sanura laughed. "A porn star stage name? That's hilarious."

It was kind of funny, and yet another easy point for Sanura. He could think of several porn star names without even trying.

"Just to be clear, no casting calls unless they're with me."

"Do you have a casting couch, Assefa?" She climbed onto his lap, silky-smooth brown thighs peeking out from under her robe. "Or are we already on it?"

Inquisitive hands slipped between the folds of Sanura's robe and settled on her luscious bare hips. Thumbs rubbed back and forth. "What about Bronco Buster?"

She swatted his shoulder. "That's awful."

"Okay. How about Connie Lingus?"

"Gods, Assefa, that's worse."

"Backdoor Becky?"

Sanura collapsed onto his chest, body shaking from laughter.

"You're so bad at this. I wouldn't choose any of those horrendous names."

"Not even Debra Deep or Mary Dickins?"

"Stop. Stop. You're making my stomach hurt, I'm laughing so hard. You're bad. And creative in a way I would've never imagined."

"Well, what's said in the solarium stays in the solarium. Now that I've made you laugh and a fool of myself, it's your turn. Or did I take all the best porno star names and leave nothing good for you?"

"You wish." Sanura kissed him, then slid off his lap. Resettling herself, she eyed Assefa with a contagious grin. "Since you have a flare for the ridiculous, my porn star name would be Queen O."

"Queen O? As in Queen Orgasm?"

"You like it?"

"It depends. Since you're only going to star in my sex movies, is the name meant to be a challenge or a compliment?"

Sanura beamed at Assefa, spirited and with more than a fair share of naughtiness in her eyes. "Both."

"Both?"

"Yes, well, I am a queen. And queens have high standards. I understand if you can't meet them each and every time we make love."

There went her mocking laughter again.

Assefa retrieved his phone from the cushion that separated them and pushed the screen, bringing the phone back to life.

"I'm going to find a dare that involves me giving you a well-earned spanking."

Sanura lunged for his phone.

Assefa avoided the witch, fending her off with a strong arm. With his other arm, he grabbed Sanura around the waist, pulled her flush against him then pinned her to him with his legs.

Unable to move, she glared down at Assefa.

He raised a single hand and brought it down on her lovely, plump backside.

Smack.

"Oww."

"Barely a sting, Sanura. But if it really hurts, I'd be more than happy to kiss the pain away." Assefa rubbed the spot. "Would you like that, for me to kiss your bare, sexy bottom?"

Her aroused scent was Assefa's answer.

"Queen O it is then. After the party, I'll give you as many orgasms as you can stand. Right now, we should get back to the game."

He let her go. Sanura scrambled back to her side of the sofa, making a show of sitting gingerly on her bottom, as if what he'd done to her was more than a love tap.

Big fire witch baby. Queen indeed.

"My turn, and I'll take another question." When Assefa hit the screen, the next question appeared. "'What's the worst pick up line you've ever used?'"

"That's a good question." Sanura drew her legs onto the cushion and sat cross-legged. "I've heard some of the lamest come-ons, especially in college."

Assefa didn't have a good answer to this question. In fact, he didn't have an answer at all that wouldn't make him sound arrogant.

"What's wrong? Come on, I promise not to laugh."

"I doubt that, but that's not it. I don't have a worst pick up line."

"Of course you do. Every guy does. Hell, plenty of women too."

"Well, I don't." He shrugged. "I, umm, never had to do anything more than introduce myself. And most of the time I didn't have to do that."

"Wait, wait, you mean to tell me you've never picked up a woman?"

"I have. I just told you that, but I never used some clever or funny pick up line. I introduced myself, smiled, and that's pretty much it. Zareb used to say something about a pogo stick that got him either smacked or laid."

He didn't mention that she'd been the only woman he'd had to chase and the only female he'd deemed worth pursuing.

Sanura stared at him dumbfounded. "You're not even trying to be cocky. You're honestly saying that a straight-forward introduction was all it took." She ran a hand through her hair. "The crazy thing is that I can see that happening. When I first met you, you did exactly the same thing, but with so much charisma and sex appeal I couldn't help but be attracted to you."

A sweet truth from his lady without the benefit of a silly question. This was why Assefa chose to play this game, as embarrassing and juvenile as the questions could be. It was a fun way to share bits and pieces of self with the one you loved in a safe and private environment. Yet Sanura didn't appear particularly pleased with the revelation, but she said nothing more and continued with the game.

Assefa read her the next truth question, which, yes gods, he wanted to know the answer to. "Would you like to try anal sex?"

"That's not the question. Stop playing around and ask me the real question."

Assefa turned the phone to Sanura so she could read the question for herself.

She swore, and face turned a lovely shade of fire witch red.

"So, are you planning on answering the question or passing?"

"I'm not going to pass." But she also didn't seem inclined to answer the question, which meant only one thing. "Maybe."

Assefa tapped the tip of her nose with his finger. "Pinocchio."

She blushed. "I'm not lying. I've never considered it before today. So *maybe* is my answer."

He could push, coax her into explaining. But he wouldn't. Sanura's discomfiture wasn't part of the game. Besides, he knew why she'd had thoughts of anal sex today. When they were fooling around in the kitchen this morning, Assefa arousing her with a cucumber, he'd rubbed his penis between the cheeks of her ass, massaging her anus each time he thrust upward. From the amazing friction, he'd nearly come in his boxers.

He tapped her nose again. "We'll talk about it later."

She gave him a relieved smile, but one tinged with the desire to explore the unknown.

Over the next half hour, they laughed and joked their way through many questions before deciding to tackle a dare.

"Okay, Sanura, here's your dare. "'Call a friend or family member and tell them about your first sexual experience.'"

Sanura smiled, a self-assured grin that told Assefa she thought this was another easy point for her.

"I'll call Cyn," she said, voice dripping with confidence. "She'll think I'm pranking her when I call and tell her something she already knows."

Sanura held out her hand, a silent request for Assefa to hand over the phone so she could call her best friend.

With his own smug smile, Assefa handed it over. "Before you make your call, you may want to read the last line of the dare."

"The what …?" Silently, Sanura read. When she finished, resigned eyes lifted and met his. "Payback?"

"Oh yes. I get to select the friend or family member." He struck a thinking pose as if this were the most difficult decision in the world.

He thought. And thought. And thought. About nothing at all except messing with his competitive, impatient witch. As soon as he'd read the question, the perfect person had come to mind. And it damn sure hadn't been Cynthia Garvey.

He affected a sigh of agonized deliberation.

Sanura twisted the belt of her robe, at the end of her rather short rope. The woman really did need to work on being more patient.

"Just tell me to call my mother already. She's the most obvious choice. You know I'll hate telling her something like that. And she'll never let me live it down. You know how she is."

He did know. And while most daughters didn't normally share details of their sex life with their mother, Sanura and Makena were close enough that the little reveal wouldn't be as awkward as Sanura was pretending it would be. In fact, Assefa had a strong feeling Sanura had just put on a little fire witch drama for him, and that Makena already knew the when, where, and with whom of Sanura's first sexual encounter.

Assefa grinned to himself. The woman actually thought she could pull one over on a were-cat FBI agent.

He flicked her nose again. "Pinocchio." Ignoring her insulted frown, Assefa reclaimed his phone, found his contacts list and the number of the person he sought. He handed the cell back to Sanura.

And the look on her face was absolutely priceless. So priceless, Assefa grabbed his phone from her frozen hand and took a picture, all before she uttered more than a shocked gasp.

"Call and tell him about your first time. I'm sure he'll love to hear all the titillating details of his best friend's daughter losing her virginity. He'll probably say something like, For the love of Dr. Ruth. What in the hell is wrong with you, Sanura?"

"That's not funny."

"Really? From here I think I see a smile."

Sanura laughed. "Gods, Assefa, Mike would say something like that."

"I know." Assefa handed Sanura the phone. "Now call him. And don't forget to put it on speakerphone. I don't want to miss a single word." Assefa propped an ankle on a knee and an arm went to the back of the sofa.

Her face dropped. "You can't be serious. I can't tell my godfather about my first time. Or talk to him about sex at all. He's sexist and judgmental and uses words like 'narcisexual' and 'eyebrow pubes' in everyday conversation."

"The dwarf certainly has a way with words, I'll give the detective that. But you're stalling, sweetheart. Either witch up or pass and lose a point."

They were tied at fifteen apiece, which his competitive girlfriend well knew.

Sanura stared at the phone in her hand, grimacing each time her finger hovered over the green-and-white phone icon. On a frustrated growl, she tossed him his cell. "You're a spiteful, spiteful man, Special Agent Berber. I pass."

Feeling redeemed but not at all magnanimous, he kissed her cheek and said in a deliberate cheery voice, "Well, that's it for me. Fifteen to fourteen. I win, you lose." He stood. "The masseuse should be here soon." Assefa stretched his arms over his head and rolled his shoulders. "And I'm ready for our couple's massage. What about you?"

In a flash, his hot-blooded fire witch attacked, causing Assefa to slip and slide backward and into … Ever the gentleman, he grabbed a fistful of her robe, bringing Sanura with him.

Splash. Right into the hot tub.

CHAPTER TWELVE

Sanura felt glorious. How could she not? She'd spent a true day of relaxation and fun with Assefa. Her conservative agent had a most delicious boyish side that had nothing to do with immaturity but all about knowing how to take advantage of the pleasures life had to offer.

He'd cooked for her. Fed her. Joked and played with her. And made Sanura forget the anxiety of the day, the pain of their partial mate bond, felidae law, the Witch Council meeting, and even, for a little while, that they were the fire witch and cat of legend, destined to die or to save the world.

Sitting on her bed, Sanura admired the glossy fractal fire art wrapping paper. An abstract piece of art, orange-and-gold flames comingled in an intricate design that, at once, had both form and stability but also wildness and fluidity. Ironically, all words she would use to describe her growing magical ability.

Taking her time, Sanura removed the paper from the white gift box. Once the box top and red tissue paper were set aside, Sanura saw the gift inside. Days ago, she'd found the gift-wrapped box on a shelf in her closet with a gift tag that read: Happy Birthday, Fire Witch of Legend. Although the gift tag had been printed in a familiar Arial font and not written in Assefa's neat script, she knew the gift was from him. Who else could it have been from?

Although curiosity had almost killed her, Sanura had waited until her birthday to open her present. She wasn't disappointed, not that Sanura thought she would be. As usual, Assefa had impeccable taste.

Pulling the dress from the box, Sanura got to her feet and went to the master bathroom. Once inside, she stood in front of the full-length mirror and held the dress up to her. Purple. Next to red, Sanura loved the rich, vibrant color. The sheath dress featured an asymmetrical illusion neckline with ornamented diamonds. Once on, the dress would skim her knees. Smiling, Sanura knew the perfect ankle-strap sandals to wear with her new birthday dress.

Excited for her birthday dinner to begin, Sanura left the bathroom so she could get dressed. Thanks to Assefa, she didn't have to worry about her hair. After their couple's massage, which left Sanura feeling boneless and ready for a nap, Assefa sprung another one of his birthday gifts on her. With a big grin on her face and dressed in comfortable jeans and a short-sleeve shirt, Tee Price of Just Be Sacred Wellness had strolled into the recreation room, where the masseuse had set up her portable massage table nearly three hours before.

"So this is where you've been hiding out lately," Tee said. In her right hand, she held a black portable soft bonnet dryer, in her left a green-and-blue hairstylist bag that read: Sacred, Natural, and Blessed. "Cynthia said you'd moved to Alexandria." Placing her supplies on the metal framed and wooden top pub table to her right, Tee, a full-human Sanura had known for ten years, took in the rec room, eyes as wide as Sanura's had been when she'd first entered the room in search of Assefa.

While Assefa hadn't been in the room, Manute and Zareb had been, lounging in leather recliners, feet propped on ottomans, and eyes glued to an Orioles versus Boston Red Sox game on the 75 inch LED, LCD television mounted over the fireplace. Oak wood floors with a mosaic design glistened, not a scratch on the finish, which explained why Manute wore socks and Zareb's feet were bare. Built-in bookshelves filled with fiction and nonfiction literature lined the back wall while a hexagonal chess table claimed the spot between the seated men.

Several gaming chairs were in a corner of the room, opposite a multimedia unit with television, two game systems, video games, gaming headphones, and an assortment of CDs and DVDs. A black-

and-gold pool light hung above the eight-foot slate pool table with hand sewn leather pockets. Normally in the middle of the room, the pool table had been moved against a wall when Assefa escorted Sanura into the room where the masseuse had already prepared her work area.

Tee had taken in the room with a similar awe. "So this is how the other half lives. Man, I wish I didn't have plans I couldn't cancel because I would accept the birthday invite just to see the rest of this house." She removed a black hairband from around her wrist and used it to pull her dreadlocks out of her eyes and into a ponytail. Tee had the most striking amber-colored eyes, reminiscent of yellow and brownish amber pieces found in the Baltic Sea area. And those exquisite orbs glowed with humor when she asked, "Does your boyfriend have a brother?"

"He does. But you're married, remember?"

"Oh, I remember, which is why I asked about a brother."

They'd laughed.

"All right, Sanura. It's your birthday, and your man spent a lot of money to book me for the day."

"The day?"

"Makena and Cynthia were in the shop this morning to get their hair done. Your friend Rachel and several of your other girlfriends came by an hour or so later for the body wrap party."

"Assefa arranged all of that?"

"Yup. Must be nice having money like that, and a boyfriend who doesn't mind spending it on you and your family and friends."

Sanura had been shocked but not surprised, reminded, once more, of Assefa's generosity. But she really needed to have a talk with him about his spending habits when it came to her. Even now, as she admired herself in the bedroom mirror, the purple dress a beautiful and perfect fit, hair in double-strand twists pinned up in a stylish braid, guilt and regret threatened.

He'd given her a birthday to remember, and there were hours left before the day would come to its inevitable end. She wished they could remain in this cocoon, a place where joy, warmth, and love reigned supreme and troubles and heartache were forever banished from her Kingdom of Dreams and Fantasies.

Despite the fairy tale atmosphere of the day, Sanura and Assefa were of this world, reality-based beings who comprehended, all too well, the complexity and unfairness of life, even of the heart.

"You're a stunning sight to my were-cat eyes." Assefa crossed the threshold of the sitting room and into their bedroom. "That's a lovely color on you, Sanura." His eyes traveled from her dress and to her face. "Absolutely gorgeous. I'm a lucky man."

The game of *Truth or Dare*, hours over, mocked their relationship. So much truth existed between them, such as the earnest compliment Assefa had just given her and the heart that leaped with love whenever she saw him. But life and the prophecy dared them to go beyond the safe confines of known truths, seeking facts not yet revealed and dares too frightening to contemplate.

"Thank you. I love this dress." She eyed him. So handsome. "I've never seen you dressed like that before. You look regal and commanding."

Assefa wore a white mbubb, which fell a few inches above his ankles. Gold embroidery decorated the neckline, shoulders, and center of the robe, as well as the cuffs of the pants and the matching hat he wore. Sanura couldn't take her eyes off him, so much did he remind her of a groom on his wedding day, awaiting his bride.

She wondered if he realized how they would look to others when he escorted her downstairs, across the lawn, and into a tent of waiting guests. Sanura also wondered if Assefa would consider marrying her without a complete mate claim or if she even had the right to ask.

Too many life-altering thoughts to ponder right now, especially with Assefa having just lifted and extended his hand to Sanura. She moved away from the mirror and toward Assefa, taking the offered hand when she reached him. With a squeeze of his hand and a kiss to his cheek, Sanura was ready to greet their guests.

Five minutes later, they were in the backyard and by the same gazebo she'd sat in two nights ago, watching Assefa's Mngwa swim out of the Potomac River and praying what she had to tell the man wouldn't end their relationship. The news hadn't sent him running, but it had altered something profound between them. Yet there they stood, side-by-side, dressed in evening finery, smiling and holding hands as if they were Lady Sanura and Lord Assefa of this Alexandria manor and nothing in the harsh, ugly world could touch them.

Not at all the truth.

Assefa led her into a white, luxury marquee party tent. Enclosed to protect against the elements, the tent, like Assefa's clothing, reminded Sanura of a wedding. Dining tables and chairs, covered in red cloth with a white table centerpiece of gardenias were situated on the left side, along with buffet tables. On a lace-covered table was a polished stainless steel chocolate fondue fountain and assorted fruits, cookies, and marshmallows on trays in front of and to the side of the fountain. Next to the chocolate lovers' paradise was a silver-and-gold trimmed champagne fountain, flowing with clear liquid. Full-human food servers dressed in white pants, white button-up shirt, and a red tie bustled about.

Jazz music punctuated the surreal moment. On the far end of the enormous tent was an elevated stage with four women whose soulful music Sanura would recognize anywhere. They were an eclectic group with experience that ranged from fifteen years to sixty. Three generations of Louisiana Creoles who'd brought their unique bayou sound north. The Bujeau women were highly sought-after because they loved what they did and it showed in every cord they struck and note they sang. Lovely didn't begin to describe the harmonic symphony they produced when they played with a single-minded purpose—to bring pleasure to their listeners. Clea Bujeau, her two daughters and one granddaughter were actually there, playing at Sanura's birthday party.

Unbelievable.

"Ladies of Louisiana. But I thought Clea Bujeau was retired."

Assefa hugged her to him. "She is retired, but I had a conversation with Mrs. Bujeau. I told her what a big fan you are of her music and how honored you'd be if she and the band played at your birthday party."

He stated it so matter-of-factly as if convincing a five-time Grammy Award winner to play at her birthday party required nothing more than introducing himself to the seventy-five-year-old woman whose impressive tone, diction, intonation, and improvisational style captivated her listeners and kept them coming back for more.

Speechless. This man and the incredible day he'd given her left Sanura speechless and so close to ruining her makeup with tears of gratitude.

"Are you a bouncer or something? Why in the hell are you standing in front of the entrance? And what do you have on there, Assefa? A dress? I told you this would happen once you took Sanura as your mate. But did you listen to me? Noooo."

There went their moment and Sanura's urge to cry. She spun around to face the rude dwarf.

Dressed in a well-fitted and wrinkle-free black suit with a light-blue dress shirt and a tie with an image of the Chesapeake Bay, Michael McKutchen smiled up at Sanura. His unibrow trimmed, salt-and-pepper hair neat and combed, green eyes sparkling with humor, and a big grin on his aging face, Sanura hadn't seen Mike this put-together since, well, since her father's funeral.

"Happy birthday. You're a vision in purple, like a meadow rue. Elegant, tall, and deceptively delicate."

"Do you think that compliment makes up for the insult to Assefa?"

Mike shrugged. "You know how I am and so does he. Besides, I've known you longer and you love me more."

Sanura couldn't help but smile at her godfather. Leaning down, she hugged him and pressed a kiss to his cheek. "How could I not love a man who compares me to a pretty perennial?"

Stubby but quite strong arms hugged Sanura back. "But you love me more. Don't forget that part or the kid just might think he's stolen you from me."

She kissed his other cheek, and he held her tighter. Mike's love, like Assefa's, unconditional and heartwarming.

"That's enough, Mike, let my daughter go so I can wish her a happy birthday. You do this every year."

With reluctance, Mike released Sanura. "Just because you gave birth to her that doesn't mean you get special privileges on her birthday."

"That's exactly what it means, Mike, now get out of Makena's way and let her greet her daughter."

Assefa waved Mike to his side. They spoke in low tones while Sanura was enveloped in a motherly bear hug. Makena said nothing, just held Sanura to her, a subtle rocking motion as she did so. So much passed between them in that single, silent hug. A hug that included the ones her father could no longer give to her. This third year of his sacrificed death.

Now that Sanura knew the truth, she better understood the melancholy that had overcome Makena her last two birthdays. Sadness and gladness mixed together in an emotional stew that kept Makena from confessing Sam's secret. Birthdays weren't days for secrets, but they also weren't days for gloom and heartache. So this year, Sanura would respect Makena's need to maintain her husband's secret, unwilling to hurt her mother with the truth.

"I love you," Makena spoke against her ear. "And I'm very proud of the woman you've become." She kissed her cheek, then pulled back so she could see Sanura's face. "If your father were here, he would tell you the same."

"I know, Mom. I know."

No, she couldn't tell Makena about the jaguar spirit, especially if she couldn't find a way to transfer it from herself and to her mother. Which, as each day passed, Sanura thought the likelihood of her being able to do so a million in one chance.

Sanura held Makena's hands out to her sides to take in all of her mother. Always so lovely, tonight was no different. Decked out in a black dot mesh bodice fit and flare dress with a contrast skirt that fell to her knees, she wore her natural hair in twists that framed her face and fell past her shoulders. Strands of gray accented the style, emphasizing what Sanura already knew about Makena Williams. She rocked her fifties like nobody's business.

When Makena stepped aside to speak to Assefa, Sanura saw Rachel standing quiet and shy in the background. Where Makena was classically beautiful in black, Rachel was colorful and romantic in a radish lace wrap dress with a ribbon belt and surplice neckline.

"I'm here."

"I see that. You came with Mom and Mike. That's good."

"Actually, when I saw Makena at Tee's today, I decided to ride with her instead of Mike. By the time I met your mother at her house, Mike was already there. Makena drove and Mike sat shotgun."

"I see. Which left you in the backseat with no pressure to make conversation with anyone."

Rachel smiled. "You know me well, you spoiled brat."

Sanura shook her head. "After today, you have no idea how right you are. Except for the brat bit. I take offense to that."

"All brats do. Happy birthday to you, girl."

They hugged.

"I want to introduce you to Assefa."

Sanura turned to see her mother, Mike, and Assefa engaged in a conversation about the tense relationship between some African American residents of Baltimore City and the Baltimore City Police Department. Excusing herself, she managed to extricate Assefa from the conversation. If she allowed them, the FBI agent, judge, and detective would talk business all evening.

"Rachel Foster, this is Assefa Berber. Assefa, this is Rachel."

To her surprise, Rachel extended her hand for a shake. As far as Sanura knew, this was the first time she'd permitted a man to touch her she hadn't known before her rape. It was only a handshake, the tent full of people, and Sanura right there. Still, Sanura chose to see this as a good sign.

"It's a pleasure to meet you, Rachel. I've heard nothing but wonderful things about you."

"Sanura gets this Disney princess starry-eyed look whenever she talks about you. It's very annoying." Rachel glanced around the elaborate tent. "I guess I now know why. You really are out of some fairy tale, aren't you, Assefa Berber? Or maybe you're an undercover prince, like Eddie Murphy in *Coming to America*."

Sanura waited to see how Assefa would respond to Rachel and her odd version of humor. Without missing a beat, Assefa smiled down at Rachel. "My name is Assefa Berber, and you are a most welcomed guest, Miss Rachel Foster. I hope you enjoy your evening." He turned to Sanura. "I'm going to escort Makena and Mike to our table. You stay and speak with your friend, and I'll be back."

When Assefa walked off, leading Makena and Mike to the left side of the tent, Rachel, like Sanura, stared after him.

"Wow! He's, umm, something else. Why did he introduce himself after you did?"

Sanura had a better question. "Did his simple introduction work for you?"

Rachel scratched her head. "It's the weirdest thing, but it felt different when he did it. Kind of like the best pick up line you've ever heard even though the man said nothing more special than his name."

Damn but Assefa Berber had an uncanny way of charming women. A part of Sanura, the jealous part that had nothing to do with her fire spirit, didn't like the easy way he managed to disarm women. Worse, her special agent knew the power he wielded, no magical pheromones required.

"Where's Cynthia and Eric? I thought they would've been here by now."

"Maybe they had to deal with Gen, who's upset that her little four-teen-year-old self wasn't invited to a grownup party. She called me this morning to wish me a happy birthday, but to also let me know how 'unfair' it was that Assefa's invitation hadn't included her."

"Yeah, that sounds like Gen." Rachel scanned the tent again. "I was only messing with your mate, Sanura. This is really nice. Did you know about the body wrap party?"

"Not until it was over."

"I've never had that done before. If I were a bit more claustropho-bic, I couldn't have gone through with it. But it was nice. And Assefa is as sweet as a red velvet funnel cake slathered with white powder, cream cheese frosting, and whipped cream. I see why you're taking the time to learn Wolof for him."

Sweet. Yes, Assefa was as sweet as that fattening dessert Rachel just described. But so much better because, unlike the high-calorie funnel cake, Assefa's sweetness was all natural and healthy for Sanu-ra.

"Oh gods, there you go again with that look." Rachel grabbed Sanura's hand and pulled her away from the entrance and toward a group of their friends. "An attractive bald guy in a gray suit is speak-ing with your man and Mike. That gives you time to make your rounds and cool down. No one wants to see a fire witch combust in a tent with alcohol and too many chiffon and silk dresses.

****

Paul Chambers reclined in the leather seat of his SUV, cell phone on the dash and thumbs tapping the steering wheel with impatience. Three years. Three goddamn years of being patient and now the

Council thought they could pull this shit. Thought they could deny his son the power and prestige due him the way the old Council had done to Paul. Well, that shit wasn't going to happen again, not if Paul had anything to do about it.

"This Council will decide who the next alpha will be, Paul, not you or your pride."

Paul had glared at Anna, the mother of his son but never his mate. Her mother and father had seen to that, threatening to disown Anna and her newborn if she took Paul as her mate and familiar. And being the spineless woman that she was, Anna had caved, giving in the way she always had. Yet over the years, she'd grown into a much stronger woman. The kind of woman who could no longer be so easily manipulated by a handsome guy who knew what to say to coax a shy, pretty girl away from home and into his bed. Her pregnancy, without the sanctity of a mate bond, was against Council law.

"So you've said. But it's been three years and we still have no alpha. He will be our leader, not the leader of witches." He'd pointed to each of the women in turn. "Water, fire, wind, earth. Each witch element has a representative on this Council, the were-cats get only one."

"We understand your concern," Makena had said, her voice as smooth and as unyielding as polished marble, "as well as the concerns of the other alphas. Rest assured, Paul, we have this well in hand. We will soon make our selection and present him to the community."

"As a fait accompli?" He'd stood during the meeting while the witches had sat, none offering him the slightest courtesy other than their time. Their dislike of him was clear on their disinterested faces. "By Council law, the alphas have the right to challenge any were-cat selected by a witch-only Council."

Makena's expression hadn't changed, although all in the room understood Paul's point. Per Council law, when a Council Alpha stepped down, he chose his replacement. Unless the priestesses had a very good reason, they could not deny him his chosen successor. Yet when an alpha died in office, without naming a successor, the responsibility of selecting the next alpha fell to the priestesses. But the law of succession was very clear. Under such circumstances, any alpha could challenge the Council's selection.

The fire witch had smiled at him, beautiful white teeth and one hell of a dangerous elemental spirit. If Paul had known about Makena Williams back then, he'd pursued her instead of Anna. If he had, he would be the Council's alpha, because the fire witch was damn sure the strongest priestess on the Council, capable of elevating a chosen mate to the post. But he'd selected poorly, and now his son would suffer. If Paul couldn't claim the alpha chair for Greg before the new were-cat was installed, he wouldn't get another chance.

"You and the other alphas are free to oppose our selection," Makena had said, a slither of heated warning in her voice, "but I would think very hard about challenging the cat of legend. Trust me when I say such a foolish decision could prove fatal."

The priestesses had smiled at him, including Anna, who'd nodded her head at the door behind him.

"We will take your concern under consideration. Good day, Paul."

Ten minutes. Ten goddamn minutes and he'd been dismissed like some kind of panhandler begging for scraps. Well, no one treated Paul Chambers that way, especially a group of witches who knew nothing of were-cat ways. Were-cats didn't accept an alpha simply because one was presented before them. If this so-called cat of legend wanted the position, he could damn well fight to earn it. This was his pride's territory, and they would cow to no were-cat.

His phone vibrated, and Paul quickly answered. Not bothering with speakerphone, he pressed the cell to his ear.

"What do you have for me?"

"He was expecting us."

"What do you mean?"

Paul looked out his car window. At seven in the evening, the sun still shone high and bright in the sky, but it would soon wane and give way to another sweltering June night. He'd parked in a neighborhood where people's garages were nicer than his entire house. And Paul owned a pretty decent home in Baltimore County. But these were multimillion dollar mansions. And while his SUV was nothing to sneeze at, it wasn't a Rolls-Royce or Bugatti. The owners of both had driven past him while he waited for news of his team's reconnaissance mission.

"There are security guards on the perimeter of the property and at the front gate."

"Full-human? Preternatural?"

"All full-human, I think. They definitely smelled like prey. But we didn't want to get too close, so we don't know how many there are. Damion and Junior didn't mention anything about guards."

No, the boys had slipped onto the property without any trouble. But had been detected and caught within minutes, which meant there were probably sensors and surveillance videos. Paul had planned for that. What he hadn't planned for were security guards, especially full-humans.

He smiled. Berber just may prove to be a worthy opponent. Using full-humans as security was an excellent strategic move. Unless Paul wanted his lions to confront and hurt the full-humans, bringing all kinds of hell down on their heads, from the Council and local law enforcement, which no sane preternatural would do, Berber had effectively tied Paul's hands for the evening. Well, not completely. There was always the direct approach.

CHAPTER THIRTEEN

"You've outdone yourself, Assefa."

Before accepting the chair, he held out for her, Makena pulled Assefa into a hug. For a second, he didn't know how to respond. She'd hugged him only once before, the day Sanura was to play bait, luring the adze to her so Assefa's Mngwa could catch and kill the murderer of witches. Then, Makena's hug had been full of fear and desperation. Tonight, she smelled and felt like motherly love. Sensations he hadn't experienced since his own mother had passed away.

He returned the embrace. In truth, Assefa couldn't recall his mother's arms or her love, but he assumed she had hugged him like this. Didn't all mothers love and hug their children? He knew they didn't. Some mothers could be cruel, selfish, and as heartless as the creatures Assefa and his fellow agents tracked and dispensed with. But this woman, this mother had him aching for home and for a family he and Sanura may never get a chance to have.

"One day soon, Assefa, I'd like to have a conversation with you about my late husband."

Assefa made sure to not react to Makena's words, although they sent his mind to questioning. Did she plan on telling him about Sam's sacrifice? Did she want to know if he harbored the jaguar spirit of her deceased husband? Or maybe she was finally considering telling Sanura the truth and wanted to begin with him, gauging his reaction before moving on to her daughter.

None of those thoughts appealed, but the conversation would open up a door to one that needed to take place between mother and daughter. Which, if the opportunity presented itself, Assefa would suggest.

True, all of this involved him as well, but Makena and Sanura would have to first work things out before he and Sanura could.

And the little velvet box in the pocket of his mbubb felt like a hundred-pound barbell, weighing down his heart. He should've left it in his lockbox. Pulling out the velvet box and looking at the engagement ring had been a stupid idea. Dropping the ring box into his pocket made him question his common sense. Assefa still wanted to ask Sanura to marry him, but he wasn't sure if he could do it now.

Makena finally accepted the chair he held out for her. Two women, full-humans from the smell of them, sat at the next table. Obviously, they knew Makena because they struck up a conversation with her as soon as she sat and poured herself a glass of water.

"Ever the gentleman," Mike said, his tone, for once, free of mockery. "This is the first time Sanura's celebrated her birthday since her father's death." Mike glanced over his shoulder and at Sanura, who stood speaking with Rachel and three other women "You've made her happy. Thank you for that."

"Thank you for the off-duty officers."

They walked a few feet away from Makena and the table.

"For what you're paying them for this gig, I could've gotten you another dozen. What's going on, kid? You were pretty vague yesterday."

He had been, requesting full-human officers to pull a last minute security detail. Trusting Mike, Assefa didn't worry who the detective would send out to his home because the dwarf would pick the best available.

"One of Sanura's Sankofa friends gave her a cryptic message."

"Sankofa, yeah, got you."

Assefa didn't need to say more to Mike than that. The dwarf knew how to blend in with full-humans. More, he was an expert at keeping his true identity a secret, as was every other preternatural in the tent.

"What do you know about felidae law?"

"Nothing. Sam may have mentioned it once or twice. But they keep that kind of stuff to themselves."

"I know. But I had to ask."

"So you're expecting trouble tonight?"

"Maybe."

"Of the fang and fur variety?"

Assefa nodded, scanning the crowd and cataloging all the were-cats in attendance he didn't know. There were five of them, four with their mates and one single jaguar shifter whose appreciative eyes were fixated on the swaying hips of two women dancing by the stage. Per Assefa's directive, Manute, Dahad, and Omar mingled like any other guest.

Similar to the scent disguise charm Sanura had made for Mike, his friends wore their own charms, gifts from his witch. Sanura had told Assefa she wanted to thank his friends for being so kind to her and for accepting her into their home and making her feel like family. So she'd given his friends a black stainless steel ring band. The value of the gift wasn't in the price of the ring, which cost Sanura no more than fifty dollars each, but the magic imbued within and the protection her magic would afford the were-cats. Tonight, Manute, Dahad, and Omar would smell like full-human prey to any were-cat they encountered. Zareb and Rashad were told to not wear their rings tonight, Assefa working under the assumption that anyone who learned the Sankofa teenagers made it onto his property would also know of Zareb and Rashad.

While Assefa had yet to figure out the level of threat of the Sankofa lions, intuition told him it would be imprudent to let them know the extent of his were-cat allies.

"If there are party crashers, I'm going to enjoy introducing their heads to their asses."

"As eloquent as ever, Mike."

"Yeah, I'm right up there with MLK and JFK."

"I'm pretty sure King and Kennedy never gave a speech and used the word ass."

"Maybe not, but they—"

"Assefa, I need to speak with you. I didn't mean to cut you off, detective, but I need to have a word with Assefa."

At the same time, Assefa's and Mike's eyes searched for Sanura. She and Rachel hadn't moved. Satisfied she was safe, he turned to Mike. "I'll be right back."

Mike nodded. "I got this. You go, and call if you need backup."

Assefa and Zareb went. Not far, just to the relative privacy of the gazebo. Neither sat.

Dressed in a gray suit, classic white shirt, and blue tie, Zareb looked like an on-duty FBI agent.

Serious and irritated eyes met Assefa's. "Someone sent scouts," he informed Assefa, his voice low, gruff, and dangerous.

"I assumed as much. How many and how far from the estate?"

"I spotted four were-cats two houses down. Rashad saw two even closer, watching the guests' cars approach the security gate before being buzzed in by one of the Baltimore City officers."

"That's fine. Whoever orchestrated tonight's scouting party know about the guards. If they've done nothing to incapacitate the full-humans by now, then I doubt if they will."

"Which means they'll either go home and try another day or grow a set of balls and come knocking."

"Precisely."

"Your directive?"

Assefa could hear music and laughter coming from the tent. Today had gone according to plan, including the men stalking his home. But he wouldn't permit them to intrude on this happy evening. He would deal with them tomorrow. Zareb could deal with them tonight.

"Be my shield."

"Not your sword?"

Assefa heard approaching footsteps. Three people, from the sound of their voice—two women and one man. Assefa knew the couple but had never met the other woman with them. Sanura would be pleased to see her friends.

"Not my sword, Zareb. Hopefully, it won't come to that."

But it would. Eventually, it would, because were-cats, at their magical core, were lethal beasts of prey.

****

Zareb walked away from the gazebo and his best friend. His shield but not his sword. A medjai was supposed to be both, his honor bound to the safety of the one he protected. But Assefa had never accepted his role the way a proper alpha should, thinking, if he ever did, he would become the man he feared, the kind of man he despised.

Not a baseless fear, Zareb conceded, considering the Berber history. But Assefa would never, could never turn into his grandfather or great-grandfather. Even his father, a man Zareb had known since boyhood, couldn't compare to his son. Assefa's compassionate and forgiving heart set him apart. Without both, Assefa would be lost.

The group of three approached. One white male who smelled like a were-cat, an older woman with hair the color of tree bark, the same shade as the male's, and a voluptuous woman with sandy-brown skin, dreadlocks, and ocean blue eyes.

When they walked past each other, the male's hand going up and waving at Assefa, Zareb and the younger woman's eyes met. Hers widened. His didn't. But his nostrils flared and his tiger roared to life.

Without slowing his pace, Zareb nodded to the beautiful woman. Now wasn't the time for flirting, his favorite pastime after sex, or for contemplating why the woman had smelled so damn good to his cat. Not prey, because the woman was damn sure a witch. A witch who should've known better than to leave her house without wearing a scent disguise charm. Either she was stupid or too lazy to make one for herself. Stupid and lazy, two kinds of women Zareb never dated. Unattractive traits in a bed partner, no less in a mate.

"Hey, Assefa," Zareb heard the male say, as the special agent strode in the opposite direction of the group, "sorry we're late. There was a fender bender on 95, which pushed everyone to the right two lanes."

"Don't worry about it, Eric. I'm just glad you got your wife and mother here safely."

When Zareb reached the end of the path, he turned around to see Assefa leading the trio into the tent. He knew who they were now— Cynthia and Eric Garvey. And the woman with them was Eileen Garvey. All their names were on Assefa's guest list. Zareb frowned, confused, and then became angry.

By the time he reached the front of the house, he was in no mood to deal with the bastard giving two off-duty officers a hard way to go, his SUV parked in front of the closed gate.

Rashad appeared to his right, an impish grin on his face. "I can deal with the asshole if he's too much for you, Z."

On any other day and with a different level threat, Zareb would've stepped back and let the young man have the experience. But the older white male in the SUV was far too much were-cat for young Rashad to handle.

Stopping in the winding driveway that led from the house and to the security gate, Zareb stepped in front of Rashad, hoping the man's keen eyes hadn't seen him.

"Go inside, Rashad."

"I was just playing."

"I know. But that guy is an alpha and I don't want you anywhere near him. In fact, go to the tent and glue yourself to Omar's side. And say nothing about this to Assefa."

Rashad may have been only twenty, and an immature twenty at that, but he comprehended the gravity of threat an alpha posed to a were-cat of his age and inexperience.

"It's an insult for him to be here without an invitation from Asse-fa."

"I'm sure that's the point. Now get your ass out of here."

Turning on his heels, Rashad walked calmly away. Smart boy, if he'd run that would've caught the attention of the alpha, making him look more like prey than he already did.

Zareb continued down the driveway and toward the arguing men.

"I told you, sir," the tall police officer with a thick middle said, "if your name isn't on the list, you aren't getting in. It's as simple as that."

A second police officer, a thin, lanky woman with breasts so small Zareb questioned whether she'd actually gone through puberty, stood on the opposite side of the vehicle from the male officer, her fingers skimming the butt of her firearm. Full-human or not, the officer sensed the threat and was prepared to deal with the man if he decided to do more than shoot off at the mouth.

"And I told you that I want to see the owner of the house. I don't have to go inside. He can come to me. In fact, I would prefer it if he came to me."

Zareb approached, and the man smiled a Cheshire grin. His driver's side window was rolled down, left arm out the window and gesturing when he spoke, the were-cat's self-satisfied smile broadened.

"Finally, someone worth speaking to. Send these nuisances back to the house so we can have a real conversation."

"This is not your territory, so I suggest you watch your tongue." He didn't like the man already, not that he thought he would. But he hated even more that the asshole was right. Caught between predators was no place for full-humans. "Thank you," Zareb said to the officers. "I'll take it from here. Please return to your post."

"Are you sure?" the female officer asked him, distrustful gray eyes on the man who could kill her in under ten seconds. He liked this woman. She had excellent instincts, which would, hopefully, keep her alive.

"I'm positive. Has everyone on the list arrived?"

"All except for one," the male officer answered.

"That's good." He gestured with his chin to the house.

After a long beat, the female officer nodded before she and her partner ambled up the driveway and to their assigned post.

"Now that wasn't so hard, was it? Taking orders from your superior?"

His shield and not his sword, Zareb fought to remind himself. "Who are you and what do you want?"

"I see he hasn't taught you proper manners. Your presumptuous tongue stinks of poor leadership and disrespect. I don't answer your questions, you answer mine."

Everything in Zareb screamed at him to drag this arrogant son of a bitch out his truck and beat the shit out of him with the arm he would rip from his body.

"I can see murder in your eyes, smell the desire for my blood in your pores. Remember this, boy, as alpha, I have the strength of my pride flowing through me. You're old enough to sense my power. Do you think you can take me? You wanna try?"

He did. And he would. But not tonight. The old alpha made a big mistake coming there. But he'd played his move. The problem, which anyone who'd ever challenged Assefa soon found out, was that they couldn't handle Assefa's countermove.

Zareb laughed at the old fool. "If you or any member of your pride trespasses on Berber property again, you'll see how disrespectful of an alpha I can be."

"And how murderous and bloody? Sounds delicious." The man returned Zareb's grin, allowing his fangs to fall from his gums. No matter the country, showing another were-cat your fangs was an act of hostility, of aggression, of intent to see him dead.

Six shifters emerged from the shadows. Were-cat magic poured from them, flooding the sticky night air with the scent of powerful lions.

"What would your alpha do if I sent you back to him defanged? I bet that'll get the runt's attention, wouldn't it? Seeing you all bloody and hurt, he'd come running then, wouldn't he?"

The were-cats began to stalk closer. The alpha laughed and unlocked his seatbelt. "The back of the truck is big enough for what I have in mind. And the tinted windows are just a plus. Win-win for me."

His shield and not his sword. Follow orders. Zareb gave the asshole and his snarling were-cats his back, hiding his knowing smile.

"You insolent piece of—"

A horn blared. Once. Twice. Three times.

Zareb turned back around, his smile no longer hidden. The black luxury car he'd spotted two minutes ago was now parked between the were-cats and Zareb, with the front of the car perpendicular to the truck. If the asshole still intended to get out of his vehicle, he would have to climb over the driver's console and exit through the front passenger door.

The door to the car opened, and out came his division chief. Six feet and all lean muscle, Ulan Berber, dressed in a black suit, white shirt, and a red-and-black tie, was a welcomed sight. In his right hand, he held a gun, the barrel of which he tapped on the hood of his car.

"Is there something going on here you want to tell me about, Special Agent Osei or should I shoot the were-cats to my right and then pistol whip the answers out of the one in the truck?"

The six were-cats looked to their alpha, whose eyes were fixed on the gun Chief Berber held in his steady hand.

No one fucked with Ulan Berber. The man was a classic Berber male—powerful, dangerous, stubborn, and intelligent, with a tendency toward unapologetic violence.

"What kind of dickless were-cat fights with a gun?"

"The same kind who would send six shifters after one. You like to win. Like having the odds on your side. I get that." He trained his gun on the red-faced asshole in the truck. "I play the odds as well. How fast are you? Fast enough to dodge a bullet to your head? Fast enough to prevent me from shooting your men where they stand? Fast enough to stop my special agent from ripping your throat out while I take care of these cubs?"

"Hardball. You like to play hardball."

"No, you misunderstand. Berbers don't play hardball. We simply destroy all challengers."

The older men glared at each other, neither willing to back down.

Zareb's claws pushed through the tips of his fingers, ready to rip into the first bastard who made a move. The biggest of the were-cats, a six-foot guy in green fatigues and T-shirt damn sure didn't look like he was about to stand down. If he didn't, Zareb would see his ass on the pavement, spitting up blood, teeth, and pride.

The old alpha laughed, but no one relaxed, not even his were-cats. "Tonight's not the night for this and this isn't the place. Too many full-humans around. They'll only spoil our fun."

With that, the six were-cats drifted away, a temporary and strategic retreat.

The asshole drew the seatbelt back into place and started his truck's engine. A moment later, he was backing up and turning his truck in the direction where Chief Berber had come. He started to drive away, stopped, opened his door, and then dropped something into the street before closing his door and finally driving away.

Once the man was well up the street and Zareb could no longer smell those six were-cats, he retrieved the item the man had left for them.

"What is it?" The chief still sounded mad and had yet to put his gun away. Only Chief Berber would think nothing of attending a birthday party with his FBI-issued Glock. Thank Sekhmet for the man's overly cautious nature.

Zareb opened the 6 x 9 mailing envelope. A single item was inside. He took it out, looked at it, and, with a growl, handed it over to his chief.

"Are you planning on showing this to Assefa?"

"I have no choice. But I won't do it tonight. I don't want to spoil his evening."

"He's not going to be happy."

The understatement of the century.

"Come on, get in the car and take me to the party before I give in to the urge to track that bastard back to his house and splatter his brains all over his pillow."

Yeah, classic Berber male. Thank Sekhmet Assefa was an enlightened Berber male. But even enlightened men have been known to take a step down the evolutionary ladder when provoked.

****

"So when are you guys planning on making the big announcement?" Cynthia eyed Sanura's left hand. "And where in the hell is your engagement ring? Don't tell me he hasn't asked you yet or that you were crazy enough to turn Assefa down."

"I was wondering the same thing," Rachel said, unknowingly adding to Sanura's sudden bout of tension. "You do know this is one of those tents rented for weddings, don't you?"

They sat at the table reserved for Sanura, Assefa, Makena, Mike, and Ulan. Cynthia's family, as well as Rachel, were given the table to her right, with Assefa's friends assigned the table directly to the left of them. Omar sat at that table now, a book in front of him but chatting with Mrs. Livingston and her husband Callum. Gayle Livingston, a thirty-eight-year-old mid-level fire witch, looked amazing tonight. Gone were the flare cut drawstring pants and matching front snap tunics she wore as a uniform, her red hair pulled back in a tight ponytail, green eyes serious yet beautiful.

She smiled at Gayle, who waved back. Tonight, those beautiful emerald eyes of hers were just as stunning, but they gleamed with amusement and relaxation. Red tresses fell in curls to her shoulders and makeup covered the freckles Sanura knew dotted the landscape of Gayle's nose. But it was the dress, more than anything else that had Sanura nearly failing to recognize the woman when she'd approached her, wishing Sanura a happy birthday.

A metallic accordion dress with V-neck, spaghetti straps, open back with crisscross straps, and an empire waist revealed all that her cabernet tunic and pants hid. Gayle Livingston, an unassuming house-keeper by day, was model gorgeous. No wonder her husband, her mate, stayed by her side, a barely-repressed snarl for any man who ventured too close. Except for Omar, who seemed unmoved by Gayle's attractiveness.

Next to the table where Omar and the Livingstons talked was Makena, Anna Spencer, and Barbara Vaughn. Every now and again, the priestesses would whisper to each other and then glance in Asse-fa's direction.

Sanura didn't like it. Didn't like the priestesses' odd fascination with Assefa, who was across the room in conversation with his uncle, Zareb, Mike, and Eric. She did, however, appreciate Assefa's effort to befriend Mike and Eric, inviting them to his home and introducing the men to his friends and family. Sam's death had not only cost Sanura a father and Makena a husband but Mike a best friend. Life didn't hand out too many of those in a dwarf's lifetime. But watching her godfa-ther now, surrounded by men of character, she could sense his happiness.

"Assefa has nailed the groom look." Rachel waved her small hand in front of Sanura's face. "Are you listening to us, or have you zoned out again?"

"No, I'm listening, and Assefa and I aren't engaged."

"I find that hard to believe," Cynthia said. "But I'm sure he'll change that before the night's up. It's your birthday, he's dressed to get down on one knee, and you're a sucker for romance. Besides, I'll bet you a hundred bucks he has a ring in that pocket he's been worrying since I've gotten here."

Both Sanura's and Rachel's head snapped in Assefa's direction. His right hand was in his robe pocket, which wasn't unusual for a man when he wore a mbubb.

"He's just standing there talking, Cyn," Rachel said, sounding bored. "I think you're reading too much into a normal physical act. Men never know what to do with their hands. Having pockets solves their problem."

While Sanura agreed with Rachel's overall point, Assefa wasn't the nervous type. He didn't need pockets or anything else to make him feel comfortable around others and in his own skin. And now that she was carefully looking, something in his pocket did seem to have Assefa's attention. But that didn't mean it was an engagement ring.

Did it?

"You're wrong, Rach. Assefa has that look on his face that all men get when they're about to pop the question and aren't quite sure what they're about to get themselves into."

"I don't know. I've only just met the man." Rachel sipped from her champagne flute and glanced around the tent. "Where's the closest bathroom, Sanura?"

Sanura had an idea. But first she needed to find … there, reentering the tent was the person she was looking for, as handsome as ever.

"If I arrange for someone to escort you to the house and back, do you promise to be nice?"

"I'm always nice."

Cynthia paused, drink halfway to her mouth. "You're a damn lie. And you tell them with a straight face and big doe eyes."

"Don't get her riled up. She probably has a bag full of stress balls under her dress."

"What in the hell are you talking about?"

"Never mind. I'll tell you later. Anyway, back to you. I have someone who would be more than happy to take you to the first floor of the house and point you in the direction of the guest bathroom."

"Let me guess, that Manute guy you mentioned the other day?"

"Someone say my name?"

Rachel turned, then, because she was short and seated and Manute tall and standing, had to look way up.

Hair as wild and sexy as ever, beard full but nicely trimmed, Manute stared down at Rachel, who, Sanura was sure, didn't know her mouth hung open like one of those one-dollar bill wielding women at strip clubs. The were-cat wore a slim-fit light-brown suit, a white tailored-fit V-neck shirt, and a stylish pair of brown leather loafers with no socks.

"Manute, this is my friend Rachel. Do you think you could take her into the house and show her the guest bathroom?"

"But, but, you can show me, Sanura. And Cyn can come with us."

"It's her birthday, Rach. Do you really want to pull Sanura away from her guests just to walk with you to the bathroom? We aren't in college, and this isn't a frat party. We don't need to go to the bathroom as a group."

The look Rachel shot Cynthia promised brutal retribution. But the woman was polite, at least in public and with a gorgeous male waiting for her. Manute's wink and thankful smile to Sanura told her he knew she was playing matchmaker and didn't mind.

Grudgingly, Rachel got to her feet and followed Manute. Who, smart man, gave the skittish witch plenty of space.

Cynthia snorted a laugh. "Gods, she's going to be spitting mad when she gets back here."

"I know, but it'll be worth it if they hit it off. Manute's great. If he weren't, I wouldn't have done that to her. Besides, if Rachel didn't feel comfortable with the situation, she would've refused, knowing we would support her."

"Yeah, I know. But tell me one thing, Sanura, who's the big guy in the gray suit speaking to my husband?"

Sanura didn't have to look to know who Cynthia was referring to.

"That's Zareb. He's Assefa's FBI partner."

"Oh, that's him. He was never around the other times I visited." Cynthia drank more of her champagne and shrugged. "I was just wondering."

"If I didn't know you so well, I would say you sound interested."

"Don't be ridiculous, I'm married."

She wasn't being ridiculous, and Cynthia, despite her words, kept glancing to her left and at Zareb.

Sanura reached over and pulled one of Cynthia's locks.

"Oww, what in the hell did you do that for?"

"I know Zareb's eye candy, but if you keep staring at him like that Eric's going to notice."

Sanura didn't get it. Okay, yes, Zareb was literally tall, dark, and handsome. Still, she'd never known her friend to take an interest in any other man since she and Eric became mates and tied the knot. And the way she kept stealing glances at the were-cat, Cynthia definitely liked what she saw.

"I get this weird feeling every time I look at him. I felt it when we crossed paths on the lawn."

"What kind of weird feeling?"

"I don't know, but it's nothing like I've ever felt before. I feel bad for even saying it. I know how it must sound to you, and it sounds even worse to me."

"It sounds like you're attracted to Zareb."

She rolled her eyes. "No, that's not it." Cynthia finished off her drink, then stared at the empty glass as if more bubbly would miraculously appear. "Don't get me wrong, he's hot as hell. I would be lying my ass off if I didn't admit that much." She sighed, toying with the stem of the glass. "Just forget I said anything, okay?"

"Ah, yeah, sure."

Sanura looked toward the group of men again. This time, however, Zareb was staring at Cyn over Eric's shoulder and Assefa was gone.

CHAPTER FOURTEEN

For what felt like the thousandth time, Assefa slid his hand into the pocket of his mbubb and wrapped fingers around the soft velvet box. He had everything planned, down to tonight's proposal. What he hadn't planned for, however, was Sanura's secret. No man could prepare for what she'd told him. It changed nothing and everything between them. Assefa still loved and wanted Sanura, but the future he'd envisioned would never happen now.

Sanura didn't understand. With each passing day, the residual energy from her father's cat spirit, now that it was awake, would become more and more a part of the fire witch. Until it was as much a part of her as her fire spirit, no matter the unnatural nature of a witch harboring a cat spirit. She thought she would one day come to terms with her father's passing and be able to let his cat spirit go. Whether from an unlikely spell that would allow her to transfer the jaguar spirit from herself and into Makena or by accepting Assefa's bite.

But Assefa knew the truth. Without knowing or even trying, Sanura would bond with the jaguar spirit, and the spirit would love and protect his witch, forming an unbreakable trinity. Assefa's Mngwa would be forever on the outside because his rightful place no longer existed. So no, there would be no chance of a complete mate bond between the two of them.

Soon, she would comprehend what he already knew, just as he would one day accept the truth. They couldn't go on like this, living under the same roof without a full mate claim. That wasn't the nature of witch-were-cat relationships, especially when they loved each other. But such bonds went beyond love.

Need. Fulfillment. Hunger. His Mngwa hungered for his mate, his fire spirit. A bone-deep need that grew with each passing day, followed by a soul-wrenching pain when his need went unrealized.

Witches didn't understand. And marrying Sanura, as if they were full-humans, would solve nothing. Marriage would only complicate matters when the inevitable happened and she moved out.

Assefa let the velvet box go and removed his hand from his pocket.

"You didn't have to follow me."

Assefa turned to see his uncle walking toward him. Long strides ate up the distance between them until Ulan stood in front of Assefa.

"Sanura is looking for you."

Using his preternatural sight, Ulan swept the expanse of land surrounding them. Assefa had walked to the edge of his property, pending darkness and trees hiding his retreat from all. Well, all except for his uncle and Chief of the Preternatural Division of the FBI.

"Who are you looking for?"

"I'm just checking, Assefa, in case you missed something."

"Do I ever miss anything?"

"There's a first time for everything. And we're all fallible." Ulan loosened his tie and leaned his back against the tree opposite from where Assefa stood. "So, do you want to tell me what's going on here?"

"About the alpha who came to my home or why I'm out here alone instead of back at the tent with Sanura?"

An afraid and unsmiling Rashad had come loping into the tent, eyes searching the area and finding Assefa staring at him. He'd approached the young man although it was clear Assefa hadn't been the one Rashad sought. In the end, Assefa learned what had put the leopard in an uncharacteristic mood.

"All of the above, I guess."

Assefa looked at his uncle, seeing so much of his father in Ulan's strong gaze. Which only made sense, since Ulan and Jahi Berber were twins. Not identical, but the physical resemblance was strong enough that Assefa had to remind himself it was his uncle to whom he spoke and not to his father.

"Let's start with an easier question, nephew."

That was good because Assefa hadn't decided if he would get into those other topics with his uncle. He would, eventually, but he didn't want to tonight.

"How long has it been since Makena's mate passed away?"

That question gave Assefa pause. Not because he didn't know the answer. He did. But because of the fake nonchalance he heard in the older man's voice. Nonchalance mixed with masculine interest.

"Why?"

"Don't sound so defensive. I'm not a big bad wolf who intends to gobble up your mate's mother. Makena Williams is a beautiful woman. I may be turning sixty in so many weeks, but I'm still a man, Assefa."

A man who'd buried a mate and wife, just as Makena had buried a mate and husband. That alone gave Ulan and Makena one point of commonality. If he bothered to think on it, Assefa could probably come up with others. But he didn't want to think about his girlfriend's mother and his uncle. Not now, not ever.

"Three years."

Ulan nodded. "She's probably not ready yet. I know I wasn't three years after your aunt's death."

The death of Ulan's mate had sent the man fleeing his family and country, accepting an offer to head a secret division of the FBI. A division that gave power and legitimacy to the agents who tracked and killed preternatural dangers to society. Preternaturals existed in every facet of full-human society, running corporations, institutions of higher education, and local, state, and national governments.

And they liked their secrets. Liked their safe lifestyles. So by protecting full-humans from all things that went bump in the night, they also protected themselves. No game of *Truth or Dare* for the people who maintained the veil of the Preternatural Division of the FBI. Chaos, fear, bloodshed, and war likely results, if full-humans learned the truth.

Well, some did know. How could none not? But those individuals were few and rare. And if they were very lucky, they wouldn't awaken one night to find a witch in their bedroom, a memory wipe spell on her lips. Months, maybe years, taken from them in a whisper of witch magic.

"And you're ready now, Uncle Ulan?"

"If it's with the right witch, I am. I'll tell you something, Assefa, it's no fun growing old alone."

For the first time in a long time, Ulan sounded like a grieving widower. Assefa remembered the shell of a were-cat who'd locked himself in his house for a month after his mate's funeral. Not even his twin could get Ulan out of the house. But he'd endured, as all Berbers did, no matter the temptation to wallow and give in to the pain and heartache.

Something akin to how Assefa suspected he would feel once things with Sanura came to a heart-rending end.

"And you think Makena is the right witch for you?"

Ulan reached up and removed his tie, stuffing it in his pants pocket. "I don't know. But I'd sure like to find out. Tonight is only the second time we've been around each other. And we've only had brief conversations, mainly about you and Sanura. She's someone I would like to get to know better." Ulan chuckled and shook his head. "You should see your face, your eyes. They aren't even glowing Mngwa gold, but I can see the deadly warning in them." Ulan pushed away from the tree. "She's the mother of your mate, it's only right that you would want to protect her. But Berber men love well and true."

"Berber men are also violent and possessive."

"That we are. But not only those things. Makena Williams, if you haven't noticed, is a powerful witch who can take care of herself. She'd never be attracted to a were-cat not her equal, no more than she would accept one into her life, bed, and heart who mistreated her."

Assefa knew all those things. Unfortunately, he couldn't fault Ulan his interest. Makena would catch most men's eye, were-cat and full-human. Beautiful yes, but also witty, smart, loyal, fierce, and so many other traits that made Makena a wonderful person, friend, judge, and mother.

"I'm a patient man, however. Yet another Berber trait. I can wait until she's ready. There's no rush. She'll choose me eventually."

"Arrogance, another Berber trait."

Ulan smiled, gleaming white teeth and masculine pride. "Yes, Berbers are an arrogant people. But, in this case, I like to think of myself as confident, hopeful. She's a fire witch, after all, and fire witches can be unpredictable, stubborn, and feisty. In all the best ways, mind you."

Something else Assefa knew. Ulan could be right. One day, Makena would be ready to see what the world had to offer her beyond the love of Samuel Williams. When she reached that point in her life, the woman would find no shortage of suitors lining up to impress her. Arrogance and confidence aside, Ulan may be in for an uphill battle if he wanted to win the heart of the witch.

But those were his uncle's future woman's troubles. Assefa had his current woman's troubles to contend with. And no amount of brooding would change anything.

"I need to return to the party before I worry Sanura any more than I'm sure I already have."

With Ulan beside him, Assefa strolled away from the trees and toward the white tent. The laid-back harmonies of cool jazz floated on the muggy evening air, drawing him closer to the woman he loved but couldn't have completely.

"Once you know why that alpha singled you out, give me a call."

"I will."

But not before he confronted the man. Otherwise, Ulan just might deem the alpha too dangerous to live. If his uncle hoped to have any chance with Makena, he'd have to show the fire witch he wasn't a brute. Which meant curbing his baser Berber instinct and not murdering a member of her Sankofa family simply because the man didn't know any better than to threaten Ulan's relative.

"One of these days, nephew, you'll have to accept the truth you've been running from your entire life."

Fifty feet from the tent, they stopped. Ulan pulled his red-and-black tie from his pants pocket and put it back on. He also straightened an impeccable suit jacket, laid down nonexistent wrinkles in his shirt, and swiped his handkerchief over black leather shoes Assefa could see his reflection in. In essence, the were-cat was primping for a woman who barely registered his existence. Sekhmet help the old jaguar, Ulan had it bad. And poor Makena wouldn't know what hit her.

"How do I look, Alpha? Good enough to woo a fire witch out of mourning?"

Ulan, the strongest were-cat he knew, besides his father, had just paid him the greatest compliment one were-cat could extend to another. But the word, the ultimate title in the were-cat hierarchical community, choked like a leaden noose around his neck.

Ulan had spoken deliberately, as he always did. But Assefa would not be moved on this issue. He'd told his uncle a hundred times before. No need to repeat the same tonight.

"I thought you said you would wait until Makena was ready."

They resumed their walk, a leisurely pace that allowed them to speak in private without feeling rushed to finish before they reached the tent.

"I did, and I am. But that doesn't mean I can't ask a beautiful woman to dance, does it?"

"I think Mike may have something to say about that?"

"The Baltimore City detective? Are you telling me the two of them …?"

Assefa shook his head, blocking out the disturbing image Ulan's question had evoked. Gods, Assefa didn't want to even think about the kind of woman who could survive being in a relationship with Mike McKutchen without succumbing to madness, murder, or both.

"Nothing like that. But he's her self-proclaimed guardian."

"You mean her watchdog."

"Same difference. He loves her like a sister, so tread cautiously."

Ulan smiled. A handsome devil in black-and-red. "Thank you for the advice. But I have everything under control."

"Berber confidence again?"

Strolling with purpose to the tent, Ulan left Assefa standing where he was. "No, nephew, that was unadulterated Berber arrogance."

Assefa shook his head again and then went in search of his own witch. Uncle Ulan had the right idea. Dancing was in order.

****

Sanura glanced around the tent, champagne flute in hand, and a smile on her face. From her spot in the back of the tent, near the champagne fountain, she could see all the people who'd gathered to celebrate her birthday. A minute ago, a suave Ulan had sauntered up to the table of priestesses, said something to Makena in low tones, and offered her his hand. After a clear pause of surprise, Makena accepted the offer with stately grace. Now they were on the dance floor, Ulan's deep-set brown eyes staring at Makena with what could only be called were-cat attraction. Makena, on the other hand, returned Ulan's gaze with polite neutrality.

She finished the last of her champagne, unsure how she felt about Ulan's open admiration for her mother. The psychologist and adult Sanura accepted and understood Makena would one day find someone other than Sam to love. This same part of Sanura also recognized that a part of her mother had died with Sam. But what was left of Makena, a vibrant woman with needs and wants, had, hopefully, decades left to her. Would she live them alone, or find someone to share them with, a chosen mate with whom she could create new and different memories?

Yet Sanura's inner spoiled child glared at Ulan. A temper tantrum brewed in her belly, screaming at the were-cat that he could not have her mother, that she belonged to someone else.

Yet Makena didn't.

Not anymore.

Sanura watched Ulan and Makena dance, the were-cat, naturally, light on his feet. He spun Makena in circles, heedless of the other dancers, who, as if choreographed, shifted and swayed and placing them just out of their way.

Her gut tightened and the residual jaguar energy within Sanura began to whine. The pain was a possessive, jealous response to what Sanura watched, Makena smiling and laughing while in the arms of a man not her mate.

She turned away from the dancing couple, unsure what to do with the knowledge that her father's spirit was still attuned to Makena. That shouldn't be possible. Should it? Dammit, all of this was unprecedented. Under such strange circumstances, Sanura had no idea what constituted normal or abnormal, no less possible or impossible.

She placed the champagne flute on the drink table and then closed her eyes. A relieved smile tugged her lips upward. When large, strong arms came up to wrap around her waist, she relaxed against him, allowing Assefa's more powerful magic to calm the jaguar and the woman.

He kissed her cheek, rocked her in tune to the music, and said nothing at all. Sanura sank deeper into his embrace, grateful he'd returned to her side.

Hands lowered to hips, leading her into a sensual dance, nothing like what Sanura watched the other dancers doing, least of all Makena and Ulan. Sanura placed her hands over Assefa's, twining her fingers through his and swaying against his hard, sturdy body as Clea Bujeau sang a ballad about lost and found love.

It felt so good to be held by Assefa, especially after the scare he'd given her when he'd slipped from the tent, telling no one where he was going or when he would return. Irrational panic had threatened, settling in deeper the more people Sanura had spoken to, none having seen her beloved. Yet it had been Ulan, the man twirling her mother around the dance floor, who'd come to her rescue. "I'll find and bring him back. No worries, Sanura. No worries," he'd assured her.

"Ulan is a good man," Assefa whispered in her ear. A hand crept from her hip and to her side. "You can trust him with your mother. He only wants to get to know Makena better. It's just a dance. Nothing more."

The whining jaguar inside her disagreed.

"Her heart is still healing. Mom still loves her husband. Mourns him."

"I know. And I told Ulan the same. But Makena won't always be in mourning, Sanura. Eventually, she'll raise her head and realize how many men have been waiting for her to be ready, to see them as suitors, as men worth getting to know."

Sanura didn't respond, but she did turn in Assefa's arms, their bodies still moving to the rhythmic pulse of the music. Arms around his neck, Sanura pressed her body close to his, closer than she should've, considering they weren't alone. A quick look around the tent, however, revealed no shocked eyes or gasps. In fact, no one seemed to be paying them any attention, except for Anna and Barbara, whose assessing eyes strayed to them more often than Sanura liked. Sanura really wanted to know what in the hell the priestesses wanted to speak to her and Assefa about.

But the meeting with the Council was hours away, and Sanura not yet ready to relinquish hold of this magnificent birthday. No less the man rubbing his hands up and down her back, sending frissons of desire through her. His hips gyrated against hers, a slow sensual dance best done in the privacy of their bedchamber.

"How much longer before this party ends?"

Sanura laughed. Her special agent sounded charmingly grumpy and uncharacteristically impatient.

"I don't know. You're the one who made all of the arrangements."

He growled. "Dammit. There's still the cake and the opening of presents." A kiss to her neck. "Do you think anyone would notice if you weren't around when the cake Omar made for you was rolled out?"

At this bit of dessert news, Sanura forgot all about Ulan and Makena, her taste buds anticipating sugary goodness. "Omar made me a cake? What kind of cake?"

A kiss to the other side her neck. "I'm close to debauching you in public and all you can think about is your birthday cake."

"I like cake. And I love Omar's desserts. And you have too much class and respect to do more to me in public than what we've just done." She pressed a quick kiss to his lips "So, what kind of cake?"

"One of these days, Sanura, I'm going to surprise you."

Oh, but the man had already done that. Today being one Assefa surprise after another. All wonderful. All unexpected.

But he didn't answer her question. Assefa didn't have to because a minute later a server came through the door, pushing a silver cart on which sat a four tier all-white cake. A red edible bow was wrapped around the second tier, its ties falling onto the third tier. On a corner of the base tier were three red gardenias with a decorative jewel in the center of each flower. And on the top tier was the motif Rachel had mentioned—a white gardenia surrounded by a ring of fire in the shape of an S.

Assefa kissed her cheek and wiped away a teardrop. "Strawberry shortcake. Your favorite."

It was her favorite and the cake was absolutely stunning. Sanura had never seen such an elegant cake. While her guests huddled around the table the cake was being placed on, Sanura lifted loving yet sad eyes to Assefa.

His eyes fell to her. A mirror of her emotions reflected back at her.

She reached out, her fingers finding his mbubb. They traveled from his chest and down to the garment's pocket. When she reached what was inside, she stopped.

Their eyes held, and Assefa didn't try to stop her when she explored the shape and size of the item in his pocket. The same pocket she'd seen his hand in, repeatedly, right before he'd disappeared for thirty minutes.

Assefa kissed her forehead, regret and disappointment contaminating their partial mate bond. "I wanted to give you a sneak peek into what our wedding could be like. When I planned all of this, I didn't know about your father. And once I did know, it was too late to change the theme."

Gods, was that her heart breaking? Or had razor-sharp Vulture talons pierced her chest and ripped the organ clean out?

"I didn't want it to be like this, Sanura." Assefa looked at the outfit he wore. "I should've worn a suit today. Anything other than this ceremonial mbubb."

A mbubb, she knew, he would've had specially made for this occasion. The day he intended to propose to Sanura, probably in front of their family and friends.

Yet there they stood, staring at each other, their hearts in their eyes while clamoring guests waited for them so they could wish Sanura a happy birthday and cut into the beautiful cake.

Sanura dropped her hand away from the engagement ring Assefa had no intention of giving her tonight. Perhaps never. He didn't want to marry her. He had, but no longer. Her truth and guilt had done this, denied Sanura a husband and Assefa a wife and mate.

"I'm sorry," they said in unison, an apology to themselves as much as it was to each other.

Assefa took her hand and walked Sanura toward the smiling crowd and her birthday cake. The S was now lit and glowed with brightness and symbolic hope. Brightness and hope, both were missing from Sanura's ravaged heart.

She plastered on a fake smile, clapped when everyone sang "Happy Birthday," and blew out her red-and-white candles, making a wish she prayed would come true but feared wouldn't.

Two hours later, after she'd been trampled under a ton of birthday hugs and kisses, stuffed with delicious strawberry shortcake, and forced to open one present after another, she'd waved goodbye and sent her family and friends home with a, "Drive safely and thank you for coming."

Now she sat at the foot of her bed, sandals, jewelry, and makeup off. Assefa's birthday dress was draped on the bed beside her, Sanura in a white charmeuse gown with diamond cut lace neckline and low cut ribbon tie back.

The chamber, lit only by the white candles Sanura had placed around the room—windowsills, nightstands, dressers—produced a warm, romantic radiance. A sensual, expectant glow that, like tonight's party, could have been another sneak peek into a future that would never be—Sanura and Assefa's wedding night.

Sanura dropped her head into her hands and let the tears she'd held inside these past two hours fall. Today, the twenty-ninth year of her birth, had been the best and worst birthday ever. She'd experienced extreme highs and one crushing, unforgettable low.

Laughter.

Tears.

Love.

Heartbreak.

Bonds strengthened yet frayed by the truth. An assault on the heart, an unraveling of the soul. A man's nature laid bare. A woman's confliction made manifest.

Liquid sadness and crimson heat streamed out of Sanura in wild spirals of fire witch magic. Shoulders heaved. Eyes reddened. Head ached. And heart slowed to a painful throb of lost opportunity and guilty need.

CHAPTER FIFTEEN

Realm of the Gods

Mami Wata cackled, malevolent eyes staring through her scrying glass and to the human realm.

"You are a bleeding heart fool, Oya. I can barely countenance your presence in this room, so great is your stupidity." Mami Wata turned cold, contemptuous eyes to Oya, yet another Titanoboa around her neck. Its long tongue slithered out and scented the air. "That fire witch is as weak as your other champions. She is unworthy of Ra's grand scheme. This you must see. Ascension is beyond her. You and your consort have weakened the witch. No favors did you do the child."

Oya, who had used her own scrying glass to watch over her fire witch, reclined on her plush bench and ignored her sister. She had learned long ago to not argue with the goddess, especially when Mami Wata thought herself cunning and above reproach.

No, telling rarely impacted the intractable mind of a god. Showing. Yes, showing was a more effective killer of a god's pride and ebullience. Still, Mami Wata spoke the truth. Oya and Sàngó, in their fervor to win, to free Oya, and to reunite forever, had indeed done the fire witch and cat of legend a disservice. But she refused to believe Sàngó's blessing and her mate claim spell had weakened her champions. Adversity made mortals stronger. And there was no greater adversity than that of threatened bonds of the heart.

Mami Wata, the blind and misguided creature that she was, mistook Sanura's tears for fragility. Yet Oya perceived the truth, even if Mami Wata could not. *I need her tears, her human heart if she is to defeat the water witch of legend, ascend, and free me. The alternative to a fire witch's tears...* Well, Oya knew what happened when a fire witch of legend was driven to madness and blazing anger. *Inferno and death.*

Unfortunately, she had witnessed the devastation before, lands and people engulfed in destructive flames of uncontainable fire witch of legend magic. Taking a slow, deep breath, Oya ignored the encroaching memories of burnt bodies, fire-ravaged kingdoms, and Ra's growl of, "Another failure."

With an arrogant arch of a brow, Oya gave nothing away when she spoke. As long as Sanura could cry, then she would survive, endure, and not devolve into a destructive fireball of hate and vengeance. *Like her sisters before her.* "Through flames, tears, and doubt, like a Phoenix, they will rise. Once they do, once my fire witch ascends, she will be unstoppable."

"I think not."

"Think what you will. But witness their indomitable spirit with your distrustful eyes." Oya pointed to the scrying glass in Mami Wata's hand. "Look for yourself, sister. Love, strength, and compassion. Sekhmet's cat of legend is unrivaled. You think you can break his spirit. I vow, he will break yours before this masquerade of a prophecy is over."

With a hiss that matched her scaly beast's, Mami Wata scowled into her scrying glass.

Oya smiled, but not with true happiness. She comprehended, all too well, the ache of a heart that loved but also betrayed. More pain awaited, over the horizon for Sanura and Assefa. From which, she could not shield them. But they would endure, survive. Not because they knew not fear, but because they had faith.

In their family.

In their friends.

In themselves.

In each other.

****

Assefa hated when Sanura cried. Worse, he despised his inability to heal her heart and take away her sorrow. If he could, he would. But how could he stand between Sanura and her grief when Assefa didn't even have the cure for what ailed him? All he had to offer her was his love and nearness.

No reassurances that all would work out in due time. No promises of a happily-ever-after. And no romantic gestures meant to assuage her heart.

Assefa knelt in front of a weeping Sanura. One hand went to the back of her head and pulled her forward. She went, wrapping her arms around his neck and burying her wet face against his bare shoulder. In silence, he held her. Her soft whimpers were the only sound in the room.

Sometimes, like tonight, Assefa wished he could release his worries and pain through the shedding of therapeutic tears. Maybe even yelling, screaming, and destroying tables and chairs would work equally as well. But Assefa was a Berber. And Berber men didn't shed pointless tears, throw inconsequential temper tantrums, or act out in a fit of uncontrollable anger. Yet, as a kid, and even as a young man, he'd done all three, but to no avail. Which was why, as a man one year away from his thirtieth birthday, Assefa could comfort the woman he loved, the woman he adored, without breaking down in front of her, even though his pain was no less deep, no less gut-churning than Sanura's.

He lifted her off the foot of the bed. By the time he settled them in the middle of the bed, she no longer wept.

"Here, wipe your face." He handed her tissues from the box on his nightstand. "That's it. You're almost done."

They reclined on their sides facing each other, Assefa in nothing but a pair of black boxers and Sanura in a sexy as sin lingerie he'd never seen before. He ran a curious finger over the lace neckline. "This is new. Did you buy it for me, for tonight?"

"Yes."

It was a sad, soft response that should've brought out the protective, gentleman in him. Instead, Sanura's sensual vulnerability aroused the man and the cat. His exploring finger dipped below the hollow of her neck, circling the tender flesh there and then going lower to the V between her luscious breasts.

Sanura sucked in a breath, licked her lips, and moaned with pleasure when his hand rescued a breast from the tight gown and took it into his mouth.

He sucked, savoring her ripe nipple with lips and covetous tongue. He'd wanted to do this all day, desiring nothing more than to have Sanura in their bed and at his mercy.

With a deft hand, he unclasped the tie that held the lingerie around her neck, all the while eating greedily from her engorged nipple. She shifted onto her back.

And Assefa took advantage.

Down the lacy temptation went, over breasts, hips, legs, and onto the floor. Sanura wore nothing but a scrap of white silk underneath, a mouth-watering thong with a single upside down red rose. The stem began at the top of the panty, ending with the fully opened petals at the mouth of Sanura's sex.

Assefa's Mngwa purred. He reached for the rose, but Sanura stopped him. Holding onto his wrist, green eyes stared up at him with longing and love.

"What if I asked you?" She sat up, glorious breasts bare and so very distracting. "What if I proposed? Would that make a difference?"

Assefa plopped onto his back, one leg bent and up while the other lay flat beside Sanura. He watched her and detested what he saw.

Desperation

Distress.

Doubt.

"It's about balance and fairness, Sanura, not whether I want to marry you or not."

"I don't understand."

Of course she didn't, because she and her fire spirit had yet to achieve equilibrium.

"I could marry you next week and be very happy. While marriage may be enough for my human side, only a full mate claim can satisfy my cat spirit. I can't take you as my wife, Sanura, and leave my Mngwa to suffer alone without his fire spirit, his mate. We are one, but we are also two. As much as I want you, I can't break the bond with my inner spirit. I've worked too hard to build it and fought and bled to earn his trust and respect. I thought I could. I thought I could propose and pretend the mate claim didn't matter as long as I made you my wife."

Eyes lowered. Shoulders slumped.

Deflated.

He'd worked so hard to give Sanura a perfect birthday. But in the end, he'd screwed it up. Honesty cut like a double-edged sword. And no witch wanted to hear how her man loved her but had no intention of marrying her out of a sense of loyalty to his cat spirit. No more than he'd relished hearing her tell him she couldn't accept his claiming bite, despite being in love with him.

Well, weren't they a pair of star-crossed lovers.

Sanura straddled his waist, forcing Assefa to lower his bent leg. Hands going to the mattress on each side of his head, his witch hovered over him, her gardenia scent tickling his senses.

"Don't give up on us, on me."

"I haven't."

She kissed the tip of his nose. "Pinocchio."

It wasn't a complete lie. But yes, a part of Assefa, the practical side of him read all the signs and had reached the only logical conclusion. He and Sanura couldn't last, wouldn't last. The only unknown in the equation was when it would end.

"Will you fight for me, Assefa?"

"What do you mean?"

Sanura sat back up. Her eyes, for the first time tonight, glistened with challenge. The same competitive challenge he'd seen in them when they'd played *Truth or Dare for Lovers*.

"I mean I'm willing to fight for you, for us. Even if that means fighting myself. My grief. My guilt. My fear. What I want to know is if you're willing to fight for me? Even if that means fighting yourself. Your stubbornness. Your pride. Your fear." Sanura smacked him on the chest. "For once, Assefa, fight with me. Argue. Curse. Break shit you'll regret destroying later. And trust, gods trust that I can handle a pissed-off special agent who can turn into a dumpster-sized cat."

"You don't know what you're saying, what you're asking of me."

Another smack to his chest. "I know because I have the same fear. But you're better than me, Assefa. My fire spirit and I are so far from being in sync it's not funny. That's not the case with you and your cat spirit. You've mastered your inner spirit in all the ways I haven't. Yet you still don't trust yourself fully."

"That's because I'm dangerous."

"I know. But not always. Not with everyone. And not under any circumstance. Judgment, my love. Yours is impeccable."

Assefa's fingers began to skim Sanura's thighs, not to arouse, but an unconscious need to touch, to feel the silky-softness of her skin under his calloused hands.

"I don't argue, Sanura, especially with women. I may disagree, but I don't like to argue."

"You prefer to walk away and hold it in. You think that's taking the high road, but it isn't. It's called running, Assefa. And you're bigger than that."

"I'm sure there was an insult somewhere in that psychological assessment of yours. The word *coward* implied but smartly left unsaid."

The idea of fighting with Sanura, the way she wanted him to, set off all his warning bells. As a child and teenager, Assefa had done nothing but fight. His brother. His classmates. Himself. He was no stranger to the ugliness that came from expressing his bone-deep emotions, especially his pain. His fights had never boded well for anyone, not even for Assefa.

And there Sanura sat, virtually begging him to go against every ounce of common sense he possessed. She wanted him to fight. Himself. And her. Could he do it? Could he fight for her the way she requested?

He would fight to protect her. Hell, he would kill to protect her. He'd demonstrated that already when he'd slaughtered two murdering adzes who preyed on witches. But protection, for a Berber, for his Mngwa, was easy. What Sanura asked of him was much more difficult to do. Because if it went wrong, Assefa could hurt her. The way he had Razi.

"Come back down here."

She did, lowering herself onto his chest.

Hands went to her hair and plucked out all the pins. Red-gold curls fell onto Sanura's shoulders and Assefa's hairless chest. Gods but the woman was so damn beautiful, even more so without clothing, makeup, or her moonstone.

He should deny her. It was after midnight and no longer her birthday. Her day of pampering had ended an hour ago, and he'd done enough spoiling to last her a good long while. Still, she'd said she'd also fight for him. An enticing offer no other woman had ever made. Assefa couldn't help but be touched and intrigued.

Women had fought for his money, for trinkets of affection, for trips to exotic locales, but none had ever fought for him. The man.

What would it feel like to have this woman, this stubborn, impatient fire witch to fight for him? Surely, with Sanura's unstable relationship with her fire spirit, the thought had to frighten her as much as it concerned him. Yet she'd made the proposal, the challenge. How could he say no?

Tender, exploring lips found his collarbone and kissed. "I want you." His neck. Kiss. "Your heart." His cheek. Kiss. "Your faith." His chin. Kiss. "Your body." His lips. Kiss. "I want all of you, including your claiming bite."

They kissed, Sanura crushing her breasts and pebbled nipples into his chest. Her pelvis pushed forward, rubbing her rose-covered sex against his throbbing and very hard erection.

"You made me wait all day to have you."

"Well, you can have me now my impatient witch." Assefa's big, bold hands found the cheeks of her bare ass. The wonderful thong gave him easy access to her desirable backside, and he couldn't help but take advantage. "You feel good in my hands, on top of my body. And don't doubt that I want you just as much."

He slipped his right middle finger between the cheeks of her bottom, while using his left hand to hold the thin string to the side and out of his way. Assefa placed his finger over top of her anus, paused, and waited.

Sanura's head lifted from his shoulder, eyes so very green with trepidation but also with sexual curiosity.

Assefa rubbed the spot. He had no intention of penetrating her there tonight, not even with the tip of his finger. But it was virginal territory he couldn't wait to explore.

"Kiss me again."

She hesitated.

"Put your juicy lips on me. And your tongue in my mouth. I want to taste you. I want your refined flavoring on my lips, in my mouth, and coating my tongue. Now kiss me, Sanura."

She grinned. "You're being wicked tonight."

He was. But the witch had no clue how wicked he could be. "You want me to fight for you, with you, then be prepared to experience me in all my Berber wickedness. Know what you've asked of me. Because once I'm all in, I'm in, sweetheart. And I'll do whatever it takes to win, to defeat all who oppose me."

She shuddered, but not from revulsion. The woman, the crazy fire witch that she was, actually found his intense, fierce confession arousing. Her excited magic and lustful scent stirred between them, and Sanura's eyes began to glow a faint red.

She kissed him. Hard. Pushing past his lips and teeth with her forceful tongue, she controlled the tempo and heat rating of the kiss. Which, damn, was set to scorching hot, so ardently did she claim his mouth, winning their duel of tongues with erotic ease.

He flipped her onto her back, Sanura's eyes going wide with surprise. But there was no protest from his witch, just an appreciative gaze when he stood and discarded his boxers. She stared at him, at his thick and ready dick, her scent of arousal growing stronger the longer she watched him.

Assefa touched himself, taking his manhood in his hand and stroking—from base to tip and back again. Up and down. Up and down. Up and down. If possible, he grew even harder, even longer under her admiring, heated gaze.

"Like what you see?" He climbed back onto the bed.

She lifted flattering eyes to his. "Always." Sanura started to shimmy out of her thong, but Assefa stopped her.

"Not yet."

Crawling between her parted thighs, Assefa spent focused minutes worshipping her globes of wonder.

Sucking.

Kissing.

Biting.

Palming.

Planting open-mouthed kisses on her flat stomach, Assefa didn't stop until he reached the red rose. He kissed there, too, giving her silk-covered mound a long tongue kiss.

Sanura moaned, as he knew she would, as she always did when he pleasured her in this way.

He kissed her again, running his lips and tongue up and down her sex, reveling in the way her body responded to his touch. Her sex wet and ready. Her moans guttural and needy. Her hips insistent and mobile.

For his mouth. His tongue.

He thought of using a claw to cut the thong off her but decided against it. The panty was sexy and he wanted to see Sanura in it again. So he caged his beastly urge and stripped the thong off her without destroying the barely-there material.

Then he resettled between her legs and went to work.

Kissing her thighs.

Laving her folds.

Sucking her clitoris.

His mouth dipped lower. Tongue peeked out and rimmed her anus.

Sanura squeaked her surprise, going up on elbows and staring down at him.

Assefa ignored her and did it again. Licking and kissing the tender flesh with his wide, flat tongue, he moved around the anus before switching to an up and down oral stimulation.

Breaths coming in short pants, she tried to watch him, which was impossible since he'd pushed her knees to her chest and she lay in a missionary position, ass up and on glorious display.

"That's so nasty," she murmured, which would have caused him to stop if it hadn't been followed by, "but it feels soooo damn good."

Sanura had showered less than an hour ago, was disease free, and had no other lover. Assefa could do this for her. The only woman he would ever consider engaging in anilingus with was Sanura. And he so did like the way she moaned and clenched whenever he hit her sweet spot.

He used Sanura's moisture to play with her. Index and middle fingers dipped into her sex before pulling out and over labia and clit, rubbing, caressing, playing, and stimulating.

"You're going to make me come." A ragged confession from his fire witch.

That was the idea. Tomorrow, or maybe the next day, he'd stop by a local drug store and purchase a silicon-based lubricant. For, well, a bit of anal fingering at a later date. Then, if he were very lucky, Assefa would turn her *maybe* about anal sex into a definite *yes*.

Releasing her legs, Assefa rolled onto his back, encouraging Sanura to move with him. She did, following his nonverbal cue to straddle him where he wanted her—her knees on both sides of his head, her dripping sex over his mouth.

Then he was devouring her again. Sanura's moans louder than before. Her hands went to the top of the headboard, balancing herself as she rode his face. She pushed and rubbed her sex against his lips, his seeking tongue, and gods Sanura had never tasted this good before, been this aroused from oral sex.

And neither had he. His erection strained upward, leaking pre-cum and crying to be inside of his wet, willing witch.

She came. Inner muscles clenched, heat rose, and sex became sticky, slick and so damn rewarding.

"Gods Assefa, I can't stop—"

Flowing for him, he knew, because his powerful hands gripped her upper thighs, holding her in place for his relentless tongue. She wanted him to fight for her, for them. Well, Berber's fought dirty, using all in their arsenal to achieve their goals, their selfish ends. And Assefa wanted Sanura, all of her.

Boneless.

Pliant.

For his love, his touch, his bite.

And sex, wicked, wild, and shameless, was but one of countless weapons in his cache. So he took and took, gave and gave until Sanura's lips were swollen and sensitive, his face drenched in her fluids, and her moans exhausted whimpers of delight.

Then and only then did Assefa enter her. Hoisting Sanura onto her hands and knees, face to the mattress and inviting backside magnificently exposed, Assefa pushed his aching erection into her, groaning with unrestrained pleasure when her welcoming body swallowed him whole.

After that, well, there was nothing but slapping, sweaty skin, hoarse cries and shouts, squeaky bed and bursts of witch-were-cat magic. For two and a half hours, preternatural stamina claimed them, ruled them, and then in a fiery rush of were-cat speed and fire witch heat, they exploded in unison.

Magic from their merged auras coalesced where their bodies joined, in intimate decadence, and radiated outward. Gold, green, and red vaporous magic, visible to only them detonated, a kaleidoscope of love, hope, and faith. Reflected, a dozen times over, their magic sang a song of unity.

CHAPTER SIXTEEN

"If you keep staring at me like that, we'll never make it downstairs."
Assefa finished making the bed, neatly placing the decorative throw
pillows in front of the standard ones. "Wasn't twice this morning
enough for you, my greedy witch?"

Sanura blushed, recalling exactly how Assefa had awoken her and
how her body had responded, no foreplay required. Afterward, they'd
taken a shower together and made love again. Assefa, the strong man
that he was, had held Sanura throughout their lovemaking, her legs
around his waist and him buried deep inside of her.

For the last ten minutes, she'd watched him strip the bed, replacing
sex-scented sheets with fresh linen. Instead of assisting the way she
normally did, Sanura couldn't help but stare at her man, transfixed by
his attractiveness, his kindness, and his wickedness. Gods, the things
he'd done to her last night. And the things she knew he wanted to do
to her if she permitted him. Which, eventually, Sanura knew she
would.

Changing the bed linen, like cleaning their suite, was a job for
Gayle Livingston, Assefa's housekeeper. But Assefa, ever so conservative, had freed the woman of the task after Sanura moved in with
him. He also, Sanura had learned, did not permit Mrs. Livingston to
touch his suits. Once a week, he dropped off a backseat full of expensive, tailor-made suits at the natural dry cleaners a mile from the
house. Yet, and this was what always brought a smile to Sanura's
face, Assefa had no problem with Mrs. Livingston washing his boxers.

Gods, the special agent was full of interesting and head-scratching
contradictions.

Bold, brown eyes dropped to her legs, and he smiled. "Another sexy dress, Sanura. I'd fill your closet with them, but you already have so many."

Today she wore a mid-thigh length sleeveless crochet-hem shift dress with a scoop neck. In red, her favorite color. Assefa, dressed much more casual than he'd been on Saturday, wore a deep navy cotton polo shirt with a contrast chambray front and a pair of navy khaki pants.

"Speaking of dresses, the one you had on yesterday was breathtaking."

"Ha, ha."

Sanura grabbed the dress off the floor. The poor thing hadn't survived all the activity in the bed last night. Neither had the sheets and pillows. By the time they'd finished, whatever had been on the bed when they'd started had ended up on the floor, including her new dress. She tossed it to Assefa.

"I guess that's your less than funny way of giving yourself a compliment."

He held the purple dress in his hand, alternating looking at Sanura and the garment. "What are you talking about?"

"The dress you bought me. It's beautiful and fits perfectly. Thank you."

"I didn't purchase you this dress." Assefa examined the dress again, eyes going from human brown to Mngwa gold. "It's definitely something I would pick out for you—classy and sexy. But I didn't get this for you."

"I don't understand. It was in a gift box in my closet. Who else could it be from, if not you? Mom buys me dresses, sometimes, but nothing as expensive as that dress. And she just would've given it to me, not hidden it in my closet for me to find. Not that I can figure out how she could've done that."

"She couldn't have, and this dress is much more expensive than you think." Assefa handed the dress back to Sanura. "Look at the front."

She knew what the front looked like. Decorative diamonds were everywhere, the selling feature of the dress, in her opinion. But she did as he'd asked, seeing nothing different than she had last night when she'd taken it off.

"I don't—"

"With your second sight, Sanura."

Focusing, Sanura tuned down her human vision and turned up her magical sight, her second sight. Normally, high-level, mature witches used their second sight to read auras of animate creatures. But their second sight could also be used on inanimate objects, determining its elemental composition.

She lifted the dress closer to her face, examining the ornaments as carefully as Assefa had done. *Carbon atoms arranged in a cubic lattice. Isotropic crystal with a tensile strength of 60 GPa.* That couldn't be right because that would mean the decorations on her dress were actually ... "Diamonds. These are honest to goodness diamonds."

"I know."

"B-but, diamonds." Sanura stared at the priceless dress, unable to reconcile what she knew to be true with any sense of reality or logic. Who in the hell made a dress with diamonds? And how had this dress found its way into her closet? She then remembered the surreal sensation that had come over her Thursday night and the speck of gold glitter on Assefa's lip.

She had been mesmerized that night, but not by Assefa's pheromones. Much more powerful magic had been at play. The same magic that had crafted the ideal birthday dress for Sanura, she concluded.

"What are you thinking?"

"That godly magic is at work here. I assumed this was a gift from you. But maybe"—she didn't want to speak the truth she now felt in her soul but knew it had to be said— "Oya visited us. Left the gift box for me to find. And maybe, just maybe, while here, encouraged the strange interlude between us the other night."

Assefa's eyes returned to their normal brown and he considered her words, as well as the dress in her hand. After a minute of contemplation, he nodded. "I think you're right, which means the goddesses have begun their battle."

"What does that mean?"

"I really don't know. It could mean anything, I suppose. When it comes down to it, not much has been written about the battles between the fire and water witch of legend, other than there were other battles."

"Maybe there are records somewhere and we just need to find them."

"That's a possibility. A needle in a haystack, as some full-humans like to say."

True, but they had to begin somewhere. Assefa returned to work on Monday, July began tomorrow, and Sanura would be back at work by the end of August. Which meant she had a little more than a month to do some serious research before her fall semester started and she was swamped with students' online work and her advisory duties.

Assefa took the dress from her hand, went to her closet, and hung it up. "So, no ascension but an invaluable gift from your goddess."

"Not my goddess," she objected with an angry rejection that came from a place deep within that whispered that she could not trust Oya, no matter how tempting.

"Whether you consider her your goddess or not, Sanura, you're bound to her. And, perhaps, she is to you, for as long as you live or until we defeat the water witch of legend."

A depressing thought. But leave it to Special Agent Berber to cut through the magical, mystical layers and get to the heart of things, no mincing of words or self-delusions.

He grasped her hand and pulled Sanura to him, wrapping his arms around her waist. "I have a bad feeling."

Yeah, so did she.

"A tsunami is on the horizon and headed straight for us."

"What are we going to do about it?"

Assefa kissed her, a soft peck to her lips.

"Fight, just as you said last night. If that tidal wave wants us, I'm damn sure not going to stand still and wait for it to devour us in its cold, rising waters."

"What if we and our beasts aren't enough to push back the explosive water, to weather the seismic sea wave?"

Worst, what if their beasts were enough? What in the hell would that mean for them, the woman and the man? What would be left of Sanura if she let her fire spirit out of her cage and unleashed her onto the world?

She mentally trembled, revolting against the horrid thought.

He kissed her again. "We should be going. Makena and her Council sisters will be here soon. While you were getting dressed, I asked Omar to prepare lunch for everyone. It'll be ready by the time the meeting is over."

Grateful, she smiled. "You think of everything. Thank you."

"Yes, well, I thought it would be the height of poor hospitality if we sent our guests home with food poisoning."

She smacked his shoulder. "I'm not that bad of a cook."

Assefa shot her a dubious look, then flicked the tip of her nose. "Pinocchio."

****

Half an hour later, Sanura and Assefa sat across from four priestesses, gaping at them. The women arrived fifteen minutes ago and Omar had escorted them into the living room. Of the four, Assefa knew Makena Williams quite well and had met High Priestess Anna Spencer and Priestess Barbara Vaughn yesterday. Today, the fourth member of the Council, Priestess Peggy Bradford, joined her sisters.

Last night, Assefa hadn't appreciated the priestesses' silent fascination with him. While cordial, Anna and Barbara had observed him with critical gazes that bordered on peculiar, if not rude. They'd stared at him as if they were evaluating his best fit for a job he hadn't applied for, but one they were willing to offer him. Which, damn the gods, they just had.

He and Sanura sat together on a beautiful antique walnut loveseat, a floor-to-ceiling window behind them. The golden-brown drapes were pulled back to let in the bright rays of the late morning sun. Sitting on the couch to his immediate right sat Makena, Anna, and Peggy. To their right, in an armchair, was Barbara, her wide-set wizened eyes catching his—assessing, hopeful, and patient.

He didn't know what to say to their offer. Actually, he did, but his father hadn't raised him to be the kind of were-cat to throw women out of his home. Which he'd wanted to do as soon as they'd brought up the preposterous request. Thankfully, Sanura was in the meeting with him and had no compunction addressing her witch elders in a way that only another woman could.

"You want Assefa to do what?" Sanura, who had been holding his hand as they'd listened to Anna and Makena explain the vacancy left on the Council by Sanura's father, dropped it and scooted to the edge of the loveseat. She glowered at Makena. "You told me and everyone else that you hadn't filled the seat because you were waiting for the perfect alpha to make himself known."

"That's true," Makena defended, voice calm yet determined.

Apparently, the judge was the only one of her sisters brave enough to deal with an angry and annoyed Sanura. The others leaned against the plush pillows and watched, their eyes ping-ponging from mother to daughter, as if Sanura and Makena were playing a tennis match and all in the arena were asked to remain silent.

"The unspoken implication was that you would eventually choose from among the current alphas or a second."

"We never said that, Sanura."

"I know the Council didn't say that exactly, but it was heavily implied. You all knew what we would think, what we would conclude. The Council's alpha is selected from within our ranks. Now you're sitting here telling us that you saved the seat for the cat of legend, for Assefa?"

"That's precisely what we're saying. I don't know why you're so upset. There's no rule against selecting a were-cat outside of our community. The Council's alpha is always the strongest, most powerful were-cat within our family. It's what your father always wanted, to be succeeded by his daughter's mate. But he couldn't name Assefa as his successor because we didn't know who the cat of legend was at the time. Rules of succession are clear in that respect. Sam couldn't very well state he wanted the cat of legend to replace him without also being able to give his were-cats a specific name of their next leader. So we had to wait and hope you and the cat of legend would find each other before we were forced to fill the vacancy with an inferior were-cat."

"Three years is a long time to go without an alpha on the Council, Sanura," Anna chimed in, her voice soft and conciliatory. "I know this is a surprise, and for that I apologize. But there's no one else capable of filling the void left by Sam. No other were-cat, not even the alphas, are mighty enough to bring all the cat families under control. Without Sam's leadership and stellar management, the large, strong cat families have grown arrogant and combative while the smaller, weaker families have retreated into skittish silos. That cannot continue. That's why we're here today."

Sanura wasn't at all appeased by anything the high priestess had just said to her, no matter that it made too much damn sense and explained so much about Gregory Chambers' warning, felidae law, and the uninvited alpha who'd come to his home.

If he'd known Sanura's father had been the alpha of the Witch Council of Elders, he wouldn't have been groping for answers these past few days. Hell, he hadn't even known the Council had an alpha as a member. To his knowledge, no other Witch Council did, which made the Sankofa community a bellwether example of how best to manage were-cat-witch power relationships. If not handled correctly, the dynamics could be messy at best, violent at worse.

His witch knew him well—his strengths and his fears. Assefa would handle the alpha who'd come to his home, thinking Assefa and his friends prey. But Sanura would deal with the priestesses. Of that Assefa had no doubt. Besides, they had a secret to maintain, which would be difficult if he became the Council's alpha.

"Just because Assefa's my mate and the cat of legend, that doesn't mean he has to also become alpha to a bunch of were-cats who neither know him nor have any reason to trust or to listen to him. Do you have any idea how the alphas will react once they hear of this? Once they learn their Council has chosen a were-cat other than one from their community?" Sanura stood, glaring at each woman in turn. "They will come after him."

"You're overreacting." Makena got to her feet. "Once they learn Assefa is the cat of legend, no were-cat in his right mind will challenge him."

Sanura shook her head. "You don't believe that any more than I do, Mom. Dad kept them under control because he proved himself as alpha of the jaguar family long before Anna's father named him as his successor. And with you as his witch and his jaguar family behind him, no one could best Dad in battle. But Assefa is alone, the only were-cat of his kind. His singularity is reason enough for the alphas to challenge him. He has friends, great friends, but he doesn't claim the mantle of alpha over them. That's not the kind of relationship he has with them, although I don't doubt they would die and kill for each other. What you all ask of Assefa is too much. He isn't family. None of this is his responsibility."

"There you are wrong, Sanura." Barbara, the oldest of the priestesses, spoke up for the first time.

The woman wore a pair of black culottes, a black-and-white sleeveless shirttail blouse that showed off what Rashad would call "teacher's arms," and a practical pair of flat black sandals. At seventy, the woman probably shouldn't wear high heels, yet she had on a pair at the party, moving about with poise and confidence.

"Assefa is your mate, which makes him part of our Sankofa family. Once you and he complete the Oshun ceremony and we bless your union, no one will question our selection of Assefa as Council Alpha. We would never do anything to put your young man in harm's way, my dear. The two of you are our future. We love you, Sanura, and we'll do all in our power to protect you and your mate."

Assefa had never heard of the Oshun ceremony, but from the way Sanura turned to him, her eyes no longer fueled with fire but filled with concern, he knew it couldn't be good.

"We know we dropped a lot in your laps," Makena admitted.

The other priestesses stood, a united front of elemental witch power. Fire, water, earth, wind, striking yet deadly, four calla lilies, a highly toxic flower with the most stunning and elegant white petals.

Assefa could appreciate the beauty and strength of such women, respecting their femininity, as well as their sheathed magical claws.

Peggy, looking weary from her medical conference, smiled down at a seated Assefa. "You're the one we've all been waiting for. But I can see doubt in your eyes, rejection even. You're too respectful to tell us to go away, which isn't at all a bad trait for an alpha to possess. But you're much stronger than you know, than you give yourself credit for being. You would make a superb Council Alpha."

"I know precisely how strong I am, Dr. Bradford, that isn't what should concern anyone in this room." Assefa rose, done with being the passive gentleman. "I've heard your offer, and I thank you. And while I'm tempted to refuse the position right now, I'll do the Council the courtesy of thinking on it further and discussing the matter with Sanura."

"That's all we can ask of you," Anna said. "But do give the offer serious thought, Assefa. You would be an asset to the Council. A true leader for our were-cat brothers. After Sam's unexpected death and three years with no direct representative, they deserve the best this Council can offer them. You are the right person. We all agree. Which, trust me, is rare for us priestesses."

"I'm sure Omar has lunch prepared. Makena, would you please show your sisters to the dining room?"

Makena lifted the corner of her lips, humor glimmering in her mischievous eyes. "I've never been so politely dismissed before. As judge, I'm normally the one doing the dismissing." She started toward the living room door, Omar having closed it after delivering a carafe of coffee and a plate of pastries, which sat untouched on the coffee table. "Come, sisters, let's give Assefa and my daughter time to speak in private. If we don't leave now, with the way Sanura's eyes are boring into us, she just might set us on fire, foregoing wooden stakes."

The four women chuckled. Not mocking, but in that way older women had of poking fun at a too-serious younger woman with more growing up to do.

Sanura fumed but said nothing until the priestesses opened the door and left. Anna, ever so gracious, closed the door behind her Council.

"She's right, I should cast a fireball and drop it onto their presumptuous heads. Just because you're my ... gods, Assefa, what are we going to do?" Sanura fell back onto the loveseat. "Even if you turn down the offer, getting out of the Oshun ceremony without explaining why will be much harder. I could probably get around Anna and Barbara, although I doubt it. But Peggy and Mom are another matter. They're tenacious and shrewd and will question our resistance to a simple ceremony."

Assefa reclaimed his spot on the loveseat. "Tell me about the ceremony. Why are you more upset about it than their offer of alpha?"

"I'm upset about both." She shook her head, agitation in every line of her tense body. "I should've told you about Dad, but I didn't think him being Council Alpha was important. He never told me his wish for my mate to succeed him as alpha. If he had, I would've expected this from the priestesses. I know they're only trying to fulfill Dad's last wish and to secure the future of the were-cat families by installing the best alpha possible, but they don't know you."

This woman was the perfect mate for him. She understood, without him providing her with all the emotional details of his childhood. Dr. Sanura Williams, brilliant psychologist that she was, truly got him. He'd never told her his feelings about being alpha, but he had revealed how much he hadn't wanted to be like his father and grandfather, ruling a country and its people. The ultimate alpha position.

"They think it's an offer that honors you and your cat. In a way, it does. But there's so much more to it than that for you."

"Are you saying you don't wish for me to become Council Alpha?"

"If you really want my opinion, I agree with the priestesses. You're the ideal were-cat for the position. You're overqualified, in fact, although you probably don't see it that way." Sanura reached out, her warm palm going to his cheek. "There's so much good you could do if you became the Council's alpha. But you can't see that yet. Until you do, you'll never be happy in the role. And I don't want to see you unhappy, always afraid you'll live down to the Berber reputation and become as dictatorial as your grandfather. You could never become him, but you have to believe that truth yourself."

He covered the hand on his cheek with his own. "Is this your way of fighting for me?"

"I'm tempted to fight against you, but I have my own demons and fears I haven't dealt with. So I have no moral standing to push you on this. But I would love to see you as Council Alpha. In the long run, I think the role would be good for you and you'd come to love it as much as Dad did. But now isn't the right time. And the timing couldn't be worse because we aren't fully mated."

Assefa had a feeling their partial mate bond was at the heart of Sanura's concern about the Oshun ceremony.

"Tell me about the ceremony. I assume it's more than a simple blessing."

They lowered their hands.

"No, it actually is just a simple blessing ceremony. A few prayers and well-wishes from the priestesses and invited guests."

"Okay, so what's the problem? I saw your face when the ceremony was mentioned, and I know there must be more to it than prayers and well-wishes."

"Yes, well, for every other couple who've gone before the Council to receive their blessing for their union, the ceremony is nothing more than an old but respected tradition. Ours, because we're the fire witch and cat of legend, would probably be a more formal and elaborate event, with the Council inviting the heads of all the families. But this is the thing, Assefa, at the end of the ceremony, the mated pair is expected to reveal their mate mark to the gathered community. It is then the guests bless the couple and the children to come from the pairing—powerful witches and mighty were-cats. The next generation."

Now he understood, which did nothing to alter the trajectory of the storm he felt coming.

"From my analysis, we have two choices—turn both offers down without explanation and let your family and friends think what they will or accept both offers and figure out how to make them work."

"Or we could split them. Accept one, reject the other."

"I don't think so. That would only raise more questions we aren't willing to answer. Unless you want to walk into the dining room and tell your mother and her sisters we aren't mates and don't know when or if we'll ever become mates, effectively telling them we've been lying to everyone for weeks. How do you think that will go over, Sanura?"

"I get your point. Damn, this is a mess. I thought we could keep our partial bond between the two of us, now I'm not so sure. And if the other alphas learn the truth, I fear what they'll do."

Sanura shouldn't fear those men. Those alphas should fear him. Lone Mngwa or no, he would back down from no one, not even a community of were-cats. The priestesses and Sanura were wrong, with such a rebellious attitude, Assefa wouldn't be the community building alpha the Council needed. Yet he couldn't help the tang of guilt he felt at the prospect of letting the women down. More, he feared what would happen to the Sankofa community if the priestesses were forced to choose a were-cat unfit for the role.

His father had found himself in the same position after Assefa's grandfather had died. So many military men were willing and eager to become the next General Supreme, none of them capable, however, of fostering coalitions and bringing peace to the war-ravaged country. So Jahi Berber had stepped into the breach, taking on the ill-suited role and transforming it, himself, and the country into nothing before seen in the Republic of the Sudan. But what would've happened to his beloved country if Jahi hadn't made that decision, hadn't sacrificed his independence in exchange for the freedom and civil rights of his countrymen and women?

And what would happen to the Council and those weak were-cat families who'd isolated themselves after the death of Samuel Williams? Would they move further to the margins, afraid of the stronger families, like that of the lion pride? Would the priestesses be compelled to accept someone like the alpha who'd come to Assefa's home last night, an untrustworthy and dangerous foe who cared more for his ego and pride than the safety and equality of all witches and werecats?

Those questions, and more, weighed on Assefa's conscience. As Sanura had said, none of this was his responsibility. So why did he feel a strange obligation to the priestesses? Women who had indeed honored him with their request. Women who'd looked upon Assefa without fear or caution but with trust and hope. Women who would bless him and bring Assefa into their family because they loved and respected the final wishes of their deceased alpha and wanted what was best for their community and the fire witch raised to protect them all.

"What are you thinking?"

The same probing question he'd asked Sanura less than an hour ago. Her response had cast the prophecy into blunt reality. His own, well, Sekhmet created his kind for one purpose. A purpose he took seriously, never wavering, always ready.

"I was thinking about a were-cat's duty."

Sanura scoffed. "You have no duty to the Council. You owe them nothing, not even my mother. She loves you, if you don't already know. She'll be disappointed if you turn the Council down, but that's it. She respects your mind and heart, and will accept your decision no matter how grudging it may come out as. So don't worry about hurting Mom's feelings, or the feelings of the others. They'll get over it. I'm worried that you may not if you accept for the wrong reasons."

Such a good woman, no wonder he wanted to take her as mate and wife. But sometimes, Sanura, like Najja, underestimated the loyalty and protective capacity of were-cats. Makena Williams, and now her Council sisters, were under his care, part of his extended family, just as Sanura's best friends were, just as Mike was. Whether he liked it or not, and he didn't, not one damn bit, if becoming Council Alpha kept his family safe and the Sankofa community stable, he would accept.

Gods help him, he was more like his damn father than he realized.

CHAPTER SEVENTEEN

The priestesses hugged, kissed, and thanked Sanura a dozen times since she and Assefa had joined them in the dining room, giving the women the "good" news. Apparently, they'd credited Sanura with talking Assefa into joining the Council. When, in fact, she'd argued the opposite, fearing the steps he might have to take to ensure his acceptance and respect among his were-cat brothers.

After filling themselves on Omar's delicious cooking, the priestesses showering the humble man with empty plates and words of gratitude, they now stood in front of the house. The winding driveway, unlike last night, held a single vehicle. Less than a minute ago, Mr. Siddig had driven Peggy's white SUV from where he'd parked it in the garage, a valet service the women appreciated.

Barbara kissed her cheek. "Assefa is a fine young man, Sanura. I knew that as soon as he introduced himself to me last night. So gracious and handsome." The woman actually clasped her hands to her bosom when she'd said that, as if she would swoon at the thought. "I can't wait to see his Mngwa. Do you think he'll grant us the honor at the Oshun ceremony? Or is Assefa the shy type?"

If Assefa had a shy bone in his body, he'd hidden it under dense layers of charm and swagger. But her were-cat was no exhibitionist or circus performer. He wouldn't shift into his cat form because someone, even an infatuated priestess, requested it of him. From the looks of Anna and Peggy, they shared Barbara's hope of seeing Assefa shed his human skin for fangs, claws, and fur.

Sanura glanced over Barbara's head and caught her mother's apologetic gaze. Makena whispered, "Ignore her." Sanura did, trusting her mother to explain to her fellow priestesses how offensive it would be to ask Assefa to act the role of a trained show dog for them and whatever guests they intended to invite to the ceremony, hoping to impress and perhaps intimidate into accepting their choice of alpha without complaint.

"Assefa and I will be in touch to arrange a date for the ceremony."

"The sooner, the better," Peggy said, car keys jangling in her right hand. "There are already rumbles within the cat families. We won't be able to keep a lid on this much longer."

Sanura already knew about the rumors, at least within the lion pride. But she wouldn't allow Peggy, bossy, arrogant, and not even half of Sanura's magic level, to dictate the details of Assefa's formal acceptance or the couple's part of the Oshun ceremony. She would allow no one, not even the Witch Council, to bulldoze Sanura and Assefa into doing things their way and on their timeline and terms. Assefa may be too polite to argue with women, but she sure as hell wasn't.

"As I said, Peggy, I'll be in touch with a date that will work with our schedules. I would also like to see the Council's press release about Assefa's nomination and acceptance of the alpha position before it goes out."

The Council's press releases were delivered as magically encrypted emails that could be decoded by members of the Sankofa community only.

The medically skilled fingers gripping the car keys tightened, as did Peggy's face. Irritated. The woman had always been easy to read. Not the best trait for a member of the Council, but Peggy was the strongest witch among the Sankofa earth witches and she possessed other characteristics which served her well on the Council. But she thought too highly of herself, thinking everyone would defer to her the way too many nurses and doctors did at Johns Hopkins Hospital where she served as the director of the department of surgery.

"You do understand if we permit you to see the letter beforehand it would only be as a courtesy. And that courtesy would not extend to any opinions you may have."

Sanura smiled down at the priestess and bit back a cutting retort. She respected the woman, although she'd never particularly liked her. Besides, she wouldn't put her mother in a position where Makena would have to side between her daughter and her Council sister. No, that wasn't accurate. No matter what, Makena would always side with Sanura. But it would be unfair for Sanura to create a pointless wedge in the Council.

"Thank you, priestess. I look forward to reading the letter." She'd managed to say that without a shred of sarcasm. Dr. Peggy Bradford wasn't the enemy, and Sanura wouldn't waste her energy on a woman who was as invested in the safety and future of the Sankofa witches and were-cats as Sanura was.

Appeased, Peggy said her goodbye and made her way to her truck. Hopping inside, she unlocked the doors for her sisters.

Anna hugged Sanura. "We'll be in touch soon. Please thank Assefa for us again, and let him know how much we look forward to working with him for many years to come."

Years, gods, this was really happening. Assefa Berber would become alpha of the Witch Council of Elders, replacing Samuel Williams. The thought brought a pang of sadness, as well as pride to her heart. And, not for the first time, Sanura wished Sam and Assefa could've met. Her father would've adored Assefa as much as Sanura and Makena did. And Assefa, well, sometimes Sanura worried about him. Even having his uncle so near, Assefa kept far too much inside, thinking himself everyone's warrior. He ceased to realize, or to accept, that even the strongest warrior couldn't win every battle on his own.

As an agent, he understood this truth. As a familiar, he did as well. But as a prideful Berber, as a courageous Mngwa, he fought as an army of one. Dangerous yet so alone.

Anna and Barbara joined Peggy in the truck, slipping into the backseat and leaving the front passenger seat for Makena. Unlike the other priestesses, Makena didn't hug or kiss Sanura, but she did stare at her with an unreadable expression.

"Thanks for returning my cell phone, Mom, and for the birthday present. It was unexpected." Sanura wanted to say more about her mother's birthday present, but Makena's eyes had drifted to Sanura's left hand, assessing.

"Still no ring? I don't understand. I was certain Assefa would propose to you last night. Cynthia, Rachel, even Mike. We all thought …" Her eyes rose, full of questions and motherly concern. "What am I missing?"

Sanura's nonchalant shrug lied. The pain of Assefa's truth was still an open wound Sanura doubted would close and heal any time soon.

"We haven't been together that long, Mom. There's no need to rush into marriage."

"You're living with the man, Sanura, sharing his bed and his life. I may not be as old fashioned as some, but this kind of living arrangement should come after marriage and the mate bond."

Sanura's eyes shot to where the priestesses waited in the car. Thankfully, with the humid day, Peggy had the car's air conditioner on and the windows rolled up.

She stepped closer to her mother and lowered her voice. "What do you mean?"

Without replying, Makena's eyes turned crimson. She scanned Sanura with her second sight, discerning eyes taking in every lying inch of the fire witch. When Makena's eyes returned to Sanura's face, they no longer glowed fire witch red but a dull, mournful brown.

Gods help her, Makena knew. But how much she knew, Sanura couldn't be sure. Then she was because a single tear dropped right before Makena fell into Sanura's arms.

Peggy's back passenger side window rolled down and Anna's blonde hair and worried blue eyes came into view. When the high priestess made to open the door, Sanura shook her head. She didn't need anyone's help with her mother. With a goodbye wave to the priestesses, and a, "It's all right. I got her," Sanura escorted Makena away from the driveway. Come what may, the conversation they were about to have was way past due.

****

Assefa was back in his living room, sitting by himself on the loveseat. Zareb sat in the chair across from him, where Barbara had been two hours ago. Unlike the priestess, who'd reclined demurely in the chair, face calm and pleasant, Zareb perched on the edge, forearms on his knees, face hard and threatening.

"I should've slit the bastard's throat."

"For coming to my home unannounced?"

"It was an insult, an attempt at intimidation."

"Only if I choose to see it that way, which I don't."

Assefa shook his head when Zareb made to reply. He didn't want to hear any more of his friend's angry ramblings. This wasn't the Sudan, and Assefa was trying very hard to not overreact to last night's scene at his front gate. Hard when an envelope left by the man sat beside him, given to Assefa by an embarrassed-looking Zareb. Zareb, a man who'd run butt naked through the University of Khartoum's library on a dare, without a slither of discomposure, even when he'd slammed into the shocked Head of Periodicals, a forty-three-year-old water witch who just happened to be Zareb's mother's best friend. Whatever was in the envelope to bring a discomfited flush to Zareb's face, Assefa knew was something likely to turn his stomach and fuel his banked rage.

Yet he ignored the envelope for now, choosing to focus on the alpha and not what he'd left for Assefa.

"Tell me who he is. I'm sure you've run his license plate and performed a cursory background check."

"Of course I did. He's Paul Daniel Chambers, age sixty-seven. He's single and lives by himself in Catonsville, Baltimore County. He has a son, Gregory Daniel Chambers. You may be interested to know that High Priestess Anna Spencer is the mother of Gregory Chambers. But I found no record of a marriage between Spencer and Chambers. As far as I've been able to gather, neither has ever married."

"Which means it's likely they never became mates. If they had, Chambers would've probably become Council Alpha."

"And would've had no reason to come sniffing around here last night. Are you thinking what I am?"

"That the conniving were-cat is trying to secure the alpha seat on the Council for his son? A vain and deadly attempt to live vicariously through Gregory Chambers? There aren't too many other conclusions for me to draw." Assefa picked up the envelope, holding but not looking at it. "I assume this is a picture of Sanura with Gregory Chambers?"

Zareb's fists balled, his nod curt. But his shoulders relaxed, as well as the tension around his eyes. His friend hadn't known what to make of the picture, which only made sense. While Zareb and Sanura were beginning to build a friendship, he didn't yet know her well.

Assefa opened the envelope and slid out the glossy photo. The content of the envelope was as he'd expected, which didn't make seeing it easier to digest. Yet Sanura had told him exactly what had transpired between herself and Gregory Chambers. Honest, even though she knew how much the thought of another man touching her, holding her against her will, would eat a whole in his stomach and strain his self-control.

On the grass was Sanura and what Assefa knew to be Gregory Chambers. The blonde man, naked except for a towel wrapped around his waist, held Sanura against him. From the angle, a profile, Assefa could see the man's deep, satisfied smile—wide and broad and all for Sanura. Yet he couldn't see much of Sanura's face. A good deal of her long hair covered her expression.

But the truth of the seemingly intimate embrace was in the line of her tense body. The hands on Gregory Chambers' bare chest were balled and her shoulders were arched upward—subtle signs that supported Sanura's story. Not that Assefa questioned her fidelity, not when she'd relayed the story to him and not now, despite how the picture might appear to others.

"Sanura told you about the encounter with the younger Chambers?" Magical embers of relief rolled off Zareb.

"She did. But she didn't know someone had taken a picture of her and the lion." Assefa flicked the picture to the other side of the loveseat, tempted to excuse himself so he could wash the filth from his hands. "I don't know whether father and son set Sanura up, or another were-cat, probably a member of Chambers' pride, saw the scene, took a picture, and then passed it along to his alpha."

"Who then decided to use the picture to try and create a rift between you and your mate." Zareb slid back into the chair, thinking. "You could've taken the picture at face value and gone after the son. Chambers had no way of knowing what your reaction would be."

"True, but I bet Gregory Chambers, as of last night, is under tight lion pride security. The old alpha probably hoped I'd be so possessive of my witch that I'd spiral into a jealous rage and go after his son."

"Giving him and his men an excuse to kill you, thereby ridding his son of the competition." Zareb rose from the chair, anger and tension returning. "That old, sly bastard. Give me permission to—"

"My. Shield," Assefa said, emphasizing each word. "Not. My. Sword." He also stood. "If I am to be alpha of that damn Council, I'm going to have to fight my own battles, Zareb. No one listens to and respects an alpha who stands behind his cats. Even Paul Chambers, as much as a power hungry bastard he may be, was the one to drive up to my gate and demand to see me. Not his were-cats, but the old alpha himself. That's why those six were-cats followed him, and why they will do whatever he says, no matter how foolish and dangerous."

And coming to the home of the enemy was, without a doubt, foolish and dangerous. Ulan alone could've murdered Chambers with no remorse, body disposal an inconsequential matter for the division chief. Then there was Zareb, Omar, and Dahad, trained by a special operations unit of the Sudanese army. Even Manute and Rashad, the youngest of his household, were skilled were-cat combatants—lethal and vicious.

But five years away from the Sudan wasn't long enough for Zareb and the others to forget the hard lessons of home. The United States was a different cultural beast than what they were used to, but a ferocious beast all the same. Here, all too many preternaturals donned the sophisticated skin of civility, hiding their true nature behind fake smiles, passive aggressiveness, and ideological warfare. The Sudan, a shameful history of oppression and civil war, was, at its core, a nation of haters and lovers. Sudanese didn't pretend to love those they hated, and those they loved received their entire heart and soul. If nothing else, when at home, Assefa knew where he stood.

Here, were-cats like Paul Chambers played games of the heart and sports with the mind. Assefa didn't like or appreciate either, but unsavory schemes weren't enough to justify sanctioning the man's death, his execution. Make no mistake, if so ordered, Zareb Osei would be Assefa's sword, killing the old alpha quick but brutal or slow and brutal. Either way, Chambers' death would be bloody.

Assefa reached down, retrieved the photo, and put it back into the envelope, which he then handed to Zareb.

"Burn this. I don't want Sanura or anyone else to lay eyes on it. The picture is misleading and insults my" —he wished he could say with pride and honesty, his *mate*. Instead, Assefa finished with— "witch."

Zareb ripped the envelope and picture in quarters before shoving the pieces into the pocket of his dark-green dress pants. "So, alpha of the Witch Council of Elders?"

"I guess I will be once the announcement is made."

For the first time since the birthday party, Zareb smiled. "It's about damn time you took on the role you were born to have. No matter what you think, you've always been an alpha were-cat."

"I don't want the job," Assefa said, irritated with how petulant the statement had come out as.

"It's suited for you. You'll do great."

"That's what Sanura said, but she doesn't know what she's talking about."

"Now who's insulting her? Your mate knows you."

"She doesn't know everything. Not how I was back home, and not what I did to my brother."

"Razi deserved what you did to him. It's past time you stopped feeling guilty about that jackass. Your psychologist of a mate would tell you the same if you opened up to her." Zareb ran a weary hand over his bald head. "I met Cynthia Garvey last night."

From the corner of his eye, Assefa saw Makena and Sanura walking away from the house and toward the river. Strange, when he'd last seen the two, Sanura was headed to the front of the house to see the Council members off. If he weren't mistaken, the priestesses had arrived in the same vehicle. But Makena had, at some point, decided to stay behind. Why?

As he watched the women through one of the living room windows, curiosity having captured his attention, it took him a few seconds to process his friend's words. He refocused on Zareb.

"What about Cynthia?"

"I met her last night. She and her family were late to the party."

Zareb's superficial response explained nothing Assefa didn't already know or why Zareb would even care. "And?"

Zareb glanced around the living room, scanning it as if he hadn't lived in this house for five years and knew every inch of the room. He shoved his rather large hands into his pockets, face guarded when he turned back to Assefa.

"It's not important."

A lie but one Assefa had no intention of calling Zareb on. His friend, while no stranger to romantic entanglements, had many dating rules, but only one he'd never broken. Zareb Osei did not date or sleep with married or mated women. He'd stolen a girlfriend or four away from a boyfriend, with a cocky the-better-man-won grin. But Zareb drew the line at women in committed and binding relationships, which Cynthia Garvey most certainly was.

Out of all the people Zareb had met last night, including several beautiful and single women, full-human and witch, Zareb had brought up Cynthia. Knowing his friend did and said nothing without a good reason, his sudden interest in a mated witch he'd met less than twenty-four hours ago didn't count as unimportant to Assefa.

"You met her mate, Eric, as well."

If Assefa hadn't been watching Zareb closely, he would've missed the flicker of anger and jealousy in his dark-brown eyes. Quick but there, and it made no damn sense. Why in the world would Zareb care about one of Sanura's mated girlfriends? True, Cynthia was a sexy and attractive woman. But so were the countless women Zareb had dated over the years. None of them had lasted more than a few months, and none of them had garnered this type of uncharacteristic reaction from the special agent.

"Yeah, I met him, talked to the man. He seems nice enough. A fire-fighter, I believe. Anyway, Chief Berber's been trying to get in touch with you since this morning. When he couldn't reach you on your cell, he called mine."

A deliberate change of topic. Assefa gave his friend that as well. When Zareb was ready, truly ready, to speak to Assefa about Cynthia Garvey he would listen. Until then, Assefa saw no point in pushing the special agent on an issue he had clearly yet to work out in his mind.

Assefa retrieved his phone from the end table next to the loveseat. Sure enough, there were five missed calls from his uncle and one text message. *Call me. ASAP.* Before his and Sanura's meeting with the Council, Assefa had set his phone to vibrate and placed it on the end table. But he'd forgotten to take it with him when they'd joined the priestesses for lunch in the dining room.

"Did Ulan tell you what he wanted to talk to me about?"

"He said something about love and sex making a were-cat deaf, dumb, and blind." Zareb chuckled. "He's right. For the last three days, your world has narrowed to nothing but Sanura Williams. But I get it. She's the one."

Sanura was the one, and Assefa had no problem admitting that truth. But what had he missed that was so important his uncle would call him five times?

"I'm going to see what else I can dig up on Paul Chambers and the other Sankofa were-cat families. I have a feeling you're going to need that information sooner rather than later."

"Begin with the Council. Most of the information you want should be part of their Council records. Speak with Makena. She can save you a lot of time. Tell her you're asking on my behalf because I want to begin learning about the were-cats who will be under my domain. There are probably records she has access to from the former alpha. If so, get those as well. I need to know what Sam knew."

Three years weren't that long, which meant Sam's records should still be fairly accurate. More, they would provide a history of each were-cat family—members, matings, offspring, strengths and weaknesses, and so on. Pertinent information Assefa would require as he transitioned into a role he neither aspired to nor desired, unlike Paul Chambers.

"You think Judge Williams will turn over her husband's files?"

"She wants me to be successful as Council Alpha. I don't think she'll have a problem sharing her mate's files with me."

In fact, Assefa now wondered if that's what Makena wanted to speak with him about. Maybe it had nothing to do with Sam's sacrifice and lingering jaguar spirit. He glanced out the window again. The women were no longer in view, of course, but Assefa remembered what he'd seen earlier. Mother and daughter had walked hand-in-hand, Makena's face gloomy, Sanura's troubled.

He had no doubt truths would be revealed between the women. He hoped the truth would heal their wounds, cauterizing the emotional injury with organic ingredients borne of their love for Samuel Williams and each other.

"Makena will need a ride home."

"Understood. I'll drive her home and use the time wisely."

"Don't play special agent with the priestess, Zareb. Just be straight with her, and she'll tell you what she can and cannot help us with."

"An ally. That's even better. Have Sanura call me when her mother is ready to return home." With purpose, Zareb strode to the living room door. "Call the chief. Find out what's going on and whether it's something we need to add to our list of shit to deal with." He opened the door and stepped into the hallway. "Or people to kill. Mark my words, Assefa, Paul Chambers will only get more brazen. The stunt at the front gate, the scouts, and that picture of Sanura and his son are only the beginning. He won't stop unless someone stops him. That's how were-cats like him are made. They push and push until someone stronger pushes back. Hard."

"I know."

Zareb closed the door. Assefa didn't have to say more. Paul Chambers would've been right at home with Assefa's grandfather's lieutenant generals—men who'd made the lives miserable for too many citizens of their country. Greedy and power hungry, the lieutenant generals abused their rank and privilege, preying on the people instead of protecting them, healing them, befriending them.

Yes, Assefa held no illusions about how this tale with Paul Chambers would end. Yet he chose to hold onto the hope he kept hidden inside his heart. In the face of all that he'd seen, at home and as an FBI agent, hope had kept him from becoming a cynical bastard. Without hope, people ceased to see and appreciate the great possibilities of life. Without hope, he would have little reason to get out of bed, to protect innocents, or to build a life with Sanura.

He'd almost lost his hope. *What I want to know is if you're willing to fight for me? Even if that means fighting yourself. Your stubbornness. Your pride. Your fear.* But Sanura's words had reignited the flame of hope within, challenging him to be better, to be more.

Not perfect. Just better.

So he would try other methods to deal with Paul Chambers, hoping, this once, the story wouldn't end in bloodshed—one more death on Assefa's conscience.

CHAPTER EIGHTEEN

Like a duckling, Sanura followed behind her mother, trusting but having no idea where Makena was going. They'd circumnavigated the house, Makena quiet and pensive. Sanura the same, unsure whether she should interject into her mother's thoughts or wait for Makena to begin the conversation. Strategically speaking, Sanura knew she should exercise patience, giving Makena the opportunity to reveal what she knew, or thought she knew, first. But strategy had no place between mother and daughter.

Makena stopped, past the gazebo but only thirty feet from the pier. The Potomac River, on this last day of June, temperature and humidity high and sweat-inducing, was mysterious, still, and frightening as hell.

Watching the water with wariness, Sanura retreated several feet. Makena, however, remained where she was, gazing at the river, oblivious to Sanura's mild panic attack.

Heart raced.

Pulse thudded.

Skin moistened.

She closed her eyes, shutting out the image of the river and thoughts of it claiming her life—drowning her in the name of Mami Wata. Water. Damn, Sanura hated the fear being near so much water evoked in her.

"I wasn't thinking." A warm, gentle hand settled against her sweaty cheek. "I'm sorry, sweetie, I was so lost in thought that I forgot."

Sanura opened her eyes, meeting the contrite gaze of her mother. "It's all right. I shouldn't still be afraid of the water. After all those swimming lessons you and Dad gave me, I should've gotten over my phobia a long time ago."

Makena patted her cheek, a loving gesture she'd done a thousand times. But there was also sorrow in her mother's familiar touch and in the brown eyes that held Sanura's. Familial magic flowed between the women, a bond of fire witches and of mother and daughter. Never before had Sanura kept something so important from her mother, and the guilt had eaten at her heart and her soul. Yet, as Sanura's and Makena's magic comingled and they stared into each other's eyes, Sanura could see, for the first time, the toll Makena's own secret had taken on her.

"I'm sorry. I should have told you the truth." Makena had spoken first, but the sentiment, the words, were echoed by Sanura.

"Let's sit."

Sanura thought Makena would walk to the comfort of the gazebo. Instead, she removed her sandals and lowered herself to the cut green grass. Unlike Sanura, who wore a dress, Makena was clad in a pair of blue boyfriend jeans and a deco blue, short sleeve peasant blouse. Perfect for lounging outside on the grass and, apparently, for disclosing secrets.

Makena sat with her knees tucked to her chest, her tall body a ball of self-protection. Sanura, however, feeling no less vulnerable than Makena, sat cross-legged, her short dress tucked neatly in her lap.

"Sam and I rarely argued, although we disagreed as much as any married couple." Like before, Makena stared off into the distance. "But we disagreed and argued over whether to tell you the truth." Makena laughed, with sad remembrance and no humor. "I slapped Sam when he told me what he'd done, then I wept into his arms. Fury, fear, and love, Sanura, can be the most devastating and volatile of emotional mixes. I hope you never experience such conflict in your heart, although I suspect you soon will."

Makena was but one generation away from being the fire witch of legend. Sanura always wondered if that explained why she and her mother were so much alike and why they were so close. But now, listening to her mother, watching her tense profile, Sanura finally grasped the easy-to-see truth. And it was such a simple truth, yet it had eluded her all these years.

"We almost lost you that night." Makena shifted her focus to Sanura, tears filling her eyes. "Sam came bursting into our bedroom, startling me awake." Makena lowered her knees, crossing her legs in the same fashion as Sanura. "Your face and little body were sticky with blood. And you were so damn hot, Sanura. Your aura radiated like wildfire and your fire magic raged hot and out of control." Makena swiped at her fallen tears, as if she wanted to wipe away the memory of that wretched night. "Sam was frantic, roaring something about Sàngó and a blessing. I had no idea what he was talking about. But it didn't matter. Not then, at least."

Sanura reached out and held the hand that shook. The hand still wet from Makena's tears and relived pain.

"I couldn't get my bearings, think what to do. You were limp, bloody, feverish, and dying, and I couldn't think of one damn thing to save your life. I just kept staring at you, where Sam had placed you in my arms, his eyes afraid in a way I'd never seen them before. At that moment, my heart ceased to beat, my breath slowed and stopped, and I saw myself dying along with you." Makena raised their linked hands and pressed them to her chest, over her soundly beating heart. "Then I felt my mother's magic around me, around you, tethering us to this plane of existence. She searched for and found our fire spirits, first mine and then yours. Yours, which should've been asleep and immature, cried and screamed with sorrow."

Tears fell, from them both, and neither made to wipe them away. Too much kept inside, and for far too long. Unconditional love, that's what Makena and Sanura shared. And she knew, before her mother told her, how Makena had saved her life that night.

"For the first time in my life, I gave my fire spirit free reign. She knew, better than me, how to connect with and calm your newly born but too-powerful fire spirit. When it was all over, my magical energy spent and you fever free, I fell into an exhausted sleep. I've never slept that deeply before or since. For two days, Sam stayed by my side, taking care of us both. On the third day, I awoke. And you were there, tucked against my side, green eyes staring up at me with so much fire witch impatience that I burst into laughter and tears."

Makena smiled wanly and released Sanura's hand. Their physical connection no more but their spiritual one, well, that could never be broken, not even by lies of omission.

"When you turned eighteen, I thought you were old enough to know the truth."

"About Sàngó's blessing and Dad's sacrifice?"

She nodded. "Your father never wanted you to know. He didn't want you to blame yourself for his decision and feel guilty about his passing." Makena patted Sanura's cheek again. "But I can see that you do. It's in your eyes now and in the way you looked at Assefa last night. I hoped I was reading too much into how lost and afraid you seemed when you couldn't find him, or how Assefa's eyes filled with regret when you opened one present after another. And while I knew the extravagant party was his gift to you, I still kept waiting for him to give you a much more personal present. But when you opened the last gift, and it wasn't from Assefa, my heart dropped and I feared the worst."

Sanura's heart had dropped as well, although she already knew Assefa would not give her the engagement ring hidden away in his pocket. That he, despite his plans to propose at the end of the evening, had changed his mind.

"Before he died, Sam made me promise not to tell you unless there was no other choice. He hoped, we both hoped, you would find your mate and pass along the remnants of his cat spirit without ever knowing it resided in you or the truth of the god's so-called blessing."

Makena had spoken the last part with such disdain Sanura had no doubt, if she could, Sàngó would've been on the receiving end of her slap instead of Sam.

"But it's awake. With my second sight and emotional connection to you and Sam's jaguar, I can see the blue of jaguar spirit magic surrounding you." Makena shook her head, disapproval in the movement. "This isn't what your father wanted, Sanura. You can't keep Sam with you this way. He died so that you could live."

"I know that. Dammit, don't you think I know that?" Agitated and tired of sitting, Sanura handed Makena her shoes then got to her feet.

After securing the second strap on her sandal, Makena rose. "Accept his bite. Give Assefa the added strength of Sam's black jaguar."

"And what will that mean for Dad's cat spirit?'

"I have no idea. No one, except that damn god of fire, thunder, and lightning knows. But a witch isn't meant to hold the spirit of a cat. It isn't natural."

"But I've been trying to find a spell to transfer Dad's cat spirit to you."

Makena shook her head again, this time with sadness and knowing. "Even if such a spell existed, I wouldn't want you to cast it. None of this is what Sam wanted, why he sought out Sàngó without telling me or anyone else. 'Could you choose between a daughter and a mate'? Sam asked me right before confessing. 'Who do you love more? Me or Sanura? Could you choose, Makena'? Of course I could never choose, which Sam knew. But I would die for you, which your father also knew. In his stubborn were-cat way, he was trying to protect both of us. I had to live for you, knowing, one day, your father would die for you. So you see, my sweet girl, I had to let your father go and respect his final wish and yes, his sacrifice."

Sanura tucked a strand of hair behind her ear, looking out at the river but no longer seeing miles of watery danger but Samuel Williams' handsome, smiling face. He was forever smiling at her, even on his deathbed. A boyish smile intended to soothe the pain of his passing, Sam, to the end, Sanura's guardian. How could she let him go? How had Makena?

"I'm not ready." A sad confession.

"What about Assefa? The prophecy?"

"I can't do anything about the prophecy. If Mami Wata's water witch comes for me, then I'll have no choice but to fight her, I suppose."

"And Assefa?"

The face reflected in the river was now that of her special agent. Unlike Sam's image, Assefa wore no smile but his FBI mask of cool detachment. For all her talk, last night, of them fighting for each other, Sanura's sense of foreboding hadn't diminished with his agreement or with Assefa's reluctant acceptance to become the Council's alpha. If anything, the threat she detected intensified with each passing hour.

"Assefa knows everything I do. I told him a few days ago." The image of Assefa vanished from the river, giving way to ripples that formed a menacing, self-satisfied smile. She rubbed her eyes then looked again. The ripples were still there, but they no longer seemed like cruel lips that scorned her while relishing her pain, her inner conflict. No, they now resembled ... "We should move away from the water."

"What? Why?"

Sanura grabbed Makena's wrist and yanked her up the small hill, heedless of how rough she was being with her mother.

"Sanura, wait. What's wrong?"

"We have to get away from the ..." She glanced behind them, the sky now overcast and ominous, as if it would open up and rain death upon their heads.

When Makena lifted her arm to the river, finger pointing, Sanura was forced to release the appendage. Her eyes were too focused on the sight down the hill to notice the finger marks she'd left on her mother's forearm.

The river ripples slithered and hissed.

The clouds broke.

And the sun's rays shone on the river bank, an unnatural beam of light tracking the slinking progress of scales and forked tongues.

Too many snakes to count slithered from the river. Red stripes were everywhere, as were rows of black spots. Dozens, it had to be dozens of them gliding from the water and onto the grass. Yellow coloration on their heads and sides twinkled in the strange beam of light, an unnerving contrast to their small, dark eyes.

Sanura stepped back.

Makena, eyes transfixed on the reptiles, didn't move. But she did whisper back to Sanura. "Rainbow snakes. By the gods, there are so many of them. And I think they've just dragged something from the river, if I can trust what I'm seeing."

Both of their eyes and minds couldn't be playing tricks on them because Sanura damn sure thought the same. Shiny, scaly bodies, while found along the Coastal Plain of the southern United States, including Virginia, typically hid amongst aquatic vegetation. But there they were, dozens of rainbow snakes, on her back lawn, bodies working together in a gruesome effort unlike anything snakes were known to do.

Makena raised her hands, palms out. "I'm going to send their scaly hides to hell."

Her mouth began to move, reciting a fireball spell Sanura knew well. But when the snakes began to unpeel themselves off whatever they'd dragged from the river, Makena's incantation slipped into disgusted silence.

Like a grotesque stripper in a horror movie, with each rainbow snake that slithered away, a piece of wrinkled skin was revealed.

Five minutes. It took five whole minutes for every rainbow snake that had been coiled around the body to release its section and return to its river home. The Potomac accepted each creature, ripples forming, not into a self-satisfied smile this time, but into a triumphant and challenging sneer.

On the repressed lawn, goose-fleshed and undeniably dead, was a woman Sanura met when she'd moved into Assefa's mansion home, greeting the newcomer with warmth and kindness. Red hair no longer held their curls of last evening, and Sanura couldn't see the green of her eyes or the freckles on her nose. But the metallic, pleated dress, what was left of it anyway, clung to the body of Gayle Livingston, Assefa's housekeeper and friend.

****

Kansas City, Missouri

"When will you return home?"

Joanna Blackwell laughed into her cell phone and at the man on the other end. Sweet, Dahad Siddig had to be the sweetest were-cat she'd ever met, including the hyena she'd taken as her mate and familiar. Not that there had been anything wrong with Troy Blackwell. He'd been an excellent provider and mate, giving Joanna two great children—boys—but he was an army man through and through. And he'd died an army man, one of over three thousand American soldiers killed in Afghanistan since 2001. He'd survived two deployments to the desert country, but not the third. An improvised explosive device took his life in 2007; guerilla warfare at its finest and its most destructive.

Joanna paid the cabbie, grabbed her carry-on suitcase, and climbed out of the bright yellow taxi cab. The black bag, while old and well-used, reminded her of those long ago getaways Troy used to take their family on whenever he had a break from his military duties. A combination of guilt and love had Troy organizing the best family trips. Joanna and the boys had fond memories and dozens of pictures to show for Troy's successful efforts. So yeah, she could've traded in her 1990s boring black bag for a newer, sleeker model with dual caster spinner wheels, a hardside case, and a fancy color design like mocha maze and heart-leaf pink. But Joanna was old school and didn't see much need in upgrading when what she had served her purposes just fine.

Or maybe she saw too much of her fifty-seven-year-old self in the nondescript bag, no longer new and sleek but still miles left in her to travel.

"A couple of days. I can't see this trip taking longer than that." At least she hoped it wouldn't.

"I miss you already," Dahad grumbled.

Joanna laughed again. Yes, her African golden cat was sweet indeed. After Troy's death, life had held little joy for Joanna beyond her sons. But TJ had been a senior in college and John a freshman, no longer boys but young men who didn't need a mother's constant attention. The first couple of years after Troy's death she'd grieved deeply, as many widows did, she assumed. But her saving grace, the one that brought her equal parts stability and guilt, was her "easy" ability to adjust to Troy's absence in their home.

For twenty-five years, Troy had given all of himself to the United States Army, Special Operations. He lived and breathed the core, *sine pari*, without equal. No, Troy Blackwell had not been a sweet man, but he had been a patriotic one, leaving Joanna at home with their boys for months at a time. She hadn't realized, until after his death, how well she'd adapted and coped with his absences, over those twenty-five years.

In the early days of his death, she would tell herself her mate was on one of his many missions. But as the months would pass by, no short, rushed phone calls from him, the venomous truth would reassert itself, a death adder ambushing her and striking with lethal neurotoxin when she least expected. Still, there had been those months in which it took very little effort for Joanna to forget and to treat Troy's absence as any other, bringing a familiar and much-needed routine to her life.

But on those nights when she was forced to confront the lie she'd so painlessly built and lived, guilt would crash over Joanna, a riptide of grief and loneliness pulling her under, away, and into squelching darkness.

Yet after the rain and storm came the sun and better days. Through the grace of the gods, Joanna had her health but, more importantly, she had TJ and John. And now she had Dahad Siddig, a were-cat as fierce and as loyal as Troy had ever been. His charm and sweetness was an added bonus she found irresistible. At her age, Joanna felt blessed to have found love again, although she and Dahad hadn't talked of marriage. But he had invited her to a birthday party where he intended to introduce Joanna to his alpha and friends. Unfortunately, she had to turn the were-cat down. This trip to her brother's home took precedence over what sounded like a high-class gathering of preternaturals and full-humans.

"Where are you? Have you reached your brother's house yet?"

Joanna stood in front of the split entry home in northeast Kansas City. Darryl and his wife Michelle purchased the home in 2012 when it had first been built. It was a gorgeous home nestled in a quiet cul-de-sac. The four-bedroom house had all the amenities of a modern home—fireplace, granite counter tops, stainless steel appliances, pool, soaker tub, and a boat load of other features her brother thought justified the high price he'd paid for the house.

Honestly, Joanna never understood why Darryl and Michelle had purchased such a big home at their age. By the time they had, their three children were grown and living on their own. When she'd asked Darryl why he hadn't purchased a smaller dwelling, or at least a single story home, he'd smiled and said, "One of these days, Michelle and I will be grandparents. We need plenty of room for the rug rats." She got that, she really did. But four bedrooms and three bathrooms still seemed like a lot to Joanna, especially since none of Darryl's children were mated. How Darryl and Michelle had visions of grandbabies dancing in their heads, she'd never know.

Cell phone in one hand, suitcase handle in the other, she stared at the house. All the drapes in the front of the home were closed, which would've made sense if it were nighttime. But at eleven in the morning Michelle would've pushed the drapes aside, welcoming the natural light into her home. Earth witches were like that, their inner spirit more in tune with the sun than the other elemental witches.

"Yeah, I'm here. But it doesn't look as if they are."

"What do you mean?"

Joanna glanced around. Her brother's home was at the end of the cul-de-sac. Cars littered most driveways, and a few kids were out, using the cars and trees as hiding spots from the round-faced child in search of them. When the little girl, dressed in sneakers, leggings, and a red-and-white graphic tee that read: Keep Calm and Call Wonder Woman, spotted a boy about ten, trying to hide in a cottage playhouse meant for toddlers, she took off in his direction.

She turned away from the happy, playing children, already knowing the little Wonder Woman wannabe would catch the boy and he would be *it*. For his sake, Joanna hoped the little boy was better at seeking than he was at hiding. If not, he was in for a long, exhausting morning.

"The house is shut up." She eyed the cast aluminum pedestal mailbox in front of the house. "It's quiet and the mailbox is full."

"Maybe they went on vacation. You told me they're retired."

"Yeah, they are." Joanna lifted her suitcase as she made her way up the five steps to the front door. "But Darryl would've told me if he and Michelle were going out of town. Granted, living in Baltimore, I wouldn't have been able to keep an eye on the house for them. But Darryl still would've told me, just so I would know where he was and wouldn't worry if I called the house and reached only the answering machine."

Which had happened. For the last two weeks, she hadn't been able to reach her brother or her sister-in-law. Not on their house phone or on their cell phones, which had Joanna calling their children, all of whom had moved away from Missouri after graduating from college. To her growing concern, they hadn't heard from their parents either, but they, like Dahad, thought Darryl and Michelle had run off somewhere for a little trip and didn't want to be disturbed.

Which okay, if Joanna were being honest with herself, they'd done that before—romantic getaways to Branson for a flashy show and golfing or to St. Louis for a riverboat cruise and a bit of gambling at the Ameristar Casino. For some reason, though, this time felt different.

Yet everyone could be right, and Joanna an over reactive fool. But Troy always told her to trust her gut. "You have great instincts, Jo Jo. You'd make an excellent Army Ranger." Well, her instincts had brought her this far, and they would take her into the house and the truth.

"I don't like this. I should've gone with you."

"You had work to do."

"Assefa wouldn't have cared if I escorted you there. If I told him I didn't, just to stay here to watch his back, he wouldn't be pleased."

"He's your alpha. Your place is by his side."

"He is my alpha, although he rarely acts the part. My point is that I should've said something to him. If I had, you wouldn't be there alone, sounding frightened and nervous."

Joanna was both, unsurprised Dahad had detected those emotions in her voice. She pulled the Kansas City Chiefs lanyard from around her neck. The key to her brother's home dangled from the silver loop. He'd given Joanna and his children a lanyard and spare key when he and Michelle moved into the house, telling her, "Who in the hell are a bunch of poem spewing black birds going to intimidate on the football field? Edgar. Allan. Poe. My ass. The Chiefs, now that's a real football team." Joanna remembered making some remark about offensive football names, which had Darryl growling at her and then tickling Joanna until she cried her defeat, forgetting all her wind witch training in the face of her older brother's loving playfulness.

Now she stood outside his home, key in the lock and her heart in her throat. The organ pounded wildly, and her wind spirit became agitated.

"I can be there in a few hours," Dahad said. "I'll have Manute make me one of those online reservations while I pack. You find a nice hotel, and I'll meet you there. But whatever you do, Joanna, don't go into that damn house by yourself."

She heard the fear and unease in Dahad's voice. And she felt the disquiet of her wind spirit, its blistering magic chilling her core as she turned the key, displacing first the bolt lock and then the lock on the doorknob.

"Do you hear me? I said wait for me. Call a taxi and get the hell out of there. This doesn't feel right."

Commanding. Sweet, charming Dahad had never sounded so commanding before. Troy yes, but not her Dahad. But he was right. None of this felt right, although her gut, her instincts, told Joanna to forge ahead, that the truth could be found on the other side of the cherry beveled wooden door her brother had purchased and hung with expert hands.

Listen to your chosen mate. Do not go inside. We will not survive if you do.

"Are you listening? I'm getting Manute now." Joanna heard footsteps, hard and fast. "Get away from that house and call a taxi. Once you do, call me back. I'll stay on the phone with you until you're picked up."

The door swung back on hushed hinges when Joanna pushed it open.

"Dammit, Joanna, answer me."

Do not go inside. Do not go inside, my witch.

Joanna paused at the threshold, sweat beading her brow. Cell phone clutched in her hand and up to her ear, she saw nothing but ominous darkness before her. And a foul smell hung in the stale air, evidence that there was nothing alive in the house that beckoned to the witch.

Metallic, coppery, rusty is how Troy described the smell of fresh blood. Older blood as fruity or even ripe. Dried blood as rancid, musty. As a were-cat, he would've known. As a soldier, he'd had far too many experiences with the scent—fresh, old, and dried.

Not so for Joanna. But she knew. By the gods, she knew. Blood and death, a stench that curled its way up her pant leg, under her blouse, around her neck, and straight to her flared nostrils, burning the hairs within and the last shred of hope that all was well with her brother and his wife.

"Don't go inside the house," Dahad barked over the line. "Don't go inside the goddamn house."

Stay outside, my witch. Stay out here and keep us safe.

Good advice. The best advice.

So why was Joanna stepping inside the mausoleum of a house, closing and locking the door behind her?

Why were her fingers boneless, unable to keep ahold of her cell phone and suitcase? The *thud* when they hit the floor scarcely registered as Joanna stepped deeper into the foyer.

Deeper.

Deeper.

Driven. She'd been driven to get there, to reach this home and her brother.

Gut. Instincts. They'd never failed her. In fact, they'd been the source of her drive, pushing her forward, compelling her compliance. The 1,061 miles from Baltimore to Kansas City was a mere inconvenience of time and space she had no trouble conquering, her gut and instincts encouraging the impromptu trip.

And they prompted her on now, guiding her through the lightless house. But witches could see in the dark, just not as well as were-cats.

From somewhere, she thought she heard Dahad screaming her name, or maybe it was her wind spirit yelling at her. Or both, she couldn't tell. She could only move forward.

Until she didn't. Until she heard a laughing sound. Familiar, so familiar. But not quite. Madness, between the echoing beats of the laughter was madness.

A spotted hyena stood before her. Teeth bared. Froth coated his mouth and saliva fell into silent pools of menace.

Carnivore.

Opportunist.

Hunter.

Scavenger.

Darryl Hughes. Joanna's brother.

Before she could process what she saw, what was about to happen, magic lashed through her, picking Joanna up in a vortex of wind and sending her flying down the hallway and toward the locked front door. Her wind spirit. Gods, her wind spirit was trying to sav—

Sharp teeth clamped onto her right ankle, and strong jaws brought her crashing to the floor.

Thump.

Turning from her stomach and onto her back, Joanna tried not to look at the crazed hyena stalking her. She took cautious scoots backward and closer to a front door that seemed miles away with each *tap*, *tap*, *tap* of claws hitting hardwood flooring.

He began to circle Joanna, cutting off her slow retreat.

Tap. Tap. Tap.

Sickly yellow eyes watched Joanna, wild and inhuman.

Darryl, or what was left of her brother inside the insane mind of the laughing hyena, toyed with her, drawing near then backing away.

Tap. Tap. Tap.

Closer. Closer.

Her ankle hurt, bled. And her wind spirit raged, demanded action from the witch to save them. But her mind blanked. All her knowledge of magic and spellcasting gone with a single malicious bite.

Joanna began to cry, not for herself or even for her brother. But for TJ and John and Darryl and Michelle's children. Grown yes, but still in need of their parents' love, protection, and guidance.

She could hear Dahad better, now that she was closer to the front door and where she'd dropped her phone. Like her boys, he would mourn her. So she cried for him too, and their new love cut short.

Hands raised in front of her, Joanna touched the cold, wet snout of her brother. His breath was hot and smelled of things she'd rather not know. Closing her eyes, she conjured an image of Darryl, teasing her the way older brothers loved to do to their younger sister.

More tears, heavy and uncontrollable.

When he struck, fast and vicious, knocking her onto her back, head slamming into the floor, Joanna didn't fight, couldn't fight. The same gut and instincts that had her jumping on a plane and rushing across the country had frozen her limbs and her wind magic.

But not her pain. Gods on high, not her pain.

Darryl's razor-sharp fangs sank into her throat, cutting deep and ripping her open. Claws tore at clothing, shredding fabric and fragile skin.

Blood spurted and spilled.

Mouth shrieked, body twitched, and the hyena feasted.

CHAPTER NINETEEN

"It's about damn time," Ulan snarled when he answered the phone. "What in the hell took you so long to get back with me? Never mind. Never mind. It doesn't matter. I assume it had something to do with Sanura."

It had, but Assefa didn't appreciate his uncle's tone. Deaf, dumb, and blind, Ulan had told Zareb. He hadn't liked that assessment either, despite the truth of it.

"Just tell me what I've missed that you think I need to know."

"A hell of a lot, nephew. A hell of a lot." Ulan sighed, sounding less like an overbearing division chief and more like a concerned uncle. "There's been a shooting in the Bronx. A mass shooting. It's been all over the news for the last two days."

Assefa hadn't turned on the radio or cable news since Thursday, too concerned with giving Sanura the perfect birthday. Deaf, dumb, and blind indeed. But what did the mass shooting have to do with him?

"Was a preternatural the gunman?"

"Full-human, like all of her victims."

"Her? That's unusual."

"I know, but that's not the part of the news report that piqued my interest."

Assefa walked to one of the living room windows. From this spot, all he could see was grass and sunshine. He wondered where Sanura and Makena were and how their conversation was going. He had faith the women would, eventually, come to a meeting of the minds. When he saw Sanura with her mother, how close their bond, he couldn't help but be reminded of all denied his sister when their mother passed away. As a boy, he'd wanted his mother. As a female, Najja needed her mother. A meaningful distinction Assefa understood better now that he knew Sanura and Makena and the overwhelming power of the mother-daughter bond.

"Pilar Salazar, does that name ring a bell?"

"She's a Baltimore City detective. I met her when you sent me to the city on the adze case." That was the serial killer case that had brought him face-to-face with his destined mate. "I don't know her well. What does she have to do with anything?"

"Friday afternoon, Detective Salazar shot and killed seventeen people before being mortally wounded by Bronx police officers."

Assefa turned away from the window, slow to process what Ulan had just said. Detective Salazar, he remembered her. She was an attractive Puerto Rican woman who assessed people through bold, brown eyes, spoke with a New York City accent tempered by southern living, and smelled of uprightness and benzoin, a sweet vanilla-like fragrance.

"She wouldn't do something like that." But she obviously had. Otherwise, Ulan wouldn't have passed along inaccurate information. "I mean, I have no explanation why a good officer would kill innocent people. And why the Bronx? Why not Baltimore or a place a lot closer than New York?"

Assefa stalked around the living room, suddenly feeling like a caged beast being hunted.

"The case has just been turned over to the FBI. They view the mass shooting as an act of domestic terrorism."

"Who are the victims?"

"That's the reason I called, Assefa. Detective Salazar drove to the Bronx and opened fire on a street filled with people gathered for the grand opening of African Rights in America. When I first saw the broadcast about the shooting, I recognized the name of the organization but not the connection to you. It wasn't until a were-cat friend of mine on the Bronx PD called, wanting to know if the shooting was another full-human hate crime or one meant for my division, that I remembered."

"You remembered that I'm a major contributor to that non-profit organization."

"Yes. You give money to so many organizations, schools, and charities, I stopped trying to keep track of them all."

Assefa's claws had slipped from the tips of his fingers, and he knew his eyes glowed gold with anger. African Rights in America was an organization founded by foreign-born Africans who'd immigrated to the United States—mainly political and humanitarian refugees who were well-educated and spoke English fluently. Foreign-born Africans from Nigeria, Ethiopia, Ghana, and Somalia, for example, settled in major urban cities like New York, Los Angeles, Minneapolis, Chicago, and Philadelphia. Washington, Boston, Seattle, and New Jersey suburbs also had their fair share of African immigrants, adding to the cultural diversity of those areas.

Yet the United States, the country of their choice, wasn't always a welcoming and culturally accepting place to live. Nativism and racism became part of their immigrant experience. African Rights in America was created to, primarily, advocate for African civil rights in their adopted home and to serve as a source of information for various economic and social services. So yes, Assefa had helped fund the organization, taking a personal interest in a way that only another immigrant could understand.

"For a yet to be determined reason, Detective Salazar targeted and slaughtered seventeen men, women, and children. All African immigrants, although there were dozens of other people on the street. Broad daylight and dozens of witnesses." A humorless laugh and a disgusted snort. "The detective had to be a sociopath or on one of those mind-altering drugs that are so popular nowadays."

From all Ulan had said, one word caught Assefa's attention.

"Children?" The claws from the hand not holding the cell phone ripped into the cushions of first the loveseat and then the sofa. "How many children?" A snarl.

"Five. Four boys and one girl. They ranged in age from two to thirteen years."

Assefa closed his eyes and tried to recall how to breathe.

"Three were shot. The other two, toddlers I believe, were trampled to death when people realized what was going on and ... well, you know how scenes of chaos and panic play out."

He did. People ran for their lives, uncaring or unmindful of what they did to survive, even if that meant sacrificing the life of a child to spare their own. Assefa couldn't blame them their survival instinct, but that made the hurt and anger suffocating him no easier to accept.

"From what my Bronx PD friend told me, it took an unusually long time for first-responders to arrive on the scene. When they finally did, the officers' yelled at the detective to put her rifle down, but she didn't seem to hear them. Or maybe she ignored them. I don't know. But they had no choice but to take out the threat. The detective must've been on a suicide mission because she didn't have on her bulletproof vest. The officers' bullets ripped her apart. 'Overkill.' That's the word my friend used to describe the detective's death."

Assefa's claws withdrew, and he dropped onto the sliced loveseat, webbing and cotton batting were everywhere, a mute testimony to his temporary loss of control.

None of this made any sense to Assefa. The woman he'd met less than two months ago, a committed detective and fighter for justice, wouldn't kill without just cause. But what just cause could Detective Salazar possibly have had to massacre those African immigrants? None he could think of, yet she had. Seventeen people dead, eighteen including Pilar Salazar.

"Are you still there, nephew?"

"Can you get access to the investigation files? Autopsy and witness reports?"

"I already put Special Agent Huntington on it. The computer geni-us was given orders to forward her findings to the two of us. The first funeral for the victims of the shooting will be later this week, will you attend?"

Assefa didn't want to, but he would. How could he not? His sense of responsibility for the victims, which he counted Detective Pilar Salazar among them, meant he had no choice but to show his respect for the recently departed.

"As the funeral arrangements are finalized, have Huntington send me that information as well."

"For all of them?"

"Yes, including Detective Salazar's."

"Assefa, listen, I know how big your heart is, but I don't think it's a good idea for you to attend all of those funerals. Send flowers, make a charitable donation in the victims' names, but for Sekhmet's sake, don't do that to yourself."

"I don't have a choice."

"Yes, you do. You aren't responsible for the whole damn world. Their deaths aren't your fault. Hell, you barely knew the shooter."

True, but that truth meant little to Assefa. There was a bigger truth at work here, invisible yet lethal. The Mngwa sensed it, and the man agreed.

"I know but—"

The living room door swung open and two witches, wide-eyed, breaths heavy, and fire magic circling them, stood on the other side of the door.

Assefa jumped to his feet, his cell phone dropping from his hand and falling into a pile of cotton batting.

"What's wrong?"

Sanura rushed into the living room, trailing fire witch magic be-hind her.

He caught her by the shoulders, yanked Sanura to him, and stared over her right shoulder to a dazed Makena.

"She's dead," Sanura sobbed. "Gods, Assefa, I can't believe she's dead."

How had Sanura known about Detective Salazar? "Did Mike call and tell you about her death?"

Sanura stepped out of his embrace, shaking her head and dabbing at her eyes with the heel of her hand. "I haven't spoken to Mike today. And I don't know how he would even know."

"What are you talking about? He's known her for years."

"Mrs. Livingston?" Sanura frowned. "I'm pretty sure they met for the first time yesterday."

"No, Detective Pilar Salazar. They've known each other for …wait, what about Mrs. Livingston?" When Sanura didn't answer, sad eyes only staring at him, Assefa posed the same question to Makena.

She finally stepped into the living room, eyes thick with the same sorrow as Sanura's.

"I'm sorry to tell you, but Mrs. Livingston is dead." Makena raised a solitary finger and pointed toward the window behind Assefa. "Out there, by the river. She's ashore now, brought there by dozens of rainbow snakes. The creepy, slithering bastards returned her body, made sure we saw what had been done to her."

Assefa's gaze shifted to Sanura, who nodded as if what Makena had said made perfect sense. It didn't. None of this did. Mrs. Livingston couldn't be dead. He'd seen her just last night, laughing and dancing with her mate, Callum.

"She has the day off. Mrs. Livingston couldn't be down by the river." A nonsensical response to what Makena and Sanura had revealed and the truth he saw in their watery eyes. But they wouldn't lie to him, especially about something like this. No more than Ulan had been trying to deceive Assefa when he'd told him about Pilar Salazar. "She can't be dead," he heard himself mumble, an emotional rejection not supported by common sense. "Gayle and Callum have three little girls. She can't be dead."

He followed Makena's mournful gaze, still looking out the window as if she could see the river and Gayle Livingston's body.

"We saw her, Assefa." Two hands came to his disbelieving face and thumbs stroked under eyes that refused to shed tears. "We didn't see Callum, so I'm not sure if he's also ..." Sanura pressed her forehead to his. "Let's just hope, for their daughters' sake that Callum made it home safely last night."

Amanda, Frances, and Kelly Livingston were triplets who couldn't be more dissimilar. Amanda and Kelly, born within five minutes of each other, had red hair, fair skin, and freckles like their mother. While Frances, born a whole two minutes before Amanda, making her the oldest of the three, inherited her father's golden hair and seafoam eyes. When they turned six, Assefa had several of their drawings turned into custom toys, which earned him three tight hugs and sloppy kisses to the cheek. At seven, he'd given Amanda drums, Frances a guitar, and Kelly a keyboard for their "girl band." The triplets loved the gifts, of course, and Gayle didn't clean his bedchamber for a month. Last year, at eight, he'd sent the family to Disney World for a week, hoping to make up for his faux pas of the year before. Once again, his birthday gift was a hit with the girls and Gayle had gifted him with a full-color portrait of the family done by an artist in Downtown Disney.

The framed portrait hung in his home office, the most precious artwork in the entire house. This year, when they turned nine, what could Assefa give them that would wash away the tears and pain of losing their parents? Because Callum would not have left this house without his mate beside him. The were-cat wasn't built that way. He and Gayle had the night to themselves, Callum's parents babysitting the triplets at their home.

Was Callum's truck still there, parked in his wife's assigned spot? He would have to ask Dahad.

Assefa wanted to eviscerate another piece of furniture. The whole damn room, if necessary. Anything, gods anything, to drive back the pounding ache of loss and the confusion clouding his thinking. Two women dead. One he barely knew but respected as a fellow law enforcement officer, the other he cherished as a friend. Secretly, Assefa had envied Callum—his loving mate and adorable, rambunctious girls.

He'd wanted that kind of family for himself. Assefa still did. But they were gone now, Gayle and Callum Livingston. Their once whole and happy family forever fractured, shattered by what Assefa suspected to be magical means and godly motivations.

Mami Wata and her water witch of legend.

"I'm sorry," Sanura whispered. "I'm so very sorry about Mrs. Livingston. Tell me what I can do to help."

So many thoughts and images competed for space in his head. But all he could manage to pluck from the barrage was an image of the triplets by their parents' gravesite, faces damp and ashen, eyes red-rimmed and swollen, and accusatory fingers pointing at him.

He hadn't protected those under his charge, which was the most basic responsibility of an alpha. Yet he'd failed the Livingston family.

"The first thing we need to do is retrieve her body and call my uncle. He'll take care of the legal end while Zareb and I will see to things here. We need to know for sure what happened to Callum. From there, we'll decide how and when to break the news to the Livingston family. But I won't make that decision until I have more facts."

"If you have something owned by Mr. Livingston, even something he touched recently, I could perform a location spell."

Sanura and Assefa turned to Makena, who he'd forgotten was still in the room. She'd come back to herself and was looking more like the self-assured witch he'd come to know and love.

"Within reason," she added. "Ten to twenty miles in all directions. If he's in the river and within that range, I'll be able to find him."

"I don't have anything like that here, Makena. I suppose I could send Rashad or Manute to his home to retrieve whatever you might need to cast the location spell."

"There's another way," Sanura added, but she didn't look pleased with her alternative. "Mom or I could touch the body of Mrs. Livingston, which would give us a direct connection to her mate for the location spell."

"I was hoping not to go that route. But Sanura is right. That's actually the best, most effective option."

Assefa had seen a location spell performed before, by his sister when her pet rabbit had gotten lost in the presidential compound. She'd been sixteen, her magical abilities far beyond her witch peers. She was much stronger now, a powerful level six wind witch. But no witch he knew, not even Najja, could locate the dead up to twenty miles from her location.

These Williams women were truly extraordinary, their magic level, like Najja's, exceeding the normal one to five range. But the exact level, for either one of them, Assefa could only speculate. Makena, at least a seven, probably an eight. Sanura? Only Oya knew.

And the water witch of legend? Well, Mami Wata held the answer to that question.

"Let me get in touch with Dahad first. If Callum's car is still here, will that do?"

The women nodded.

"Good, just let me find my cell and call—"

An anguished roar pierced the maudlin air, cracking windows and stabbing Assefa in the heart. He knew that wail, the tortured cry. He'd heard it only once before when Dahad Siddig learned his mate, their two sons, and one grandson had died in a plane crash. It had been the worst sound he'd ever heard, like a volcano erupting and spewing out hundreds of colicky babies.

Assefa ran out of the living room and toward the sound he'd wished never to hear again. But on this day of truth, lies, and sorrow, when bad things often happened in threes, Assefa feared what he would learn once he reached his friend.

****

Sanura shot after Assefa, not knowing what else to do when he'd bolted from the room. Gods, the room, what in the hell had happened to
the loveseat and sofa? Shredded. Had Assefa done that? If so, why?
Before five minutes ago, he hadn't known about Mrs. Livingston, but
he'd said something about Detective Salazar. What did the detective
have to do with anything?

She heard shouting, cursing, and the loudest, most heartrending
bellows coming from the back of the house. Down the hallway and
through the kitchen she ran, Assefa so far in front of her she could no
longer see him. But she heard his voice, commanding but with an un-
dercurrent of gentleness and restraint.

They may have only shared a partial mate bond, but it was a powerful bond all the same. The emotions she detected now from her
special agent had her staggering to an abrupt halt. But it was the sight
in front of her that had Sanura stumbling forward and grasping for the
magic that connected her to Assefa.

Dahad's midsize car, a mere few feet out of the parking spot where
he kept it in the garage, was open on the driver's side. But no one was
inside the car. Omar and Zareb were on the ground with Mr. Siddig,
holding the screaming, thrashing man down.

"Let me go. I have to get to her before it's too late." He sobbed.
"Gods, it's already too late. I should've gone with her. Should've protected her."

Manute and young Rashad watched on, Mr. Siddig's car keys in
clenched in Manute's left hand.

For a long minute, no one moved or spoke, not even Assefa, who
stood by Mr. Siddig's restless legs, Zareb holding them firm while
Omar restrained the older man's arms above his head. They simply
stared at the distraught man, including Makena, who now stood next
to Sanura.

"I heard her screams and could do nothing to save her," Mr. Siddig wailed, a tormented confession that had him fighting Omar and Zareb with renewed effort. "But the bastard didn't care about her screams, her frightened whimpers. He ripped into her anyway until the screams dimmed and finally stopped. Then I heard what came next." He closed tear-ravaged eyes. "Every slurp. Every crunch. Every squish and swallow. I heard it all. Him devouring her, my lovely Joanna. Gods, I should've protected my witch. Now she's dead."

Assefa knelt beside Mr. Siddig, as calm as she'd ever seen him. A perfect alpha mask, she knew, because the rage and pain not revealed on Assefa's face or in the voice that spoke, was there in the tether of magic between them.

"Release him," Assefa said, voice as rich and soothing as steaming hot chocolate after an arduous trek up the Himalaya. "I'll take care of Dahad. He's mine."

Obeying without question, a shell-shocked Omar and a grim-faced Zareb let Mr. Siddig go. They got their feet but remained by their friend's side.

Sanura whispered in Makena's ear. If she'd been thinking straight earlier, she would've done it sooner.

Makena nodded and then walked over to Rashad. The young man trembled and cried. She wrapped an arm around his shoulders, spoke into his ear, and then led him in the house and away from the emotional drama no twenty-year-old should have to witness.

Sanura thought, as soon as Zareb and Omar let the older man go, he would make a run for his car, which she'd assumed was what he'd done earlier before being tackled to the ground by his friends. But he didn't. Mr. Siddig simply wept, ragged tears that shook his entire body.

Assefa, on his hands and knees, scooped Mr. Siddig into his arms. He pulled the man's back against his durable chest, legs on either side of the older man and held him while he cried for the woman he loved, the woman he couldn't save.

All the were-cats cried. All except Assefa, who embraced his friend with strong, masculine comfort. On their knees Omar, Zareb, and Manute went, huddling around their fallen comrade. Hands went to Assefa's shoulder, his leg, his arm while three hands found Mr. Siddig's shoulder, leg, and arm, completing a circle of friendship, of strength, of family.

Assefa was truly these were-cat's alpha. He led, and they followed. And when they hurt, he hurt with them. More, when they suffered, he comforted them. If he could see himself now, heart bleeding for his friend but in absolute control, a Sudanese prayer on his eloquent lips, Wolof melodic, Assefa would never question why these men chose him as their leader. Or why the Witch Council of Elders wanted him as Council Alpha.

Without conscious thought, she'd moved closer to the men. Their voices, in unison, repeated the prayer Assefa began. And while Mr. Siddig still cried, he no longer shivered his agony at losing his Joanna.

Joanna Blackwell, gods, Sanura didn't know the woman well, but Makena probably did. If Sanura recalled correctly, Makena and Joanna were around the same age and Joanna had two sons—were-cat leopards.

Assefa lifted composed brown eyes to her and asked Sanura a single but significant question. "Can you make him forget what he heard?"

Three more sets of eyes rose to Sanura, the same question in their gazes. To Omar, Zareb, and Manute, Sanura was not only the fire witch of legend but their alpha's biological mate, which meant she had the same level of responsibility to their household as Assefa.

Assefa knew differently, however. Yet he'd been the one to pose the question. He had to know how risky a memory wipe spell could be. Their partial mate bond might not be enough to help Sanura select and erase the single memory while leaving all others intact. Precision, it all boiled down to precision, to accuracy.

There were spells so powerful and dangerous the Witch Council banned the teaching and use of them to witches below a level four. Even then, high-level witches were cautioned to use the spells carefully, if at all. Memory wipes fell into the powerful and dangerous category, insanity, even death, the result when cast improperly. Or, for unscrupulous witches, cast properly.

She knelt behind Assefa, her arm going around his neck and hugging him to her, as he held Mr. Siddig.

"I can perform the spell."

With his help, she could. Yet Sanura would have to perform the spell flawlessly, or she could take more than the desired memory.

"But there's a risk Mr. Siddig may not be willing to pay."

"I know, but I believe in you, trust you with Dahad's life and his mind."

Gods, Assefa had no idea what his faith meant to Sanura. How it buoyed yet injured, mates, but not quite. He'd given her another gift yet he was also keeping her to their agreed-upon promise.

To fight.

Sanura kissed Assefa's cheek before pushing to her feet. She had a magical working to perform.

"Please take our friend inside the house. I have a delicate spell to cast, and I'd rather not do it on the dirty ground."

CHAPTER TWENTY

"What did you do to him?" Assefa sat on the edge of Rashad's bed. Like this, quiet and still, Rashad appeared younger than his twenty years. Assefa placed a hand on Rashad's chest, over his strongly beating heart and recalled when he first met the boy.

"A relaxation spell." A reassuring feminine hand touched his shoulder. "It's just a relaxation spell to calm the boy and help him sleep. Sanura asked me to take care of him."

Assefa should have known. In the midst of Dahad's emotional crisis, the psychologist had known what to do, enlisting the aid of her mother to help the youngest of his friends.

"Thank you, Makena."

"We're family, Assefa." The hand on his shoulder squeezed and Makena leaned in, pressing her mouth to the crown of his head and kissing. "Sanura told me everything, and I'm sorry. Be patient with her. She'll figure it all out and do the right thing. She loves you."

"I know."

"So do I. You're the son Sam and I always wanted." Leaning over top of him, Makena hugged Assefa with one arm extended around his chest, her mouth inches from his head. "You're like an iceberg. What you show people, what's above the water, is only ten percent of who you truly are. The depth of the man, the were-cat, lies beneath the water's surface. And that's the person who will be the Council's alpha. The man who is already the alpha of his household. And the man who will help Sanura tame her fire spirit and defeat Mami Wata's water witch."

He smiled, in humility and gratitude. Gods, the Williams women would be the emotional death of Assefa and his mighty Mngwa.

Makena kissed his head again before releasing Assefa from her motherly spider's web. "I called my sisters after I put young Rashad to sleep. They should be here shortly. I also called Cynthia."

Assefa removed Rashad's shoes and pulled the white-and-blue comforter up and over him.

Standing, he turned to face Makena. "Why did you call the Council and Cynthia?"

"If Mr. Livingston is in the river, it won't hurt to have two level five water witches at your disposal. And I need the rest of the Council to cast a four element ward around the property."

"Sanura already has magical wards in place." She'd cast the protective spells the day after the sirens had come calling. But they were only for the buildings on the property, not the acres of land as Makena had just suggested.

"I know, but the power of a Council, combining their magic, is much stronger than a sole witch's spell, especially since you are so close to a body of water. For a water witch, that's like leaving your door open and inviting the local burglar to come inside and rob you. We don't want to make an attack on you and Sanura any easier on the water witch of legend than it already is with the Potomac River so close to your property. That's something else Cynthia and Anna can help us with. There are no stronger water witches in our network than the two of them."

"It seems like you've thought of everything."

"No, although my sisters and I have had twenty-nine years to prepare for this. But there's so much we cannot plan for and protect you and Sanura from. Or your friends," she added, with a concerned gaze sliding to Rashad's bedroom door. "How is Mr. Siddig? I assume Sanura is with him."

"I asked her to perform a memory wipe spell. I couldn't think of anything else to do to ease his pain, his mental torment."

"Then you should be going. To perform the tricky spell, Sanura will need the aid of her familiar."

Makena was right, but Assefa stayed put.

"What's wrong?"

"Will our partial mate bond be enough? I mean, I've served as Sanura's familiar a couple of times, but never for a spell this delicate before. If we aren't in perfect sync, Dahad could suffer brain damage."

Or they could kill the man, which Assefa didn't want to utter aloud. Although, he had no doubt Makena well knew all the possible contraindications of a poorly executed memory wipe spell.

"I understand your concern and, under different circumstances, I would advise against it. But you're a powerful were-cat and Sanura's a talented spellcaster. Even with a partial mate bond, your combined effort should be enough."

"Should?"

The fire witch shrugged. "Magic, like the elements, can be unpredictable. No spell we cast is guaranteed to work, no matter our witch level, knowledge, and skill. The unforeseen can and does sometimes happen, despite our best efforts. As a witch, Sanura understands and accepts this truth. As her familiar, so must you. Claws and fangs will always cut, rip, and shred. That's the known, the stable factor in the witch-were-cat relationship. But magic, well, sometimes it's as steady as a three-legged table."

Assefa grasped Makena's hand, raised it to his mouth and kissed the back of her hand.

She shook her head and smiled. "You're an unrepentant charmer. What did I say to earn such a gentlemanly gesture?"

"You're an unrepentant pragmatist. I respect and like that trait in you."

"Because you share the trait. But let me tell you something, Assefa, people like us need people like Sam and Sanura. Dreamers keep us balanced as much as they challenge us to think beyond the confines of our minds and the tidy boxes we place them in. They have a wide lens vision and soul just as expansive."

"And we don't?"

"Not like them."

They began walking toward the bedroom door.

"Then what do we have?"

Assefa permitted Makena to walk through the door ahead of him. Before leaving, he took one last look at a peacefully sleeping Rashad. He would speak to him when he awoke, do all he could to reassure Rashad. Despite his bluster and silliness, Rashad was a sensitive boy who had no one in the world to care and love him except the were-cats he called friend and brother. And Dahad Siddig was as close to a grandfather as Rashad had ever known. No wonder the boy had nearly broken down, seeing Dahad in pain and out of control.

He closed the door. A right would take him down the hall and the front steps that led to the first level, where Dahad's room was located. The left led to his and Sanura's bedchamber, Sanura's home office, and a set of back steps Omar often took when he traveled from the kitchen and upstairs to his bedroom.

"I saw Callum Livingston's truck." When he'd heard Dahad's mournful scream and charged out of the living room and toward the garage, he'd seen the white SUV parked in Gayle's assigned spot. "As I said before, Callum wouldn't leave here without his mate."

"Cynthia and Anna will find him."

Assefa couldn't offer the Livingston triplets more than that, the bodies of their parents to bury. Cold comfort for the girls he loved like nieces. Like Rashad, they were now orphans, condemned to a life of faded memories and washed-out tears.

"I need to make a few more phone calls."

Assefa pointed to the open door of the office. "You may use that room there. It will afford you privacy. If I'm still in with Sanura and Dahad when Cynthia and the Council arrive, Zareb will help you with whatever you need. I'll let him know."

"Thank you."

They began to walk away, going in different directions. But Assefa had to know, so he asked over his shoulder, "If Sanura's a visionary with a deep soul, then what am I?"

Assefa heard Makena stop and sensed she'd turned to look at him. He didn't move, keeping his back to the fire witch, as if that would prevent her from knowing how much her opinion and analysis mattered to him. And there were so few people's opinions Assefa valued, especially above that of his own.

But with this woman, on this topic, she'd piqued his interest and uncovered a latent question.

"You're the rest of the body, Assefa. The calm mind. The steely shoulders. And the determined heart. Incomplete and imperfect, like Sanura."

Incomplete and imperfect, two words that aptly described how Assefa always viewed himself. And while his inner cat assured him that mating with Sanura's fire spirit would complete him, the man knew that perfection of mind, body, and soul did not exist.

Not for humans.

Not for preternaturals.

Not even for gods.

He listened and waited as Makena proceeded down the hall and enter Sanura's office before he resumed walking. A couple of minutes later, he stood on the outside of Dahad's bedroom, Omar and Zareb flanking the door, Manute leaning against the opposite wall.

"Why are the three of you out here?"

"Once we got Dahad settled and pushed the furniture out of the doc's way, Sanura thanked us then asked us to leave her alone with him."

"You did what?"

Zareb stared back at Assefa when he glared at the man as if he had an IQ of a pet rock.

"Why in Sekhmet's name would you leave my witch alone in a room with an unstable and distraught were-cat?"

"Because Dr. Williams is the fire witch of legend." "Because she's kind of scary when her magic rises to the surface."

Omar and Manute had spoken at the same time. And Assefa was no more interested in their opinion than he was in Zareb's self-assured posture. Yet he heard nothing coming from Dahad's room that had his hackles rising. In fact, he heard no voices at all. Which meant, thankfully, Sanura was safe and Dahad composed.

"Zareb, I need you to meet Makena in Sanura's office. When her Council sisters and Cynthia arrive, escort them to the river. Whatever they need for their spell, if anything, you and Manute get it for them."

"What? What's at the river?"

Ah hell, with everything with Dahad and Joanna, he'd forgotten the men knew nothing about Mrs. Livingston. With one ear trained on Dahad's bedroom, Assefa gave the men a cliffs-notes-version of what Sanura and Makena had told him they'd witnessed down by the river. By the time he'd finished, Manute had slumped to the floor, Omar's eyes had hardened to brown pinpoints of anger and sorrow, and Zareb had stalked away, cursing in Wolof and in English.

It had taken Assefa years to create a safe and happy home for his friends. Yet in a matter of hours, minutes, Mami Wata and her water witch threatened to unravel all that he held dear. His men, his friends, were falling apart right before his eyes. This couldn't continue. Assefa wouldn't let it continue.

He entered Dahad's room and stopped dead in his tracks.

The lights were off, and all the furniture had been pushed up against the tan walls. In the center were Sanura and Dahad, surrounded by four candles—two blue and two green. Each lit candle was placed at a cardinal point of Sanura's chalk-drawn magical circle.

The witch had wasted no time while he'd been upstairs with Makena and Rashad, slipping in and out of their room, for her spell-casting supplies.

Dahad sat cross-legged in front of a kneeling Sanura. His blue-and-white judo shirt, leather loafers, and socks had been removed, leaving the older man in a black, ribbed tank top and dark-blue pants. Eyes closed, Dahad no longer wept, but the pain of Joanna's death was etched in every line of the were-cat's solemn face.

With a soft *click*, Assefa closed the door behind him and walked farther into the room. Without needing to be told, he joined Sanura and Dahad in the circle. He sat in the spot he knew Sanura reserved for him, the third point of the triangle. A blue candle burned behind Assefa and green candles flickered to the right and left of him, with the second blue candle on the other side of the circle.

"The color blue has many meanings to witches," Sanura had once told him. "Trust, calm, stability, peace. But the power isn't in the color itself, but the witch's faith attached to the color and to her magic."

She'd shared other colors and their meanings, and Assefa had remembered them all. The color green represented health, nature, peace, and harmony, which aligned with the emotional and magical intent of the spell Sanura was about to cast.

Sanura raised a steady hand and laid it upon Dahad's cheek. The older man didn't move, didn't acknowledge Sanura's tender touch beyond a tear that slipped from him.

"I can take away the painful memory, Mr. Siddig."

Sanura's voice, psychologist calm and reassuring, the way it had been when Assefa had first met her. Mike had asked Sanura to meet them at Johns Hopkins Hospital to speak with an adolescent witch whose parents were murdered by an adze. Elizabeth Ferrell had been the sole survivor of a horrific night of bloodlust and violence. Yet she'd opened up to Dr. Sanura Williams, putting her trust and faith in a woman whose warm touch and dulcet voice had an uncanny effect.

They felt like home, hugs, and heaven.

"Or I can do nothing at all. The choice is yours."

Dahad's eyelids opened half-mast, red, puffy, and moist. Then his right hand came up to cover the one on his face. "I can't stop hearing her screams. No matter how hard I try, I hear them. Over and over and over."

"You won't always hear them. Today you will. Tomorrow. And many days after that. But not always, not forever. You will heal. The mind and heart are capable of bringing us so much heartache, but they also have the capacity for great strength and perseverance."

Heavy, weary lids opened all the way. They stared at Sanura with so much pain, so much grief Assefa wished Sanura hadn't given the man a choice. And while she may be a powerful witch, Sanura was also a doctor of the mind. For her, this was about more than patient informed consent.

She understood the grieving process, not just as a physician but as a daughter who'd lost her father and had yet to fully accept his death. But she was working through it, a slow journey but a necessary one for personal growth, psychological health, and emotional sovereignty.

"But I want to forget now. Does that make me a coward?"

Sanura used her other hand to wipe away Dahad's tears. "There's nothing cowardly about wanting relief from a bleeding and broken heart, Mr. Siddig. None of your friends will think less of you if you grant me permission to cast the memory wipe spell. But the question you must ask is whether you will think less of yourself."

They dropped their hands, Sanura's to her side, Dahad's to his lap.

"Are you saying I'll remember asking you to perform the spell on me?"

"Yes, if I only remove the memory of what you heard on the phone. Everything before and after will remain with you."

"But you could remove more than those few minutes, couldn't you?"

What was Dahad saying? He couldn't possibly want Sanura to wipe his mind of all memories of Joanna.

"Wiping weeks and months, even years of memories, is far easier than minutes and specific memories. It's the difference between using a needle to pop a balloon and threading a needle with yarn. Is that what you want? For me to wipe all memories of your witch?"

Assefa felt as if he should intervene since it was he who'd asked Sanura to take this step with Dahad. At that moment, holding a quivering, grief-stricken Dahad, all Assefa wanted to do was alleviate his friend's pain. So he'd turned to his fire witch, knowing she possessed the power to do what he could not. Yet watching and listening to Dahad now, contemplating erasing chunks of his memories of a woman he loved but did not think he could cope with losing, Assefa's anger blazed to life.

Mami Wata and the water witch of legend were playing a dangerous, cruel game with him. Instead of attacking Assefa outright, they were systematically, strategically peeling back the layers of his heart, exposing the organ for the sentimental, weak creature that it was. But it was his friends and their loved ones who'd taken the brunt of the assault, mere pawns in a war between two selfish and unfeeling goddesses.

Dahad and Joanna.

Gayle, Callum, and their daughters.

Pilar Salazar and the seventeen African immigrants.

And only Mami Wata knew how many other lives she and her water witch had taken, tainted, and destroyed, all in the name of some damn prophecy. Now Dahad Siddig, a man who'd lost his entire family in a fatal plane crash, an "unfortunate act of the gods" Uncle Ulan had once called it, was now considering sacrificing so much more than the loss of Joanna.

"I don't know what I want. And I'm ashamed at how weak I feel and by how much I want to run away from my thoughts and pain."

"Once you begin running, it's difficult to stop. And once I remove your memories, they're gone forever. Is that your wish, Mr. Siddig, to never remember the good times you shared with Joanna? Her smile? Her laughter? Her touch? Her love?"

Tears bled from Dahad, a stream of doubt, self-loathing, and anguish. He shook his head. "I want all of those memories. I don't want to forget her. But I want to be able to sleep at night without dreaming about how she died and how terrified she must've been when the end came. I wish I was stronger. I would like to get over her death without magic. But I don't think I can."

"It's not a question of your strength, Dahad," Assefa said, "but a matter of safeguarding your heart and mind. Just for the record, your alpha will not think less of you as a were-cat or as a man if you consent to the spell."

Dahad held Assefa's gaze, a depth of understanding in his weepy eyes. Never had Assefa referred to himself as anyone's alpha, despite having earned the unfailing allegiance of Siddig, Zareb, Omar, Manute, and Rashad. For so many years, he'd refused to acknowledge the title or act in the role of a true alpha. But those days were over, Assefa knew. He could no longer deny the truth or his friends' appeal. To continue to do so would only expose them to more danger. For the war that was already at his front door, Assefa had to be more, be better, be an alpha.

Ninety minutes later, emotionally spent and magically exhausted, Sanura and Assefa strolled, hand-in-hand, across the lawn and toward the Potomac River. Neither spoke, which was fine. They'd just spent nearly two hours magically linked and threading that needle with yarn Sanura mentioned earlier. An apt analogy, as it had turned out.

Sanura truly was a master witch. She had the finest of touches as she explored Dahad's brain with her magic. The spell turned out to be more complicated than Assefa had thought because present and past memories melded together in an intricate knot of feelings, facts, and interpretations.

With his help, however, Sanura managed to untangle the Gordian knot of Dahad's mind, freeing him of the last minutes of Joanna's brutal death while leaving his other memories of the wind witch intact.

They passed the gazebo, Assefa spotting a crowd of familiar faces when they cleared the top of the small hill. The full Council was there as were Cynthia, Rachel, and Zareb. They stood several feet from the dock, backs to Sanura and Assefa, eyes on the wind-roughened waters of the Potomac.

The river began to hiss, rage, and grow. Up the water went, twenty-foot spirals of blue-black waterspouts, an intense columnar vortex of river water and dozens of kingsnakes.

Sanura shouted.

Assefa transformed.

And the waterspouts attacked.

CHAPTER TWENTY-ONE

The sky rained snakes. Opportunistic creatures of vibrant colors that killed its prey, including other snakes, through constriction, swirled in the raging water storms. Menacing and moving toward the shore like a fluid tornado of death, eight waterspouts twisted and turned. Kingsnakes shot from them like arrows from an archer's lethal bow.

"Watch out!" Sanura yelled, already knowing it was too late to prevent what was to come.

Dozens of red snakes with black-and-white stripes bolted from the waterspouts. Their shiny shields of dorsal scales careened through the darkening sky, landing in the grass and on stunned witches.

But the shock lasted no longer than the time it took the first wave of kingsnakes to touch down and the first waterspout to make shore.

Splash. Slam.

Down went the witches and Zareb, knocked off their feet and surrounded by water and slithering snakes.

Splash. Slam.

Splash. Slam.

Two more waterspouts attacked, the weight and ferocity of the water keeping the witches and were-cat on their hands and knees and vulnerable to the looming kingsnakes.

As if commanded at once, dozens of red snakes attacked, attaching themselves to legs, arms, wrists, ankles, and necks, whatever body part they could get ahold of.

Barbara screamed, swallowing river water and thrashing like a madwoman.

Peggy made to stand but was forced back to the soggy ground as more snakes worked their way up her body, wrapping around her like a corset of old.

Makena's eyes raged fire engine red, as scarlet as the snakes around her neck, choking the life out of her.

Zareb was somewhere in a half man, half tiger state, his body heaving and convulsing as he fought to force his change while being squeezed by a dozen or more vicious kingsnakes.

A horrid sight. Zareb's hands, feet, and face were that of a tiger, but the rest of him existed in a grotesque suspended animation between humanity and animality. His growls, filled with fury, also exposed his physical and spiritual pain. Were-cats did not have an in-between state. Nothing resided in the in-between but fear and loneliness. Man and beast, in the in-between, were ripped from each other, their magic a taut tether all that kept them connected.

Splash. Slam.

Splash. Slam.

Assefa's Mngwa, shredded clothes hanging from his humongous form, waded into the water, batting, clawing, and ripping snakes with speed and accuracy. But there were so many of them and the water-spouts kept coming.

A wide-eyed Rachel hid behind a kneeling Cynthia, who shielded the earth witch with her body and her water magic. In fact, no water-spout attacked either Cynthia or Anna, who was crawling toward the still screaming Barbara.

Cynthia stood, hands up and in front of her.

Two more waterspouts barreled toward the group, flinging snakes at the snarling Mngwa, who stood in knee-high water surrounded by a pile of severed and slashed snake flesh.

"Damn you back to the river of your birth. Be gone from this land of rock, grass, and trees." Cynthia stepped forward, dreadlocks falling onto tense, determined shoulders, water witch magic a blue-and-white haze around her. "Heed my command," she yelled over top of the swirling but slowing waterspouts. "Be gone from this land of rock, grass, and trees."

"Be gone from this land of rock, grass, and trees," Anna chorused, kneeling beside a shivering Barbara.

Sanura ran to her mother and began freeing her from the snakes, burning them off her with each heated touch.

"Be gone from this land of rock, grass, and trees," the water witches spoke in unison. "We command you. We command you. We command you."

Once free of the scaly encumbrances, Makena sloshed through the water to reach Peggy, who was having difficulty using her earth magic to defend herself. Two vicious gray-banded kingsnakes had their bodies coiled around her neck, preventing Peggy from uttering a single spell.

"Be gone from this land of rock, grass, and trees." Hands up, water witch magic potent and thickening the midday air, Cynthia and Anna moved closer together. "Be gone. We command the water. Heed your mistresses and be gone."

Sanura kicked snakes out of her way as she ran past the fighting Mngwa and to Zareb. As she did her mother, Sanura burned the slithering beasts from the special agent. Once free, his Bengal tiger burst forth, healing Zareb's bruised flesh before taking form with angry relief and vengeful white fangs.

Cynthia and Anna, arms stretched to their sides, one hand linked with the other witch, combined their water magic. They repeated their incantation, pushing the waterspouts away from land and back into the water. Even with their collaborative will and magical might, the waterspouts still raged, still harnessed the power to harm, to kill.

And the kingsnakes were their weapons, catapulted at the group as if they were missiles intent on destroying the castle walls. And a wall they indeed hit. A wall of water witch magic, a blue-and-white fortified defense stronger than any siege weapon of forked tongues and shiny scales.

"Heat of fire, heat of flames, burn, burn, burn." Sanura directed her fire magic at the swirling waterspouts and the river supporting them. "Heat of fire, heat of flames, burn, burn, burn."

Bubbles began at the base of the five waterspouts the water witches were keeping at bay.

"Heat of fire, heat of flames," Makena began from the other side of the watery, slithering battlefield, "burn, burn, burn."

A gasping Peggy flattened her hands into the grass. Her voice, hoarse when she spoke, resonated with formidable earth witch magic. "Soil of life, roots of history, feast, feast, feast."

The earth beneath began to shake, shallow tremors that grew each time Peggy recited her spell. "Feast, feast, feast," she commanded.

Cracks opened in the grass and out sprang bulky, gnarled tree roots. The roots reared up from the displaced grass and dirt like the Kraken's tentacles from beneath the Greenland Sea, seizing the kingsnakes in its coarse, unbreakable grips.

And crushed, crushed, crushed.

From the corner of her eye, Sanura saw Rachel follow Peggy's lead. Although she was only a level one earth witch, she could add her magic to the priestess', upping Peggy's earth magic from a four to a five.

The snakes were burned, strangled, and ripped to shreds. Dozens upon dozens of them.

The Potomac River bubbled and boiled, defenseless against the combined fire magic of Sanura and Makena Williams.

And when the oldest of the witches got to her feet, clothing drenched, hair matted to scalp, face haggard but eyes glowing white with wrath, the hot air bowed in supplication and departed.

In came the freezing cold directed at the stalled but resilient waterspouts. Bone-chilling wind surged toward the remaining waterspouts, corralling them and pushing the vortexes deeper into the boiling river, an unheard spell on the pissed-off wind witch's lips.

The area was bathed in a symphony of elemental witch magic—dense, demanding, and absolutely unforgiving.

Unless Mami Wata herself appeared, this unexpected battle was over. But the ugly, cruel brutality of the day wasn't.

Dissolving like an effervescent tablet into the caldron of boiling water the fire witches had turned the river into, the waterspouts gasped and fizzled their liquid defeat.

Assefa's lawn, once immaculate and inviting, was now water-logged and smelled of burnt snake skin.

Waiting for her fire magic to cool, Sanura scanned the faces of her family and friends. The Mngwa and the tiger had their muzzles to the ground, searching for whatever snakes may still be lurking. Every now and again, Sanura saw one of the big cats raise a claw and slice a kingsnake in two.

Rachel, Peggy, and Barbara huddled together while Anna and Cynthia still had their blue eyes cast to the oddly swirling water.

She prepared a fire spell when the swirling picked up the pace, its momentum growing with each passing second.

The water witches, hands still clasped, detected the unseen danger as well, their magic, like Sanura's, poised to defend.

A final waterspout rose from the river, spinning in rapid rotations. But it didn't remain above the water for long, nor did it spew forth more constricting snakes. With one hard jettison, it flung its sole cargo at Sanura.

Thwack. Thud.

Down she went, a bloated dead body on top of her.

****

You have violated critical rules of war.

Tossing her scrying glass into the air, where it hovered within reach and at eye level, Mami Wata, back to her sister, smiled her most wicked and self-satisfied smile. Today had been a most delicious day indeed. And it had hours yet to go.

Daughter of Yemaya, you will not sully this holy war with short-sighted acts of cruelty and barbarism.

Sekhmet, the disembodied voice in the room, threatened to ruin this glorious moment for Mami Wata.

"There is nothing holy about this war or those of the past, daughter of Ra. You and my mother may be tasked with monitoring what takes place between myself and Oya, as if either of you have the moral standing to judge my war strategy, but I have stayed within the parameters of this duel."

The lion goddess' growl shook the prison room Mami Wata shared with Oya, an earthquake in the realm of the gods.

Mami Wata fell to her hands and knees, unable to remain standing with the floor cracking and crumbling beneath her.

You live but for the mercy of Ra. You exist to do his bidding, not to wreak havoc on the mortal realm as if you had no more sense and discipline than a rabid warmonger.

As the room exploded around her, Mami Wata covered her head, ears throbbing from Sekhmet's roar. Her long, thick hair blew like an uprooted tree in a tropical cyclone and her bare flesh split and bled when invisible claws raked over her.

Through the pain, as well as the humiliation of being treated and punished as if she were a baby god caught pilfering the sun god's solar disk, Mami Wata refused to play the villain to the goddess' hero. When it came to the gods, on any given day, sometimes within the same day, they could be both.

Through a haze of pain and anger, Mami Wata peered over her shoulder and to the other side of the room. Just as she'd been before, Oya reclined on her Mngwa print chaise lounge, green eyes boring into her from a spot untouched by Sekhmet's wrath.

Mami Wata turned away from her younger sister, uncomfortable with the glimmer of love and pity she saw staring back at her. She did not need or want her sister's love, and she certainly did not appreciate her pity. The mere thought of Oya pitying her had Mami Wata surging to her feet, heedless of the claws and cyclone laboring to compel her submission.

She would not submit. She had never submitted.

"Ra desired a villain. I am that villain. Witches and were-cats fear me, and well they should. I care nothing for their mortal hearts, minds, or souls. They are too easily controlled and manipulated, especially the full-humans."

You go too far, water goddess. It is not yet time for the Day of Serpents.

Lion claws freed Mami Wata from their biting grip and the tropical cyclone withdrew, reforming the shattered west side of the prison room as it made its chilly retreat. Within seconds, the room was once more whole, an infinitesimal example of a god's divine power. What Mami Wata had done minutes ago, waterspouts and snakes, required no more than a thimble full of her power. Yet the knowledge she had gained and the fun she had had was well worth an angry visit from Sekhmet.

And you were not given permission to use my were-cats as part of your plan to test the heart and will of the cat of legend.

Ah, now Sekhmet's anger became clear. Mami Wata should have known the warrior goddess had not taken issue with the deaths of mortals.

"Not were-cats, Sekhmet. I only played with one of your furry creatures. And it was not even one of the prettier creations you birthed. Hyenas are hideous but quite mentally malleable."

You try my patience, daughter of Yemaya. I will countenance no further ill use of my were-men. Stay within your domain, water goddess, and out of mine.

"And the death of the full-humans?"

Casualties of war. Mami Wata could hear the shrug in the warrior goddess' voice. *They served their purpose. They died for the greater good. Ra will reward them their sacrifice.*

So Sekhmet had only come to chastise Mami Wata on her handling of her precious were-hyena, a territorial backlash she should have anticipated. Yet it was her unstated message she most took to heart.

All was fair in love and war. This was war. And Mami Wata loved no one.

She smirked. Some of Sekhmet's precious were-cats would still serve Mami Wata's cause. Unlike the were-hyena in Kansas City, whose mind she had so relished tormenting and twisting, converting him from a man of love and principles to one of hate and hunger, Mami Wata need not lift one magical finger to get what she wanted. The goddess only had to sit back and wait and watch.

And, of course, savor the cat of legend's pain and his bitter taste of defeat.

This summer would be the longest and shortest of Assefa Berber's life.

****

"How is everyone, Dr. Bradford?"

The earth witch's scrutinizing eyes cast around the dining room, where they'd all retreated after the battle down by the river. Cynthia and Rachel sat beside each other, quiet and tense but surprisingly composed for all they'd seen and been through. Barbara, like Assefa and Sanura, sat across from them. The older woman appeared every bit her age—haggard but with a dogged strength Assefa couldn't help but admire. Zareb stood at the head of the table, surreptitious eyes skidding to and away from Cynthia, agitated fingers tapping on the large natural wood table.

Assefa held Sanura's hand, which he'd taken as soon as he and Zareb met the group in the dining room after shifting back into their human form and dressing. The fire witch sat between Assefa and Makena, whose eyes registered the same concern for Sanura as his own.

She hadn't spoken a single word since being buried under the cold, rotting corpse of Callum Livingston.

Gods, the thought of the murdered man and his wife set Assefa on edge. He'd feared the man was dead. But having that fear confirmed in such a vicious and insensitive way put Assefa in the mind of bloody murder. Mami Wata or the water witch of legend, the death of either a succulent craving for his vengeful Mngwa.

Peggy claimed the white, nail-head trimmed Parson Chair at the other end of the table, slumping onto the cushion as if she'd pulled a double shift in a hospital emergency room.

"A few shallow snake bites." The doctor raised her arm, showing rows of thick, red cords where kingsnakes had been. "Except you and Sanura, everyone else sustained skin contusions. Thank the gods."

That was good news, but Peggy hadn't stated the situation accurately. The kingsnakes hadn't been able to penetrate his dense Mngwa fur, although they had tried. Sanura, he suspected, had propelled the snakes with the sheer heat of her wild fire magic. Even now, her skin was almost too warm to touch. Yet Anna and Cynthia, the only water witches in the group, had gone unmolested by the waterspouts and the snakes, which the good doctor had to know.

Assefa thought of raising the issue, but was forestalled when the high priestess said, "Mami Wata and her water witch are trying to cause dissension in our ranks."

Cynthia glanced down at her injury-free body and relatively dry clothing. "Anna and I were spared while the rest of you took the full brunt of the water and snake attacks."

"When I saw that river yesterday," Rachel began, "I thought it beautiful and serene." She wiped a shivering hand over her brow and snorted a humorless laugh. "If I never see another body of water, it will be too soon. But yeah, the water witches were left unmolested."

Rachel looked down the table and at Peggy. "We all saw it, no need to pretend that we didn't."

"Or try to protect Anna and Cynthia from their friends," Makena added. "We decided long ago to not lay unfounded distrust at our water sisters' feet because of Mami Wata and the prophecy. High Priestess Katherine did enough of that during her tenure on the Council. And we won't allow those days of discord to return. If we begin second guessing each other now, where will it end?"

No one replied, but all eyes shifted to Anna and Cynthia. The women stared back, unwavering in the face of open scrutiny. And while Assefa could sense their anxiety, neither smelled of lies and deception.

"No one here thinks the two of you are in collusion with Mami Wata or the water witch of legend." Sanura disengaged her fingers from his and settled her hands on top of the table. She smiled at her high priestess and best friend. "We trust you. I trust you. You protected us when we needed your water magic the most. That's what witches do for each other, shielding our sisters' backs with our power."

A fog of uncertainty and tension that had settled over the dining room lifted and cleared with Sanura's honest words and unfailing faith in her water sisters.

Anna nodded in unhidden relief, and Cynthia returned Sanura's smile. They were truly sisters of the heart, the same as Zareb and Assefa were brothers of the soul.

Rachel, who must've been with Cynthia when Makena called, deciding to tag along for the ride, broke the silence with a jarring and gut-wrenching question. "Umm, was that Callum Livingston who fell onto Sanura?"

For the breath of a thundering heartbeat, no one spoke. The Council and Cynthia were asked to come there to help Makena locate Callum. Assefa assumed that's what the group of women, along with Zareb, were doing down by the river when he and Sanura had come upon them. But the witches hadn't exactly found the man, no more than Callum had simply fallen onto Sanura.

Sadly, his body had been spat from the river as if he were trash, a wad of worthless gum on the bottom of Mami Wata's godly shoe.

"Yes," Assefa said, confirming what all in the room had to be thinking. "My uncle has sent a couple of agents from the Preternatural Division to collect the Livingstons. They should be here soon."

The bodies would then undergo a magical autopsy before being taken to a local witch-owned funeral home. Once in the care of the funeral director, Assefa would drive out to speak with the Livingston family about their loss. He would only have a word with the triplets' grandparents, of course, who would then have the unenviable task of explaining to the girls their parents would never pick them up and take them home.

The rancid thought felt like a Bowie knife being plunged into his chest and through his heart—deadly but not fatal. Assefa had too much to live for and too many people to protect to allow anyone, even an entitled and privileged god, to permit the pillaging of his heart, mind, and soul from vile plots and unscrupulous deeds.

He would defeat the god and her water witch. Assefa didn't know how, but he had no doubt he and Sanura would prevail. His concern, and it was a monumental one, was how many innocent people, including family and friends, would die before they managed to do so.

Rachel held the large black towel Omar had given her tightly around her shivering shoulders. When they'd sloshed into the house, sodden bodies and haggard eyes, Omar had arched one questioning brow at them before escorting the group away from his spotless kitchen and to the mudroom.

"If you like, I could find out what happened down by the river."

"I don't understand. What do you mean?"

Rachel's lips lifted in a shallow smile. "Yes, I realize I'm the least powerful witch at this table, but even low-level witches, on occasion, have their uses."

"That's not what Assefa meant, Rach." Sanura folded her hands on top of the towel that covered her damp dress. "Assefa wouldn't insult you or your earth witch magic. He posed an honest question. He doesn't know what makes you special in a way that the rest of us aren't."

While it was true Assefa didn't know to what witch power Rachel referred, it was obvious the teacher of foreign languages had a chip on her shoulder about her magic level. Which, in all honesty, Assefa could understand, especially since her best friends' magic levels far outpaced her own.

Rachel's gaze met his, an apology in her autumn brown eyes. But she didn't offer it. Instead, she explained.

"Earth witches draw their power from the land, the ground. The closer we are to it, the more potent our spells. We love the soil as much as we cherish the heat from the sun that give life to trees, plants, flowers, and grass."

"I know all of that about earth witches. Tell me what I don't know about you."

"What you don't know about me is that I have a rare magical ability to commune with nature."

Assefa didn't see what was so special about that. As far as he knew, all witches could commune with nature in some form or fashion. It was what made them elemental earth witches.

He stared at Rachel Foster, unimpressed by her lack of an interesting or useful revelation.

"What Rachel is trying to say, and rather poorly for a teacher of young minds," Peggy interjected, "is that she can actually communicate with plant life. To her, it's like another foreign language to decode and master. To me, the flora on this property sound like white noise across the spectrum of my magical senses. I've never known another earth witch with her particular talent, level one or level five. It's amazing really, and wasted on a witch who fails to recognize her own magical worth."

Priestess Peggy Bradford gave and took, complimented and insulted. Assefa hoped her bedside manner with her patients was better, but from the oblivious, haughty way she held her head, he didn't think so.

No matter, Assefa now understood what Sanura had meant by "special." And he was definitely interested. But first they needed a plan of action. So much needed to be done and Assefa had three were-cats in Omar, Zareb, and Manute and seven witches at his disposal. He wouldn't squander such powerful resources.

"Here's the plan. Two water witch agents have been dispatched to this location. Once they arrive, they'll take care of Gayle and Callum. In the meantime, I don't think I have to tell anyone here to stay away from the river. That includes the high priestess and Cynthia. I don't want Mami Wata or her water witch to use or hurt either of you because you're close to Sanura and have access to this household."

"Makes sense," Cynthia agreed. "They have to know that after what they did at the river and to the Livingstons that Anna and I will stand between any water magic attack and our friends. Maybe that was the reason why we weren't attacked. Maybe they wanted to gauge the strength and loyalty of your water witch allies in the face of danger and death."

"Perhaps you're right. And if that turns out to be the case, then you and Anna may now have targets on your back."

"Any witch or were-cat who dares to take a stand against Mami Wata and her water witch is a target," Makena said. "Based on what happened to the Livingstons, they have no decency in who they use to harm you and Sanura. Danger and maybe our deaths are unavoidable, but the Council is sworn to serve and to protect. The same as you, Zareb, Ulan, and Mike. We are here because we want to be here, Assefa. So give us our marching orders, Alpha, and we will carry them out."

Assefa didn't think he would ever get used to having people call him that, but now wasn't the time to travel down the well-trodden road of insecurity and fear.

"Okay, well, you mentioned the need to cast a four element ward around the property. Once the agents have come and gone, I would like the Council to cast the ward."

"Cynthia and I can cast one where your property meets the Potomac River." Anna looked to Cynthia, who nodded her head. "We can make it strong enough to stop a level eight, maybe level nine fire witch from getting to you and Sanura from that liquid door. But if her magic level is greater than nine, then the water ward will slow but not stop her."

Again, Assefa wondered about Sanura's magic level. Apparently, from the way all in the room, except for Makena, slid their gazes to Sanura, so did everyone else, their thoughts clear. If the water witch were as strong as they believed Sanura to be, the wards would be a mere inconvenience and nothing more.

"Can you breach a level nine ward?" Rachel asked Sanura.

"I never tried." She sounded as if she didn't want to answer the question, as if doing so would reveal to everyone how different she was from them.

Assefa reached for Sanura's hand and held it, his silent way of reassuring her that no one in this room would judge her, least of all him.

"If I released my fire spirit, I could do it. It would take a lot of magic, though, but it can be done by a level ten or above witch."

Zareb whistled. "That's one insanely strong water witch. A tsunami of magic no witch should possess."

"True," Assefa said, "but we only need the wards to buy us time we wouldn't have without them. Minutes?" he asked Sanura.

"Five, maybe ten."

That worked for Assefa. There was plenty his men could do with five minutes warning. When he glanced at Zareb, he saw the same strategic conclusion in his partner's eyes.

"A four element ward around the property and a secondary water ward by the river," Assefa summarized. "Can you align the wards so they won't cancel each other out?"

Barbara nodded. "Of course. It only makes sense. We'll also tune them to everyone's magical frequency who's in this room, as well as the four other were-cats in your household. Meaning, no other preternatural will be able to come within a hundred feet of your property without suffering an electrical shock to their magical senses. The shocks will increase the longer they remain inside the protected barrier. I suggest warning your uncle and Mike to call before they drop by. As a witch, Sanura will be the only member of this household who'll be able to grant another preternatural entrance onto the property. It takes a high-level spell to create a temporal rift in the ward, which Sanura knows how to cast. Other than that, the Council's ward will dispel any uninvited visitors."

Like the lion alpha from last night and his were-cat scouts. Pleased, Assefa continued.

"Once all the wards are set," his gaze shifted to Rachel, "I'll have Manute watch over Rachel while she," Assefa didn't know what in the hell to call what the earth witch could do, "talk to the trees and grass." That was a sentence he never thought he'd utter. "After that, we'll reconvene here. We need to talk about Paul Chambers, felidae law, and the Oshun ceremony."

Anna's eyes widened. "What did Paul do now?" Ah, an impressive snarl from such a demure water witch.

CHAPTER TWENTY-TWO

She could still feel him, the heavy dead weight of Callum's body on top of her. In life, he had been a handsome man, quick-witted and big-hearted. Yet in death, gods, in death Callum Livingston left her cold and nauseous. After killing the siren sisters and not losing her dinner afterward, she'd thought herself made of sterner stuff. But the villain-ess sirens had been her enemy while poor Callum had been a kind and devoted family man who didn't deserve his fate.

When Assefa's Mngwa had pushed the body off Sanura, freeing her from her prison of slimy flesh, she hadn't moved immediately. Instead, she'd stared up at the clear sky, the dark clouds no more and the sun shining. And she swore she saw a face in the clouds—a face that resembled her own. A face that nodded and lips that mouthed, "Don't let her win. Get up, my fire witch."

"This is really nice." Cynthia rocked in the wicker lounge chair, looking around the enclosed porch the same way she did every other part of Assefa's home—with a combination of disbelief and awe. "Every time I come here, I see something different." Cynthia raised her blue eyes from the tiled porch floor with a geometric vector design that bore the unmistakable face of Assefa's Mngwa. "I've never seen anything like that design before. Nothing but triangles, but when put together like that, it's so beautiful. I mean, the design is the clear focal point of this porch."

It was. Manute and Rashad were talented, the vector Mngwa in-spiring and fierce.

Despite the hellacious day they'd all had, Sanura couldn't be prouder of her family and friends, especially Rachel.

Sanura pulled her bare feet onto the stylish chicory wicker sofa, with three Aztec Grain cushions that had her sighing in comfort. No longer in a wet, dirty dress, she and Rachel had showered and changed while the Council and Cynthia set the wards. After they'd finished, the other witches had followed Sanura's lead. While her clothes didn't fit any of the women perfectly, except for Makena, Sanura managed to find something comfortable and appropriate for all of them to wear home. Even the short but busty Barbara, who smiled too broadly when she'd given the priestess one of Assefa's large T-shirts to wear. What she failed to tell the woman was that the shirt was a gag gift given to Assefa by Zareb and that FBI didn't stand for Federal Bureau of Investigation but Female Body Inspector.

Assefa had taken one look at Barbara, who'd beamed up at him expectantly when he saw her in his shirt, and said without a trace of humor, "That shirt was made for you, Priestess Barbara. Keep it, with my compliments." Her smile, if possible, had brightened even more. When Assefa had strolled away from the older woman, he shook his head at Sanura and whispered, "You're shameless."

"How do you think Rachel is doing?"

Cynthia glanced over her shoulder and out the see-through patio wall. From this location, the Potomac River wasn't visible. "She should be fine. Anna and I set the ward perfectly. She and Manute are as safe as they can be."

Sanura agreed, but that wasn't what she'd meant. "Her low witch level still bothers her."

Although, when it counted most, Rachel put on her big girl panties and added her magic to the battle. It mattered. Every ounce of magic they'd been able to muster against the snakes and waterspouts had mattered. She wished Rachel understood that all magic, regardless of how minimal, counted.

Cynthia turned back to Sanura. "Oh, that. Yeah, I realized that today. I get it, I guess, but she's too damn sensitive sometimes."

Rachel could be, but Sanura and Cynthia would never know how it felt to live and work among people so much more physically and magically powerful than them. No more than Rachel could understand how possessing a lot of power brought its own set of insecurities.

"Speaking of the grumpy witch." Sanura rose from the sofa, walked over to the sliding glass door, unlocked, and opened it. "All done, tree whisperer?"

Rachel pushed past Sanura. "You aren't funny. But yes, I'm finished." On her way to the sofa, Rachel threw Cynthia a disapproving look that said, "I know the two of you were talking about me, and I don't like it."

She plopped onto the far left cushion, the one she'd seen Sanura sitting on. Unfazed, Sanura claimed the cushion on the right, leaving the middle cushion vacant for Rachel's attitude.

Rachel swept a hand through hair in need of Tee's expert attention, the waterspouts having destroyed the hairstylist's hard work from just a day ago. "I wasn't mean to your special agent, so the two of you can stop gossiping about me."

"No one said you were."

Rachel snorted. "Don't give me your clinical voice, Dr. Williams. No, you didn't have to *say* anything. But I know it's what you're thinking." She pointed an accusatory finger at Cynthia. "You too."

Cynthia rolled her eyes. "I've seen you mean before, Rach, so I know what it looks like. You weren't mean to Assefa, but you were kind of rude. We know how you are, what makes you great but also what makes you a real pain in the ass. And you know the same about us."

Another snort, self-deprecating and not the least bit feminine. "A real pain in the ass, huh? I guess Aunt Peggy and I are related after all."

Cynthia grinned. "You said it. We didn't."

Rachel peeled off the too big pair of flip flops Sanura loaned her and pulled petite, shapely legs onto the sofa. Sitting cross-legged in a pair of black-and-white leggings that fell to Sanura's knees but nearly skimmed Rachel's ankles, she appeared nothing short of a five-year-old playing dress up.

"You didn't, but you did call her a bitch one time."

More than once, actually. But Sanura wouldn't correct Rachel's faulty math and memory. One time or another, they'd all said things about Peggy Bradford that were neither kind nor respectful, no matter that most of their sentiments were quite true. Despite the priestess' character flaws, there was one aspect of the woman Sanura never questioned. Peggy loved her niece—her oldest sister's daughter.

"Yes, well, when I was younger I said many things I shouldn't have. Statements I've come to regret but can't take back."

"So you regret the stuff you said about my aunt?"

"Hell no. Besides, I only said those mean things to the two of you. It's not as if I called the priestess a bitch to her face. But gods, I think she says stuff just to get a rise out of people. To see how far she can push them before they snap and make a complete fool of themselves by cursing her out or by walking away in seething frustration."

"And when they do, she looks down her nose at them with superiority and disdain." Rachel laughed. "I've seen her do it a million times."

So had Sanura. But she didn't want to spend these few minutes with her friends talking about Priestess Peggy. If she and Assefa survived this prophecy madness, the three witches would have plenty of time to gossip about the priestess and countless other pointless topics.

And, from Rachel's drained eyes when she'd entered the room, she didn't think her friend was yet ready to share what she'd learned from the flora. But she would have to soon. Once Manute reported back to Assefa, he would pull them together for a status report. After that, well, her special agent would be off, delivering news of death to the Livingstons.

Sanura leaned forward on the sofa, looking first to Rachel and then to Cynthia. "Listen, I have something to tell you."

"Something serious from the way you look."

"It is, Cyn."

She wouldn't insult them by asking her friends to promise to keep her secret. Trust between the water, earth, and fire witches had been a given since middle school. Even longer for Rachel and Sanura, who'd met when the Fosters moved to the Williams' Mount Washington neighborhood when Sanura was eight and Rachel six.

Over the next fifteen minutes, Sanura told her friends everything that had plagued her heart and mind since meeting, falling in love, and moving in with Assefa. By the end of her monolog, she'd confessed all, including her talk with Makena about Sam's jaguar spirit and Assefa's refusal to marry her.

Apparently, she'd left her friends speechless, who stared at Sanura with incredulity for several seconds after she'd finished.

"Wow," Rachel breathed out. "That is truly, truly ... truly ..." She snapped her fingers. "What are the words I'm looking for, Cyn?"

"Messed up?"

"No."

"Screwed up?"

"No, no." Rachel bit her lower lip, appearing like the brat she liked to accuse Sanura of being. "Fucked up," she whispered with a devious, taunting grin that had Sanura wanting to push her friend off the sofa and onto the hard tiled floor.

Sanura narrowed her eyes and glared at Rachel, who stared back at Sanura with a sheepish grin on her face. Times like these, Sanura had no doubt that Rachel Foster and Peggy Bradford were indeed from the same family. Neither woman had a tactful bone in their over intellectual body.

She sat back, reclining against the soft but firm cushion. Then, with reluctance, had to concede. Her predicament was pretty fucked up. But it was just something about hearing it come from a neutral party that made it seem all the more real and distressing.

"Yeah, that's better than the ones I came up with. Too apt. So, what are you going to do about it all?" Cynthia asked.

"I need help getting through the Oshun ceremony."

Rachel and Cynthia nodded their understanding.

"You mean you need us to help you and Assefa trick everyone into believing that you're mated."

Simple for Cynthia since she and Eric were actually mated when they'd gone through their Oshun ceremony.

"The good thing is that you and Assefa are partially mated, so your auras are merged." Rachel tapped her chin with her index finger, thinking. "That helps if one of the alphas challenges Assefa. He could demonstrate his strength through the combined might of your bond. No one will be able to tell the difference."

True, but Assefa, if challenged, wouldn't rely on their partial mate bond to "demonstrate his strength." That wasn't how her proud special agent worked. If challenged, he would face the rival using nothing but his own might. Which, considering who in the hell Assefa Berber was, would be more than enough to see him to victory.

"The biggest issue will be the lack of a mate mark. Everyone will want to see them, especially since you guys are the fire witch and cat of legend. They'll be curious to find out if your marks are similar to or different from any other mate mark."

"That's what I was thinking, too." Cynthia ran a hand over her left shoulder, where her mate mark was—a beige-and-white cougar paw print with five long, pointy claws curled as if preparing to swipe at an invisible prey. "For this particular problem, Rachel is better able to help you than me."

Rachel laughed. "And the two of you used to make fun of me."

"Of course we made fun of you," Sanura said. "Who ever heard of an eighteen-year-old girl paying for college by working at a tattoo shop? A restaurant, office, retail store, sure. Hell, even a strip club. We knew several girls who did that to make ends meet. But Ink and Blink Tats? I never got the blink part."

Cynthia chuckled. "I think it meant they finished tats in the blink of an eye. Which kind of makes sense, I guess. Still, it's a lame name for a tat shop."

"Lame or not, I made enough money to pay for books and a used car. But you can't possibly want me to give you and Assefa a permanent tattoo. And what will happen when the two of you become full mates and the real marks appear? How do you plan on explaining having two mate marks?"

Full mates. She'd said those words as if that future was a foregone conclusion. Faith. Rachel had faith in Sanura and Assefa, in a happily-ever-after, which spoke volumes for a woman with trust and security issues. Sanura wondered how things had gone between Manute and Rachel last night when he'd escorted her to the bathroom, and today when he'd served as her bodyguard down by the river. With all of the madness since her birthday party, she hadn't had an opportunity to speak with her.

Yet she hadn't done more than give Sanura a frosty Foster glare when she'd returned from the bathroom, a smiling and intrigued Manute trailing behind her. But no, Sanura did not want a permanent fake mate mark. Like Rachel, she had faith. Well, at least hope that a complete mate bond would be in her and Assefa's not so distant future.

"Magic ink. Now I see how I can help," Cynthia blurted into the silence, her eyes alight with dawned comprehension. With her water magic, Cynthia could create a semi-permanent magical ink that could last days, maybe even weeks.

"With the combination of your skills, I think Assefa and I will be able to get through the Oshun ceremony without everyone learning of our deception."

"It's a good plan," Rachel said. "To be honest, it's not as if you guys need to let everyone gawk at the tats. You can just flash the designs to the priestesses, who will confirm the mate marks to those in attendance. Barbara and Peggy will probably want to make more of a show out of it than that, but you and Assefa can easily decline."

Even if the marks were real, Assefa wouldn't allow himself to be paraded about on display, treated like a rare museum find for the Council.

Cynthia leaned over and grabbed the unopened bottle of water she'd placed on the floor beside her when she'd claimed the rocking chair. She hadn't touched the water in over an hour. Now she twisted off the top and took several sips before screwing the top back on and placing the bottle between her jean-clad thighs. "Have you run this plan past Assefa?"

"Not yet." She would speak to Assefa later, when they had a few minutes alone together. Right now, Assefa had too much on his plate, and she still didn't know why he'd mentioned Detective Salazar earlier. The Oshun ceremony, well, he'd only consented, like the alpha position, out of a sense of obligation. The least Sanura could do was formulate a plan. She would not have her special agent embarrassed in front of a bunch of strangers, some of whom would like nothing better than to find fault with the Council's alpha selection.

Rachel slid over, claiming the cushion next to Sanura. She pointed to Sanura's cell phone on the coffee table. "I have a few design ideas, but maybe you want to do a bit of research to find something you like and that makes sense with Assefa's Mngwa."

Good idea, because the mate mark was an outward manifestation of the bond between the couple's inner spirits. Assefa's Mngwa and her fire spirit.

"And please don't ask me to be so uncreative as flames for him and fangs for you."

"You say that as if most witch-were-cat mate marks aren't that simple." Cynthia shook her head. "Eric has five water droplets on his left inner thigh. Don't get all Jacob Lawrence on them, Rach. Keep it simple."

Rachel ignored Cynthia. Reaching across Sanura and to the coffee table, Rachel grabbed Sanura's phone and began typing. Five minutes later, she handed Sanura the phone, two colorful images on the screen.

"What do you think?"

Until now, Sanura had agreed with Cynthia. The mate marks she'd seen hadn't been special or particularly inventive, although she always thought her parents' marks quite beautiful and unique to them. But seeing the images Rachel had selected brought a pang of sadness and want to her heart.

"I won't make them exactly like the pictures. I have a few ideas of my own that I think you and Assefa will like." When Sanura said nothing, just stared at the images on the screen, Rachel poked her in the side with a, "So, what do you think?"

What did she think? What did she think? More like what did she feel? *Like my heart has ceased pumping.* "Perfect." A low breath of sound. *Too perfect.*

She had no doubt Assefa would agree to her plan. But he wouldn't like it. Not because he was above a victimless lie, but because the deception, the fake but perfect tattoo, would remind him of Sanura's rejection of his claiming bite.

"Don't worry, Sanura." Rachel slid a supportive hand over hers. "In time, all will be fine. Count on your friends to see you through."

The same words Sanura had spoken to Rachel after her rape, cradling the crying witch in her arms, Cynthia huddled on Rachel's bed with them. Cynthia's anger had been palpable, her tears unshed, and her magic threatening to burst water pipes in the house Rachel no longer thought of as her haven.

"Dr. Williams."

Omar, as polite and formal as ever.

She turned in the direction of his voice. Omar stood in the doorway that led from the enclosed patio and to the house.

"Excuse me, Dr. Williams, Assefa has requested everyone return to the dining room for a status report."

****

Assefa hadn't been this emotionally battered in years, not since his final confrontation with Razi. Even then, no one had died, although, with all the blood, he was sure his brother would follow their mother into Anubis' jackal arms. But Razi lived, and Assefa would survive this ... Test? Challenge? Attack?

Pushing back the duvet, but making sure not to toss it onto a sleeping Sanura, Assefa rolled out of bed. Standing, he stretched his naked, sated body. After retiring to their bedchamber, Assefa and Sanura had sought pleasure and peace in each other's arms. Their destructive destiny was a curse to all those around them, even people on the fringes of their lives.

Pilar Salazar was dead.

Seventeen African immigrants were dead.

Gayle and Callum Livingston dead.

Joanna Blackwell dead.

And those were just the innocent lives Assefa knew had perished because of a prophecy he and Sanura were forced to live out. A prophecy, from what Assefa could figure, benefitted no one. Regardless of the outcome of the war between fire and water, the gods would endure, as would mortals, even if thousands or millions of them died. A holocaust, for certain, but one that wouldn't see the earth ravaged of all human and preternatural life.

So what was the point of all of this? Bragging rights for Mami Wata or Oya? Were the gods truly so shallow and heartless? Cruel even. Recalling the image of a horrified Sanura under the bloated corpse of Callum Livingston, Assefa knew the gods had to be. Because what other explanation could there be to explain the prophecy and the loss of lives and innocence?

Assefa had no answers. He wished he did. But would knowing change the trajectory his and Sanura's lives had taken since meeting each other? He had no doubt knowledge, for once, would make little difference. Yet a lack of knowledge and true understanding did not mean Assefa held no power or control over his thoughts and actions. And the same was true for his witch.

Assefa strolled to the master bathroom, closing the door before turning on the light so he wouldn't disturb Sanura. The woman needed her rest. She'd performed a complex spell on Dahad and had just as an emotional day as Assefa. She'd also worked with Rachel and Cynthia, for hours, on a spell in her office, only venturing from her lair once the women were happy with the result.

Watching himself in the mirror, Assefa could see the toil of the day in his frustrated, fatigued eyes. Here he was, on the cusp of becoming alpha to countless unknown and likely hostile were-cats. A position any were-cat, other than him, would feel proud to undertake. Yet his stomach rumbled with primitive rejection, even while his mind fought to accept the inevitable.

And it was inevitable, as much as what he would soon do was unavoidable. He could no longer run away from this particular fate. In that, Dr. Williams was correct. Running changed little, other than your location but rarely your destination.

He climbed into the shower and permitted too-hot water to beat down on shoulders and back, easing the tension in his muscles. During the status report meeting, Assefa had shared news of Detective Salazar's unexplained attack in the Bronx, which Makena had known about but thought Sanura had also seen the massacre on the news. He'd also relayed the situation with Paul and Greg Chambers, the priestesses, especially Anna, furious at "Paul's audacity to defy his former alpha's final request."

Assefa suspected Paul Chambers was in for his own unexpected visit. But that confrontation was between the former lovers and would likely yield very little beyond a migraine for the high priestess. Perhaps, if Chambers were very lucky, Anna would put him out of his misery before Assefa would be forced to take matters into his own hands.

Stepping out of the shower, Assefa snatched a towel from the bathroom closet and dried off. Gazing at himself again in the mirror, Assefa saw nothing but Berber man looking back at him. The imposing build and tenacious chin. The imperial nose and cunning lips. And skin the color of bubble-rich lava found on the surface of the Moon. Yet the Berber eyes, cold and merciless, did not stare back at him. Most days they were hidden behind the soft, tender eyes he wore for people like Sanura and Makena.

Paul Chambers, if he persisted, would meet those Berber eyes. And the old lion alpha would die. That wasn't what Assefa wanted, but his mind had already calculated the probability, and the numbers did not bode well for Chambers. Another inevitability Assefa wouldn't be able to walk away from. He blew out a breath, his stomach settling at the reluctant acceptance.

Five minutes later, dressed in only a pair of blue printed running shorts, chest and feet bare, Assefa closed the door to the bedroom balcony. He looked over and down. They were there, just as he knew they would be. Standing, from oldest to youngest, fit, rippled bodies shone under the brilliance of the full moon, their clothing choice the same as his own. For what was to come, the fewer the clothes the better.

He took a deep breath, because this moment, these few seconds left to him marked the beginning of the end. Running was no longer an option. The appeal gone, if it had truly existed in the first place. No, only his fear had been real, as well as his cowardice. "Being an alpha," his father had once told Assefa, "isn't a job but a way of life, a way of being. Next to becoming a father, it's the most terrifying decision I've ever made." He'd hugged Assefa. Standing in front of the limousine that would drive Assefa to the airport and away from all he'd known, Omar, Zareb, Dahad, Manute, and Rashad already inside, his father's words had no effect on his stubborn, naïve ears.

"I love you, son. Be safe. Be happy. And when the time comes, return home and be our nation's alpha."

He still didn't want to become General Supreme. And he didn't think he ever would. That wasn't his destiny. But this mansion and these people, he jumped over the balcony's wrought iron railing, were his destiny, his tiny nation to serve and to protect.

Landing, well, like a nimble cat, Assefa stood in front of his friends, his brothers of the heart. They stared at him, saying nothing as he led them away from the house and deep into Berber property. After a few minutes of walking in the direction opposite of the Potomac River, they stopped.

"This is where you want to do it?" Zareb, in a red knee-length pair of graphic running shorts, scanned the area around them and shrugged. "It's as good a place as any, I suppose."

It was. In fact, this was the same spot Ulan had found him last evening, brooding after having run away. It seemed appropriate to return there tonight, a symbolism only he would understand. He touched the thick bark of one of the towering trees that flanked the men, a small, secluded woodland on his sprawling property.

He wondered if Rachel would find solace there, now that he knew of her special earth witch ability. She really could commune with the trees, her story of how Gayle and Callum had come to their watery end painful to hear but less physically violent than what he'd envisioned.

"Hand-in-hand, they walked into the river," she'd told the assembled group. "No hesitation. They just went. Even when the water reached their shoulders, they kept moving forward, never once looking back."

No, not physically violent, but violent all the same. No sane person, and the Livingstons were definitely sane with three children to live for, would take a stroll into a river over three thousand feet above sea level, as if it were a sandy beach instead of a liquid grave it had become for them. No more than a law-abiding detective would drive to the Bronx and open fire on over a dozen strangers. Or a were-cat maul his sister and wife to death, as Joanna Blackwell's brother had done. Two agents, dispatched by Ulan after receiving a phone call from Assefa, found the dead women. But no trace of the murderous hyena who'd killed them, eaten flesh from bone and leaving gruesome carcasses behind. A report from the division's forensic anthropologist wouldn't be in for another day or two, but Assefa knew.

They all knew. An out of control were-cat was on the loose in a major American city, his mind no more his own than Gayle's, Callum's, or Pilar's had been when death had come for them, contorting their will and shattering their lives.

"I've never seen it before." Rashad stepped closer to Assefa, his eyes on his upper arm. The younger man smiled with envy and hopefulness. "I can't wait to find my true mate. I know she's out there and I have to be patient. But your mate mark is on point. I should've known it would be."

Assefa lowered his arm from the tree, careful not to reveal the deception in his eyes and voice. With the exception of the day Sanura had thought the men's were-cat training session a true battle, Assefa shifting from Mngwa to man on the back lawn, he'd been careful not to show too much of his body to his friends. Luckily for Assefa, the men had been too frightened of the fire witch of legend to pay his naked body any attention.

While a mate mark could appear on any part of the body, the witch and were-cat having no control where it formed, most materialized on the lower back, upper arm, or calf. Dahad's mate mark, however, before it disappeared after his wife perished in a plane crash, ran from under his ear and to the top of his shoulder blade. A desert rose plant, luscious pink-red blooms and stout, twining roots, his mate's earth spirit.

So when Sanura had come to him with her plan, inquiring if he would allow Rachel to ink a fake mate mark on him, he'd turned away from her, a quick rejection on his lips.

"I'm sorry, I know this isn't how you wanted it to be."

It damn sure hadn't been.

"We can come up with another plan for getting through the Oshun ceremony, Assefa." She'd hugged him from behind, her forehead going to his shoulder, her arms around his waist. "Or you could bite me now, and the mark would be real."

He hadn't even been tempted, although Sanura's offer was sincere. She wasn't yet ready to part with her father's jaguar spirit. And he wouldn't use the ceremony and her guilt to get his way. So he'd let the earth witch mark his body with Cynthia's magical ink. Rachel's design choice was painful for how well she'd captured the bond they were pretending to have.

Now all his friends were taking in the fake mate mark, Rashad circling it with an exploring finger.

"On point," Rashad said again, so much awe in his voice. "Flames are everywhere. The entire body of the Phoenix is engulfed in magical flames. And the wingspan of the bird covers the width of your huge arm, its tilted head on your shoulder."

"It's flying, or rather soaring." With a move Assefa knew to be unconscious, Omar glanced down at the jogging pants he wore and what it hid. Like Assefa, Omar had a secret. Unlike Assefa, Omar was still running from what most frightened him.

"And the flaming Phoenix has lightning bolts in its talons and bright blue flames coating the red. Or are those fire blue winds?" Zareb asked. His eyes sharpened, then his baldhead nodded. "I get it. A flaming Phoenix, Sanura's inner spirit. Wind and lightning, magical gifts from Oya. The fire witch of legend, three elements, one deadly witch. Rashad's right, the mark is pretty awesome. You should've shown it to us before."

He would've, if it had been real instead of a counterfeit. But the mate mark, real or false, wasn't the reason the men were out so late.

Manute, who stood the farthest from Assefa, mumbled something about Rachel and a prickly pear cactus. He had no idea what made his friend say something like that but hoped Manute hadn't been so rude as to compare the earth witch to the desert plant when they were together earlier. Although, Sekhmet help the were-cat who took Rachel Foster as mate because the petite woman was damn sure full of sharp, pointy barbs.

"Are you all ready?" Assefa asked, bringing an end to the discussion about Rachel's clever design and superior inking skills. "I would like to be back in my warm bed before my witch notices my absence."

Not that Assefa intended to keep tonight's ritual a secret from Sanura. She had to know such rituals occurred when a were-cat became alpha. But the Oshun ceremony was in two nights, which had occupied her mind most of the evening. What would happen tonight, between Assefa and his friends, required no preparation. The only prerequisites were trust, friendship, and Mngwa magic.

The men dropped to their knees in front of Assefa, their gazes locked on him.

For witches and were-cats, so much of their culture was steeped in rituals and mythology. Superstitions ran rampant in many witch-werecat communities, the Sudan and the United States among them. And while Assefa was not a superstitious man, he valued traditions and respected others' need for ritualistic practices. But what he was about to do contradicted every alpha inauguration ritual he'd ever heard of or read about.

According to Sudanese tradition, he should move behind his friends, his soon-to-be were-cat clan. Then, one by one, sink his fangs into them, drawing a slither of their cat's chi into him. This act would magically fuel the Mngwa, forming a metaphysical bond and adding to his strength, making him alpha to their beta.

But this practice always struck Assefa as selfish and one-sided. If a were-cat deserved to be called alpha, then he should give instead of take, rewarding the men's trust and loyalty instead of receiving what didn't belong to him.

This was why he would never claim Sanura as mate until she was absolutely ready. His bite, his loving Mngwa bite would be a selfless act of giving, at least that's how he wanted Sanura to view the moment that would make them whole, make them one.

Assefa joined his friends on the ground and gestured for them to form a circle.

They did, with Zareb to his right, Omar to his left. Manute, Rashad, and Dahad completed the circle. Like King Arthur and his Knights of the Roundtable, his were-cats were equal to that of their chosen alpha. They would follow him, take orders from him, not because Assefa would demand it of them but because they had the right to say no and to walk away, without dishonor or fear of retribution.

Zareb shook his head. "I should've known you would have to do things your way."

Yes, he should have.

"Not that I was looking forward to you biting me with those big ass Mngwa fangs of yours."

Rashad made kissing noises at Zareb, puckered lips and all. "Afraid of a little passion mark, Z?" Rashad laughed, then backed down when Zareb snarled at him.

Assefa shook his head. For all the boy had seen and heard today, Rashad had an amazing knack for bouncing back. His resilience a trait Assefa respected and relied upon, especially in these ugly, trying times of gods, witches, and war.

"Let's join hands."

Assefa opened his palms and linked hands with Omar and Zareb. The other men did the same until they made one physically connected circle.

"I thought about what I wanted to say to all of you. Considered reciting one of my favorite prayers to express my feelings and thoughts on this momentous night. But when I sat down to write, nothing came, no matter how long I sat or how hard I thought."

He squeezed his friends' hands, closed his eyes, and let his mind drift, drift, drift to the home of his first friend.

Assefa strolled through the thick, heavy foliage where his Mngwa slept on his side. The sun shone big and yellow overhead, giving light and life to this patch of undergrowth. A vegetation island home where only one creature dwelled.

Kneeling, Assefa reached out and found the body of the sole resident.

His paws.

His legs.

His shoulder.

His head.

Golden eyes opened, as did a mouth on a wide yawn.

It's time, my friend. You've been alone too long. A tiger, leopard, cheetah, lion, and African cat are waiting for you. Will you befriend them, the way you befriended me?

The Mngwa's long tongue came out and licked the face Assefa had lowered while he spoke to his inner cat.

Will you love and protect them, the way you have loved and protected me?

Assefa reclined beside his Mngwa, head on the beast's side and hands in his dense mane. When Assefa was but a shy, bullied boy, he would retreat to his mind, allowing his Mngwa to care for him, to soothe his hurt and his fears.

Fear of anger, of blood, of death.

You still have fear in your heart.

I know.

But it's a good kind of fear, Assefa. It no longer paralyzes you but makes you cautious in a way that an alpha needs to be. But you are mistaken, as long as I had you, I was never alone, never lonely. But you, well, a man's needs are different from a spirit's. I will wait for her. I have waited for her. Just as your friends have waited for you.

The Mngwa rose, shaking out his long gray-and-black fur.

On his knees, Assefa accepted the face that lowered, whiskers tickling him as he leaned forward and pressed his forehead to the head of his cat spirit.

Brown eyes met golden, and they became one.

Golden Mngwa magic poured from Assefa, up his arms and out through his hands. Like a ripple effect, the magic flowed from one linked hand to the next, until a golden halo of magic surrounded the men.

The halo pulsed with raw cat of legend power.

In the magic went, burrowing through hair and skin and into bloodstreams and organs.

Deeper. Deeper. Deeper.

Mngwa mystical energy exploded in a kaleidoscope of magic when it came into contact with the other cat spirits. Each man's aura radiated around him, visible and thrumming with magic and power. A piece of Zareb's blue aura broke off, shooting into the night sky like a missile. A yellow missile from Manute followed. Orange from Rashad. Omar's green. And Dahad's purple.

Above them, the missiles of beastly magic merged, twining and shifting until they'd created a multi-colored Mngwa of combined were-cat energy.

This was his clan. The power of his friends, his brothers.

Assefa lifted a hand skyward, a golden lasso of magic running from his shoulder and to his balled fist. With a fierce slash downward of his arm, the Mngwa charged toward the men, running with bright, blinding speed.

As the Mngwa barreled down on them, the image began to disintegrate, breaking apart into deadly, sharp claws. Then the claws were slamming into his friends, the tips piercing their backs and sending them forward from the force.

In. In. In.

But not out. Not through.

Just in.

Their combined magic—clan magic.

In Omar.

In Zareb.

In Rashad.

In Dahad.

In Manute.

Assefa stood, sent out his magic lasso around his friends, his new clan.

"From this night forward, we are the Clan of Legend. We are not myths but men of destiny, beasts of valor. We love. We protect. And our bond will never be broken. This I vow. This I promise my brothers. Your friend, your alpha."

CHAPTER TWENTY-THREE

That night, Sanura dreamed of snakes, water, and death. But she hadn't cried out or awakened drenched in sweat, as she'd done when nightmares plagued her as a child. Instead, her body had, instinctively, sought comfort from the one person she knew could keep her safe.

Assefa Berber.

Yet he hadn't been there. His large, warm body was gone. And Sanura's eyes had popped open, searching the dark room for her special agent. Dragging herself out of bed, she'd looked first in the bathroom and then the sitting room of the suite. He hadn't been in either place, so she'd crept down the hall, passing Manute's, Omar's, and Rashad's bedrooms, their doors open, lights off.

Deciding the men were likely together, Sanura felt better about Assefa's MIA status, but the prospect of returning to their bedroom alone had held no appeal. Forcing her legs to move and her mind to thoughts other than snakes, water, and death, Sanura had strolled back to the bedchamber and climbed into bed. She'd thought herself too tense to fall back asleep. She'd been wrong.

And the nightmare returned.

Eventually, so did Assefa, who Sanura now watched.

He sat on his side of the bed, red-striped boxers on, chest bare and head hung low.

Reaching out, Sanura placed the palm of her hand to the center of his back. "Good morning." She began to rub—up and down. Sanura considered asking Assefa what was bothering him but thought better of posing such a stupid question, in light of yesterday.

Assefa looked over his shoulder at Sanura. The same shoulder that bore the burning Phoenix—her fire spirit.

It was an amazing design, even better than the Internet image that had inspired Rachel's creativity. This Phoenix was much fiercer and life-like than the original. The blue-and-red firestorm wings literally moved each time Assefa flexed his incredibly massive arm, giving the illusion of flight.

Rachel had told them there were three stages involved in healing from a tattoo. The first stage was the open wound stage where the tattoo was washed and bandaged to prevent infection. "The area usually stings, swells, or feels like a mild case of sunburn," she'd informed them. During the second stage, the scabs formed during the initial stage would begin to flake and fall off, creating dry skin and some itching. By the final stage, all the scabs would be gone but the area could still be a little dry and tender to the touch. For full-humans, the healing process would take about a month. For preternaturals, like Assefa and Sanura, by the time the couple saw Rachel and Cynthia off for the evening, the inked area looked healthy and perfect. The colors vibrant.

And Assefa irritated in a way their tattooed skin hadn't been.

Although they'd made love last night—sweaty, glorious, and loud—Assefa hadn't once touched, no less looked at Sanura's tattoo. Which was just the opposite of her reaction to his. For her part, she couldn't stop admiring it, laying fingers and lips upon it. A heat of possessiveness overtook her each time Sanura saw her fire spirit emblazoned across her man's arm. Gods, she had no idea the effect the mark would have on her feminine senses.

But it wasn't real. The mark wasn't their real mate mark, blessed and given to them by the gods. Yet seeing the Phoenix on Assefa damn sure felt real. The sight stirred a primal hunger within Sanura, an ancient beast of passion, of desire, and of love.

Apparently, Assefa felt none of those things, which hurt Sanura's feelings. His less than thrilled reaction made sense, intellectually. His submission to her plan had been a reluctant one, at best. So she shouldn't have expected any more from Assefa than he gave her, certainly not a happy grin when his tat was done.

When she'd finished his design, ever-sarcastic Rachel had beamed with pride and then surprised herself and everyone else when she'd hugged Assefa and thanked him for "being such a wonderfully big canvas." He'd met her self-satisfied grin with a wooden nod and a brittle, "Thank you."

A minute later, Assefa had his shirt back on and was striding out of their bedroom, the only room in the house where absolute privacy was guaranteed. Tattoos not mate marks, a lie, a secret, their deception. Assefa had wanted no part of it, uncaring as to the design Rachel had in mind for Sanura. So his nonchalance had stung, but it was no less than what she deserved.

"Did I wake you?"

She shook her head, right hand still rubbing the taut muscles of his broad back. "Where did you go last night?" When he moved to face her, Sanura's hand fell away.

"I had to make it official."

Sanura sat up in bed, propping her back against the headboard. When she'd gotten out of bed earlier, as naked as the day she was born, she'd thrown on a nightgown and robe before she went in search of Assefa. And she wore the knee-length, short-sleeve nightgown now.

"Make what official?"

"Me as alpha to a hodgepodge group of were-cats."

Ah, she understood. She'd been a girl when her father had become alpha of his jaguar clan. But she remembered a dozen jaguar shifters at her house one night, before her mother scooted her upstairs and into bed. Fifteen minutes later, she'd heard the men and her father leave the house. She didn't know when he returned, but the next morning, at breakfast, he seemed different somehow—stronger, quicker, and more self-assured. Which, for Samuel Williams, a confident man whose strength no one questioned or challenged, that was saying a great deal.

Assefa, on the other hand, exuded his usual off-the-charts might and the first chilly signs of his FBI mask. After the events of yesterday and what he had scheduled for today, Sanura wasn't surprised to see the return of this side of Assefa. The way he watched her, chocolate eyes flat and unfeeling, he'd already retreated behind his wall.

She wasn't ready for this. Wasn't ready to lose her sweet, kind Assefa. But he wasn't only that, Sanura fought to remind herself. He'd told her. Time and again, he'd told her. *A Berber male.*

Yes, he was. But what did that mean precisely? Her Assefa, no matter his family's violent history, wasn't a cruel or domineering man, given to acts of brutality and unkindness.

Her hand rose to his face, his cheek. She knew this man. His heart. His goodness. "You didn't strengthen yourself by taking chi from your friends."

A statement of certainty, not a question.

Buttressing were-cat power was the way of alphas. Even her father had followed the tradition of chi sharing. Never had she heard of an alpha doing otherwise during his inauguration. But Assefa was one of a kind, in so many breathtaking ways.

He turned his face into her palm and kissed, eyes no softer for his gentle gesture of affection. "I have a lot on my plate today, Sanura."

A reminder, as well as a subtle warning from her lover. The fun, sexy, and relaxed Assefa, who'd given her such an incredible birthday, was no more, replaced by the determined, fearless, and intense Special Agent Berber.

"I know." She wanted to help but knew his errands could only be accomplished by him. "Don't go too far." He would know what she meant by that. He'd ruined the sofa and loveseat in his once pristine living room, uncharacteristic for her cool, collected special agent.

His smile, devastating for all the unspoken pain and anger it held, sent a rush of arctic wariness through Sanura. She'd asked him to fight for them, but she hadn't thought through all that may mean to a man like Assefa Berber. Losing control for him, she began to see, held a different meaning for Assefa than it did for Sanura.

His loss of control, unlike her own, wouldn't be chaotic and thoughtless. If or when Assefa lost control, it wouldn't be because his mind and temper snapped, pushing him over the edge of reason. No, he would simply, deliberately, coldly shed morality and ethics and cloak himself in impenetrable layers of violence and blood.

Hardhearted.

Vicious.

Calculated.

The disarming smile faded, Assefa's handsome face and deep voice devoid of emotion as he shared now what he hadn't last night.

"Mrs. Livingston collapsed in my arms when I told her about her son and daughter-in-law. She weighed nothing. I held her thin frame easily. But her heartache made me feel like Atlas holding up the sky." The hand on his face traveled to his chest, over his beating heart. "Mr. Livingston could only gape at me, green eyes first going wide with disbelief then lowering as his body collapsed into a chair, my words a hammer to his gut."

She should've gone with him, but he'd insisted he deliver the bad news alone, telling Sanura, "You don't know them. It doesn't make sense for you to come."

She didn't know the older Livingstons, which made him right. But he was also wrong. She should've gone with Assefa, not for the Livingstons' sake. There was little a stranger could do for them. She should've gone for Assefa's sake, helping him carry the burden of his friends' deaths.

"A couple of years ago, Gayle brought the triplets to work with her. Callum was out of town, and the babysitter was sick, so she brought the girls here. I think she thought I would mind, but I didn't. She put them in the recreation room with a tote full of movies and an admonishment to 'not move.'"

Assefa's face softened as he relayed the story. But not his eyes. If anything, they became harder, like obsidian rocks found within the calderas of Newberry Volcano.

"I went into the recreation room looking for something or another and wound up seated between the girls watching *Pinocchio*. They couldn't believe I'd never seen a cartoon before, so they pulled me down beside them and made me watch." A shrug. "It made them happy and kept them quiet and out of trouble. Since then, I've watched dozens of cartoons with the girls."

He made a sound, somewhere between a grunt and a sigh. "I went to school, studied, read, and received leadership and political training on being General Supreme. To my father, watching television, and the like, was a waste of time and my intellect. He did permit extracurricular activities, like martial arts and weight training, however, but only because he viewed them as an extension of being a strong and fierce alpha."

Did Assefa know how his words tore at her heart? For the triplets' loss, as well as for the lonely child Assefa must have been and the man who wanted a family of his own, to get all the things right that his father had gotten so terribly wrong. A family that, without a full mate claim, they would never have. And that was assuming they survived the Day of Serpents.

He kissed her hand again and placed it in her lap. "Put my mind at ease, Sanura, and stay home today. Or if you must go out, take Omar and Manute with you. I don't trust that lion alpha, especially since the Council intends to announce my appointment as alpha tomorrow. With the Oshun ceremony tomorrow night, I suspect he'll try something here or there."

"You think he'll challenge your right to become alpha?"

"He will, which doesn't concern me. What does concern me is what he did last night, coming here with six shifters and threatening Zareb. Paul Chambers is not only pompous but dangerous."

"Dad didn't trust or like Mr. Chambers either, and neither does Mom. Do you think your plan will work?"

"My plan is a short-term solution to a bigger issue. What I'm going to do this morning will only serve to anger the old lion alpha. How he reacts will determine what next steps I'll be forced to take."

Okay, well, Sanura damn sure didn't like the sound of that.

"What does that mean?"

Assefa pushed to his feet. "I need to dress. As I said, I have a lot on my plate today."

"Wait. Wait." Sanura flung back the covers and jumped out of bed. "What do you mean by next steps?"

Assefa opened the doors to his closet, sliding them to the side. Two rows of tailor-made suits met his discerning gaze—two-button, four-and-five button, double breasted, casual leisure, three piece vested, pinstriped. So many, and these were only the suits in this single closet. He had more, much more.

And he wasn't talking, just picking out shirt, tie, socks, and cufflinks to match the two-button charcoal gray suit he'd selected.

In no time at all, Assefa was dressed—mask on, posture rigid and eyes unreadable. He holstered his gun and then kissed her goodbye, all without answering her question.

****

Baltimore, Maryland

At fifty-six and the alpha of the jaguar clan, Rodney Jordan had a lifetime of experience. Which meant he'd done and said plenty of stupid and crazy shit in his day, and had seen others do and say far worse. The news, no matter the cable station or country, was replete with stories of the stupid, crazy, vile, and unthinkable. And today, well, this day was neither stupid, crazy, vile, nor unthinkable. But it had been unexpected. He'd yet to determine whether, when he looked back on this Monday years from now, if he would think of it as a pleasant surprise or as strategic handling by a were-cat with too much money, charisma, and power.

Something told Rodney, as he reclined in his chair, light-brown eyes taking in all around him, no matter the outcome of today and the days that followed, the Sankofa were-cat community would never be the same.

Last night he'd received a call from Assefa Berber, on his unlisted home line, no less. The man, who'd Rodney only heard of through the rumor mill, and then confirmed by Paul Chambers as being the cat of legend and Sanura's reputed mate, had spoken in a confident, cultured voice, inviting Rodney to spend the day with him.

"Mr. Jordan, I apologize for the lateness of my invitation. If you make yourself available, I will consider your flexibility as a personal favor."

The apology and request had sounded sincere enough, despite there being an undertone of command. No one commanded an alpha, especially not a were-cat young enough to be Rodney's son. Yet there had been something compelling in Berber's voice, in the way he said just enough to peek a cautious were-cat's interest without exposing any of his cards.

"You're a smart man, Mr. Jordan. I'm sure you'll arrive at the best decision. A car will be at your home by eight. Have your second there thirty minutes before. I'll email you our itinerary so you can prepare properly. I look forward to meeting you, alpha. Good evening."

Then the man had hung up, leaving an open-mouthed and slightly amused Rodney staring at the phone in his hand. The call had lasted no more than three minutes, but Berber's true message had made the intended impact. Berber knew far more about Rodney Jordan than a stranger should while the jaguar knew virtually nothing about the man who thought to take Sam's place.

He hadn't liked or appreciated Berber's smooth arrogance. No more than he enjoyed receiving an email from the man or the agenda he'd laid out for his Monday. A day he should've been at work, not flying to New York and sitting through two funerals. Worse, he took umbrage with his own anticipation at the thought of meeting a brash were-cat who thought himself worthy of the title Council Alpha.

Rodney disliked it all. Yet the funerals had moved him, as did the unveiled grief he saw in Berber's eyes. Grief he could've hidden, but chose to reveal, uncaring or perhaps simply unafraid of how such emotions would appear to the predators around him.

Now, observing the man, the soft emotions displayed during the funerals were long gone. In front of Rodney sat one marble hard son of a bitch. To Berber's immediate right, and standing, was Berber's second, a big bald guy in a suit as expensive-looking as the one Berber wore. Not that Rodney was unaccustomed to seeing men in well-fitted suits.

As County Executive to Baltimore County, Rodney wore a suit every day. He did, however, take issue with Berber's email asking him to wear a suit to today's meeting as if he were a know-nothing teenager and Berber his mentor in all things proper and male. Which, fair enough, considering he intended to take the men to two televised funerals, his request made sense. But that wasn't Rodney's point. The point was that this newcomer to their community, in a matter of a night, had managed to contact and convince the alphas of every were-cat family in the Sankofa network to attend today's morbid excursion without knowing what they were getting themselves into until the plane had taken off and the man explained.

That had taken fangs of steel and strategic maneuvering. Being seen at the funeral of victims of a horrendous hate crime by a Baltimore City police officer was great press County Executive Jordan, who planned to run for reelection next year. Awful but true. Rodney knew the other alphas had come to the same conclusion, once they grasped the full scope of what seemed like an odd meet and greet by Berber. The man didn't play around. He'd given them a glimpse into his world, and what it would be like to have a rich, powerful man as their alpha, their benefactor.

Assefa Berber was no mere special agent. Any cub could see that, and Rodney hadn't been a cub in a long damn time. He would bet the outcome of his re-election bid that Special Agent Berber had deep and far-reaching connections. And the men around the table, influential in their local domains, hadn't managed to break through that glass ceiling that was state and national power and politics.

Eduardo Ruiz Soto, President of University of Maryland, College Park, and leopard alpha.

James Harrison, Baltimore City's Fire Chief and tiger alpha.

Shawn Wade, County Attorney for Howard County and cougar alpha.

Maurice Dunn, Chief of Baltimore City's Office of Professional Responsibility and cheetah alpha.

All the Sankofa alphas and their seconds were present and accounted for. Well, all except for Paul Chambers and his son, Greg. Rodney smirked to himself. Paul, always a loudmouth, amoral schemer, may just find himself six feet under if he weren't careful. This Berber fellow, for all of his youth, poise, and intellectualism, wasn't a cub that could be toyed with, bullied, or beaten into submission. Hell, he wasn't a cub at all, and Rodney's cat spirit had been on high alert since last night's phone call.

Now they sat around a familiar conference table, in a building and a room they hadn't been in since Sam's passing. This made him disapprove of Berber even more. Who in the hell did he think he was?

The alpha of alphas? Not yet, young man, not yet.

This North Baltimore building was one of five apartment buildings Sam owned. When he was alive, he would convene monthly meetings of the alphas, using this site and conference room as their designated meeting location. Yes, Berber had done his research. Apparently, Makena and the priestesses had already given him keys to the proverbial kingdom.

"Three years with no alpha and now this?"

Indecipherable dark-brown eyes, which had been focused on who-ever had interrupted their meeting by first calling and then texting Berber, snapped to Rodney.

He turned his cell off and slid it into his jacket pocket. "Yes, and now this, Mr. Jordan. In my line of work, forewarning is a luxury, never an expectation."

"Right, you and your second are FBI agents."

That was all Rodney had managed to scrounge up on the men before this meeting. The lack of substantive Intel had galled him, left Rodney feeling amateurish and vulnerable, which made him angry and irritated.

"Zareb and I deal in death and protection."

"Meaning what?"

"It means we're often too late to save innocents like the two people laid to rest today. It also means there are too many creatures out there who hunt and kill and get away with it because their crimes are one of thousands. Unsolved, Mr. Jordan, but not unsolvable. Not if you have the right resources and people who care."

Maurice, white shirt sleeves rolled up to his elbows, black suit jacket on the back of the seat he always sat in, nearest the window and farthest from the door, leaned forward. "And you expect us to believe that you care? About innocents? And about a bunch of were-cat families you don't even know?"

"I expect nothing from you, Mr. Dunn. Whether you accept me as your alpha will not change the fact that I *will* be your alpha. The only uncertainty that remains is the type of relationship we'll foster."

"I guess, being from another country, you've never heard the idiom that you can catch more flies with honey than you can with vinegar." Maurice sat back in his chair, and considered Berber, arms crossed over a lean chest and dark brows arched at a defiant angle.

Of average height and build, normal size for a cheetah shifter, Maurice, Eduardo, and Shawn had the most to lose if Berber turned out to be a total bastard of an alpha. The men's were-cat families were small and weak, so easy to dominate and control by an unscrupulous alpha. Not true for the other families, although Rodney had a feeling Berber was unconcerned by the numbers and might of the lion pride or the tiger and jaguar clans.

He should be.

"You'd be surprised what I've heard and know, Mr. Dunn." He smiled, humorless and without a glimmer of teeth. "Let me enlighten you. Were-cats require no coddling or hand-holding. We value honesty and straightforwardness, even when we disagree with what is being said. I don't sugarcoat, placate, or manipulate. I leave such weak-minded tactics to lesser men. Today isn't about me asking to be your alpha or pleading my case as the best were-cat for the job. The priestesses offered, and I accepted."

"The priestesses' decision must go through us," James spat, face pink with resentment. "We choose our alpha, not them. We decide who will rule us, not them." James' voice rose with each sentence, specks of spittle flying as his anger grew. "They have no right to choose for us. They put us off for three years when they could've chosen any one of us to fill Sam's seat. We were right here all this time. And we're still here."

The tension in the air thickened, as James pressed, voicing three years of discontent at the Council passing over each of them and their seconds without an acceptable explanation. Rodney knew how James felt, his righteous anger, the insult of rejection. But Rodney couldn't lie to himself, the way the others were doing. They knew. They all knew Sam's wish.

He'd searched for years for the cat of legend. "Help him, guide him," a dying Sam had begged Rodney. "He'll be just a boy, no older than my Sanura. He'll need an older cat to rely on, to trust. Will you do that for me? For him?"

Like the sentimental fool he was, Rodney had promised. What else could he do? Sam Williams was more than his alpha. They were friends, Rodney Sam's second when he'd been alpha of the jaguar clan. And it had been Sam who'd helped Rodney make the transition from second to alpha when Sam ascended to the rank of Council Alpha.

He should step in, remind his brothers of Sam's wish. If Berber were truly the cat of legend, which he didn't doubt he was because the priestesses wouldn't nominate any were-cat other than the Mngwa of myth, then the alphas were duty-bound to accept and acknowledge the upstart as their alpha.

No matter what.

Rodney opened his mouth to speak, to fulfill his promise to his dead friend and alpha, but the harsh scraping of Berber's chair when he pushed to his feet silenced James' hostile ramblings and stilled Rodney's tongue.

Icy, dark-brown eyes locked on James. Berber removed his suit jacket and folded it across the arm of his chair, keeping James in his sight the entire time.

His second, whose own chilly gaze scanned the other men around the table, took several steps back, giving himself room, to attack on his alpha's command, Rodney assumed.

Rodney's jaguar began to growl deep in his belly, ready to fight, to defend his brothers. The problem was that it had been James and Maurice who'd escalated the conversation and insulted the man. What choice had they left Berber but to rise to the challenge?

"Everyone here is free to challenge the Council's selection. That is a right I respect and support." An expensive gold-and-onyx watch was slid from his right wrist and shoved into his pants pocket. "If you think you are more qualified to be Council Alpha, then I am prepared to accept challengers." Berber removed a shiny, black gun from his side holster and handed it to his second, who had a matching weapon on his right hip. "We can fight here as men or at Sankofa as were-cats. The place or form doesn't matter to me." He glanced around the conference room, taking in the wooden bookcases, buffet credenza, mobile lectern, and electric presentation screen that shouldn't be down while not in use. "Although Makena will have our hides if we destroy this nice room." A shrug. He began to remove his tie. "She'll understand, and I'll pay for the repairs."

James stared at Berber, his face as red as Rodney had ever seen the man. But with anger or fear, he couldn't tell.

"Y-you want to f-f-fight my alpha?" Andre, James' nephew and second looked between his silent uncle and the unmoving, unblinking Berber.

"That's not what I'm proposing."

Andre, a brunette with moss green eyes like James, visibly relaxed. That was until Berber added, "All of you. Whoever wants to challenge the decision of four priestesses I respect and will protect with my life, may do so. Right now, or thirty minutes from now, which is how long it will take us to drive from here to Sankofa Preparatory School and change from men to beasts."

Shawn laughed, low and filled with cougar anxiety. "You can't be serious."

But one look at Berber and the answer was clear.

"All of us?" Shawn glanced to Eduardo, James, Maurice, and finally at him. "Do you believe this guy?" Shawn leveled a finger in Berber's direction, although his words were for the seven other men around the table. "He seriously thinks he can take all of us."

Shawn, who was closest to Berber, stood, and smiled the playboy smile that garnered him so many female voters when he ran for County Attorney. "You're one cocky son of a—"As fast as a pickpocket in a Mardi Gras crowd, Shawn swiped sharp cougar claws at Berber's throat.

Oh shit. Mistake. Big god damn mistake.

Slam. Crack. Crunch.

Shawn's face was pressed against the solid oak conference table, his arm at an unnatural angle. A bone jutted through the skin of his elbow, pushing against the cotton of Shawn's dress shirt while Berber's huge hand held him down by the nape of his neck.

And, for Sekhmet's sake, his stoic eyes never changed. Nothing about the man had altered, not even his scent. He didn't smell of anger, irritation, or even triumph at having taken down an alpha with embarrassing ease.

Worse, much worse was that Rodney, who sat a mere three chairs down from Berber, hadn't seen the man move. From the shaken looks of the others at the table, neither had they.

Berber ignored the whimpering Shawn and addressed the group. "I don't wish to fight any of you. It's counterproductive, especially when we all know the outcome. Let me be plain, I can and will defeat all of you if you push me. I can read each of your cat spirits."

He can what? Read our cat spirits? No were-cat should be able to do that, not even the goddamn cat of legend.

Berber kept speaking, as if the bomb he'd dropped wasn't Little Boy to a were-cat's Hiroshima, shredding a were-cat's most coveted secret and strategic advantage.

"I know your strengths, which are considerable. But they won't be enough, even combined, to defeat me. Not hubris or cockiness, just a fact. Nature and the gods can be cruel, giving some more while others less." He glanced down at Shawn, who'd gone still and silent. "Your cougar spoke to you, Mr. Wade, warned you against attacking me." With a jerk, he lifted Shawn off the cracked table and onto wobbly legs. "You should've listened."

Berber nodded to Shawn's second who hustled to retrieve his alpha, fear and deference having the man moving with swift efficiency.

With a jaw and nose that had to be broken, Shawn slumped into his chair, face beginning to swell. If he were lucky, his were-cat healing would kick in sooner rather than later. Because, damn, that facer he'd taken to the table had to hurt like a son of a bitch.

And Berber hadn't broken a sweat, no less his stony expression.

Yeah, Rodney didn't think he'd have to do much, if any, guiding of the new alpha. The priestesses had done right by Sam, which was more than he could say for his alpha brothers.

"Respect, trust, fear." Berber raised a finger as he enunciated each word. "An alpha can lead by respect, trust, or fear. Right now, I can see that you all fear me. That's not what I wanted, but it's often the way of things, especially in the beginning."

He lowered his hand and reached for his suit jacket. After slipping it back on, he accepted the gun from his second and secured it in his holster.

"Trust and respect are earned, alphas. From me to you and from you to me." He pointed to Shawn. "He's earned my respect. A man willing to stand up and fight for his conviction, even against a bigger, stronger foe, is a were-cat I'd like to call brother and friend."

Shawn, holding his broken arm with the uninjured one, glared at Berber. But he couldn't hide the pride he felt at the man's compliment. His scent betrayed him.

"Will you be all right, Mr. Wade?"

Shawn's nod of response was slow, his eyes filled with pain from the shallow movement.

Yeah, his jaw and nose were definitely broken.

Berber reclaimed his chair at the head of the table. With a nod to his second, the big, bald guy strolled to Shawn, handed him a handkerchief for his bloody mouth and nose, and then proceeded to the other end of the table where he sat.

"Now then," Berber began, his voice authoritative, eyes no softer for the kindness he'd shown Shawn by not killing him or stripping the cougar of his title, which, as alpha, he could do, "let us get down to business."

CHAPTER TWENTY-FOUR

Baltimore County, Maryland

Paul Chambers grinned at the woman sitting across the dining room table from him. It wasn't the charming smile he used to give her when she was young, naïve, and ripe for rebellion and seduction and Paul a predator of virgins and power, but the fuck-you-and-your-Council smile of a man who was about to screw Anna Spencer again.

This time, he would actually enjoy the fuck, coming all over the high priestess's ill-conceived alpha plan.

The grin grew, flashing sharp, white teeth and followed by a slow wink just to piss the water witch off. Yeah, he liked that too, toying with the woman who should've been his mate and first-class ticket to the Council. Instead, she'd been a scared momma's girl, too weak to stand up to Katherine Spencer and tell the caustic crone to go to hell.

But there she was, three decades too late with a strength and confidence she hadn't possessed back then. And it was Paul, instead of Katherine, Anna had the nerve to stare down, animosity and distrust in those rigid blue eyes of hers.

If Greg hadn't been in Paul's home when Anna had come calling, uninvited and furious, he would've flipped her off and slammed the door in her face. But their son had been present, staying with Paul ever since Saturday night. After he'd left that picture for Berber, no way would he take any chances with his son's life. So he'd forced Greg to stay with him where he'd be safe. The strongest lions in their pride, six of them, were now Greg's temporary bodyguards.

Yet Berber hadn't gone in search of Greg, as Paul thought he would. What kind of were-cat could stand seeing his mate pawed over by another male and not seek retribution? Apparently, Assefa Berber could because there'd been no sign of the so-called cat of legend. Either Berber had ice water in his veins and cared no more about Sanura Williams than Paul had about Anna when he'd taken her to bed and knocked her up, or the special agent had a level of self-will Paul would glory in crushing.

But first he had to deal with the mother of his son. Looking far too much like Anna, Greg, casual in a white oxford shirt, slim fit jeans, and a pair of classic brown boat shoes, he sat beside Paul, who wore what he did most days, patterned dress shirt, solid pants and matching tie, and Italian leather loafers. Hell, if it weren't for the fact that Paul knew he'd been Anna's only lover back then, he would've suspected she'd laid up with another man, so little did Greg resemble Paul. Greg was all fair skin, blond hair, blue eyes, and tall, lean musculature. And Paul, while as tall as his son, had shoulders and arms like a linebacker, eyes as dark as blackberries, and thick hair just as dark. Well, not so thick nor so dark these days. Age and maternal genes had not been so kind to Paul whose widow's peak emphasized his forehead making him look, apparently, like a Cro-Magnon man, as the asshole Rodney Jordan took too much pleasure in calling him.

Anna's eyes shifted from Paul to Greg, softening into a whirling pool of affection and worry when they landed on their son.

"Don't worry, Mom."

Ah, just like Greg. The boy's heart and resolve were too soft by half. Something else he'd inherited from his mother. For all that Paul despised Katherine Spencer, he'd held a grudging respect for the witch. She was tough and unyielding. A bully in the best sense, when you weren't the one on the receiving end of her power play, as Paul had been too many times. If Greg had to take after any of the Spencers, it would've been best if he'd been more like his grandmother than his mother. It would've made this coup much easier on Paul.

No matter, in this, father and son were of the same mind.

"You have no idea what you're doing."

"Of course I do, Mom. I'm going to be Council Alpha."

Greg smiled at his mother, as handsome as ever. Too handsome to have pined after Sanura for so long. But if not for his small obsession with the fire witch, Paul wasn't so sure he would've been able to talk his son into making the moves necessary to assure his spot on the Council. Every man had his motivations. For Greg, it was Sanura, a woman he thought he could obtain if he became alpha.

Paul knew Greg's desire for a life with Sanura to be the misguided dream of a romantic with more lust than common sense. If Sanura wanted Greg, she could've had him years ago. The witch didn't strike Paul as the type of woman who would drop her mate for Greg simply because Greg defeated Berber and became Council Alpha. And, with Paul's help, Greg would defeat Berber.

Once he did, Greg would have his pick of beautiful and powerful witches, forgetting all about the pretty but unattainable Dr. Williams.

Anna shook her head, silver dangle earrings swaying from side to side. "Don't challenge him. It's meant to be, Greg. It's what Sam wanted."

"Sam's dead, Anna, and his wish no longer matters."

She ignored Paul, her concentration and words all for Greg.

"Your father thinks he knows what's best for you. But he doesn't. Whatever he's told you, whatever he's promised you, the last thing you want to do is challenge the cat of legend."

Paul scoffed. "You see, Greg. I told you."

"Told him what?"

"That you had no faith in him. I told Greg you would try to talk him out of this, and here you are. You're no different from your mother. She thought you were too weak, too passive to lead the Council. But you proved her wrong. Didn't you, Anna?"

Oh, but the woman was a stunning sight when she was mad, as she was now. Her face glowed with barely-controlled anger. And Paul bet if he fucked her right there and now, it would be worth all the scratches to his back and snarled curses to his ears because there was no better bed partner than an angry witch.

This was turning out to be a good meeting after all. Any time he could thumb his nose at a member of the Council, Paul's day brightened.

"This isn't about me, Paul, and you know it. It's about our son and his safety."

Greg pushed to his feet, walked around the circular glass dining room table, and sat in the chair next to his mother.

"I know you're worried. I can see it in your eyes. But there's nothing to worry about. You and the priestesses didn't have to go to an outsider. We have all the strength we need right here, within the lion pride."

"I know the lions are strong, proud, and formidable. But to challenge Assefa, gods Greg, I've seen his Mngwa."

She'd what? Not even the cubs who'd stolen onto Berber's property had managed to see the man in cat form. But Anna had? Why? When?

Paul slid forward in his chair, forearms going to the table, ears alert as not to miss any detail that might give Greg an advantage in the battle to come.

"You've seen the cat of legend?" Greg's soothing voice of only a moment ago turned inquisitive. "You've actually seen the Mngwa of myth?"

She nodded.

"Well," Greg urged, when she said nothing more, "tell me about him. How big? How fast? How strong?"

Yes, yes, those were Paul's questions as well. Even more, he wanted to know Berber's weaknesses. Surely, if Anna had seen the cat she had to have noticed some weakness Paul and Greg could exploit. Even if she didn't know what she'd seen, if the woman would talk, tell them all, Paul was certain he could figure out Berber's Achilles' heel.

"Too big. Too fast. Too strong. For you." Anna's eyes traveled from Greg to Paul. "And for you. You have no idea. I had no idea. He changed so fast. I've never seen a were-cat shift in a blink of an eye. But he did, Paul. Not only that, the Mngwa is huge."

"How huge?" Paul asked. He had to know. "Larger than a Siberian tiger?"

"Does it matter?" She gave Paul a withering look before turning back to Greg. "Your lion is impressive, son, even larger and stronger than my father's lion. But that Mngwa was unlike any other cat I've seen. You know I love you and will always support you." Anna grabbed Greg's hands, holding them with the same ferocity Paul could see in her eyes. "But I can't support this action. It's too dangerous. Even if you manage to defeat him, it will be at a serious physical cost. He doesn't back down. I've seen the Mngwa in action, and I've had a chance to get to know the man. Both are dangerous but in different ways. Assefa Berber, while kind and generous, is a tactician, seeing angles where others see only planes. And his Mngwa is just as stealthy, just as strategic and vicious in battle."

Battle? What in the hell had happened since Saturday night? What battle did Anna see the Mngwa fight? And who had been the Mngwa's foe? Details, Paul needed more details.

"Tell us what happened. If you tell me everything you saw and know about the Mngwa and Berber, our son will be victorious. Don't you want Greg to be Council Alpha? Would that be so bad, for your son to hold the seat once held by your father? To serve alongside his mother?"

Paul knew Anna wanted just that because she'd coveted a position on the Council as much as Paul had. The only difference between the two of them, then and now, were the lengths they would go to to achieve their mutual ends. Paul would do anything. Anna, well, she had a conscience and too many ethical standards that got in the way.

But she loved their son. More, she harbored just enough jealousy of Makena Williams and the happily mated life she'd had with Sam to want to see her son as Council Alpha above the chosen mate of her friend's daughter. Even though she wouldn't admit it, not even to herself, she'd been insulted when Sanura had chosen full-humans to date over that of her were-cat son. Anna and Paul may not have gone through the tri-part handfasting ceremonies, bonding their inner spirits, but they were still biological mates. Which meant he knew the water witch very, very well, including all the unpleasant emotions she hid deep inside, but refused to act on.

Maybe, just maybe, he could convince Anna to step outside her box, as she did when they were young and her domineering parents and conservative witch-were-cat rules were their enemies.

"If we work together, as a family for once, Anna, we could help our son. Assefa Berber isn't one of us. He's not Sankofa. He isn't even American. Our son deserves this chance. He's already my second, but he could be so much more than that. He could be the alpha of all alphas. You could give that to him. Just tell us about Berber and his Mngwa."

Anna's eyes dropped, as did the hands holding Greg's. "We went to him," she said on a pathetic whisper. "You're asking me to betray my friends and everything I hold dear."

"I'm asking you to love your son more than you love your Council sisters."

A below the belt shot. But he'd never been a fair fighter, and he wouldn't start now, not with so much at stake.

"Mom, please." Greg enfolded his mother in his arms, Anna's face to his shoulder, her arms around his waist. "You know I'm strong, and that I'd make a good alpha. Besides, you'll be there to help me, to show me how granddad ruled the Council."

Greg had adopted Paul's manipulative charms after all. He was a cut off the old Chambers block. Gregory Chambers would be Council Alpha, one way or another.

****

Baltimore, Maryland, Sankofa Preparatory School

Assefa stared out a window and down onto the quad. Four floors up, he had an unobstructed view of witches and were-cats filing into the area. Foldable chairs were everywhere, rows upon rows of them, reminding Assefa of an outdoor high school graduation. The guests appeared just as anxious as graduates' parents, waiting for the commencement ceremony to begin and the procession of the graduating seniors.

"When Cynthia and I had our Oshun ceremony, there couldn't have been more than twenty people who attended."

Eric stood next to Assefa, his gaze, like Assefa's, on the growing crowd of people. "It's at least two hundred people down there." Eric raised his finger and pointed. "The witches sit according to element type. Right over there, all the way to the right, is where Cynthia will sit when she goes downstairs. She'll be with the other water witches." His index finger moved each time he spoke, explaining the seating arrangement to Assefa. "Earth witches are next to water. Between the earth and water witches are the tiger and cougar clans. Then there's wind and fire witches. After the fire witches are the remaining cat families, with the lion pride closing the circle, which places them next to the water witches where the circle begins."

Assefa appreciated Eric's explanation, although Sanura had already filled him in on the details of the ceremony, including each group's assigned seat.

"Witches in the middle, surrounded by were-cats." Assefa respected the practice. Even his bastard of a grandfather would approve. For all his despotic ways, Assefa's grandfather never sanctioned the abuse of women. But there were other ways to harm a woman, such as imprisoning or killing her husband or son for daring to speak out against the Berber regime.

"It's our job to protect our daughters, mothers, sisters, and mates."

It was, and Eric, the little time that he'd known the man, had become an ally and a friend. Ever since Assefa had shared his Mngwa's chi with Eric, when he was dying from felinethrombosis, a disease that prevented him from transforming into his cougar, they'd formed a bond that went beyond Cynthia and Sanura being best friends.

"I bet this is all Peggy's doing. She turned something that's supposed to be intimate into an extravagant Sankofa event."

A "spectacle" Rachel had called it, when she'd escorted the small group of friends into her foreign language classroom and had taken one look out the window near her desk.

"The crowd doesn't bother me." Crowds never had. He just wanted this ceremony done and over with. A lie of omission was one thing, but deceiving hundreds of people was something else entirely. He and Sanura no more owed those gathered the truth than they deserved to be lied to and tricked. But there was no help for either. The tattoos were done, the guests had arrived, and the ceremony would begin in less than ten minutes. All that was left was—

"You know Paul Chambers will challenge you tonight, right?"

Of course he did. Like Peggy Bradford, Assefa suspected Chambers enjoyed a crowd, turning tonight into a true were-cat spectacle.

"I know."

Eric pointed in the direction of a group of men, dressed in business casual attire, moving toward a row of chairs. Assefa recognized two of the men—Shawn Wade and his second.

"He used to be my alpha. Well, technically, he still is. But cougars, even your friends, don't look at you the same when you can no longer turn into one of them. Some pitied me when I could no longer shift while others kept their distance as if felinethrombosis was contagious. Real assholes." Eric, a man a couple of inches shorter than Assefa, placed a hand on his shoulder. "Sam was a great Council Alpha. The best thing Mom did was to leave that drunkard that was my father. The second best thing she did was to move to Maryland and join the Sankofa community. Most of us are decent people, Assefa. Shawn's not a bad alpha, but he tries too hard to act the dominant, so afraid of being smacked down by the lions and tigers."

"I won't allow that to happen."

Eric slapped him on the back. "I know you won't." He cleared his throat, paused, and then cleared his throat again. "I was wondering. I know it's unorthodox, but I was wondering about your clan. I mean, Omar, Zareb, Manute, Dahad, and Rashad are all different cats."

Eric cleared his throat again, eyes straying, once more, to Shawn Wade, who sat in the front row of the section of seats reserved for members of his cougar clan. One of those seats belonged to Eric Garvey.

"You're correct. It is unorthodox, Eric."

"I'm not referring to your hodgepodge clan."

He knew that. But Assefa wasn't a poacher, not of were-cats or women. And he wouldn't begin his tenure as Council Alpha by inserting himself between another alpha and a member of his family. There were better ways to handle Eric's hurt feelings and Shawn's weakness as a leader.

"There will always be a home for you in my clan, Eric. But for tonight, sit with your alpha. Show him the respect his rank entitles him. Once this challenge business is complete and I'm officially instated as Council Alpha, we'll begin the hard work of breaking down walls and building bridges."

He'd already begun. Yesterday had gone according to plan, even the verbal and physical attack. Assefa had learned a lot about his alphas and their personalities, especially Rodney Jordan, who'd looked on with a mix of aggravation, curiosity, and reluctant respect. After Shawn's outburst, the men around the table talked for hours. Assefa opened up the discussion by sharing part of himself with the alphas and their seconds. If he expected their trust and honesty, he had first to demonstrate his willingness to offer the same to them. So he'd told the alphas who he was, not just an FBI agent and owner of a pharmaceutical company, but the son of General Supreme Jahi Berber.

He'd ignored their shocked, even fearful expressions, and pushed on, explaining why he'd left home, became a special agent, and accepted the priestesses' offer. Assefa had omitted much, but the point of the sharing wasn't to divulge all but to set the tone and the expectation for their future working relationship.

"Forming, storming, norming, performing, and adjourning," Sanura had said to him when he'd returned home in time to have a late dinner with her and they'd discussed his day. "Bruce Tuckman's five stages of group development. It's a good model, and Tuckman was an excellent psychologist. Those stages are universal, no matter whether you're dealing with full-humans or preternaturals, women or men, business executives or a high school math department."

The were-cat families were already formed, which meant, as the new alpha of alphas, he came onboard already in the second stage of development—storming—competition and conflict.

Sanura, Cynthia, and Rachel, who'd been chatting on the other side of the classroom, talking about female stuff Assefa had no interest in and wished his keen hearing hadn't picked up, joined the men near the windows.

Cynthia stood next to her husband and Sanura to Assefa's right, while Rachel hopped onto the desk nearest the set of windows. Kneeling, she pressed her hands to the window pane and peered down onto the quad.

"You would think they'd have better things to do on a Tuesday evening than drag themselves here for a simple blessing ceremony." Rachel glanced over her shoulder at Sanura and Assefa then down to their linked hands, Sanura having taken hold of his hand when she joined him at the window. "You guys are like King T'Challa and Queen Ororo before Marvel broke them up."

"Who?" For a woman whose first language was English, sometimes Rachel Foster made no sense at all to Assefa.

"She means Black Panther and Storm. They're comic book characters," Cynthia explained, but it wasn't much of a clarification since

Assefa had never read a comic book. Cynthia shook her head at Rachel. "Tattoos and comic books. Gods, Rach, how did we ever become friends?"

Rachel cast a superior glower at Cynthia. "The more important question is how you ever became Headmistress of the Lower School when you needed a student two years younger than you to tutor you in geometry, chemistry, and Latin."

"Who in the hell in the twenty-first-century needs Latin? None of our spells are even written in Latin. And you had the nerve to charge me twenty-five dollars an hour. What fourteen-year-old does that?"

An enterprising one, Assefa thought, but kept his capitalistic opinion to himself.

Rachel shrugged. "You should've studied more. Anyway, my point is that the fire witch and cat of legend are the couple everyone wants to see. People have always treated Sanura as if she were some kind of goddess and queen. And now that she's found her king, everyone wants to see him up close and personal. When T'Challa and Ororo married, heroes from all over the Marvel Universe attended their 'Wedding of the Century,' just to get a glimpse of the power couple." She tapped a fingernail against the window pane. "And that's why they're all down there, on short notice and on a weekday. The Council is sending a message. This is more than a simple Oshun ceremony. It's a declaration to the Sankofa community of things to come."

Rachel jumped from the desk, her white high-heeled sandals matching her white linen pants, the peach blouse she wore a pretty complement to the oddest woman Assefa had ever met.

One minute she was grumpy and sensitive, the next serious and shy, and now this. Whatever this was. Rachel had an offbeat sense of humor, if one could call half the things that spilled from her mouth as humor and not just plain old sarcasm delivered by a pixie with a Cheshire grin. Whatever her peculiarities, the earth witch was correct. Not about him and Sanura being like T'Challa and Oro-whoever, but the Council using tonight and this ceremony to set the stage for future shifts in power.

Rachel and Cynthia had been asked, by High Priestess Anna, to escort Sanura and Assefa into the quad and to offer the first blessings. They thought they'd been given the honor because they were Sanura's best friends, but Assefa didn't buy it. Not one bit. When the four of them walked through the crowd and toward the Witch Council of Elders, the declaration Rachel referenced would be made. The declaration being, "Get a good look. They are your future Council."

Of course, with Rachel being only a level one earth witch she would disagree with his assessment. But he'd listened carefully to the way Priestess Peggy spoke to and about her niece. Her pride in Rachel was palpable, especially when they'd reconvened and Rachel gave her report. She'd told the assembled group about her conversations with the grass and two trees, her voice sad but strong when she relayed the awful details of Gayle and Callum's final minutes.

Sanura would replace Makena. Cynthia Anna. And Rachel Peggy. By the end of tonight, Assefa would have filled the vacancy left by Sam, making the outsider and newcomer to the Sankofa community alpha of the Witch Council of Elders. That only left Barbara's protégé. That wind witch had yet to reveal herself, but he didn't doubt the Council already had someone in mind. Considering Barbara's age, the woman would soon retire from the Council, which meant she'd have to make her selection soon.

But now wasn't the time to get into the Council's unspoken but clear succession plan with Sanura and the others. The lion pride had just arrived, last and nearly late.

Sanura squeezed his hand. "Are you ready?"

To lie and to deceive? To bear witness to the unveiling of her fake mate mark? To kill a son in front of his mother and pride?

No, Assefa wasn't ready for any of this, but he was committed to seeing each distasteful deed through to the miserable end. And if he couldn't bear to look at himself in the mirror for a week or a year, he would simply chock it up to the cost of being a Berber, an alpha, and the cat of legend.

Assefa placed a kiss to Sanura's forehead, released her hand, and turned away from the window and toward the classroom door.

"Let's go."

They all went.

CHAPTER TWENTY-FIVE

Her heart beat too fast, and her palms were sweaty. So many people. Too many people. They shouldn't be doing this, not this way, not with dishonesty as the secret ingredient in this ceremonial dish. She wished, seeing all these people gathered to witness the blessing of her mate bond, that she'd permitted Assefa to bite her all those days and weeks ago. Or that he'd accepted her offer the other day. Instead, he'd refused, telling her, "You aren't ready yet." Perhaps he'd been right. But that left them with no good options.

A minute ago, Eric had kissed Sanura's cheek and shaken Assefa's hand, wishing them good luck before darting off to join his cougar brothers. Now, the two of them, along with Cynthia and Rachel, stood to the right of the fire path. On the stoned fire path was Makena, dressed in her white priestess robe. The edge of the hood, wrists, and bottom were outlined in a swirling red-and-orange flame motif.

The hood covered her face, and Makena never glanced back at the group. Tonight, right now, she was about priestess and Council business. Sanura wished she'd had an opportunity to speak with her mother before the ceremony, to apologize, again, for lying to her. But Makena had been busy with her Council sisters, finalizing the details of the last-minute ceremony.

From the look of things, they'd done an excellent job. Candle lanterns were everywhere. Egg lanterns, in an oval shape and made of stone, lined the four elemental paths. Between each path were rows of chairs occupied by dozens of witches and were-cats. Some, like Rodney Jordan and Maurice Dunn, she'd known her entire life. Others she'd attended school with, was taught by or met during one Sankofa event or another over the years. They were her family. They were Sankofa.

Makena stood on the southern path, representing fire witches. Directly across the quadrangle from Makena, illuminated by glowing egg lanterns that cast a bright light in all directions, stood Priestess Barbara on the wind path. Her short form was covered in her ceremonial Council robe, wind turbines the chosen motif of the wind witches.

Priestess Peggy, outfitted in the same white Council robe as her sisters, was to Makena's left, her foot tapping an impatient beat as she waited for the first stroke of midnight. Peggy had no special decorative lining on her robe, opting for a series of black-and-white floral motifs that ran down the center of her sleeves—African violet, impala lily, proteas, and African iris.

Anna waited on the eastern path. As high priestess, her robe was black with a singular design over her chest—a tree with roots of water and flaming leaves that blew in a whipping wind.

When the Orunmila Library's bell sounded the first of twelve *bohms*, the priestesses began to walk down their respective path. Hoods on, robes flowing, lanterns shining, the women appeared as if they floated on currents of magic and mystery. With each *bohm*, they got closer to their destination, and not a sound could be heard in the quad above the melodic bell.

Bohm.

Bohm.

Bohm.

The priestesses stopped at the end of their path, each at a cardinal point and surrounding the Tree of Ma'at. The Tree of Ma'at, a towering tree planted by the first Council, represented truth, balance, and order. The placement of the tree, in the center of the quad, was meant to express the individuality of each element but also unity.

The high priestess touched her palm to the rough bark of the tree, beginning the opening of the ceremony. "I am water—clear, sparkling, absorbent, fluid, elusive, and mystical."

Anna's water witch sisters rose to their feet, bodies facing their high priestess. "We are water—clear, sparkling, absorbent, fluid, elusive, and mystical."

"I am water," Anna continued, hand still on the tree, head bowed. "Beautiful, dangerous, reflective, soothing."

The water witches repeated.

"We are of the earth," Anna and the water witches said in unison. "We are life, and we are death. We are one. Sisters. Forever. Always."

"This isn't right," Cynthia whispered to Sanura. "This isn't the opening of the Oshun ceremony."

She knew that. None of this made sense. It wasn't yet time to nominate new Council members. Sure, everyone expected Barbara to announce her Council designee in the next six months or so, but not the others.

Anna dropped her hand from the tree, turned toward the hushed crowd and lowered her hood. Blonde hair spilled out and blue eyes looked past everyone and straight to Cynthia.

"We are water," Anna intoned, her arm raising up and stretching forward. "We are water."

The water witches shifted, their eyes going to Cynthia. "We are water. You are water. Come, sister," the water witches said, their arms going up and out like Anna's. "Come, sister," they repeated, voices as mesmerizing as the element they wielded.

"Umm," Rachel said, pushing a rigid and shocked Cynthia toward her sisters, "I think you better go before they come over here and drag you to the high priestess."

"But, I don't want to—"

"We are water, come, sister."

"Dammit," Cynthia cursed under her breath. But she went. Anna and her water witch sisters had left her no choice but to comply.

"This was never just about you and Assefa. I see that now." Sanura looked down at Rachel, who wore an angry frown. Arms crossed over her chest, she glared across the quad and at her aunt. "She's going to call me out in front of all of these people. I just know it. Then I'll be forced to kill my mother's sister after I'm mortified when the earth witches refuse Aunt Peggy's call."

Sanura lifted her eyes and watched as Cynthia, eating up the distance between herself and Anna in long, furious strides, reached the Tree of Ma'at in record, incensed time. Even more than Rachel, Cynthia hated being blindsided, which was precisely what Anna and the water witches had done. Cynthia had never made any secret about her lack of desire to join the Council, no matter her powerful magic level. Now, for all intents and purposes, she was the undisputed water witch nominee to replace Anna when she stepped down from the Council.

Not that Cynthia would become high priestess simply because Anna had been. No, damn Makena's scheming fire witch soul, that undesirable job would fall to the strongest witch on the Council. Which meant, if she permitted the priestesses to manipulate her into joining the Council, Sanura would become—*No, no, no.*

"Your mother's going to nominate you tonight." Assefa's soft whisper, spoken against her ear, confirmed her fear. As if being the fire witch of legend weren't bad enough, now this. "I didn't think the priestesses would do it officially tonight, but it makes sense." He kissed that sensitive spot just below her ear. "What's good for the goose is good for the gander, as you Americans like to say. "Welcome to my world, High Priestess Sanura."

She smacked his chest. "There's nothing sexy about a smug Assefa."

He swatted her bottom. "Assefa is always sexy." In a flash, he reached out and caught Rachel by the arm just as she tried to skate past them and out of the quad. "Oh no you don't."

Assefa held Rachel's wrist, not hard, she could tell. But firm enough to prevent her from leaving. Yet she didn't yell, push him away, or look the least bit frightened by being physically controlled by a man. A large man at that, bigger than that asshole Stephen, who'd raped her.

Sanura didn't get it. What was it about Assefa that put the skittish Rachel at ease? She was tempted to ask but Priestess Peggy was speaking and people were beginning to look in their direction.

Assefa shifted his body in front of Rachel, effectively blocking her from everyone's sight. Then, in tones nearly too low for Sanura to hear, he said, "I allowed you to mark my body with magical ink. Do you know why?"

"No, enlighten me Obi-Wan Kenobi."

"Because of that right there."

"What? My smart ass mouth I shoot off when I'm scared and don't know what to do?"

He raised the arm he held, brought her hand to his chest and tucked her fingers into a tight fist. "This will never be your greatest weapon. That's not how a woman like you fights or survives. Your brain, your willpower, your grit. The smell of fear is in the air. It's all around. And it's aimed at me. These people are already frightened of me, and they haven't yet laid eyes on my Mngwa. But you, Rachel Foster, smell of almond oil and self-doubt." Assefa kissed Rachel's knuckles, sweet and reverent. "I let you mark me with your ink because, when we first met, you had the audacity to mock me with a haughty, challenging expression."

"That makes no sense."

"Sure it does. Tonight, when you're plotting your aunt's murder, it will dawn on you."

Sanura understood now. Rachel had trusted first, which allowed Assefa to trust her in return. But what still eluded Sanura was why Rachel would trust a man she'd just met at all.

"We are earth," Sanura heard Peggy say. Pulled by her resonant voice, the trio turned in the direction of the priestess. Her hood no longer covered her head and she addressed the rows of earth witches in attendance. "We are earth—lush, rugged, abundant."

No one spoke. Not one earth witch echoed their priestess' words or stood in agreement and unity.

Silence.

Silence.

Silence.

"I told you." Rachel sounded dejected, hurt. "No one wants a level one earth witch as their next—"

"We are earth."

"We are earth."

Two earth witches stood.

"We are earth."

Three.

"We are earth."

Four. Five. Ten.

All of them.

"We are earth."

Peggy smiled, wide and with extreme arrogance. She reached out her hand to Rachel. "We are earth—sun-drenched, snowcapped, wind-swept. Come, sister, you are earth, breathtaking and awe-inspiring."

Sanura leaned down and hugged her friend. "You can do this."

"Only if you, Assefa, and Cyn are by my side."

Rachel didn't need them to hold her up, but Sanura offered the re-assurance anyway. "We'll always be there when you need us, come earth, water, or fire."

Rachel laughed and pushed away from Sanura. "Gods, that was so corny."

"It was. Now stop stalling and go."

Walking much slower than Cynthia had, Rachel made her way to her aunt's side. In fact, for every one brisk step Cynthia had taken, Rachel took three short, slow ones.

Sanura couldn't help but chuckle. The woman was truly a force of nature, making her priestess wait longer than what was necessary or kind. By the time Rachel reached the earth path and stood in front of Peggy, the witch was seething. Then, to make matters worse, Rachel executed a low curtsy, which sent a wave of laughter through the crowd.

Leave it to Rachel to mock what's supposed to be a serious and respectful rite of passage.

"I am wind." Barbara touched the Tree of Ma'at with both of her palms. "I am the wind—gusty, bracing, turbulent." She pushed back her hood then blew a kiss to her wind witch sisters, who remained seated. "We are the wind, sisters, invisible and plentiful, torrential yet humid, blustery but calm. We are many, untouchable yet felt by all."

Finally, the eight rows of wind witches stood, eyes all for their priestess. "We are wind, untouchable yet felt by all."

Barbara smiled and blew her sisters another kiss. "Yes, we are."

Silence descended once more and Sanura felt the more than two hundred set of eyes on her before Assefa said, "They left you for last."

"Lucky me," Sanura muttered.

She moved onto the fire path, hating, as much as her friends did, being the center of attention. Sanura didn't know how, but she would figure out a way to make her mother pay for this. Right now, well, she couldn't singe Makena's robe in front of so many people. Later, Sanura promised herself when Makena lowered the hood of her robe, zeroed in on a glowering Sanura, and said with humor and self-congratulation in her voice, "I am fire. We are fire. But she is the fire witch of legend."

Makena walked a few feet down the fire path—she on one end and Sanura on the other.

When the fire priestess moved, rows upon rows of fire witches moved with her, getting to their feet in a show of happy allegiance.

Sanura glanced over her shoulder and at Assefa. There was no turning back, for either of them. But that had been so since the moment they'd met, death bringing Assefa to Baltimore and into Sanura's predictable and boring life. Well, there was certainly nothing predictable or boring about Assefa Berber.

He smiled, chocolate eyes softening as he held her gaze. "You are the fire witch of legend. Claim it. Own it. But most importantly, control it."

She stared at him for long seconds, and Assefa stared right back, dark eyes going hard and giving her nothing but stony determination.

Sanura turned back to face her mother, who smiled and nodded at Sanura. Makena had the most annoying habit of leading Sanura to where she needed to go, whether she wanted to or not, then refusing to give her that last final push. Leaving the decision to go forward or run in retreat up to Sanura.

Most of the time, Sanura cast fear or uncertainty aside and stepped forward into the unknown. Yet there had been times when she'd fled, too afraid of what existed on the other side of the precipice. Refusing Assefa's claiming bite had been the most recent and egregious retreat. Yet he stood a mere ten feet behind her, their bond not shattered because of her weakness, her lack of forward motion in their relationship.

This rite of passage, accepting her role in the prophecy as the fire witch of legend, meant little in the grand scheme of things. Loving Assefa and fighting and winning against Mami Wata's beasts and water witch, that's what mattered the most.

"I am fire," Sanura stated loud and clear, the way Makena had trained her to do when she was five and brought before High Priestess Katherine's Council, the women bestowing kisses and blessings on "Oya's chosen one."

"We are fire," her sisters responded.

Sanura stepped forward. "We are warmth, light, free."

"We are fire. We are warmth, light, free."

Another step and another. "We are survival, life, apocalyptic." Sanura stopped half way to her mother and turned to her sisters of fire. "I am the fire witch of legend—blazing, raging, untamable. And you are my sisters—glowing, roaring, and smoldering with fire magic that echoes my own, singing a song of unity and sisterhood."

Knowing exactly what to do to make this moment perfect and real and not about the lie that were their fake mate marks, Sanura reached out her hand to Assefa. Handsome in a black suit, white shirt and no tie, he stood at the foot of the path, hands in his pants pockets, legs apart, back straight and head held high, Assefa oozed were-cat charm and might.

And Sanura wanted to eat him up, so delectably badass and classy was her special agent.

Assefa strolled toward her, his swagger bold and commanding. He grasped the hand she held out to him, twining their fingers as well as the magical electric pulses touching him always created. They were on display, every eye in the quadrangle glued to them. They wanted to see the fire witch and cat of legend, well, now they had.

But there was still one thing left to do before Sanura and Assefa accepted the blessings of the Council and the community. The high priestess, if this were the traditional Oshun ceremony, would've led the community in prayer, blessed the newly mated couple, and then bore witness to the mate marks. But the Council had turned the ceremony on its head, forcing Sanura and Assefa to face their destiny.

If this was how the priestesses wanted it, then so be it.

Sanura and Assefa faced each other, glowing paper lanterns suddenly above them, magically held aloft by four wind witches. A literal spotlight on this moment between lovers.

"I like that skirt on you." Assefa's eyes dropped to the burgundy, black, and green pencil skirt she wore. "So sexy."

Were-cats seated close to where they stood on the fire path said nothing but Sanura knew they had to have heard Assefa's comment. But he wasn't paying the other cats any attention, his focus all for Sanura.

He touched the hem of the short-sleeve burgundy blouse she wore, before lowering his voice. "This too. I'll peel it off you when we get home."

Umm, yeah, well, now was not the time for flirty Assefa to come out and play.

His hand rose to her face, glided a finger across her upper then bottom lip, a carnal back and forth that had Sanura melting and wishing them already at home and alone.

"So beautiful, my witch and my heart. Mine to keep safe and to protect—your armor, your Mngwa of myth."

It was then, with those strongly uttered words, Sanura realized what Assefa was doing. Their mate marks were fake, but their bond, their love, were quite real.

So he was claiming her in a way that left no room for doubt that Sanura was his and he was hers. Openly. Sensually. Lovingly.

"Remove my jacket and shirt so they can see the truth of our bond."

Raising her hands to Assefa's chest, she slid them up his broad shoulders, taking quiet pleasure in the feel of his twitching muscles under her hands. And the way he watched her, with self-satisfaction and heat, told Sanura Assefa knew how his body affected her, even in a crowd of onlookers.

As the jacket fell from his body, Assefa caught the expensive garment before it hit the stone path. She should've known. The man loved his clothing too much to permit one to come into contact with the ground, even a ground free of dirt and debris.

A man from a row nearest them rose and made his way to the fire path. Zareb, Sanura realized once he moved closer and freed Assefa of his suit jacket. As Zareb stood by the path, a sentry on duty, Sanura saw, for the first time, the other members of Assefa's clan. They were there, as she knew they would be. Dressed, like Assefa, in tailor-made suits, leather shoes, and no necktie. Ulan was present as well, handsome, cocky and with a familiar unreadable countenance. That expressionless look, apparently, was a Berber family trait.

At the end of the row, next to Manute, sat Lieutenant Walter Ramsey. Ramsey was Assefa's special guest, a man Mike detested and had gotten into a physical altercation with a few weeks ago. Assefa had managed to separate the two before Ramsey, more than double Mike's size, decided to stop toying with the dwarf and have him for dinner.

Ramsey and Assefa had met during the adze serial killer case. Unbeknownst to Sanura, they'd kept in touch, Assefa a big believer in growing one's network of friends, allies, and business partners. She was glad the police officer had come, although she prayed he wouldn't be needed.

Two of the white-and-yellow paper lanterns lowered as Sanura began to unbutton Assefa's dress white shirt. After undoing the first button, she saw he wore a cupped black undershirt, which was unusual for Assefa. Typically, he wore a V-neck undershirt because the collar didn't ruin the look of his dress shirts. By the time she finished with the fourth button, she knew two things—the undershirt was actually a T-shirt, and there was writing on the front of the shirt.

When the final button was pushed through the button hole, Assefa didn't wait for her to remove his shirt. He shrugged the shirt off and tossed it to Zareb, who then turned and retook his seat next to a smiling Rashad.

"Wait, don't—"

Before Sanura had a chance to read what was written on Assefa's T-shirt, he'd yanked it over his head and was pulling it down and over her. With a lack of finesse and care that only a man could take when putting clothing on an uncooperative woman, Assefa pulled until the shirt was over Sanura's head, her arms through the short sleeves, and the shirt, which fit her like ... well, one of Assefa's oversized FBI T-shirts, fell to mid-thigh.

Men laughed and the women shook their heads in sympathy but also in good humor. After the brief tug-of-war to get the shirt over all of her hair, the hairstyle she'd spent thirty minutes getting just right, had to look a fright. Standing this way and that.

If she looked like the Bride of Frankenstein, Assefa didn't notice or care, because he smiled at her as if he saw a woman wearing a bland black T-shirt and a pencil skirt and heels every day and thought her lovely in spite of her tacky wardrobe choice.

Then she saw it, really saw what the man had on. Apparently, he'd worn two black T-shirts under his dress shirt.

"Don't cry," he warned softly when Sanura's hand came up to stroke the four white letters on his shirt. "You're a fire witch," he senselessly reminded her, "you aren't supposed to cry."

Sanura didn't feel embarrassing tears coming on. But she did feel as though she didn't deserve Assefa. Every time she thought she did, he would do something else amazing and wonderful that made her question why he'd chosen her to give his love and heart to.

"S-O-U-L." Her eyes flickered up to Assefa's. He nodded to her own shirt, and Sanura looked down at her chest. There, in the same white font was another four letter word. "Mate."

Her heart burst with love for this man. This man who, with his patience, understanding, and faith kept surprising and knocking Sanura off her feet.

They were soul mates, for better or for worse, in sickness and in health, to have and to hold from this day forward.

Assefa folded up the short sleeves of his shirt, revealing the Flaming Phoenix that was her inner fire spirit.

Another one of the paper lanterns moved closer, shining onto Assefa's displayed arm and casting the image into the night sky, a high-definition magical projector that all in the quadrangle could see.

Heads and eyes craned upward, including Sanura's. Gods but Rachel had done a fabulous job. She'd never seen anything like it before and neither had those who'd gathered.

The fire witches cheered and clapped and were all-around loud in their approval. A few were-cats whistled while others called out their endorsement.

After a minute or two, the crowd settled down and the projected Flaming Phoenix winked out, returning the spotlight to Sanura and Assefa. Or rather, Sanura, who still had to show her mark to everyone.

She tensed. Assefa had yet to see the design, which made her nervous. More, she'd decided, at the last minute, to reject Rachel's design and opt for one she'd come up with on her own. Not only had Assefa not seen the tattoo, the last he knew, Sanura was getting a yin/yang design on her stomach with the yin side half of Assefa's face and the yang side half of his Mngwa's face.

Taking a deep breath, Sanura steeled her resolve and pulled up both the T-shirt and her blouse to just under her breast. She held them there, eyes fixed on Assefa's who had yet to lower his eyes to the stomach she now bore for the Sankofa community and him to see and to judge. Assefa wasn't the only one in the relationship who wanted to make a statement tonight, to express their faith and trust in the other.

More importantly, she wanted Assefa to know that she knew him, that she saw him, that she understood him, and that she loved him—all of him. All. Of. Him.

Assefa didn't lower his eyes. Instead, he got down on one knee, his face level with her stomach.

For what seemed like an eternity, he didn't speak, didn't touch the tattoo, didn't do anything but quietly absorb the symbol, not of a biological and physical claiming, but of a spiritual and emotional affirmation.

Oh, gods, Assefa pressed his mouth to her stomach, open and hot and erotic as hell. Arms wrapped around her waist and held, cheek replaced lips and she felt his words of gratitude seep into her moist skin, travel through her bloodstream and straight to her wildly beating heart.

One of the paper lanterns descended and Assefa sat back on his heels, giving the wind witch a clear view of Sanura's stomach and the tattoo. Like before, the witch projected the image into the sky, the warm darkness of the July evening the screen onto which all took in the design.

A small boy slept, thumb in mouth and thin frame tucked tightly in a fetal position. All around that precious, vulnerable child, massive and imposing, was a cat. A beast. The Mngwa of prophecy. Not menacing. Not bloodthirsty. Not heartless. But protective. Gentle. Watchful. And vigilant.

Her Assefa.

His Mngwa.

Her gift.

His love.

The roars began with Zareb and Assefa's Clan of Legend, swiftly followed by Rodney Jordan and his jaguars, then was picked up by Eric, Shawn Wade, and the entire cougar clan. Wave upon wave of were-cat magic washed over the quad, swallowing up the summer heat and drawing Assefa to his proud Berber feet.

He whisked Sanura into his arms, hugging her tightly and thanking her with promises of hours of "sweaty debauchery."

She shivered.

He smiled.

And the priestesses began their blessing, hands linked and standing in front of the Tree of Ma'at.

"On this day of Oshun, Orisha of love, two came before us, but they will leave here as one. One heart. One soul. One love. Her fire to his cat. His Mngwa to her inferno. Unified. Bonded. Unbreakable."

"Water blesses you," Anna said, lifting her hand and creating a ball of swirling water that hovered in the center of her palm.

"Fire blesses you." A fireball appeared above Makena's hand. The same size as Anna's floating ball of water.

"Earth blesses you." Peggy opened her left hand and a gardenia surrounded by a ball of green magic bobbed up and down.

"Wind blesses you." Barbara clapped her hands four times. On the fourth clap, the swirling water, blazing fire, and white gardenia appeared directly above Sanura and Assefa. The elements twirled, entwined, and rained down upon their uplifted faces.

Warm, gardenia-scented water fell onto them, coating their faces and purifying their souls.

"We bless you," the Council said together. "We bless you. We bless you. We bless your mate bond."

Over two hundred people pushed to their feet, a single, purposeful movement crisper than a military formation. "We bless you. We bless you. We bless you. We bless your mate bond."

High Priestess Anna spoke over the loud crowd, her voice traveling on Barbara's powerful winds.

"Let us pray for the fire witch and cat of legend. Let them be safe. Let them be strong. Let them be victorious."

The crowd cheered, feet stomped and the fire witches threw magical fireworks into the air, pushed higher into the sky by the wind witches.

"And let us welcome Assefa Berber to our Sankofa family. Our new," Anna paused, as if for effect, "Council Alpha. If any were-cat dares challenge the Council's selection let him speak now or forever be silenced by cowardice or acceptance."

The cheers and applause faded slowly away, dimming and then disappearing until only stark reality remained.

A solitary, but not unexpected, voice whipped through the darkness, slashing but drawing no blood.

"On behalf of the lion pride, I reject the Council's selection and offer a nominee of my own."

Paul Chambers. Of course. This night wouldn't be complete without the lion alpha rearing his power-hungry head just when the ceremony was near its end.

"Who is your nominee, alpha?" Anna asked the requisite response she and everyone else knew the answer to.

"I nominate my second, Gregory Chambers."

Before Anna could finish the formal language of the challenge, Assefa pointed to Paul, who smirked at him from the end of the fire path.

With a smooth, calm voice that didn't bode well for Greg, Assefa said two words.

"Challenge accepted."

CHAPTER TWENTY-SIX

Assefa Berber was a smug son of a bitch. Paul stepped onto the fire path, his son right beside him. He'd had to stomach this farce of an Oshun ceremony and the naming of the Council's protégés for the last twenty-five minutes. He couldn't tolerate it any longer, the way the Council fawned all over Sanura's friends and lover. And what in the hell had gotten into Peggy and those earth witches of hers? An outsider in Berber was one thing, at least the were-cat seemed to be about something, but Rachel Foster. That runt's power barely registered on the magic meter.

This was utter bullshit. The witches were ruining the Council and someone had to put a stop to it once and for all.

Paul scanned the crowd for the other alphas, men he'd known for years but none he'd call friend. They were easy to spot. Once he'd challenged Berber, they'd gotten to their feet. In any minute, they would make their way from their clan and behind Paul and Greg, a united alpha front against the cub who thought to rule them.

Anna had turned out to be no goddamn help at all. She'd gone on and on about stupid snakes and waterspouts and a dead witch and her husband, neither of whom were members of the Sankofa community, which meant Paul couldn't give two cents about their deaths. When he'd pushed for more details about Berber and his home, raising his voice, she'd clammed up, and Greg had cast him a hard look that said he wouldn't tolerate any bullying or disrespect of his mother. So Paul had backed down and left the two alone in the dining room, hoping, with him gone, Greg would be able to pry more information out of Anna.

He hadn't. Well, except for one tidbit. The witches had cast an impenetrable ward around Berber's property, which was damn sure good to know. Yeah, the man was no slouch. But he was also no alpha of alphas. That job would go to Gregory Chambers, Paul's challenge the first step in fulfilling his dream.

Paul smiled at Berber, who met his gaze with a bored expression. Sanura stood beside him and the priestesses remained where they were, beside the Tree of Ma'at. In this challenge, they were nothing but neutral parties, while the gathered were-cats would serve as judges in the battle between lion and Mngwa.

Greg pointed to his left and then right. "What are they doing?"

"What do you mean?"

"They all just sat back down. What in the hell is that all about? They're supposed to be up here with us."

Sure enough, when Paul looked again, Rodney, Maurice, Shawn, Eduardo, and James had sat their sorry asses back down.

He wanted to roar, to shift and rip their traitorous throats out. How dare they. How. Dare. They. He'd thought it odd, suspicious even, when none of them had returned his phone calls or text messages yesterday. He'd wanted to outline a plan of action for tonight's challenge, make sure everything was in order and they did their duty as brothers. But none had answered or gotten back with him.

"Why don't they have our backs?" Greg whispered, sounding angry but also afraid. "You said they would have my back. That Berber would back down once he realized that between him and the Council Alpha seat stood not only the lion pride but every were-cat family."

"We don't need those assholes. Our pride is the only one that matters. The others may have sold out to Berber, but you'll teach him that Sankofa lions won't be cowed by anyone, not even the so-called cat of legend."

"Paul Chambers has offered a challenge and Assefa Berber has accepted." A paper lantern appeared above Berber and one above Greg. Anna spoke again, her voice carrying easily over the hushed crowd.

"What say you, Gregory Chambers? Will you fight for the position of Council Alpha, representing the lion pride in honorable combat?"

The other alphas may have abandoned them, but Paul had a contingency plan, which would see his son as alpha. The Golden Fleece was still within reach.

Greg stepped forward, voice sure and strong when he spoke. "Yes, high priestess, I will face Assefa Berber in honorable combat."

"Gregory Chambers, as the challenger, you are entitled to select the form. Human or cat? Assefa Berber, as the Council's nominee, you may select the time and place of the battle. Do you both understand?"

"Yes, high priestess."

Berber's response was nothing more than a rigid nod.

"Gregory Chambers, human or cat?"

"Human."

Smart man. Big and fast, yeah, he remembered Anna's words. More, he could still hear the fear and worry in her voice when she pled for Greg to not challenge Berber. While Berber may be big, without his gun, fangs, and claws propping him up, Greg would have no trouble defeating him.

"Assefa Berber, time and place?"

"Before I answer, high priestess, I'd like to bring a challenge of my own."

What the man trying to pull? "That's not the way things work here, Berber."

"That's for the Council to decide," Peggy said. "Not you. What kind of challenge, special agent?"

"The kind that will put an end to this. I want it known that my clan and I are inferior to no other were-cat family in the Sankofa community. By challenging me, Paul Chambers has also challenged my clan. My clan brothers are prepared to defend their name and honor in group combat. Chambers is free to select his strongest lions. You want to know the time and place? The time is now, and the place is here."

The quiet crowd was silent no more, all talking at the same time about the gauntlet Berber had just tossed down to Paul's pride. Well, Berber wasn't as smart as Paul had given him credit for being.

Paul snapped his fingers and six lion shifters got to their feet. They were the absolute best of his lion pride—military grade and vicious as hell. If Greg weren't his son and heir, Paul would've backed one of them as Council Alpha. This group combat would be over in a matter of minutes, if not seconds.

"I accept. Now, where are your six?"

Before the words were out of his mouth, six men had stood. Two of them, the bald were-cat, he'd recognized from Saturday night, as well as the older man who'd pointed his gun at Paul. This was getting better and better. He owed that interfering bastard and now his men would collect.

Paul shoved his thumb in the direction of a huge African American guy. The man had to be close to seven feet, three hundred pounds of pure muscle, and shoulders wider than a fuckin' battleship.

"Who in the hell is he?"

"A member of my clan. You have six, and so do I. When my clan wins, there will be no further challenge from the lion pride. They will accept their pride's defeat with honor, and you will step down as pride leader."

"What? That's not part of the challenge. You have no authority to—"

"Council Alpha has the authority of alpha appointment and dismissal, or have you forgotten, Paul?"

Damn Anna to hell.

"He's not Council Alpha yet, Anna. He has a battle to win. Or have *you* forgotten?"

Anna didn't reply, just shifted her gaze to the smug son of a bitch special agent and asked, "Assefa Berber, since you made the challenge for your clan, what form? Human or cat?"

"Beast form."

"It is settled. Gregory Chambers and Assefa Berber, during the battle, will be in human form, while the lion pride and the Clan of Legend will be in cat … I mean beast form. The battle will commence in fifteen minutes. Prepare yourselves, shifters, for this is a battle to the death or submission."

"Why do you think Berber said beast instead of cat?" Greg asked when they were away from the quad and in the men's changing room of the gymnasium.

"Don't worry about that right now, son. You need to focus on taking down Berber."

Greg had stripped out of his work clothes and pulled a pair of tennis shoes, sweatpants, and a T-shirt from his locker and dressed. The other lions had done the same, all having comfortable clothing in their lockers they threw on after they showered from a workout in the werecat training facility.

That would be where the beast-on-beast battle would take place, streamed live by the wind witches paper lanterns. The battle between men, however, would be on the quad, in front of everyone.

His Mighty Six knelt in front of Greg, their bare backs to him.

"Umm, what are you guys doing?"

They canted their heads to the side.

"Bite them."

"You can't be serious. I'm not alpha of our pride. I have no authority to take their chi."

"As alpha, I'm giving you authority, now bite them."

"And you said Mom was the one who had no faith in me, when it was you all along. I'm not going to cheat. If I can't win fair and as a man, then I don't deserve be Council Alpha."

"Fair? None of this is fair, Greg. Do you want to be subservient to Berber and his clan or for me to lose my position in the pride?"

A position Paul got because he threatened the former lion alpha, telling him, "Unless you want your wife and the Sankofa community to know about that jailbait full-human you take to a motel every

Thursday, you'll hand over the pride to me." Greg's grandfather, then Council Alpha, had balked at the promotion but had given in eventually when no other pride member stepped up to challenge Paul. But Greg didn't need to know all of that.

"Of course not. And we won't. You won't. I can beat the guy. I don't need a boost."

"He's alpha. He already got a boost from his men. All you'll be doing is evening up the odds. That's not cheating. It's being smart, strategic."

"No matter how you try to fix it up, what you're asking me to do violates the rules of combat. What each were-cat brings to the fight is what will determine who wins and who loses."

"And what if you lose? Die? How do you think your mother would take your death?"

Anything. Paul would do and say anything to make Greg understand what his high moral ground could cost them. If he didn't care about Paul losing his rank as alpha, he certainly gave a damn about protecting his mother from pain.

"You didn't have to go there, Dad."

Yeah, he did.

"This isn't right." Greg released his fangs and bit into Wilson Conroy, a burly five-seven former Marine.

It had been Conroy who'd stumbled upon Greg with Sanura, taking a picture of the two with his cell phone and forwarding to Paul. He hadn't known how Paul would use the picture but Conroy's calculating mind recognized a tactical advantage when he saw one.

Too bad Greg did not.

For Greg, the picture Paul had left for Berber and his insistence his son draw chi from his brothers weren't morally right. But Paul couldn't care less about his son's overdeveloped code of ethics.

By the time Greg drank from the last were-cat, pumped up on the chi of six formidable lions, his code of ethics had burned away, replaced by the euphoria that came with being full of magic, power, and the animal instinct to kill.

****

"Why won't you let me kick some lion ass? I can do this."

"Not this time, Rashad."

"I was talking to Assefa. Mind your business, Manute."

"I am minding my business. We're all each other's business. A clan, remember?"

"Manute's right." Assefa, who stood on the outside of the security gate that led to the were-cat training facility, was surrounded by his clan, uncle, and Lieutenant Walter Ramsey. "I know how strong you are. We've trained you to be one hell of a cat, but those six lions are killers. They won't stop, even if you submit. They'll rip your throat out and think nothing of it."

And that Assefa would not allow to happen. He'd managed to draw out the six lion shifters who'd come with Chambers to his home. They would serve as the example of what would happen to any misguided were-cat who thought himself mighty enough to test Assefa and his clan.

Zareb slapped his big hand on Rashad's shoulder. "What do you think the rest of us will do if something happened to you?"

Assefa didn't want to think about one of those lions hurting the youngest of them or what he would do to the unfortunate were-cat who laid one claw on Rashad.

"I know what you guys are saying. But you're benching me like a third-stringer."

Assefa stepped toward Rashad. "No, we're asking you to protect us from ourselves. You know what we'll do, what *I* will do if you're severely hurt or killed. You aren't at peak strength yet. Those lions are."

"So that's it? I'm out and Bigfoot is in?"

"No. Starting right now, you're Sanura's bodyguard. Zareb and I have a flight to Kansas City in about fourteen hours."

Before that he, Sanura, Mike, and Makena would attend the funeral of Detective Salazar. Then, on Thursday, they would all sit with the Livingstons as they laid to rest Gayle and Callum. Not a week Assefa was looking forward to, his heart already tight with bereavement and anger.

Hell, and there was Joanna's funeral. Assefa didn't have the specifics yet. But he was sure, by the time he returned home, Sanura would've contacted the Blackwell family on behalf of their household, offering condolences and obtaining funeral details.

"You're going to track down and kill Joanna's murderer?"

Dahad's voice cracked just a bit when he said the dead witch's name. He was coping with her death as well as could be expected. Not being able to recall her murder had helped, but Dahad had a long way to go before he would feel whole again.

"I'm going to put her brother out of his misery. He's a victim, just like Joanna and the others."

"I know. I just want that hyena off the streets before he kills someone else."

If the police and coroner's reports from the Kansas City Police Department Special Agent Huntington acquired were correct, Darryl Hughes' hyena just might be responsible for a series of maulings of homeless people. The most recent attack was at some shantytown, only days before Sanura's birthday party. In the news, the police blamed coyotes for the kills, although forensic evidence did not support the claim. But what else could the full-humans do when faced with evidence that made no sense to them and a scared public demanded answers?

Any answer, even if was a lie.

"You trust me to guard your mate." Rashad grinned, youthful and with gratification. "I like that." He shoved Manute. "The alpha asked me, not you, to guard his fire witch, which is ten times better than rolling around in the dirt with a bunch of lion assholes." As an after-thought, he glanced at Omar. "Those asshole lions, not you, big man, not you."

As he did every day, Omar silently dismissed Rashad's lack of forethought with an arched brow that could mean damn near anything.

Assefa extended his hand to Lieutenant Ramsey, who took the offer. "Thanks for coming."

"You freed my city from a serial killer, saved a lot of lives. My shifters didn't know what we should've been looking for, so it made it nearly impossible to track the thing down. Besides, it's time we began playing nice with other shifters. Aligning with your clan is a good start."

True, but if Assefa had his way, he would bring Ramsey's family into the Sankofa community. A lofty goal for the new Council Alpha and one that would stir up the dynamics of the witch-were-cat community. The only reason Ramsey had made it past the school gates was because he wore a scent disguise charm. Otherwise, the were-cats would've been all over him for trespassing. As it was, the lion shifters were in for one hell of a surprise.

Lions tended to fight one way—independently. His clan fought two ways—self-sufficiently and as a pack. Lieutenant Ramsey would have no problem fitting in.

"If you like, nephew, once I'm done here I could take a chunk out of that lion alpha for you. He could stand to lose a few pounds of flesh around the middle."

"Gods, you're dead serious." Omar appeared more resigned than disgusted by Ulan's very real threat.

"I am. Chambers will have to be dealt with, eventually."

"He'll learn his lesson tonight, Uncle."

"He won't. The others may, but not him."

No Paul Chambers wouldn't, dammit, which was why Assefa had assigned Rashad to Sanura. Omar or Manute would've been a better choice, but he'd insulted the were-cat's pride enough for one day.

Sanura had already agreed to accept Rashad as her shadow and to Dahad driving her where she needed to go while Assefa and Zareb
hunted. Together, Rashad and Dahad would get the job done. And it
wasn't as if they were guarding some helpless woman. Chambers
would be a fool to go after Sanura, but the world was full of fools.

"I can't kill a man in cold blood because of a crime he may commit
in the future."

"I know that's not your way. As your Division Chief, I would never approve. But as your uncle, I'm telling you the man won't stop
unless you give him a reason to stop. And from my experience, death
is the best reason of them all."

Assefa shook his head. Not a denial of Ulan's words, but a rejection of his bestial desire to end the lion's threat to his family without
first exhausting all non-lethal avenues.

He looked at each were-cat in turn, knowing they awaited his order
for the upcoming battle. As alpha, he owed them a clear, firm directive. "If you have no choice and the lions refuse to submit, kill
them."

"Will you do the same with Gregory Chambers?" Ulan asked.

He would try very hard to not kill the man, to convince him to
submit. Assefa only hoped Greg had more sense than his father. If not
…

"I'm a Berber."

Enough said.

CHAPTER TWENTY-SEVEN

"A goddamn wolf. He brought a god damn wolf to a battle between cats." Paul Chambers, in a snarling fit, spat his anger and displeasure at the priestesses.

The Council, along with Assefa and Paul, stood behind the Tree of Ma'at, their backs to the aerial display of the were-cat training facility. In beast form were Chambers' six lion shifters and Assefa's clan of brothers. All that separated the beasts were one hundred fifty feet of dirt and the alphas—Rodney Jordan, Eduardo Ruiz Soto, Shawn Wade, Maurice Dunn, and James Harrison, who stood at the halfway mark. The alphas would serve as referees, observing the battle for signs of submission or dirty tricks. Apparently, a challenge that involved death as an acceptable method of determining the next Council Alpha, as long as the fight was clean, hadn't struck the founding Council as absurd.

"You can't let this stand. I demand you make Berber switch out that mangy mutt for that cub he's trying to protect." Chambers raised his finger, pointing it at the priestesses.

Assefa had enough. His father hadn't raised him to stand by while a man attacked a woman, even if that attack was verbal. He went to step between the lion alpha and the women. Before he could, however, a witch spell reached his ears, followed by a cold, harsh gust of wind that flew past Assefa and straight into Chambers' chest, sending the man flying back and on his disrespectful ass.

"That was just a taste, Paul." Barbara, beautiful and fierce in her ceremonial Council robe, scowled at the downed were-cat. "Your vitriol will not be tolerated. You demand nothing from this Council." Barbara used her winds to lift Chambers off the ground and to his feet.

"Believe it or not, Paul, I'm the most reasonable of the priestesses. I know that's normally Anna's role, but she's a bit beside herself that you'd put your interest above her son's safety. Makena would sooner hurl a fireball at you than listen to another minute of your pompous wrath. And Peggy, well, she's never liked you."

"Assefa broke no rules of the alpha challenge," Makena said. "We have no explicit rule that prevents any shifter, including a wolf shifter, from participating in the challenge or even serving as Council Alpha."

"But the intent—"

"We understand the intent." Peggy cast disapproving brown eyes over Paul. "But intent does not a rule make. Lieutenant Ramsey will remain on the field of battle. You concern yourself with the inconsequential, Paul, and decisions that are above your power grade." The earth priestess nodded her head in the direction of the seats reserved for the lion pride. "Go sit down so we can begin the clan battle. You're dismissed."

Assefa waited for the were-cat to strike the priestess, Chambers' brown eyes blazing with red-hot fury. He would reach Chambers first, though, even before Priestess Barbara had a chance to utter another spell.

The man, surprisingly, held his tongue and his temper. But the effort had been a monumental one. The smell of banked violence poured from Chambers. No, this were-cat would learn no lesson tonight and Peggy Bradford had just made a dangerous enemy in the lion alpha.

In silence, Chambers stalked away from the group, fists balled and mumbling vile curses the priestesses pretended not to hear.

After Chambers had left, Anna seemed to deflate. "That was unpleasant. He's unpleasant. Times like today, I can't believe I was ever so stupid as to have been taken in by him."

Makena gave Anna a one-arm hug. "People enter our lives for many different reasons. Paul is the dirt that even dirt tries to rub off. But he gave you Greg and every child is a blessing, even if the father is not."

Assefa didn't want to hear what a blessing Greg was to Anna, not when the lion's blood would soon stain his hands.

Pleading blue eyes and motherly hands reached for and found Assefa.

He didn't need this, Anna Spencer's silent wish for him to not kill her son. Didn't she understand? Didn't any of them understand? Assefa and his Mngwa didn't live for violence or enjoy the hunt and kill. They only ever did what was absolutely necessary to secure the peace and to save innocents. But they took no true pleasure in the blood, the fear, the win.

Makena peeled Anna's hands away from the fistful of black shirt she'd taken ahold of.

"Don't do this to him. It's not fair. Assefa didn't ask for any of this. He's playing the hand we dealt him."

A sob broke from Anna. "I know, but Greg ..."

"Is a grown man who knows his mind. Paul may be using Greg for his own ends, but Greg is no cub being led around by the nose. He knows how to say no to his father when it suits him. You have to accept that Greg wants this challenge as much as Paul does."

Assefa turned his back on the priestesses and walked away from them. He didn't want to hear anymore. He agreed with Makena and appreciated her words, but he felt no better about the upcoming battle with Gregory Chambers.

Sanura patted the seat beside her when he reached the row where she, Rashad, Cynthia, Rachel, and Eric sat.

"Aren't you all supposed to be sitting with your own group?"

Rachel shot him a mischievous smile. "We decided we liked the seats of your Clan of Legend better. We're like those people in the nosebleed section who move to the front during intermission and hope no one notices they weren't in those seats before."

"I noticed. And every seat in the quad is a good seat to watch the battle. It's in the air, for Sekhmet's sake." Assefa's eyes traveled to

Cynthia and Eric. "And what's your excuse for abandoning your group?"

"I go where my mate goes."

Cynthia poked Eric in the ribs with her elbow. "Thanks a lot. We're here for moral support."

"You are?"

"Don't look so surprised. You're in a bad predicament, and we want you to know that we're here for you."

"You are?"

Sanura kissed his cheek. "Yes, they are. Now stop acting like that and accept someone else's kindness for a change."

A feeling of warmth and gratitude pricked his tough skin and wound its way inside, bringing a genuine smile to his lips.

"Thank you."

Rashad whooped and clapped, his eyes on the lit sky. "Yes, it's about to begin."

The priestesses were inside the were-cat facility, which was on the other side of the campus. At this distance, neither Assefa nor the other were-cats in the quad could hear what was being said inside the closed-off field. The size of a football field, the were-cat facility was nothing more than a rectangular arena of dirt and patchy grass with a twenty-foot metal security fence that shielded the sight of the activities within from the casual observer.

When it came to fighting and training, were-cats needed only open space—a basic and easy to meet need.

The Council spoke first with the alphas and then with the shifters. Although they were already in beast form, the men could understand the women. Turning into an animal did not alter a man's mind to that of an animal. After five minutes, the priestesses made their way to an observation box in the left corner of the arena.

Sanura whispered, "How bad will this get? I mean, how far will your clan have to go?"

"How much of our training session did you see that day from your office window?"

"Enough. I thought they were trying to kill you."

"We train like that for a reason."

"For times like today?"

"Yes."

"I didn't understand then. I do now. But I still don't like it. No more than I like this kind of challenge. Promise me you'll move to modify the rules of alpha challenge when you're officially Council Alpha."

He would. But there would always be a need for such a procedure. But the death part was archaic and needed to go.

When Assefa lifted his eyes to the sky, he smiled at the impressive sight. Ramsey, a 325-pound black wolf stood between Manute's spotted cheetah and Omar's reddish lion. Ulan's 340-pound black jaguar towered over Dahad's fifty-pound African golden cat while Zareb's massive Bengal tiger was on the far left of the row.

Booming, mocking laughter erupted several rows behind Assefa.

"An African golden cat. My gods, Berber, I can't believe you allowed a runt like that into your clan." Paul Chambers laughed more, raucous and with disrespect. "Where did you get him from, a rainforest?"

Rashad jumped to his feet and whirled on Chambers, who sat ten rows behind them. "Shut your mouth, you ignorant piece of shit."

The laughter died away and Chambers pushed to his feet. "Do you want to say that again, boy?"

Before Rashad made a tense situation worse, running headlong into Chambers' trap, Assefa reached out to the young man through their new link and connected with the magic they shared.

As if he'd spoken in Rashad's mind, the young man's gaze shifted to Assefa whose command for him to calm down and to retake his seat showed in his eyes.

When Rashad made to protest, Assefa pushed more Mngwa magic into him, grabbing his leopard spirit by the scruff of the neck and hauling him away.

Rashad cursed under his breath but sat.

After a minute and more mocking laughter, Chambers sat as well. But he didn't stop throwing lobs Assefa's way, criticizing the size of his clan in comparison to the size of his lions.

From this distance, Assefa saw nothing remarkable about the six lions. They were of average height, length, and build. All appeared to weigh between 275 and 350 pounds.

The Bengal tiger, black jaguar, and lion weighed that and more. Zareb, Ulan, and Omar were Assefa's big hitters of the group. They would do most of the heavy lifting. Then there was Ramsey's black wolf at 325 pounds and Manute's 150-pound cheetah. And while Manute's and Dahad's cats had nothing on the lions in terms of sheer mass and power, Manute's cheetah was damn fast and stealthy while Dahad's golden cat, with his reddish-brown fur, stocky, long legs, short tail, and large paws made for an ideal distraction and sidekick.

If Chambers' men were anything like him, they would fail analyze the overall threat of their opponents, making them vulnerable in a way they had yet to fathom.

"Will they be all right?" Rachel asked. "I'm not doubting your clan, but those lions look ready to devour poor Mr. Siddig whole."

"Don't worry about Dahad. The man can take care of himself."

Dahad also had a lot of pent-up anger at losing Joanna to release. Today, he would have all the opportunity he needed to take out his frustration over his witch's death. The lions weren't to blame, but they would make excellent cannon fodder for the cause.

More, his clan brothers had Mngwa chi running through their bodies, which made them so much more than they appeared. And Ulan, well, the man was a Berber and descended from the first known Mngwa, which made him formidable on a terrifying level.

"They'll all be fine," Assefa said when Rachel appeared no less worried from his first assurance.

Then he said nothing else and Rachel asked no more questions. Everyone's eyes were pasted to the sky, the battle imminent, lions approaching his clan.

The six lions shot forward. Fringes of long hair sailed back as they ate up dust and distance.

Faster, faster, they ran.

The Clan of Legend remained where they were, in an east to west line, with the tiger on one end, the lion on the other, and the jaguar in the middle with the cheetah, wolf, and African golden cat.

Faster.

Faster.

The six lions barreled down on his were-cats, who held their ground.

Sixty feet.

Forty.

Twenty.

The cheetah and African golden cat took off—Manute's cheetah to the right and Dahad's African golden cat to the left.

Two of the lions broke from the charging pack, one going after each of the smaller cats.

Omar, Zareb, and Ulan closed the gap in their line, with Lieutenant Ramsey's wolf fading behind them, a quarterback taking shelter behind his front line.

Fifteen feet.

Ten.

Crash.

Four lions smashed into the tiger, jaguar, and lion, finding the line of fur and fangs impenetrable.

The four lions roared.

And the black wolf bolted to the right and around them, heading after the lion who was chasing Dahad's long-legged cat.

Omar's lion attacked, first and fierce. *Slash. Slash. Slash.* Muzzle and eyes of the nearest lion enemy.

The black jaguar leaped at another lion, using his slender body and speed to go for the lion's right hindquarter and biting down with sharp teeth.

Before the other two lions could charge, the Bengal tiger ran straight toward them.

"Gods, Assefa, Zareb is doing the same thing he did when he fought you. I told him he couldn't win that way."

"He can," Assefa whispered. "Just wait and watch."

The Bengal tiger ran, lowered his head and shoulder like a running back and collided into the two lions. Knocked backward and off their feet, they crashed to the ground. His speed and strength propelled him forward and toward the lion who'd gone after the cheetah.

The cheetah, who'd circled the enclosure at a speed that had his pursuer losing steam fast, darted past the tiger and straight to the combatting lion and jaguar.

Slam. Crunch.

The cheetah buried his fangs into the back leg of the lion, digging in and yanking with all his might.

The lion under attack roared.

The jaguar evaded his snapping maw and took an even bigger chunk out of his hindquarter, clawing the skin and drawing blood and whines of pain.

The cheetah and jaguar double-teamed the lion, each attacking from a different side. Then the cheetah was gone, running off and leaving Ulan to finish his prey.

Omar exchanged blows with the lion he was pitted against, rising onto his hind legs and throwing his massive weight into his next attack. They fought, snapping and slashing each other.

The golden cat ran toward the two battling lions. He clamped down on the tuft of the enemy lion's tail and yanked for all he was worth.

Surprised by the attack from behind, the lion stumbled and lost his footing.

Omar took advantage, sinking his long, severe teeth into the other were-cat's throat, locking the grip in hard and deep. With fierce, unrelenting tugs, down the lion went, Omar on top of him.

Before the golden cat could parry, the lion who'd been chasing him came out of nowhere and picked Dahad up by the scruff of his neck and tossed him aside. Snarling, the lion attacked, batting the golden cat's head with powerful strikes.

Rachel squeaked. Her balled fists went to her mouth, and her small frame tensed as she watched Dahad take a beating.

"Get up," a man from the crowd yelled. "Come on, little guy, get up. Get up."

Others yelled the same, encouraging Dahad on, although the older were-cat couldn't hear them.

But he didn't have to hear them because Ramsey and Manute were there. The wolf and cheetah jumped into the fray, with Lieutenant Ramsey literally jumping on top of the lion and attacking his back. The cheetah pulled the golden cat out from under the lion's big body. Now, much of the red in his coat was from blood.

But the golden cat was up, shaking off the attack with nothing short of a miracle.

"That's bullshit," Chambers wailed. "That runt should be dead."

"But he isn't," a female responded from two sections over. "That adorable cat is a member of the Clan of Legend. You're just upset because those six bullies you use to intimidate so many of our younger and weaker were-cats are having their hides handed to them."

The witch and Chambers exchanged more words. But Assefa wasn't concerned about them. Despite it all, Dahad had to be hurt, Mngwa chi notwithstanding. But, hell yes, the were-cat was up and going after the lion as if he were the larger cat.

Together, Dahad, Manute, and Ramsey brought the largest of Chambers' lions down, with the wolf still on his back and doing bloody, painful damage.

When the downed lion stopped snarling, snapping and fighting, Maurice Dunn, cheetah alpha, intervened, saying something no one could hear. Yet they all understood what was going on. This was the second of Chambers' lions who'd submitted. Rodney Jordan had already stopped the battle between Ulan's jaguar and the lion he fought.

That were-cat was still on the ground, back in human form, broken leg and body a gruesome landscape of bruises, gashes, and a neck wound that could have been fatal if Mr. Jordan hadn't intervened in time.

Omar's opponent fought on. They wrestled, with Omar taking slashes and bites and giving his own in return. On the face of it, the lions looked evenly matched. But Assefa knew otherwise. Omar wasn't giving this fight his all. Assefa had seen at least two openings where Omar could've ended the battle. Yet he hadn't taken the killing blows.

"He's too weak to be the mate of a Berber, my only daughter." Assefa could still hear his father's dismissiveness and insensitivity as he uttered those words to Najja as the family sat at the dining room table, eating the meal prepared by the Executive Chef and delivered by Omar.

When Omar slung the lion to the ground, bringing down the full force of his weight onto the were-cat, Assefa saw the side of Omar Jahi Berber thought didn't exist, the side that should've fought for his mate.

But he fought now—vicious and skilled.

Fangs plunged deep and ripped throat. Blood gushed, soaking mane and hair. Omar kept up the attack, even after the lion ceased to fight, ceased to move, ceased to do anything other than submit to a superior fighter.

The remaining three lions pounded toward Omar's lion, growling and roaring their anger.

Zareb and Ulan cut them off. Zareb lunged, tackling two lions and ripping into one before he hit the ground.

Ulan's jaguar engaged the third lion, snapping and keeping him distracted while Zareb handled the other two.

And handle them Zareb did, cutting his claws down one of the lion's side before seizing his mane and dragging him backward and down. Once down and the underside of the belly exposed, the Bengal tiger slashed into the vulnerable area, tearing into flesh and making it rain blood and pain.

By the time Omar's Bengal tiger raised his crimson mouth from the unconscious lion and ran after and tackled the second lion, the jaguar, cheetah, and wolf had the third lion surrounded.

Eduardo Ruiz Soto, leopard alpha, either brave or stupid, jumped between the lone lion and Assefa's were-cats, waving his hands up-and-down. Lieutenant Ramsey and Manute paused but didn't back away. Ulan, on the other hand, continued to snarl, hard gaze locked on the powerful lion behind Ruiz Soto.

Cynthia leaned in and asked her husband, "Why won't the jaguar back down? The fight is clearly over."

No, the fight wasn't. The lion hadn't submitted and was still a threat. Ulan knew that even if Ruiz Soto didn't.

As if to prove Assefa right and the lion a petty coward, the were-cat shifted and made a dash toward a wounded Dahad.

Sanura, Rachel, and Cynthia jumped to their feet, as did many other people, screaming at the cat to, "Watch out!"

Assefa waited for the inevitable. And it didn't take long.

Crack. Crack.

Zareb from the left. Omar from the right. The lion, back and ribs broken, crumpled to the ground.

"How in the hell did they reach Dahad so fast?" Cynthia's high-pitched voice registered her confusion. "What in Yemaya's name just

happened? The tiger was, at least, twenty feet away, dealing with another lion. How did he move so fast? And Omar's lion. Gods, he was
just chewing the shit out of Paul's were-cat, then he was smashing
into that other lion. And where did little Dahad go?"

Rachel clapped her hands. "He's over by the priestesses." She
sounded both relieved and mystified. "But I thought he was too
wounded to move. Damn, was that a were-cat version of playing pos-
sum?"

"What did you do, Berber?" Paul Chambers screamed.

Assefa stood, his back to the lion alpha. "I did what every alpha
should do. I gave of myself to my men, my brothers." He turned to
face the man who had learned absolutely nothing from seeing his men
defeated and then pointed to the fidgety man sitting next to him.
"What did you do, Chambers? Are you ready to confess your sins, or
do you want to keep playing this game?"

"This is no goddamn game."

"No, it isn't. But there's still time to do the right thing. Withdraw
your challenge and this can end now, in peace instead of with more
bloodshed."

Assefa saw Gregory Chambers move before he'd finished his sentence. The man, hyped-up on lion chi Assefa could smell as soon as
Chambers returned to the quad, dashed from his seat and toward Assefa.

Pupils dilated, Greg charged Assefa, but five of his pride brothers
intercepted him, catching and holding the wild, cursing lion shifter
back.

"Calm down," was repeated by the men. They knocked over and
broke chairs as they fought to get Greg under control.

Chambers snarled his fury, kicking, punching, and biting the men
who fought to restrain him. The section cleared. Witches and were-
cats gave Chambers and the men a wide berth. People from the other
sections had taken notice, no longer paying attention to what was occurring in the were-cat training facility across the quad.

"Let him go."

The were-cats holding Greg looked at Assefa with uncertainty.

"Are you sure?" Kevin Ellison, a forty-year-old African American lion shifter asked, his cut lip bleeding onto his chin from the punch he'd taken from his pride brother.

"Yes, Mr. Ellison, Let Chambers go. We'll conclude this challenge once and for all."

With reluctance, the five were-cats released Greg, whose father, swearing at the men, ran to his son's side and helped him to his feet.

Ellison dusted himself off and wiped the blood from his lip and chin, as soon as he got to his feet.

"I guess I shouldn't be surprised you know who I am."

Assefa knew everyone in the lion pride, thanks to Makena emailing him Sam's meticulous notes. He'd read dozens of files on every were-cat family in the Sankofa community before he met with the alphas. But that's not what Ellison meant.

"Thanks for not hurting my boy, Mr. Berber. Junior is a good kid, if not a hardheaded one sometimes. He and Damion didn't mean any harm when they trespassed on your property. They overheard something they shouldn't have. That's on me. What they did with the information is on them. Young as they are, they're old enough to know right from wrong. So, if you want them, when you officially join the Council, you'll have two work-study students at your disposal."

Kevin Ellison Jr. had been the Lebron James fan Rashad had caught on the Berber estate. The other teen was his friend, Damion Chaney.

"Work-study? As in service learning?"

"They aren't exactly the same, but that's typically how the priestesses use their work-study students. Like I said, Junior and Damion are good boys—bright and full of ideas. Too many creative ideas, as you've seen for yourself. I've taken away Junior's keys and access to the car for the rest of the summer, for that stunt at your home. And

Damion's parents have increased his work hours at the family restaurant from part-time to full, leaving him too exhausted to think of dumb stuff to do with Junior. But when the school year begins, their senior year, they're all yours if you want them."

Assefa shook Ellison's hand. "Thank you. I look forward to getting to know the young men. And you," Assefa added, already seeing why Sam had considered Ellison as Chambers replacement.

When pouring over Sam's files, Assefa had found a short list of pride members the Council Alpha thought would make an excellent alpha of the lion pride. Ellison was at the top of a list of three that did not include Gregory Chambers. While Sam's notes on Greg were mostly complimentary, he thought him, "Too conflicted of mind and weak of heart to be more than a follower."

Unfortunately, Sam died, having made no change in the lion leadership. Perhaps if he had, tonight's violence would've been avoided.

Ellison strolled away just as the lights from the aerial display ended, plunging the quad into darkness, save for the lanterns still burning on the four elemental paths.

"I guess that means the battle is over and the priestesses will be back here soon." Sanura touched Assefa's hand. "Let's wait for the Council."

"I would, but I don't think he will."

They looked at Greg, who was tossing chairs out of his way, creating a makeshift fight area, Assefa assumed.

"What's wrong with Greg? I've never seen him like this before."

"He drank from a few lion shifters, probably the ones Zareb and the others just fought."

"But that's a privilege reserved for an acknowledged alpha."

"Which is the reason why he's unable to handle the power. Even as a second, without the magical recognition from the entire lion pride, he can't properly digest and manage the lions' chi."

All around them, people folded and moved chairs out of the way. Greg had finally stopped his temper tantrum and now stood fifty feet from Assefa, scowling at him. His chest heaved and eyes glowed electric blue.

"You can't fight Greg when he's like this. It's like a full-human high on PCP."

"I have no choice. This ends today. Now."

Assefa pulled off his T-shirt and tossed it to Rashad.

CHAPTER TWENTY-EIGHT

"What are you doing?"

Assefa toed out of his leather shoes, and then removed his socks, placing them in the shoes.

"I think that's pretty obvious."

"Of course it is. But why are you ...?"

Off came his dress pants. He folded his shirt and pants before handing them and his shoes to a smirking Rashad, who retreated to where they'd been seated. The chairs, however were now folded and gone.

Sanura gawked at a half-naked Assefa. Her eyes had to be deceiving her. Surely he wasn't wearing—her head swiveled in all directions, trying to determine if anyone else had noticed. And, for Oya's sake, it would've been harder to search for women who weren't silently taking in her special agent because so many of them damn sure were.

She closed her eyes and tried, very, very hard, to not cause a scene.

"Why in the hell are you wearing those in public? And why did you take your shirt off?"

"Why are you speaking to me through clenched teeth and with your eyes closed? What's wrong with you?"

Sanura opened her eyes and the sight before her confirmed what she already knew. Assefa Berber was one sexy, virile man. His hairless chest, expansive and solid, tempted the eye to travel to his thickly defined six-pack abs and then up and over to muscular shoulders and long, ripped arms. But the sight got better, or worse, now that they were in public and so many female eyes were on him.

To her dismay, Assefa wore a pair of black-and-gray compression tights, which highlighted his assets in a most impressive and infuriating way.

"Why do you have those on?"

"Because I knew Chambers would choose to fight me in human form, and I wanted to be prepared. Did you think I would fight the man in my suit, Sanura?"

"Of course I didn't think that. But why don't you have more clothes on?"

He smiled at her, with an arrogance and patience that made her hand ache to smack him.

"Baggy clothing gives an opponent too much to grab onto, which is the reason I'm shirtless and wearing these pants. They're meant for physical performance, flexibility, and their durable. That T-shirt Greg's wearing and those sweat pants he has on, I'm going to toss his ass all around this quad with them. He won't be able to do the same to me. Skin doesn't grip well, especially when it's wet from perspiration or blood. But fabric is like a handhold."

Dammit, everything Assefa said made perfect sense. Loose fitting clothing would be a hindrance and disadvantage to Assefa, she got that. Still, if one more witch whistled at her man she would do something worse than what Assefa's friends had done to Paul's lions.

"You and that amazing body of yours will be the cause of some too-appreciative witch's death. Maybe two witches." *Or a dozen*, her fire spirit hissed.

Assefa took hold of her hand, kissed it, and then placed her palm over the fire Phoenix on his left shoulder.

His message was clear, but the truth did nothing to assuage her jealousy or calm her fire spirit.

"I thought you said you weren't the jealous type."

"I lied, and you damn well know it."

His arrogant smile was back. This time, however, she wanted to kiss his conceit away, in front of all these admiring witches.

He pulled her to him, Assefa's hands going around her waist. "I have a red pair I bought just for my sexy fire witch. When I return from Kansas City, I'll wear them for you. And if you're very nice to me, I'll give you that special dance you like so much."

Sanura shuddered at his deep, sensual voice and thoughts of Assefa in body-hugging red tights giving her a lap dance.

Assefa's lips lowered to her ear. "Mmmm. I can smell your desire for me."

She turned her face until her lips grazed his. So soft. So sweet.

"You're being wicked again."

"I know. It's the calm before the storm."

It was. Greg rocked on the balls of his feet, his body taut and ready to battle, ready to kill.

When Assefa left her in the care of her friends and Rashad, he didn't smile, kiss her, or tell Sanura he loved her. He gave her no sweet goodbye message. Instead, Assefa said to them all, "My fight. Don't interfere."

"What makes you think—"

Assefa's ferocious golden Mngwa eyes cut short Sanura's retort.

"Rachel, make sure Sanura and Cynthia stay on the sidelines. And Rashad, if you step one leopard paw into my fight, we're going to have a one-on-one training session when we get home. Do you understand?"

As peeved by Assefa's directive as Sanura but unwilling to argue with his alpha, Rashad grunted his agreement.

"Good. I'll be back soon so we can get the hell out of here and go home."

Yeah, Sanura was ready for this night to be over and to return home with Assefa and his clan. But tomorrow and the days immediately afterward weren't ones Sanura were looking forward to. She had at least managed to talk Assefa out of attending anymore of the shooting victims' funerals. He'd grudgingly agreed, but Sanura knew he'd made the decision more for her peace of mind than for his own. She wished it was the other way around, but she would take what she could get.

"Um, Sanura, you do realize that practically every witch here is checking out your man, right?"

"Shut up, Rachel."

"I'm just saying."

"Well, don't. Aren't you supposed to be making sure Cyn and I don't get overly emotional and interfere?"

Rachel laughed. "Gods, the mightiest were-cat ever put the weakest witch in the world in charge of the fire witch of legend and an overpowered water witch." Rachel laughed harder and was joined by Eric and Rashad.

Sanura looked over Rachel's head and to Cynthia, who appeared no more amused than she did. Then the grass around her began to grow, Sanura barely catching the last word of Rachel's whispered command. Before she knew it, Sanura's feet and ankles were covered by heavily coiled grass, weighing her down and keeping her where she stood.

As swift as his cougar, Eric prevented Cynthia from falling when she tried to escape her own prison of grass.

"I'm going to kick your ass, Rach." Cynthia's eyes bore into Rachel, who wore a smug smile that reminded Sanura of Priestess Peggy.

"You and Sanura won't do anything to harm my grass friends or me. Why do you think Assefa assigned me the fun task of watching over the two of you?" Rachel, imitating Priestess Barbara, blew kisses at Sanura and Cynthia. "A man shouldn't be that handsome and smart. And he knows us so well, too well actually. Even me, who he only met a few days ago." A shrug. "Oh well, the battle for alpha is about to begin."

It was. She'd deal with Rachel and her grass conspirators later.

****

A mere thirty feet of grass separated Assefa from Gregory Chambers. Triple that distance were the witch and were-cat spectators, surrounding the men in a tight circle of hush and magic. He scented them all, the excitement of some and the anxiety of others. Yet it was Greg's scent that troubled Assefa—unstable and violent.

"When a beta were-cat drinks from another beta were-cat, it's like lapping up the dregs, the least desirable part of the donor."

"Shut the hell up and fight, Berber. I have no interest in hearing you speak. Let your fists do the talking for you."

"Last chance to turn back."

"I said shut the hel—"

In a burst of Mngwa speed, Assefa closed the distance between himself and a snarling Greg.

Bam. Uppercut.

The crowd erupted into sound.

Grabbing hold of Greg's T-shirt, Assefa caught the lion shifter before he fell backward and drove him to the ground.

Thud.

The men hit the ground, Assefa on top but to the side of Greg. Taking advantage of the top position, Assefa leveled blow after blow, punching Greg in the face, stomach, and side. But Greg was no slouch, he could take a punch and knew how to protect himself with hands, legs, and forearms, defending from the bottom and striking when he could.

Greg struggled, trying to maneuver Assefa into an open guard position, with Greg's legs around Assefa's waist. The open guard position would give Greg an advantage, permitting him to perform all sorts of joint locks and chokeholds.

But Assefa stayed to the side, pressing his forearm into Greg's throat with his left arm while rising just enough to knee him in his side and ward off his legs with his right arm.

Greg bucked and kicked. He hit Assefa in the back of the head with hard punches and scratched the side of his face, shoulder, and arms, drawing rivers of blood with lion claws instead of fingernails.

Dammit.

Assefa dug his forearm in deeper, pressing on Greg's carotid artery and trachea. If he exerted more pressure, he would break the were-cat's windpipe, which wouldn't kill him but the recovery would be damn painful.

"Submit," Assefa growled in Greg's ear. "Or I'll break it."

Greg fought harder, his strength increasing the wilder he became, the more out of control he acted.

Assefa rammed his elbow into the man's solar plexus, hoping the pain from the assault would bring him back to his senses. But the blow had the opposite effect.

Greg, possessing a strength he should not have, reached up, dug his lion claws into the forearm at this throat and wrenched it free.

Before Greg could do more, Assefa jumped to his feet, blood running down his face and arms. A rough knee strike to Greg's temple sent the man back to the ground when he made to get to his feet.

He lay sprawled on the grass, head to the side and eyes open and savage. His hands sported long, lethal claws coated with Assefa's blood.

Technically, with the small change to beast, the battle should be over. But no one stopped the fight, which meant the priestesses and alphas hadn't yet returned to the quad. Which was very good, because Assefa wanted to finish the battle tonight, one way or another.

He swiped at the blood that threatened his eyesight but ignored the rest. He'd bled before and he'd bleed again. The blood wasn't his concern. What did concern Assefa was the man on the ground. In his intoxicated and unstable state, Greg wasn't thinking clearly, which meant he would go to any lengths to win, even if that meant putting himself in danger.

"Get your ass up, Greg," Paul yelled at his son. "You got him on the ropes. He's bleeding all over the place. Finish him."

As usual, Chambers had no idea what he was talking about. Assefa no longer bled, although the sticky substance made his injuries appear worse than they actually were. And his cuts were already closing, Mngwa healing quicker and more effective than the average were-cat's.

Greg began to push to his feet, but Assefa was on him again, using his superior speed to evade his attacks while delivering his own.

Crack.

Crack.

Crack.

Broken nose, shattered jaw, dislocated shoulder.

Greg dropped back to the ground.

And Paul's yelling renewed, screaming at his son to, "Get your sorry ass up."

Greg got up, his own healing accelerated due to the magical powers of his brothers.

"That's it, now make him pay. Show him what you're made of."

Greg charged Assefa with extraordinary speed, throwing fists, knees, and elbows.

Assefa blocked some and weathered others. Greg was a good fighter, just not a better fighter than Assefa.

They exchanged blows, standing in the middle of the circle of spectators and going all out, hitting and being hit.

Assefa laughed, actually laughed when Greg got under his guard and punched him in the chin. How many times had he and Zareb fought like this? Or Assefa and Razi? Even with the chi of those other lions coursing through his body, Gregory Chambers did not hit harder than either of those were-cats.

Greg's punches hurt, sure, but nothing the man had in his arsenal could bring Assefa to his knees. He'd spent the last three minutes demonstrating that, hoping Greg would see this fight wouldn't go his way, no matter how many times he alternated between attacking Assefa with human fists and cat claws.

A head-butt had Greg stumbling backward and his nose broken for the second time. His face and shirt were splattered with blood, some Assefa's but most Greg's. Sweat pants were ripped and dirty and blond hair wet from perspiration and blood.

Assefa took a second to gaze at the people watching the fight. Oddly enough, none of the witches and were-cats who stared back at him did so with hostility or fear. They seemed as ready for the fight to end as he was when it began. These were good people, just as Eric had said. Like Assefa, they didn't revel in violence and blood, although they'd seen their fair share of both tonight.

Assefa found the Council in the crowd, huddled together and between his clan and Sanura and her friends. He didn't linger on them, not even Sanura, who watched him with love and pride.

He still had a challenge to finish, and a distraction could be the difference between winning and losing, between life and death.

"Sanura's only with you because you're the cat of legend. After I defeat you, she'll see that I'm the better man, have the more powerful cat." Greg spat out a mouth full of blood. "I'm going to rip you apart and feast on your entrails."

Assefa had no words for the man. There was no point contradicting someone not in their right mind. Instead, Assefa decided he'd given Greg enough time to come to his senses. Submission was no longer an option. Which meant, short of taking his life, Assefa had only one other choice left to him. He'd have to knock Greg out. Not exactly easy when he was hyped-up on cat chi.

Oh well, he would have to try.

Assefa felt the drying blood on his hands and under his fingernails, the spiky and warm grass under his bare feet and the thudding of his heart as he saw himself physically dismantling his opponent.

Then Assefa was off, sprinting toward Greg in a blur of speed meant to scare, confuse, and incapacitate.

Clash.

Assefa used his big shoulder to Greg's gut to take the were-cat down.

Ribs broke, and teeth clattered when Greg's back and head struck the ground, jarring his body and causing him to cry out in pain.

When Assefa attacked, this time, it was with the intent to beat Greg into unconsciousness, which meant his strikes were harder, faster, and more relentless. Greg's guard did him no good, Assefa simply powered through it.

He would not be stopped this time, not even when Greg sliced into him, nearly severing Assefa's right ear. Assefa kept pounding, finding vulnerable flesh and hitting, locating unprotected eyes and gouging, and catching fingers and breaking.

Assefa hyperextended Greg's elbow. He held his arm between his thighs, Assefa's left leg across Greg's chest and the calf of his right leg across his face. When Greg didn't submit, Assefa arched his hips against the elbow, increasing the pressure until he heard the bone *snap.*

Greg screamed.

Assefa straddled Greg's waist, using his knees and legs to pin his arms to his side before wrapping powerful hands around Greg's throat, compressing both of his carotid arteries. Greg struggled but didn't have enough strength or energy left to defend himself. So Assefa choked him.

And choked him.

And choked him.

With a full-human, pressing both carotid arteries, the way he was doing now, would cause unconsciousness in fifteen to twenty seconds, death occurring in two to four minutes if the person didn't or wasn't stopped. For a were-cat hyped-up on forbidden cat chi, it took two and a half minutes before Greg stopped fighting and slumped in Assefa's brutal embrace, body bloody, broken, and boneless.

With a soul exhaustion that came from nearly beating and choking a man to death, Assefa stood.

No one spoke.

No one moved.

No one seemed to be breathing, not even him.

He walked away from Greg and toward the only person he wanted to see, to touch, to tell him he wasn't a brute but a man.

But when he reached Sanura, her eyes were wide with horror. For a second, for a heart-scorching second, he thought those sickened eyes were for him and what he'd done. But they weren't. They were cast over his shoulder and to something behind him.

People screamed and shouted.

Assefa turned around. And saw a 400-pound lion growling at him.

Ripped and bloody clothes hung from the ferocious beast of prey.

"No, Greg, don't." Anna's plea fell on deaf ears. Greg, the suicidal fool, was already running toward Assefa, snapping madly.

"Ulan, Zareb, Omar, Ramsey, protect the Council. Rashad, Dahad, and Manute take care of Sanura and Rachel." Assefa didn't have to tell Eric what to do. He was already clawing at the grass around his mate's feet. Rashad was doing the same for Sanura, who looked scared and mad enough to set Greg ablaze.

Assefa took off, running away from his friends and family and right into the path of the charging lion. He didn't want to do this. He prayed he wouldn't have to do this. But Greg had left him no choice.

No goddamn choice.

From one stride to the next, Assefa shifted into his Mngwa and met Greg's lion. Then there was no more screaming, no more shouting. But there was a mighty roar—from his angry Mngwa.

The Mngwa bulldozed into the lion, hitting him with his massive body and shoving him backward. The lion dug his claws into the ground and tried to hold his ground. The Mngwa pushed harder, using his forceful legs and hips to drive the lion backward.

Raising sharp claws, the Mngwa slashed at the lion. He connected with a side and ripped from north to south, cutting into the lion's thin, single-layered coat and releasing oozing blood.

The lion reared back and snapped at the Mngwa, catching a shoulder and working to lock in three inches of canine teeth around a mouthful of thick fur. With effort, the Mngwa slipped out of his grip, yanking with hard, jerky movements until he'd gained his freedom.

He pounced, slashing at the heavy, muscular lion again, this time going low instead of high. He swiped out at the lion's forelimb, cutting deep. With blinding swiftness, the Mngwa was on the other side of the formidable lion, swiping at his other forelimb.

The lion staggered, weakened by the attack to his powerful, prey-hunting forelimbs. But he wasn't defeated or ready to end the fight, not nearly.

Pained and running awkwardly, the lion charged again.

The Mngwa ran, forcing the fast but low stamina and weakened lion to chase him. Around and around the quad they went. The lion, with his damaged forelimbs, was unable to reach anything close to the fifty miles per hour a lion his size was capable of running. Instead, he loped after the Mngwa with half his maximum speed, which the cat of legend matched and exceeded with ease.

When the lion finally halted his pursuit, heaving with pain and wasted exertion, the Mngwa pivoted and darted for the lion.

Smash.

Lowering his head like a battering ram, the Mngwa barreled into the lion's exposed side, powering the big beast down with a satisfying *crack* and *thud*.

Crunch. Crushing jaws opened and took hold of the lion's neck, biting and squeezing. Biting and squeezing.

Squeezing.

Squeezing.

Squeezing.

The Mngwa could taste the lion's thick blood, feel his withering pulse, and hear the heartbreaking sobs of Anna Spencer and the threatening snarls of Paul Chambers.

"Please don't kill my son."

"I'll kill you, Berber. I swear, if it's the last thing I do, I'll kill you."

The lion fought, twisting and tugging and trying to get free. But he only succeeded in shifting onto his back and giving the Mngwa a better angle from which to sink his teeth in deeper.

Which he did.

Completely on top of the lion, the Mngwa's large, wide mouth held the lion in an unbreakable vice. The Mngwa's self-control and the lion's temporary unstable mental state were all that stood between Greg and certain death.

"Will you do the same with Gregory Chambers?" Ulan had asked Assefa, wanting to know if he'd make the were-cat pay the ultimate price for challenging a Berber, for challenging the cat of legend. He could do it. The Mngwa need only squeeze a bit tighter, bite into the lion's soft flesh a tad deeper. And Greg would be no more—his fate sealed under his stupidity and his father's selfishness.

Priestess Anna wept, pleaded, but made no move to defend her son with her water magic. Which was good, because Sanura would, instinctively, counter attack. Then what would happen? A battle between Sankofa's fire and water witches? Gods, the unpleasant thought and the very real likelihood that such a scene could and would play out, had the Mngwa using all of his considerable strength to drag the barely-breathing lion across sixty feet of grass and to his sobbing and stunned mother.

Anna Spencer, blue eyes flooded with tears and gratitude, dropped to her knees. She covered her son with her shaking body.

The lion whined his pain, his near-fatal throat wound causing him to sound more like a neutered cat than the King of the Jungle.

The Mngwa backed away, snorting at the thought. Gregory Chambers was king of nothing, and he certainly would never become alpha of the Witch Council of Elders.

The cat of legend roared his victory and his clan roared back.

CHAPTER TWENTY-NINE

Baltimore County, Maryland

Sanura wanted to deal with this loose end before Assefa returned home from Kansas City. As he'd promised, Assefa had fought for them. More, he'd fought for her family and friends. Now it was time for Sanura to fight for him, to give the man she loved something he would never ask of her but deserved.

She stood beside the sleeping man's bed. In repose, Paul Chambers looked more like a kind grandfather than the heartless bastard he was when awake and frothing at the mouth. Because of him, Greg had nearly died at the hands of Assefa's Mngwa. And while Sanura held Greg responsible for his actions and poor choices of a day ago, she couldn't forget that he'd been the one to warn her about felidae law.

They would never again be friends, Sanura unable to trust the were-cat fully, but she harbored no ill will toward him. But she did toward his father. She'd seen the murderous gleam in his eyes when the Mngwa almost killed his son. And she'd seen the way those killing orbs had turned to Rashad. For the lion alpha, the youngest of Assefa's clan would look like easy prey. Which he would be if caught alone. For now, the leopard shifter was protected behind the wards of their home. But Rashad was a young man full of energy and had a girlfriend. He wouldn't stay cooped up in a house simply because Sanura was worried about his safety. And come August, he would be back in school, beginning his junior year at Howard University. So, with a bit of patience, Paul would eventually have his revenge.

Sitting on the side of Paul's king-size bed, she marveled at how easy it had been to enter his home undetected. An advanced-level anti-sensory spell was all it had taken to get this close to the were-cat and not have him smell or hear her. But it had been a fireball to the lock and knob of his backdoor that had granted the witch access to his house.

She mouthed two spells. One to end the anti-sensory spell and the other to invoke a binding spell. She knew the moment Paul regained his acute were-cat senses, it was a second before she smacked him across his face, hard and with a satisfying sting to her right hand.

Dark eyes flew open, a threatening scowl immediately forming. And there he was, the bastard she knew and despised.

"What in the hell are you doing in my home?" Before Sanura could answer, Paul flashed white canines. "It doesn't matter, Sanura, I'm going to enjoy making you scream and then mailing your decapitated head to your mate."

Paul made to lunge at Sanura's throat, only to grunt in pain when flesh came into contact with Sanura's binding spell.

"You little bitch. Release me now or I'll—"

Smack. "Or you'll do what, Paul? Claw my eyes out? Rip my throat out? Kill someone I love? What will you do?" *Smack.* "What do you think you can do to me before I do something far worse to you?"

Sanura ran fingers through what was left of Paul's dwindling hair, grabbing a fistful and yanking him forward. The binds cut into his naked upper torso, including the matted layer of gray-and-black hair that covered his chest.

He winced in pain but didn't scream. The man was an alpha, tough and capable of withstanding a lot of physical pain.

Sanura smiled and uttered one word: "Tighten."

The binds did, and still Paul didn't scream.

"Tighten." Paul's face reddened and contorted in muted agony.

"I made a bet with my fire spirit. She said you'd scream before I reached the fourth level of the spell. I gave you more credit and argued you'd hold out until the sixth level. But now I'm not so sure. From the tears in your eyes, I think my fire spirit may win the bet. But you're still getting off lucky because she wants to set this bed on fire with you in it and unable to run away from her flames. The thought disturbs me, but not as much as it probably should. I'll think on my weakness later. After I settle things with you."

"W-what do you want?"

"What I want is for you to forget about Assefa and his clan brothers."

"D-done. Now untie me. Let me g-g-go."

Too easy. Nothing about Paul Chambers ever came easily.

"Do they feel like fangs cutting into your flesh, Paul? I've never tried making my binds feel like fangs before. So this is the first time. I envisioned Assefa's Mngwa's fangs, which you would've experienced up close and personal if you followed through with your plan to hurt him by killing Rashad. That would've been a mistake, by the way. He would've come after you with all that he is, and you wouldn't have survived his fury. What Assefa would've done to you, in his eerie, calm rage, is too awful to think about. But no worse than what you would've deserved."

And Assefa would've hated himself afterward, no matter how justified he would've felt at the time. After nearly killing Greg, Assefa could barely look at Anna, even when the priestess had hugged and thanked him for sparing her son. At times, Sanura knew Assefa still thought of himself as a monster, a killing beast. Intellectually, he knew differently, but psychologically, emotionally, he sometimes questioned his humanity.

"Let me be transparent, so there's no misunderstanding between us. I've done a lot of spell research lately, reading old and dusty grimoires. I didn't find what I was looking for, but I did discover many new spells I'd never heard of before, including a twist on one of my favorite spells."

Sanura checked her watch. She needed to be back at the house before the mild sleeping spell she put the men under wore off. Rashad and Dahad had been watching her too closely since Assefa and Zareb left on their mission. Rashad, taking his job as bodyguard way too seriously, had even bedded down outside of Sanura's bedchamber. She literally had to step over the man on her way out of the bedroom, feeling a twinge of guilt when she glanced down at his innocently sleeping form. She always wanted a younger brother, and now she had one. Paul would not harm him or Assefa.

"I don't believe you won't go after Rashad or do something else to make Assefa pay for ruining your alpha plans for Greg. You're too stubborn and unforgiving to let it go. Tighten," Sanura said and Paul screamed—an agonized screech that did nothing to soften Sanura's heart or change her mind. "It seems my fire spirit wins."

Sanura glanced at her watch again, before getting to her feet. "Fangs ripping, tearing, shredding, your mind will remember the pain, your body will suffer the consequences. Remember, remember, re-member."

"What are you doing? What are you saying? *Argh, stop, stop, it hurts. It. Hurts.*"

"Fangs ripping, tearing, shredding, your mind will remember the pain, your body will suffer the consequences. Remember, remember, remember."

Paul screamed and screamed and screamed.

"You can stop your own pain, Paul." She had to leave. She'd stayed too long as it was, toying with her prey instead of delivering her message and getting out of there. "The binds around you are per-manent. You'll never see them and won't even feel them. Well, that is, unless you try, through thought or deed, to hurt anyone beyond self-defense."

Sanura turned her back on Paul, who whimpered and cried. He still hadn't learned his lesson. If he didn't soon, he would suffer for the rest of the night. The binds wouldn't kill him, the pain was only psy-chological, but they felt quite real. The way they did now, because Paul Chambers, the vile and vengeful were-cat that he was, couldn't stop his hatred of Sanura long enough to spare himself pain.

Oh well, he would probably pass out before morning came.

Sanura tucked a strand of hair behind her ear and exited Paul's dwelling. Cloaking herself in magic before she closed his backdoor, Sanura walked through the yard and to the front of the house and then down the street and around the corner to where she'd parked her car. During her retreat, a tall, lithe form stalked her, quiet and assessing.

"What do you want?" Sanura stopped at her car and released the magic cloaking her. "Why did you follow me to Paul's house?"

Ulan Berber, dressed in, what else, a black suit, smiled down at Sanura in a way he'd never done before. If Sanura had known a were-cat tracked her, she would've cast a different kind of cloaking spell. One that worked on full-humans as well as preternaturals.

"I didn't follow you. I was already there."

He was what? That was kind of scary, considering she'd been in the house and hadn't detected his presence.

"And I must say, you have an interesting take on aversion therapy."

"Are you judging me?"

"No, I'm applauding your bloodless yet ruthless strategy. I must say, what you did was much better than what I had in mind."

"And what did you have in mind?"

Ulan pushed back the right side of his suit jacket, revealing his holstered weapon.

Yeah, okay, point made. The man was a killer.

"My brother's going to love you."

Love her? Gods, what in the hell did it say about Sanura that a man publically dubbed as "Bloody Berber" would find what she'd just done endearing?

Sanura unlocked her car and got inside. Before she closed the door and sped away, Ulan caught her door.

"Give me permission to court your mother."

"What?"

"You heard me."

Yes, she did. But the man was speaking nonsense. "You don't need my permission. My mother will do what she wants, with whom she wants."

"I know I don't need your permission, but I want it anyway."

"Why?"

"Because Makena won't look twice at a man whom her daughter doesn't approve of."

"You were going to shoot and kill Paul Chambers tonight. Why should I approve of you dating my mother?"

Ulan laughed, rich and melodic. Like Assefa, Ulan Berber was an attractive man who knew his worth and exuded confidence.

"And you cast a spell that has the potential to torture Chambers for the rest of his life, maybe even break his mind. Now you tell me, Sanura, which of us is the more lethal predator?"

She glared at Assefa's uncle, unable to argue his point and disliking him for calling her on her double-standard.

"I won't give you my permission, but I also won't stand in your way if you wish to pursue my mother."

Ulan smiled again. Yeah, the man was too handsome for his own good. "Thank you. Now, tell me Makena's favorite restaurants and flowers."

Sanura yanked the door out of Ulan's hand and slammed it. He was unbelievable. She rolled down her window before pulling off. "Do you plan on attending the Livingstons' funeral?"

"Yes. Will you call me Uncle Ulan after you marry my nephew?"

"No."

"What about Dad after I marry your mother?"

"Do you want me to pay you a late night visit?"

He laughed.

Sanura drove away.

****

Kansas City, Missouri

"He's in there."

Assefa stood outside the home of Darryl and Michelle Hughes, Zareb beside him and yellow police crime tape over the door in front of him.

He ripped the tape.

"If he is, then the other agents would've captured him by now and we wouldn't be here."

"He's here because she wants me to find him. Wants me to see her unholy handiwork."

"You mean Mami Wata? You think she shielded Hughes from the other agents, hoping to draw you to this home when they couldn't find him?"

"She knew I would come. She did all of this to get me here. I suppose playing with us mortals is how she likes to spend her pastime. We're all expendable puppets to the goddess. I wonder if she even cares about her water witch, or whether that woman is nothing more to Mami Wata than another pawn on her chess board."

With a hard shove, Assefa popped the door lock. Taking the lead, Zareb pulled out and raised his Glock. Trailing behind his partner, firearm also out, Assefa entered the house and closed the door behind him. The home smelled of strong cleansers, but the more powerful stench of death remained.

Assefa pointed to the door at the end of the hallway on the right, and then tapped his nose, letting Zareb know he smelled the hyena shifter.

Guns raised, they walked, side-by-side, down the wide, dark hallway and to the room where he smelled the were-cat. At the opening of the room, they paused, listening for movement within. When Assefa heard nothing but soft breathing, he knew they had no choice but to storm the room. Crouching, Assefa entered low and Zareb high. They burst into the room, gun hand steady, enhanced eyes searching for the man they sought.

And there he was, Darryl Hughes, in human form and sitting on the edge of a sofa, naked and with the barrel of a gun under his chin. And not just any gun, dammit, a double-barreled .45 ACP 1911 pistol. It was a beast of a gun, two barrels, two bolts, two magazines, and two triggers. In essence, Hughes threatened himself with two guns.

Assefa lowered his weapon. Zareb did not.

"Mr. Hughes, I'm Special Agent Berber and this is my partner, Special Agent Osei. We're here to help you."

The living room, like the rest of the home, was dark and unwelcoming, Hughes' face just as depressed and morbid. Dried blood clung to the mouth and hands of the sixty-six-year-old retired construction company owner. Thin and fit, Hughes held the gun with sure hands, his eyes tear-filled and weighed down with pain and self-loathing.

Assefa expected to find a rabid hyena, had prepared himself mentally to take down a carnivorous threat to the city. What he hadn't prepared for was a lucid were-cat in mourning, which made this mission far worse than he'd anticipated.

On silent feet, Zareb positioned himself on the right side of the living room, his Glock aimed at Hughes. Assefa stayed where he was, on the left side of the room and less than thirty feet from the suicidal hyena.

"I know who you are. The cat of legend."

Assefa holstered his sidearm, which garnered him a scowl of disapproval from Zareb. Holding his hands palm-up, Assefa did his best to appear non-threatening. Yet he stayed where he was, unwilling to spook Hughes into shooting himself.

"If you know I'm the cat of legend, then you also know I'm not here to hurt you. I only want to help. Tell me how I can help you, Mr. Hughes."

Long, slim fingers slid closer to the gun's's trigger. "You can't help me. It's too late for me. I killed them. I killed so many." Hughes wept, wiry shoulders shaking with the pain of his brutal confession.

Moving slowly, cautiously, Assefa bent one knee and then the other to the carpeted floor, bringing him nearly eye level with Hughes. Even at this level and with his enhanced speed, Assefa didn't think he could reach the man before he took his life. Ironic, since Assefa had come to this city with the intention of killing him. But how could he take Hughes' life when his mind was once more his own? Worse, the poor man obviously remembered all that he'd done.

"My mate was first. Gods, I woke up one morning and was so hungry for fresh meat that I shifted right there in the bed. My human mind was grateful Michelle wasn't in the bed with me. But my hyena, he was so damn hungry. So I followed the sound of the morning news playing on the television and the smell of bacon cooking in the kitchen." Hughes' hands began to shake, including the finger poised just above the trigger. "She was watching her favorite cable news show and cooking me breakfast the way she's done since our handfasting forty years ago."

Zareb looked over at Assefa and shook his head, letting him know he didn't think he could take a non-lethal shot that wouldn't result in Hughes jerking and blowing his brains all over the sofa and back wall.

Hughes cried with heavy, body-wracking sobs as he told how he'd attacked and killed his wife. Her screams were cut short when he'd ravaged her face, crushing bones and suffocating her under his one hundred thirty-pound body of spotted fur.

"It was my body, but it wasn't. I couldn't control a thing I did, no matter how hard I tried. I kept telling myself to stop, to leave those innocent people alone. But I didn't stop. I couldn't stop. I just wanted to feed, over and over until I was full. Even then, I kept attacking, kept killing. I threw up every time I returned home. But when night would fall again, I was back on the streets. Hunting. Terrorizing. Men, women, and children."

He slid the barrel of the weapon from one side of his neck to the other, agitated and angry.

This wouldn't end well. It couldn't end well. Even if, miracle of miracles, Assefa or Zareb were able to disarm Darryl Hughes, what would they do with the man? Take him back to the Preternatural Division of the FBI? His division had neither a prison to hold preternatural criminals nor a medical facility to help them with their mental instability.

"Nothing you did was your fault, Mr. Hughes. You have to know that. You were controlled, manipulated into hurting your wife and those other people."

Since Hughes hadn't also mentioned murdering his sister, Assefa made sure to not remind him of the foul deed. But he didn't have to because the man began to weep and tremble again, screaming his sister's name with such wretched agony Assefa's Mngwa whined in impotent sympathy.

Nothing, dammit, there was nothing Assefa could think to say or to do to help this man cope with the killing machine he'd been turned into.

"I want to die. I just want to die. But she wouldn't let me. She made me wait."

"Wait for what?" Zareb asked.

"For him to arrive. She wanted him to see, to know."

Assefa knew not to ask the obvious questions. But his partner didn't.

"To see what? To know what?"

"To know this is all his fault. The killings. The deaths. The pain. And to see—"

Assefa lowered his eyes a second before Darryl Hughes ended his life, a loud *boom* and a soft *splat* the were-cat's delivered message from Mami Wata.

Assefa sank onto his bottom, head cast down, not yet able to force himself to take in the grisly sight of a man driven to murder and suicide.

Zareb sighed. "At least he's no longer suffering."

A small consolation after all the goddess had put the were-cat through. Zareb knew it, and so did Assefa.

"I want to kill her. With my bare hands and very slowly, I want to kill Mami Wata."

"She damn sure deserves to die. Unfortunately, you can't kill a goddess."

No, he couldn't. But he could kill every last one of the beasts she sent after him and Sanura. If he wasn't motivated before, Assefa was damn sure motivated now. And when he finally came face-to-face with Mami Wata's water witch, he would make her pay for the crimes of her goddess.

Assefa owed the victims that much, to avenge their deaths, even if he died seeking bloody retribution.

CHAPTER THIRTY

Alexandria, Virginia

Sanura sat across from Assefa in the hot tub. This was the first opportunity they'd had to relax and use the solarium since her birthday. That day had been all about relaxation and fun. Only a week had passed since then, but it felt more like a year.

Assefa's eyes were closed, and his head reclined on the back of the hot tub, with water covering him to his neck. He'd been like that for twenty minutes, quiet, still, and distant. In truth, since returning from Missouri and attending the Livingstons' funeral, Assefa hadn't been himself. He wasn't brooding exactly, but he was preoccupied, withdrawn.

Still, he hadn't shut down on Sanura completely, sharing some of the gory details of his trip to Kansas City, down to the conversation he'd had with one of Darryl Hughes' victims. The kid had been living in some god-awful shantytown when Hughes' hyena had come hunting. The teenager had survived when so many others in the tunnel had not, including the man who'd fought off the hyena while the kid, Jeremy, ran away screaming into the night. It had been too dark for Jeremy to see the attacker, but what he heard was enough for the police to pin the attack on urban coyotes.

There had been more to the Jeremy story, but Assefa was disinclined to relay every detail of his trip. All he said was, "That's one brave kid. I gave him my business card and told him to call me when he's ready to have the operation. It won't erase his pain, but it will help him move forward, be the person he sees when he looks in the mirror. If nothing else, the attack helped him reunite with his mother and the police close a missing person's report filed by Mrs. Whitehead two years ago."

Without context, nothing he'd said made sense to her. But it hadn't mattered. The big picture was clear. Assefa hadn't been able to save Darryl Hughes and the others, but in Jeremy Whitehead he saw an opportunity at redemption. Not that Assefa needed redeeming or that he wouldn't have helped Jeremy anyway, but men like Assefa Berber and Samuel Williams defined their value as were-cats by how many souls they saved and people they protected.

Sanura understood and respected Assefa for caring so deeply about others. What worried her was how personally he took his "failure" when he couldn't save everyone.

Reaching behind her, she retrieved an item from the pocket of a robe she'd dropped on the floor before climbing into the hot tub. Keeping it safe and dry above the water, Sanura waded to the other side of the hot tub, settling down beside Assefa when she reached him.

Despite the fact that she knew he heard and felt her approach, he didn't stir.

After a minute of watching his handsome profile, she kissed his cheek. "May we talk a bit?"

As if they weighed a ton, Assefa's eyes seemed to take forever to lift and open. Yet when they did, they were as gloriously beautiful as ever—dark and warm. But more, much more. She wondered what he'd been thinking about as he enjoyed the soothing heat from the tub.

As if he read her mind, Assefa's eyes flashed Mngwa gold and he asked, "Do you think you can help me figure out how to kill a god?"

She burst into laughter until she realized he hadn't been joking.

"A what?"

"A god. Mami Wata to be specific." He sat up, water sluicing down and over a body honed to sexy perfection. "I know it shouldn't be possible, but I think together we can figure out how to kill her."

"Wait. You mean to tell me that's what's been on your mind the last two days?"

He nodded.

Sanura laughed again, not with humor but in disbelief. "We can't kill a goddess, Assefa."

"Well, not with that attitude, we won't."

"My attitude isn't the problem here. Your audacious goal is the issue."

"I think we can defeat her."

If only. Assefa made the idea of killing a god sound so reasonable, doable. But it wasn't. Why would he think they'd ever be able to manage something so phenomenal as killing Mami Wata?

"I know you're Council Alpha and all, but you're still mortal. Don't let the fancy title go to your head."

Assefa's charming, self-assured response of a smile warmed her in a way the hot tub never could. Here she thought her special agent had been emotionally bogged down in all the doom and gloom that had become too much of their lives. But no, Assefa had been plotting a god's death. Sanura couldn't be prouder of him. She'd never known a person with more resolve and grit than Assefa Berber.

Not that she thought it possible to actually kill Mami Wata. But damn, the were-cat kept surprising her, causing Sanura to view him in new ways. Every time Assefa did something unexpected and wonderful, Sanura discovered that it was possible to love him even more, which made her feel even better about her decision.

"So, what are you hiding in that hand of yours?"

Her right hand was closed, her arm propped on the floor and behind Assefa. How in the world did he even know she had something in her hand?

"It's for you. But answer one thing for me before I give it to you."

"Sure, anything."

"What did you mean when you said my heart speaks to you in many languages?"

Sanura thought she knew. But she needed to be sure.

Assefa smiled again, his eyes turning a little sad as he reached up and tucked a wet strand of hair behind her ear. "It simply means you aren't ready to accept my bite or to let your father's jaguar spirit go. Your heart is torn, which makes it unable to speak in a single voice, one coherent language." Assefa pressed a forgiving and understanding kiss to her lips. "It's all right, sweetheart, I know you're trying and that you'll get there eventually. My Mngwa told me he could wait to have his mate, and I believe him."

Sanura didn't know how Assefa did it. She admired and envied the close and stable relationship he had with his inner spirit. The only time Sanura and her fire spirit agreed was when Sanura gave into her baser instincts and did something violent like cursing a man for threatening her family and friends. But Assefa's explanation was as Sanura thought.

She pulled her hand from behind Assefa's back and opened her palm to reveal a small box covered with shiny silver wrapping paper and a tiny black bow on the top.

"You're right, I'm not yet ready. But I will be, and I love you with all my heart. You're the very best of men. Every day I'm with you feels like a blessing, a dream. A dream I never want to end because I don't think I would survive if we weren't together."

"I don't know what to say."

"You don't have to say anything. Well, not right now." She extended her open palm to Assefa. "What I'm trying to say is that this is for you."

Makena had gifted it to Sanura on her birthday. It wasn't the birthday present she'd been expecting, but it was by far the best gift her mother had ever given her.

Assefa held the box in the middle of his large hand. His head canted right then left, eyes quizzical, mouth set in a confused thin line. He stared at the box as if it were the most complex of puzzles.

"Are you going to open the box or continue to stare at it and drive me crazy?"

"I've never received a gift from a woman before. I mean my sister, of course, on my birthday. But it's her birthday too so it would be kind of hard for her to forget. But never from a girlfriend. I guess they thought since I was rich, anything I wanted or needed I could buy myself. Which is true, but that kind of thinking misses the point of gift giving."

His words were spoken low, eyes fixed on the small package instead of on Sanura. She could feel the pulse of sadness and pleasure rippling along their merged aura. The dual emotions also played out across his face. Eventually, pleasure won, and he smiled. When Assefa finally raised his eyes, she could see the smile was there too—big, genuine, and grateful.

With wet hands, Assefa unwrapped the gift. Tossing the paper over his shoulder and onto the solarium floor, he opened the box, looked inside, and then at Sanura.

She waited for his reaction, swallowing her nerves and plastering on a smile she hoped wouldn't give her away.

Long, thick fingers lifted the gift from the box. It sparkled in the candlelight, Sanura having placed a dozen white candles around the room, wanting to set a romantic mood for this very moment.

For long seconds, Assefa stared at the gift, saying nothing, and Sanura's anxious smile began to fade. "What is it? I mean, I see what it is but . . .?"

Sanura took the gold necklace from Assefa's hand, onto which hung a priceless gift from her mother. "This was my father's wedding ring. Actually, it was his second wedding ring given to him by my mother on their tenth anniversary. Remember I told you about my father saving me from a fire in one of his apartment buildings by changing into his jaguar form?"

"Faulty wiring, right?"

"Yes, well, I was only five and my memory is sketchy. But I remember the heat, the flames, and the blur of my father's transformation. It was as if the flames burned his flesh from the bone only to be regurgitated as fine black pelt. Then I was in his teeth, wind blowing my hair as he ran faster than I thought was possible."

Now, as a woman, she wondered if the cause of the fire had truly been faulty wiring. She'd probably never know, but her fire spirit found the thought of fire killing a fire witch too ironically twisted to not question. She pushed the thought of attempted murder away and focused on the man in front of her.

"When my father shifted, he didn't have time to strip down first. In his haste to save me, he destroyed his wedding ring. A year later, my mother gave him another ring as an anniversary gift."

Assefa touched the plain gold ring and necklace Sanura held in her hand. He said nothing, which was often his way when Sanura spoke of her father.

"The gold is from a mine in Nigeria, my mother's homeland. A Nigerian metallurgist crafted the ring, which was then blessed by my grandmother. She imbued magic within the ring to protect my father, especially during transformation when the body shifts shape, which, as you know, is when the were-cat is at his most vulnerable."

Sanura gathered her last bit of courage. Assefa told her he wouldn't marry her without also claiming her fire spirit for his Mngwa. She didn't think he'd changed his mind, despite what he'd said a few minutes ago about his Mngwa being willing to wait for his mate. Her heart may still speak in conflicted languages, but her mind wasn't at all unsure about what she wanted and who she wanted to be with for the rest of her life.

"I would like to gift you with my father's wedding ring as a promise of intent. I intend to love you whether you smile or wear your FBI mask. I intend to love you so much that I'll never cook for you but will allow you to cook for me. I intend to wear dresses and skirts so you can pretend not to stare at my legs. I intend to poke fun at your conservative ways and beat you at *Truth or Dare for Lovers*. I intend to buy you comics with T'Challa and Ororo so you can see that we're much cooler than Black Panther and Storm. Most of all, I intend to be the mate you deserve and need. You're mine, and I'm yours. When we finally marry, I intend to make you the happiest of were-cats because you've already made me the happiest of witches."

Sanura took a deep breath, having said all of that without breathing or blinking or even pausing between sentences.

And there went Assefa's silent stare again. Thirty seconds. A minute. Two. How could he, after all that she'd said, not have anything to—"

Strong arms reached out and lifted Sanura onto Assefa's lap, her thighs suddenly straddling his waist. Then he was plundering her mouth, kissing Sanura senseless.

Arms went around Assefa's neck, the necklace dangling from fingers digging into shoulders. Gods, they hadn't kissed like this since the night of the alpha challenge. As soon as they'd returned home and gotten behind their closed bedroom door, Sanura had stripped Assefa, searching for injuries. There had been none to find, all having already closed and healed. Assefa had dragged them into the shower, all the while kissing Sanura and telling her how much her support and faith had meant to him.

They'd made love twice that night. The first time hard and fast in the shower. The second time harder and faster in their bed. Afterward, they'd fallen into a deep sleep.

But after Kansas City and the funeral, they'd been neither passionate kisses nor lovemaking, Assefa not in the mood to do anything other than hold Sanura when they slept.

Well, gods, he was in the mood now. His sex hard, long and pressing against her stomach.

Not wanting to break the heated embrace, but needing to finish what she started, Sanura eased out of the kiss. As soon as she did so, her lips, and other parts of her, bemoaned the loss of contact.

"Will you accept my promise to become your full mate and loving wife, having faith that our bond and my love will see us from here and to there? Will you allow me to place my gift around your neck?"

Sanura loved Assefa's smiles, not only because they were a barometer of his deeper feelings, but because he didn't bestow them on just anyone. But when his smile revealed his single dimple, as it did now, Sanura knew her special agent was truly happy.

"I accept your promise, and I would love to wear your father's ring."

He lowered his head, and Sanura slipped the necklace around his neck. And while Sam may have been the original owner of the wedding ring, Sanura purchased the necklace on which it hung specifically for Assefa.

"When you shift, the necklace will adjust to your size." Sanura had holed up in her office for five hours, testing and reworking her spell to get it just the way she wanted. "It's aligned to your Mngwa's chi. A magical kiss from my fire spirit."

He twirled the ring in his fingers, admiring the craftsmanship. "'A magical kiss.' Do I even want to know what that means?"

Probably not. "Just know that as long as you wear the necklace our bond is damn near impenetrable. Once we complete the final ritual, though, we'll be even stronger."

"Strong enough to kill a goddess?"

Doubtful.

"I love you."

"I love you too. Wait, did you speak in Wolof?"

She had. Sanura intended to take more lessons before she sprung her surprise. But tonight seemed like a good time to let Assefa know how committed she was to building a life with him.

"I haven't mastered the accent yet but, with Rachel's help, I'll get it."

"You sound great, already." Assefa kissed her lips, toying with her tongue before pulling back. "My father's birthday is at the end of August. He called me yesterday and requested I return home for a family birthday celebration. So, what do you think? Want to come with me?"

426 · N.D. JONES

"To the Sudan? To meet your father?" She sounded like an idiot, but Assefa had shocked her into stupid rambling.

Laughing, he kissed her again. "Yes, my father will be there. He's the leader of the country, after all, and we'll be staying at the presidential compound."

Assefa rubbed his hands up and down her sleek, wet back, looking pleased with the prospect of taking Sanura home to meet his father.

This was really happening. Slowly but surely, they were lowering their walls and letting each other into every aspect of their lives.

She kissed him, wanting their happily-ever-after. Yet it wouldn't be today. Not even tomorrow or next month. But she'd made promises to this man, this intelligent, brave, and sensitive man who held three little girls when they'd cried for their dead parents, scooping them into his arms and weeping with them. This man, who called his sister, Naj-ja, to tell her he loved her because Darryl Hughes could no longer say the same to his sister. This man, this spectacular man, who thanked Sanura for dealing with Paul Chambers, not once judging her method or questioning her morality.

When Assefa made love to her, hot water sloshing around their heaving bodies and onto the solarium floor, putting out candles and casting their union in sacred darkness, Sanura made him another promise.

"Together, we'll figure out a way to kill a god."

Realm of the Gods

Gloating had never appealed to Oya, although, with a sister and rival like Mami Wata, the emotion did tempt. Sanura and Assefa would prevail where all the others had failed. This Oya knew with certainty. Yet such confidence in the fire witch and cat of legend did not mean the goddess foresaw their success or possessed the power to spare them pain along the rocky road to victory.

Unfortunately, for them to win they would also have to suffer, to lose, and then to find their way back to the light and to each other. Divinity cost and divinity deceived, such was the immortal existence of gods.

"It is not yet over."

No, it was not.

Oya stood, tired of sitting about but knowing, after her forbidden trip to the human realm to see Sanura and Assefa, she could not leave this four-walled prison. The sun god had a long and unforgiving memory, which he exploited every five hundred and so odd years.

Stretching long limbs, Oya wished for the simpler days of her youth, when she was courted by the god of fire, thunder, and lightning and the world a yet explored territory Oya could not wait to traverse. Her life, however, had not been granted for her to live it "frivolously" as Ra had once scolded her.

"There must be balance. I granted Yemaya her wish of a daughter of water and she birthed Mami Wata. But the goddess is more a festering plague on the land than a springtime rain of harvest. Balance, Oya, Ma'at demands balance. Now there is you, Yemaya's daughter of fire, wind, and lightning. Do not disappoint me the way Mami Wata has and you will receive this King of Gods greatest blessing."

Greatest blessing. No, Oya had only ever earned Ra's wrath. So many mortals had suffered because of her, because of Mami Wata, and yes, because of the King of Gods.

Mami Wata, dark hair spilling down her back and front, covered her nude form. She stared out one of the glassless windows, scrying glass in her left hand, the right stroking the head of her Titanoboa.

"Did you hear me, Oya? I said this is not yet over."

"How could I have not heard you, sister, when we are the only occupants in this prison room, no less this part of the realm? What you want to know is why I did not respond to your juvenile attempt to draw me into yet another argument. I will not be baited by you, Mami Wata. You are simply too exhausting."

"Now it is you who attempt to bait me." She hurled her scrying glass at Oya, who ducked when it sped toward her head, embedding itself like a knife in the wall behind her.

Oya laughed—sour and throaty. Reaching back, she freed the handle of the glass from the wall, dusted it off, and then sent it back to her sister on a placid breeze that stopped and hovered when it reached Mami Wata.

The water goddess snatched her glass and then turned her back on Oya, eyes returning to the soul-less panoramic sky.

"You are annoyingly naïve, Oya. Their bond will not endure, no more than they will kill a god. *This* god."

"You thought you could defeat my fire witch by destroying the heart of her Mngwa. But you were wrong. The death of the detective did not break him. The murder of those full-humans did not break him. Neither did the drowning of his housekeeper and her husband nor the slaughter of his friend's chosen mate and the suicide of her brother. His heart, his mind, his resolve is stronger than you want to admit, which makes you worse than naïve. It makes you blind, incapable of discerning wishful thinking from observable data."

Oya conjured a bistro set with a round glass top, a single chair with a metal finish, red wine in a stemless glass, and a plate of penne pasta with red sauce. As a god, Oya did not require such sustenance but she found the taste of mortal food and drink quite delectable. So she sat, placed a napkin in her lap, picked up her fork and began to eat.

Closing her eyes, she savored each bite of food and sip of wine. Oya relished the indulged pleasure so much she had nearly missed her sister's silence. It was not like Mami Wata to allow another to have the last word, which meant—

Oya shot to her feet, dinner forgotten and napkin on the floor. "What in Ra's name have you done?"

"Oh, sister, do you not know that love betrays, bonds are meant to be broken, and that water extinguishes fire? The Day of Serpents will soon be upon them, Oya, and your pathetic champions will be no more. Not divine, just dead."

THE END

If you enjoyed "Of Beasts and Bonds," the author invites you to leave a review.

ABOUT N.D. JONES

N. D. Jones lives in Maryland with her husband and two children. She has a M.A. in Political Science and is pursuing a doctorate in Community College Leadership.

A desire to see more novels with positive, sexy, and three-dimensional African American characters as soul mates, friends, and lovers, inspired the author to take on the challenge of penning such romantic reads. She is the author of two paranormal romance series: Winged Warriors and Death and Destiny. N.D. likes to read historical and paranormal romance novels, as well as comics and manga.

Visit N.D. at:
Website: https://www.ndjonesparanormalpleasure.com
Facebook: https://www.facebook.com/fantasyromanceauthor/
Goodreads: https://www.goodreads.com/NDJones
Twitter: https://twitter.com/NDJonesauthor
Pinterest: http://pinterest.com/ndjones001

Get "Fire, Fury, Faith" audiobook for FREE when you join the author's mailing list at ndjonesparanormalpleasure.com.

OTHER BOOKS BY N.D. JONES

Winged Warriors Series:
"Fire, Fury, Faith" (Book 1) Available in eBook and audiobook
"Heat, Hunt, Hope" (Book 2) Available in eBook, paperback, and audiobook

Death and Destiny Trilogy
"Of Fear and Faith" (Book 1) Available in eBook and paperback

As a thank you, the author gifts you with a link to her music playlist for "Of Fear and Faith" http://spoti.fi/1NJ6rhv and "Of Beasts and Bonds" http://spoti.fi/21aGNde.

Coming Next Year:
Final book in the Death and Destiny Trilogy

At the end of each book in the Death and Destiny Trilogy, N.D. gives a clue as to the title of the next book in the series. To enter contest for a chance to win an Advanced Reader's Copy of the third book, join N.D.'s website mailing list. In the comments section, record your guess as to the title of the third D & D book. Only one entry permitted. Winners will be notified six weeks prior to the official release date, and will be sent an electronic copy of the ARC.